CHASING

SANE

Karen Smith Gibson

Acknowledgements

To my Editor, Mike Valentine without whom trying to navigate through this novel would have been murder!

To Mary Mule, who was my inspiration and reason for *almost* trying the SANE thing myself. Still miss those treats from State Fair days, Mary!

A huge thank you to Stacey Davenport who gave me the real deal on the law as it stood 15 years ago and how it has evolved today! She made Sandra Derringer rock!

And finally, to those who believed from the first paragraph and encouraged me to the last…thank you!

Prologue

The sleepy road is still wet from a recent storm, some areas still holding puddles of dirty water cleaved by tires. As cars ride down the wet, warm pavement, the lights sneak through the windows of the expensive condominiums lining the street. The hour is late, pre-dawn, in fact, and most of the occupants who live within the walls of the condos are safely sleeping in their beds, dreaming dreams of the complacent. A few residents are just now waking to their alarms and the majority hit the snooze button for just a few more minutes of uninterrupted peace. However, Teri has been awake for hours, tortured and raped by a psychopath.

She is on the floor now, cowering between her bed with its wilted linens and the metal folding door partially open; a silent witness to her degradation. She is lying with her hands bound behind her. Beside her battered face is a blood-spattered pair of cotton panties that she has managed to get out of her mouth. Her breath comes in ragged sobs. She is still blindfolded and having trouble listening for the slightest noise over her pounding heart and terrified cries. She frantically thinks, *He said he would watch me for awhile and decide whether to kill me or not. Is he still here? Oh God, I don't want to die! Please God, please help me!*

She tries not to scream out in frustrated terror. She forces herself to stop breathing and to just listen. But she hears nothing; no breathing, no snickering laugh. Even the smell of him is fading; that cloying smell of a man who never learned the art of cologne. It still lingers in the air, an aroma missing the body that wore it.

Working up the courage she spits out, "Just do it, you shit! Kill me already. Come on!" Then she waits and listens once again. She hears no grunt of anger, no footsteps rushing at her. There is nothing but the distant sound of traffic sporadically traveling down the wet road outside of her condo. She takes a chance and rubs her head against the tan Berber carpet beneath her until she has worked the blindfold far enough over her right eye to take a quick glance around the room.

Her heart stops once when she sees him standing in the corner, silently watching her pitiful efforts - but then realizes with the help of the sweep of headlights from another car that the illusion is merely her coat hanging from a hanger jammed in haste into the upper slats of the closet door. *That's right,* she thinks in a moment of clarity, *it was raining last night, and my coat was so wet. I hung it there to dry.*

She looks around now and sees her phone lying where it fell after it was knocked from her hand before she could dial the first number of 911. She tries desperately to slide her hands out of the lamp cord that holds them, but realizes she cannot. *Damn it! I need help! I need the police. What if he comes -*

She wouldn't allow herself to finish the thought. She is just beginning to get a handle on her panic, and she clings to that one thought: Get help. In a moment born of the need to survive and seek help from anyone willing to give it, she sees a pencil lying within inches of her right knee. She maneuvers her way round to get it in her mouth and uses it to dial "911." The phone rings and another swath of light dances across the room.

Suddenly, she is accosted by the video playback in her mind of when he removed his mask to lick her belly while he taunted her with, "I'm gonna take my time and there's nothing anyone can do it about it." He had leered at her as his pointed, hot tongue danced around her belly button. That leering face caught in a beam of light from a passing car was the only thing she could glimpse through the millimeters of space at the bottom of the blind-. *Oh my God! I saw his face! I know that face! I know him!*

As the realization hit her, a professional voice asked, "911. What is your emergency?"

Her answer was a tortured scream...

Chapter 1

5:03AM

The ringing phone interrupted a dream Kaitlin Tuscadero was having where her daughter was two again and screaming in the middle of K-Mart. Slowly, the cloud of the dream dissipated. She realized the screaming child was the ringing phone. The fact that her husband was elbowing her in the side was another clue hard to miss.

"Katie....Kate...answer the phone!"

What if it's for you? she wondered grumpily. How she would love to answer it and find the caller asking for her snoring husband. Then she could clock him on the head with it and say, "Aha! It's for you after all!"

Okay, so I'm not a morning person. At least not this early in the morning sans a healthy dose of java, she mused. Brushing a lock of hair out of her eyes, she glanced at the luminous dial of the bedside clock while picking up the phone: 5:06 a.m. *Well, hell,* she thought, *I have to be up in an hour anyway to get Izzie to preschool. Silver lining and all that bullshit.*

""Lo?" she managed.

"Ms. Tuscadero? Kaitlin Tuscadero?" said the efficient and obviously awake voice on the other end.

Family and close friends called her Katie or Kate. Everyone else called her Kaitlin or Ms. Tuscadero. She did not recognize the voice, so she answered, "Yes, speaking. And you are?"

"Sorry," the voice seemed abashed, "but Eileen said you were to be called right away. This is Ashley from St. Michael's ER. We have a....a um...."

"An assault victim?" Kate prodded, now knowing how this was going to end.

"Yeah...uh, yes. Eileen said you were on call and to let you know as soon as possible." Ashley explained.

"Yeah, it's okay." Kate said trying to reassure the young voice on the other end. "I'll be there in about 30 minutes."

She hung up and turned to Vinnie giving him a quick kiss on his stubbly cheek and whispering warmly into his ear, "That was the hospital. I have to go. So, you need to take Izzie to school today, okay?"

Vincent Tuscadero grunted and turned over to watch his wife comb her fingers through her long auburn tresses. He tucked a tanned and toned arm behind his head and asked, "Is it another one, ya think?"

Without looking at him, Kate continued to get dressed. She always showered at night so as not to waste precious time trying to get into the hospital to do a rape kit on an assault victim. "I hope not. I didn't get any information over the phone. It could be anything."

Sadly that was true. It could be anything from a distraught parent insisting their daughter had been raped by the boy she'd been seeing for six months to a true case of incest. It could be a three year old or an 83 year old. It could be a man, woman or child. Sexual assault did not have any preference when it came to choosing its victims. Those that sought help and reported such a crime skewed the results to a majority of female victims, but Kaitlin had seen them all.

Being a sexual assault nurse examiner - S.A.N.E.- was a specialized nursing field still in its infancy throughout most of the United States. She, herself, had only been certified for a year, but had already testified in four court cases.

Kate finished dressing, stuffing her pockets with her profession's accessories. "I'll probably just stay on for my normal shift after this exam, so I'll see ya this evening, love." Kate said as she quickly gave her already dozing husband another quick kiss. She playfully tickled his hair-covered belly, "Hey, you have to take Izzie now, don't forget."

He opened one eye, smiled slightly at her and rolled his furry belly away from her tickling fingers. His voice was muffled by his pillow, "I gotcha covered. See ya tonight, babe."

She quietly took the back stairs into the kitchen and started some coffee. While it was brewing, she added some "pretend" sugar and cream to a waiting travel mug. She ran back upstairs to put on a bit of color and groaned at her advanced stage of bed head; one of the drawbacks of showering at night. Quickly, she sprayed some water on it and combed it through. Scrunching up her natural waves, she knew with practice that the drive in would just about dry it thoroughly.

She peeked in on her slumbering angel, Isabella - Izzie to her and Vinnie from the third day of her life - and squelched the urge to go in and kiss her warm, pink cheek. Vinnie needed his sleep in order to deal with Princess Izzie when she awoke. He catered to her a bit too much and therefore, they would be running late, as usual. Internally, she sighed at her three year old daughter's beauty and knew she was blessed.

She could smell the coffee, and ran back down the stairs. She quickly filled her cup and headed out the door. Unlocking the car, she threw her purse, logbook and lab jacket into the passenger's seat. It was already muggy this early August morning in Richmond, Virginia, and she immediately turned on the car's air conditioning. Normally, with the price of gas creeping up lately, she would deal with the heat using the old 460 air-conditioning method (what breeze one could get traveling 60mph with 4 windows down). However, in August, in Richmond, she splurged - gas prices be damned!

She had left the radio on again, and it startled her by coming on in the middle of a hard rock tune. But it was a catchy tune and Kate found herself singing and seat dancing on the way in to the hospital. The song ended and the news started in with its latest scandal. Kate's career was picking up the aftermath of bad news; therefore, she avoided it elsewhere whenever she could and turned off the radio.

Her eyes caught sight of her logbook, and she was jolted back to the issue at hand. Could the person awaiting her at the hospital be another victim of Richmond's serial rapist dubbed "The Window Shopper" by the press? For the last six months, this creep was believed to be responsible for four rapes. That number did not count this one, if it was indeed his work.

Each rape kit collection that Kate had been involved in was entered into the logbook. The date of the first call, sex and age of the victim, nurse on duty and assigned to the patient, officer that had received the completed and sealed kit and perpetrator sex and approximate or known age. She had found this information useful when a case made its way to court months later. Glancing at the quick notes on each case in the logbook allowed her to recall the case in question. She was allowed to make notes as needed as the rape kit progressed, but certain statements said in front of witnesses or other useful information had helped her in the past when she was called upon to testify. The rape kit generally spoke for itself, but there were times when she was asked to recall events of the day or night in question. As any lawyer could tell you, "Let me consult my notes" always validated to the jury what one was about to say.

In the last few months, The Window Shopper had a starring role in her logbook. She was unfortunate enough to have gathered evidence on three of the four cases. His MO was the same with each case. Obviously familiar with both the victim's residence and routine, he would surprise the victim between the hours of 2 and 3 a.m. He liked to surprise them in their sleep. He would watch them sleep for an indeterminate amount of time, waiting for them to wake up. He needed the victim to be aware of his presence first before attacking them. Then, he would quickly overpower them, restrain their hands behind their backs and blindfold them. He would then begin a sadistic game of cat and mouse, raping them multiple times, threatening to disfigure, burn or kill them. He also liked to listen to them beg. He would always tell each victim that he was going to watch them for a varying amount of time - 10, 15, 20 minutes - and decide whether to kill them or not. By the time the women realized that he was gone, he had probably been gone for some time.

No one had ever seen his face. Not one victim could accurately pinpoint his voice. One victim stated that he had a gravelly, deep voice while another commented on his smooth, normal tone that had frightened her more than his yelling at her would have. No distinguishing marks, no idea of how tall or his ethnicity. No one recalled any noticeable accents or had the slightest idea of the color of his hair. He always wore a black ski mask and black gloves. Each woman stated that he removed his mask and gloves after they were blindfolded, but the blindfolds were secure, and they could not see anything after that.

Kate did not wish harm on anyone. But, she secretly hoped that if this were another victim of The Window Shopper that the victim had seen something, or heard something. Anything that could give them some kind of information that would stop this sadistic bastard! The DNA they collected was no good without a suspect to match it up against. And if this victim was one of his and **did** know something that could stop this vicious merry-go-round of pain, Kate hoped she'd be willing to talk.

So far, one of the Window Shopper's most frustrating trademarks was to leave each of the women with a warning. After a night of terror, she was told that if she were to tell anyone of "their time together" he would return to kill her slowly and "with a great deal of pain." Maybe The Window Shopper had not made a mistake. Maybe not one of the victims could remember anything to help the case.

However, even if they did, Kate had been in the room when the women spoke with the officer taking their reports. They all had the same haunted look in their eyes and basically said the same thing, "He knew everything about me, everything. He's been watching me for months. He told me things he could only have known if he had been watching me. He's been 'window shopping' he told me and chose me. He's been in my house/apartment/condo before, and he can get in again....He told me he could. He's going to come back and kill me....It's just a matter of time. I've told you everything I can. I can't talk to you anymore."

So, maybe, just maybe, thought Kate, if this is one of his "choices" she will tell us something to cut his shopping frenzy short. He was becoming more violent and toying with each victim more. It was only a matter of time before raping them lost its luster and he started to need to watch them die to get the same thrill. He was already toying with the idea and the next one may not see the inside of an ER but end up at the morgue instead.

Kate turned into the parking lot designated for ER staff and saw Bill Patterson standing outside the entrance smoking a cigarette. He caught sight of her when her car gave a chirping sound confirming that she had indeed locked it. With seeming telepathic abilities, he looked her in the eye and nodded, and she knew.....The Window Shopper had made another purchase.

Chapter 2

Sergeant Bill Patterson snuffed his cigarette out in the designated spot next to the vacuum doors as Kate walked across the parking lot in his direction.

"Hey, Katie. They wake you up?" he yelled in greeting.

Kate smiled at him. "No, I was just finishing my morning aerobics when I got the call. I had to take a quick shower before leaving the house to wash away all the pounds I got rid of."

"Bring me any?" Bill said, indicating her traveler's mug as she caught up to him at the ambulance bay.

"Had I known that you would be the one to greet me this morning, I most certainly would have. But you don't call, you don't write," she joked with him and for added measure took a long slow drink from her cup, savoring the taste within. Finishing she added, "Besides, you already have a cup," indicating the white Styrofoam cup in his hand.

"This shit?" he quipped, "This is the standard cup of battery acid. Not your high dollar Costa Rican Tunanni coffee."

Kate laughed. "Tarrazu coffee, not Tunanni."

"Whatever. That stuff you pay way too much for," Bill retorted.

"Well, you know what I say," said Kaitlin. "When it comes to coffee and chocolate: spare no expense."

They both chuckled over the never-ending debate. Slowly, they sobered as each remembered in a different way why they were here at this early hour.

"So, is this your case, then? Our guy?" asked Kate.

"Yeah, I think so," answered Bill. "Same M.O., but he started practicing the art of murder tonight. Judging from the ligatures on her neck, he strangled her to the point of unconsciousness a few times. There's more than one mark there."

Kate shuddered and it had nothing to do with the temperature. Bill continued, "She's pretty messed up, understandably. Don't know if she's going to talk to us or not. But, we'll collect the kit and put it away as evidence if she lets us."

Kate knew that the victim had agreed to a rape kit because they had called her in. But many times, that's all that a victim would agree to - the collection of the kit. Sometimes, it went no further than that. When a suspect was apprehended, the victim would or would not agree to come into the station for a positive identification. Even if identification was secured, the victim could or could not agree to press charges or testify. The kit was only the beginning of a very rough and long road.

"Well, I'll get the kit done, and hopefully there will be something we can use when this guy's caught. Maybe you guys can get her to tell you something the others haven't. Is she talking yet?" Kate asked.

"No. Really hasn't said much. Just 'yes' and 'no' answers right now. Just kind of doing that staring off into space thing. You know what I'm saying?" Bill asked.

Kate knew the look all too well and acknowledged his question with a slight upward tilt of her head and lifting of the eyebrows as if to say, "I hear you."

She walked into the air-conditioned waiting area of the ER and showed her ID badge to the security officer who was still manning the information desk at this hour. While he called back to find out in which cubicle her patient waited, Kate saw two other officers standing over by the coffee machine; a young male officer and a younger female officer. *Wow, they get younger every year, don't they?* They were standing close by each other but not speaking. Both were busy sipping their coffees in the gratuitous white Styrofoam cups. The female officer looked haunted, while the male officer kept glancing at his partner. His body language spoke loudly of his loss on how to help his partner through this. First rape scene, thought Kate. She'd seen it before in other officers and recognized it for what it was: shell shock.

The security guard gave Kate the number of the cubicle where the patient awaited her and buzzed her through. Upon entering the inner sanctum of the ER, Kate was immediately spotted by Eileen Talbot, one of the nurses. Eileen was also a close friend of Kate's. Therefore, Kate could tell by the look on Eileen's face that this was going to be a bad one.

"Sorry, Katie," Eileen began. "But your number's up tonight. I've got her in room 10, and she's still in what she was wearing when they brought her in. I did give her a warmed blanket because the poor thing was mottled, she was so cold. So, you'll just have to add that to the evidence pile."

It was a common practice to give a warmed, clean blanket to any trauma victim or someone complaining of being cold. The blanket warmer was a nice addition to the ER; an addition she and Eileen had championed. However, it was a known forensic fact that any fibers or hairs could transfer to whatever the victim was wearing or came into close contact with. It was not unusual for blankets, towels, washcloths and other things to disappear out of hospital circulation for awhile until they had been checked for evidence. The blanket would need to be added to evidence on this case as well.

"Alright," Kate started as she set her traveler's mug behind the counter. "Can I leave this here for a little while?" she asked the young lady who must have called her earlier.

"Sure, Ms. Tuscadero," she replied with hushed somberness. *Yep, she knows who I am and what I do. No need for introductions then*, thought Kate.

"Yeah, but don't drink any of it," Eileen joked with the young monitor technician. "That's her special brew and I'm sure she knows exactly how many cc's are left in that mug."

Kate rolled and crossed her eyes at the bewildered young lady until she laughed with them and the tension in the air dissipated somewhat. "I don't know *exactly* how much is there," Kate joked before walking away towards room 10.

"The kit already in the room?" she asked Eileen.

"Side table," Eileen answered and gave Kate a supportive smile.

Kate stopped outside of room 10. She made a point to prepare herself to enter this traumatized woman's world. She pulled on her professional and caring cloak and said, "No wrong, no right." It was her go-to statement that reminded her to remain non-judgmental and just collect the evidence that presented itself. Any judgments on her part could interfere with a complete and thorough collection of the kit and could possibly hinder prosecution later.

Kate opened the door while opening her mouth to introduce herself and speak with the victim before beginning the collection. She was unprepared for the sight that greeted her widened eyes and the only sound to escape her lips was a breathed out "oh...."

Chapter 3

5:30AM

He carefully tied a black thread around the lock of hair lying on the counter. He did so slowly so as not to damage one strand. Finishing, he secured it with a tight knot and looked at it lying there – a black linear wound against the white faux marble counter. He marveled at how it curled slightly at the end, but when part of the living woman the hair had hung straight. He wondered if she was one of those women who ironed her hair. He did not remember seeing any evidence of such a thing on any of his many trips to her condo.

He picked it up now, feeling the silkiness of it between his rough fingers, remembering how it was to grab it by handfuls. The sweet memory of the instant submission wrought from grabbing a fistful of a woman's hair caused him to close his eyes and enjoy the wave of domination he always experienced. With eyes still closed, he raised the lock of hair to his nose and inhaled deeply of its scent. Ah, the freshly washed smell of a woman's hair. There was nothing quite like it.

Still holding the lock of hair to his nose, he opened his eyes and saw his reflection in the bathroom mirror before him. The lock of hair appeared to be a poor excuse for a mustache on his angular face, and he smiled appreciating the humor in that. Slowly, he pulled the lock of hair away from his face, remembering the accidental obtaining of it. This particular lock of hair had come from the nape, buried under top layers - so as not to be missed. She had been unconscious, so it had been a clean cut with the knife. He had taken the time to wrap it in a pink tissue pulled from the box on her night table and put it in his bag's side pocket. He knew at the time it would be a treasure and should be treated as such. It was his first treasure secured that was part of the living woman, not just a trinket from her bedroom.

He looked at his reflection again and studied his muscular frame for any marks. He had done a quick once over in the mirror before his shower, but he wanted to make sure that nothing incriminating would present itself later. He had gotten better at subduing them faster, but sometimes an errant swinging fistful of claws would find him before he could secure their hands behind their backs. Kicking feet sometimes landed a good hit to his thighs or legs, leaving a bruise - but those were easily covered and never all that bad. Besides, for every bruise he received, he would leave three or four more. He figured it was only fair.

He saw, again in the mirror, the three claw marks the bitch had left near his right collarbone. Not very deep and hardly worth the antibiotic ointment he had applied after his shower, but they were there, nonetheless. Normally, his chosen victim would see him standing in their bedrooms and turn their backs to run or to reach for their phones. This, of course, only presented the opportune time for him to pounce. He was always quickly able to subdue them. However, this one had just stared at him with what he took at the time to be a defiant stare. She had not asked him what they all eventually did, "Who are you? What do you want?" No, she had just stared.

Then slowly, she had started to get out of bed, not removing her eyes from him. At first he thought, *she doesn't see me....she heard something, but she isn't sure what she heard.* This only served to increase the sense of hunter in him and he was flooded by waves of superiority. Then a car had driven by outside and a beam of light had quickly passed over him. Just as he had planned it all those nights ago standing in the exact same spot staring at an empty bed. However, instead of a scream or even a sharp intake of breath, she had frozen and remained silent; continuing to look him in the eye.

This lack of submission, this refusal to accept his obvious advantage over her enraged him. He took three quick, giant steps towards her, grabbing her upper arms. Then she screamed and made a futile attempt to push him away, her left hand pushing and pulling at his black T-shirt. Pulling at the collar of his shirt had allowed her nails to scratch his upper chest. With all the adrenaline pumping at the time, he had barely felt it. It was the anger at the audacity of this bitch to try and hurt him that had caused him to grab those swiping claws and push her back onto the bed. Using his knees he had held her arms down, sitting on her chest and placed his gloved hands around her wiry neck. Yet, still she fought! So, he squeezed and squeezed that little neck until she stopped.

At first he thought he had killed her. Then he slowly realized she was still breathing. He discovered he had somehow strangled her to the point of unconsciousness only. He had brought her to the brink of death without allowing her to drop over the edge. The realization of the power in that nearly caused him to explode in his pants sitting right there next to her unconscious body. And although he planned to ride this particular woman time and time again, he was not going to waste his precious fluid on a thought when she was lying supine beneath him, ready for the taking.

Seeing her long, beautiful hair - a woman's pride, his mother had told him - splayed upon her pillow gave him the idea of stealing a piece of it. So, he had. He practiced throughout their time together to perfect the new trick of bringing a woman to the brink of death. The thought of it now caused him to get an almost painful erection.

To take his mind off of it, he directed his thoughts to more practical things. It was his practice to review the attack afterwards, recognize any errors in judgment, play through different optional scenarios and therefore, be better prepared for the next "purchase."

Perhaps her refusal to react immediately to his presence was because pretty Teri wore glasses; a fact that he had forgotten in the tenseness of the moment. Maybe she had gotten out of bed to figure what was in the corner, not who. He was sure that if she had figured out it was a "who" she would have reacted sooner. So, it was fortunate that he waited for that passing beam of light to let her see that he had finally come to call upon her.

When she had seen him, she had probably frozen like a deer in headlights. What he had seen had not been defiance! She had just recognized him for the victor that he already was. She had known, deep down, in her femaleness that she now belonged to him to use as he would. No woman would ever dare look upon his physique and think they had a chance. He berated himself for doubting his own virility and the power that was innately his.

He should have backhanded her hard to snap her out of it. That action alone would have spun her around to fall face first on the bed. Then, he could have subdued her without any marks. Oh well, he thought, the marks she had left from her pitiful attempts to escape his grasp would heal in a few days, and he would be none the worse for wear. But, he had probably bled on that shirt, or left tiny, microscopic torn fragments from the rough handling of it, so he would have to dispose of it.

He carried the lock of hair with him as he walked back into his bedroom towards his stereo. In the back of one speaker, he kept his treasures - small trinkets from each of his ladies' bedrooms. He added the lock of hair making a mental note that he would need to get a nice silk or velvet drawstring bag for it. They should not be that hard to find. In fact, he would get several so that he could add to his collection. Locks of hair were so much more personal. In addition to that, he thought, what better way to steal a woman's pride than to take a piece of her hair without her knowing?

He took a few precious minutes to look over his growing collection realizing that soon he would need to find a larger spot for it. He had so much shopping still to do. With regret, he replaced the panel in the speaker box and began to get dressed for work.

He wanted to get an early start today. He had already chosen his next potential purchase, and he had so much planning to do. The press had dubbed him "The Window Shopper" and he quite liked it. However, they had no idea how much time and effort he put into each "shopping" trip. Yes, places to go, people to see. The anticipation of the "purchase" was almost better than the purchase itself.

He smiled at his reflection in the dresser mirror as he straightened his tie. By day, he was a copier repairman. At night, he was Thomas "The King Snake" King. He was the antithesis of a superhero, but just as indestructible. He grunted at his reflection in the mirror. *Yeah, that's right, baby,* he thought, *indestructible.*

Chapter 4

Kate had been a certified SANE nurse for little over a year and had seen some horrible things. But she was quite unprepared for the traumatized woman she saw before her. The woman had not been cleaned up in order to save any evidence that could be vital for the rape kit. Kate knew that before going in. But if this were the work of The Window Shopper, he had been much more brutal this time.

The woman sat on the stretcher wrapped in a hospital blanket. The blanket exposed one shoulder, the early signs of fingerprint bruising visible on the upper arm. Her black hair was a tangled cloud of horrors unspoken, and it appeared to be matted with blood at the hairline on the right. Her face, besides being tear-streaked and pale, had suffered blows to the right eye, left corner mouth and jaw line. Her left bottom lip had split and a shiny clot was quickly forming there. The vicious assault had left the beginnings of colors, which would show their true brilliance in a few hours, as well as swelling. A bag of ice, nestled inside of a towel that could be entered into evidence later, lay beside her on the stretcher. From the small amount of blood on the towel, it had probably been used briefly, but now lay forgotten.

Her neck showed multiple ligature marks in angry reddened-gray linear patterns as well as circular marks near the lump made by her Adam's apple. She gulped at the air and swallowed hard during Kate's visual appraisal and the ligature marks undulated but clung to the soft tissue there; the claim on her throat complete for now.

There were numerous other cuts, scrapes, abrasions and bruises covering the exposed portions of her arms and legs. But what had caused the words to die on Kate's lips, what had caused her stomach to flip and her heart to freeze was the combination of the haunted look on the woman's face and the fact that she rocked.

She had been staring off into space, rocking back and forth when Kate had opened the door. However, instead of stopping to acknowledge Kate or continuing to stare off into the world she had created for herself and rocking, she had acknowledged Kate with those haunted eyes and continued to rock. That gesture said I know you are here, and I know you are here to try and help me, but you cannot. I will be lost forever regardless of what you do.

Kate had seen the look before - too many times. She also recognized the characteristic rocking for what it was - an attempt to self-soothe. A part of us that returned to that time when rocking made it all alright. Together with the rhythmic, breathy one-toned hum that she emitted, she presented a picture of a fragile, frightened and trapped animal that when touched would shatter.

Kate cleared her throat and said, "My name is Kaitlin Tuscadero. I am a nurse who specializes in collecting evidence in sexual assault cases. I can start whenever you're ready. I can leave the room and give you a few more minutes, or I can just sit here with you. I will not touch you without getting your permission to do so. I will tell you everything that I am going to do before I do it. You are in control of this situation and of your own body. I will only do what you allow me to do and only when you tell me I can. You... are in control."

The woman stopped her incessant humming and her rocking, but would still not make eye contact with Kate again. For what seemed like a whole minute, she sat there not saying anything. Kate shifted her weight to set the kit down on the counter top next to the door and the young woman spoke.

"What do you mean by 'specialized'?" she asked, again not looking at Kate, but at some invisible point on the opposite wall.

"I'm a sexual assault nurse examiner. I have been trained and certified to perform exams and collect any evidence on reported sexual assaults." Kate explained. When the woman did not comment any further or look over at her, Kate glanced at her information sheet known as a face sheet for the woman's name: Theresa Ann Sanderson.

"Ms. Sanderson?" Kate began, "is it okay if I examine you and collect items for this sexual assault kit I have with me?"

The woman shifted her eyes to her left, peeking through a few hanging strands of hair to look at the kit. She began to rock again.

"What do you have to do? What are you collecting?" she asked in a voice full of distrust.

"I will not examine or touch any part of your body that you do not want me to. You can stop the exam at any time or refuse any collection of any one item. You are totally in control of this exam in that regard. I am looking for fluids, hairs, fibers, anything that may still be with you since the assault. Anything that, should you decide to press charges later, could count as evidence. Again, you are in control of this situation. We will work together and we will only go as far as you want to go. We have all the time we need...you and I." Kate spoke in a low and easy manner.

The rocking stopped once again and the woman looked at Kate, her eyes probing the nurse's face.

"What's your name again?" asked the woman.

"Kaitlin Tuscadero."

"No, I mean, what do people call you? Kaitlin?" the woman asked.

This was tricky, thought Kate. A sexual assault nurse examiner had to remain completely objective in order not to taint the collection of a rape kit or recollection of events later. A remark from a plaintiff that the SANE nurse had been "very friendly" or "helped me to see what happened" or anything of that nature could potentially discount what was collected. A good defense attorney could then claim that the SANE nurse had "extreme prejudice" towards his client, blah, blah, blah.

On the other hand, the woman had to believe that Kate, in the role of the SANE nurse, posed no threat to her in order to collect a complete kit. The process about to be undertaken was a long and arduous one. It required the victim to allow the SANE nurse to poke and probe places that had recently been brutalized. Many envelopes and swabs existed in the kit, and it could take up to four hours to complete an exam.

"Nurse" Kate answered and smiled tentatively. The woman looked back at her as if she had spoken Greek.

"Or 'Hey, nurse' depending on how long they've been waiting. So, you can call me nurse or Kaitlin is fine if you want," Kate finished.

The woman nodded and said, "My name's Theresa, but everyone calls me Teri. I figure if you're going to be doing what you're going to be doing, we should be on a first name basis, right?"

Kate was somewhat taken aback. The woman had gone from a humming rock-a-bye victim to a resigned patient in the space of a few minutes. Kate decided to test the waters.

"Are you ready to begin then?" she asked.

The woman drew back a little, although Kate herself had not moved.

"No, wait a minute. Not yet. I'm not ready yet," she said hurriedly.

Kate sat in the plastic chair beside the counter. She longed to be opening the kit and laying everything out in the order in which it would be collected. However, she realized that she would need to demonstrate her earlier promise to put Teri at ease. So, Kate sat back in the chair, crossed her legs and laid an arm casually atop one knee. Her body language said, *We have all the time in the world. No hurry.*

"Okay, no problem. We can begin whenever you're ready," Kate said.

"How long have you been a nurse?" asked Teri, sliding a few dirty clumps of hair behind her right ear. She struck the pose of someone interviewing a potential employee and Kate played along.

"Well, let's see. I've been a nurse for about six years," Kate replied.

"Do you like it?" Teri asked.

"Very much," replied Kate, wondering how long this would last. "What do you do?"

"I work in Human Resources at Co-op Electrical," Teri stated, starting to tremble.

"Do you like it?" Kate asked, mimicking Teri's line of questioning.

"Um...yeah..it's...um...I..." Teri started and then began to shake harder, her hands searching aimlessly to find something beside her. Then they were in her lap. Then they locked within each other. "I was...I mean...I..." and then she broke.

Her face contorted and her mouth opened in a silent scream as her limbs drew closer to her core. Her shoulders shook with a silent sob and a shiny line of saliva stretched slowly down through space and landed on her whitened knuckle. Her lungs sucked in the air around her, and she released harsh sobs that threatened to break her small frame. Somehow, her widened mouth formed the words, "Oh my God" in a drawn out cry. The tenuous clot that had formed on her bottom lip had broken under the stretch of her grimace and fresh, red blood cut a new path down her chin. In a high, keening wail she said, "He hurt me... and he tried to kill me again and again. I didn't do anything to him. Anything! Why? Why?"

Kate wanted to rush over to her and hold the woman's violently shaking form to absorb some of the shock for her. The woman in her wanted to rock her and shush her and tell her it would be all right. However, she would be lying. In addition, she would be contaminating evidence. So, she clenched her hands in her lap and let the storm in front of her rage on.

Eileen opened the door and Teri jumped, but continued on. Eileen looked to Kate and Kate gave a quick shake of her head without taking her eyes off of Teri. Eileen slowly closed the door and left Kate alone with Teri. Like a passing summer squall, Teri's sobs became quieter and began to slow until she was crying softly, reaching for a box of tissues on the metal table beside her. She blew her nose and upon seeing blood on the tissue, grew somewhat alarmed. Kate motioned for Teri to check her chin and Teri wiped away the blood there, leaving the tissue bunched up at her lip to staunch the wound.

During the onslaught of her grief, the blanket had slipped away and Kate could now see the pajamas she may have been wearing at the time of the assault. At least, she hoped that's what they were. Teri wore a plain T-shirt that used to be white and a pair of navy running shorts.

Sometimes, Kate would arrive at the hospital to find the victim already in a hospital gown and their clothes (usually not the clothes worn during the assault) neatly folded on a chair beside the stretcher. In worst case scenarios, victims would be sitting on the stretcher freshly showered or reporting an assault that had taken place more than 24 hours ago.

This was Kate's home hospital, and she had in serviced the ER staff on several occasions as well as the county police officers. Once the assault was over, and you had a living victim, you now had walking evidence! CSI would handle the scene of the assault. However, everything about the victim, from fibers left on her clothes to skin under her nails, was evidence. ER staff and police officers were warned to keep the victim as found.

"Do not let them wash anything. Do not let them change clothes. If found naked, wrap them up in a new blanket provided for by the police or ambulance personnel" was the speech given many times by Kate herself. Still, sometimes, women were allowed to dress before coming in. Kate had asked ambulance and police personnel to make sure, if possible, to have them wear the clothes they were wearing during the attack or at least clean clothes from home.

As Teri's tears dried up, she seemed to harden. Instead of the dazed and ashamed look that Kate saw many times, she recognized another common reaction among victims soon after a sexual assault, although more rare. Teri was showing signs of anger; rage. She noticed for herself the shallow lacerations around her wrists from the binding earlier. Kate had noticed these earlier herself and had made a mental note to swab each.

"So," Teri said, still not looking at Kate, "you're here to get the evidence to nail the son-of-a-bitch for doing this to me?"

Kate uncrossed her legs and looked purposefully at Teri. She chose her next words carefully.

"We will be looking for fibers, hairs...anything that we can lift off of your clothes or skin that we can hopefully match up to someone when that person is found. Many times, the evidence collected can help with the prosecution of an individual once a perpetrator has been found and an arrest has been made," Kate explained.

Teri lifted her eyes to look into Kate's. "So, the kit's no good unless you have someone to pin the contents on. Is that what you're saying?" she asked.

"Hey, the kit's always a good idea," Kate answered. "It's best to collect everything right after something has happened because you're more likely to have more to collect. But, yes, you are correct in what you're saying. I'm not going to lie to you. It will sit in evidence until we have a suspect to try and match the contents up with."

"Uh-huh," said Teri and looked once again at her hands; her left hand in particular. She turned the hand back and forth, inspecting it as if it were foreign to her. She looked at the broken and dirty nails like a woman considering a manicure. Then she held that hand out in Kate's direction with the back of it facing Kate. It hung there trembling with rage or trepidation, Kate wasn't sure.

"Well, you can start with this hand," Teri said with a defiant tilt of her head and rage in her eyes. "Because, I used this hand to push him away. This hand tore at his skin and that skin is sitting right under these nails. This hand will prove he did it."

Kate was stunned and could not speak at first. Should she call Bill back in here? They had him! The first bit of evidence worth anything! What to do first? Collect the kit? Swab under those nails before something happened to that evidence? Kate's mind stumbled for a millisecond over that revelation, but her mouth opened with an audible click on Teri's next statement.

"You see, I know who did this to me. I saw his face and I know who did this. And this hand," she said holding it up like a beacon, "is going to prove it!"

Chapter 5

Tommy decided to make his first stop the hospital this morning, since they were guaranteed to be open. He could service the two copiers there and maybe pick up an egg and cheese sandwich and hot coffee at the cafeteria before hitting his other stops for the day. He wanted to make sure that he was off by 3:00 so that he could turn in the van and be sitting in his car in front of the office complex across from the Willow Lawn shopping center by 5:00. He was continuing his "shopping" trip today, and he needed to learn Allison's routine. She was a clock-watcher and therefore, always out of the office and walking to her car by 5:05.

Last Friday, Al - a stupid nickname used by her big-haired friends - met some Barbies at the local Mulligan's down Broad Street closer to the West End. Miss Allison had flirted with the pretty-boy waiter while having a little too much to drink. She had hopped into the car with one of her stupid, obnoxious friends - the one that chewed gum constantly - and they had all gone dancing at one of the local meat markets in the Slip. Shockoe Bottom, a.k.a. The Slip, was *the* hotspot for all the 20-somethings; offering comedy clubs, loud pubs, excellent restaurants and myriad dancing clubs in downtown Richmond. Located by the James River, with cobblestone streets and the ability to walk to any venue, it was always crowded and boisterous on any given evening.

He hoped that she didn't repeat the same routine because following around a party girl could get expensive. Never mind having to fend off the lip-licking sluts that just wanted him to buy them their next drink. He had watched her now for the last three weeks on Mondays, Wednesdays and Fridays. Next week he would change it up and do Tuesdays, Thursdays and Saturdays. He never "shopped" or "purchased" anything on Sundays, because on Sundays, he had to take his bitch of a mother to church.

He found it ironic and almost damn comical that the woman he escorted to church every Sunday and whom everyone just adored was one of the most evil women he had ever known. Growing up with the monster that was his mother had been a lesson in survival from day one. She never let him forget that she had "allowed" him to live *"and for what? So you could make my life a living hell, that's what!"* She had planned on aborting him on a Monday morning, he had heard more than once. However, she had gotten drunk the night before and overslept; ignoring the alarm. Somehow she had assumed it was a sign from God or some shit and had decided to clean up her act and have the baby after all.

To have a baby with no real income, no father and no real idea of how to raise a child.....great thinking there, Mother dear! And the "clean up her act" bit lasted maybe a week. They bounced from roach-infested place to creepy-neighbor place. All the while, his mother would claim that God would "see them through." God would put food on the table while she used what money they did have on cigarettes and cheap bottles of wine. "If God didn't want us to drink wine, he wouldn't have let his son take pure water and turn it into wine, now would he? Go play or something, you're bothering me."

God would heal his ear infection; the ear that no longer worked now due to a busted eardrum from said infection. God would find them the next rat trap after she could no longer come up with enough excuses for not having the money. "Sorry, Jeanie, but I can't let you go another month without paying. You and the boy got to go," was the scripted speech of each landlord. But, the ridding of sin in her erstwhile child? Well... Janet King would take care of that, yes sir! She would beat the sin right out of that boy! She would beat him if she even *thought* he had done something wrong. And by doing so, she had created the monster he was today. Good job there, Jeanie baby!

He realized his knuckles were white on the steering wheel and his breathing had become audible as his heart pounded against the cage of his chest. He concentrated on calming himself down. He took several deep breaths; one of the few helpful hints he got from all of those inept counselors he had seen through the years. *In through the nose, hold.....and out through pursed lips, he thought, slower.... slower.......there, better now.*

Back in control, he mentally switched gears and concentrated on the job in front of him. Yeah, he summarized, he would get an early start, finish up and be ready for tonight's adventure by 5:00. His stomach rumbled thinking of the greasy, hot egg and cheese sandwich that awaited the job's completion at the hospital. As he pulled into the ER parking area, he saw Henrico's finest standing outside the bay doors, drinking coffee and smoking cigarettes. Dumb asses, he thought, still smoking after all that info out there about what cancer sticks laced with addictive properties cigarettes actually were. No wonder they had no clue about who he was! He could "shop" for years. When it came to the cops, his credit was obviously going to be good for a long, long time.

He gathered up his service kit from the floorboard behind the passenger seat and stepped out of the van. He gave a friendly smile and wave at the officers as he passed them. He loved moments like this! A nod and a friendly wave on the outside and visions of mutilation on the inside.....priceless, truly priceless! he thought as he walked through the pneumatic doors.

He gave a nod and a wink to.......Ashley, that's right!... as he walked by the front desk. He knew she continued to watch him as he made his way over to the copier; the young ones always did. They still carried enough innocence within them to recognize the aura of danger he wore like a tough leather jacket. To them, he reeked of the bad boy scent that virgins swooned over. Once she was ruined by some lying punk of a boy, she would become hardened and think only of herself, ceasing to notice men like him anymore. She would look for the next pretty boy with lies to tell and Tommy would not even be a blip on her radar screen anymore. They were all that way. It was just a matter of time.

However, he welcomed the anonymity that their jaded, vacuous minds afforded him. It was what allowed him to walk in their homes and "purchase" what he had been "shopping" for. The jaded, pretty women did not even notice he was there and never remembered his name. But they knew him later. Oh, they never forgot about him later, he smiled to himself.

He set about servicing the copier closest to the nurse's station. He couldn't help overhear their conversation. To his delight, they were discussing him! Instead of his usual practice of filtering women's inane conversations for statements regarding absent boyfriends or the newly acquired status of single, he tuned in order to catch every word.

"They're pretty sure it's him. Same MO and all."

They knew already? Wow, ERs must be like a bunch of gossiping women, trading horror stories before the bodies were bandaged!

"Yeah, this one's pretty banged up. He even tried to kill her!"

Oh honey. If I had wanted her dead, she'd be dead.

"Kate's finishing up the exam now. She asked for a set of scrubs about 20 minutes ago." Tommy almost dropped the toner cartridge he was holding.

She's here?! In this ER?

"Which room are they in?"

Yeah, which room?

"Exam room 10," Little Ashley answered, sipping her coffee with an aura of all-knowing. Tommy's eyes quickly scanned the numbers above each glass cubicle for room number 10. *There it is!* he thought, right next to the second copier which services triage. How lucky could he get?!?

However, he was right in the middle of servicing the first copier providing general maintenance. He couldn't just stop working on that copier to start on the second without causing people to wonder what the hell he was doing. Just then an older, casually beautiful nurse came up to the station and seemed to be looking right at him.

"Hey, um....." she started.

"Tommy," he supplied the name she was looking for.

"Yeah, sorry, I knew that," she said with a smile.

Lying bitch! Tommy thought and smiled back.

"Um, would you mind taking a look at the other copier for just a second? I realize you're in the middle of this one. But that copier over here keeps putting this line down every copy and well....we're so busy in triage and everything," she finished, giving him the pretty please look that women assumed worked on every swinging dick.

Tommy plastered his award-winning smile on his face and said, "Be happy to!" *You have no idea how happy*, he thought. *You just gave me the excuse I was looking for!*

As he followed Eileen toward the other copier, he missed the conspiratorial whisper from Ashley to her once-again attentive audience, "And *this* one saw his face!"

Tommy pretended to be perplexed as Eileen demonstrated the troubles the copier was giving the ER this morning. He knew exactly what it was; the drum. However, he hemmed and he hawed, with his arms folded and his index finger pressed against his pursed lips as if to say, *this might just take awhile.* As Eileen left Tommy to solve the puzzle of the mysterious line, Tommy allowed his eyes furtively to glance at the door of exam room 10.

The door was shut, the glass partition having been slid and locked into place. Each room had curtains hung on the inside of each partition to give patients privacy when needed. Not even a shadow could be seen.

This was such a treat for him! He was never able to see his prizes again once he had "purchased" them. He resisted the urge to cruise by their places of residence and be the first to acknowledge them in their places of business after the fact. The excitement of it caused him to sniff loudly repeatedly, an old and annoying habit. He almost sounded like he was trying to snort something. He caught himself, swallowing several times in a row as his mother had taught him to do all those years ago.

Come out! he silently begged, *come out and let me see you again. Let me see the humbled servant I have created. Let me see all the brilliant colors that I gave you now that they're fresh and angry. Don't make me wait to see them yellowed and green with age. Come out, come out, wherever you are!*

Then his heart jumped in his chest when he heard a muffled woman's voice on the other side of the door and the sound of what could have been a hand on the door handle. He strained to hear what was being said. The door opened and from his position of kneeling by the open copier, he saw her. Not his previously purchased prize, but a nurse - a very attractive nurse - carrying a white kit sealed with red evidence tape. *What the hell?* he thought.

Then the nurse spoke to the officer standing by the door. *Where did he come from?* "Here you go. Is the other room ready for her?"

How long had the officer been standing there? Had he noticed Tommy listening and looking? Tommy busied himself with buffing the drum in his hand, but kept his ears open.

"I'll ask Officer Beck on my way out. I'll have her come and let you know," reported the officer by the door in answer to the pretty nurse.

She thanked the officer and disappeared back into the room, but not before he heard Teri's voice from deep within that room somewhere saying, "What next?" Then the door was sealed shut again, and he was left both deaf and blind once more.

Slowly, he buffed the drum, trying to draw out the time. Ever so slowly he turned it in his capable hands. After a few seconds, a female officer approached the door, hesitated and then knocked.

The same nurse opened the door and slid it closed behind her. The officer reported, "Sergeant Patterson said that he cleared it with Eileen, and we can take her to the nurse's lounge for the interview." Tommy was stumbling over the word "interview" when the same nurse who had interrupted him before was back.

"How's it coming?" Eileen asked him while looking at the shiny drum in his hands. He had the feeling that she knew he had been listening and was *not* pleased.

"Just need to pop this back in and you'll be back in business," He smiled. When she didn't move away, he added, "Just take a few more minutes, and then it'll be ready for use."

"If you don't mind, I'll wait," she said, shifting some papers from one hand to the other. "I need to make some copies pretty quickly."

Tommy cursed silently when he realized that he had left the other copier out of service to attend to this one. *Damn it!* he thought as he realized the officer was leaving, and he had missed the rest of the conversation.

Tommy was sure that she had noticed him eavesdropping and therefore, did not push the issue anymore. His chance to see his pretty prize was gone and he accepted it like the cool hunter that he was. He finished re-installing the drum while the bossy nurse waited and printed out a test sheet.

Reluctantly, he returned to the other copier and quickly finished the work there. Stalling now would only draw unneeded attention to him in connection with Teri. He was sure that he was right as he felt Eileen's eyes on his back as he bid everyone a good morning and started down the hallway leading to the cafeteria in search of the highly anticipated egg and cheese sandwich.

Teri slowly emerged from exam room 10 in hospital-issued scrubs, trying not to notice everyone trying not to be obvious in noticing her. She followed Kate and Eileen as they made their way around the nurse's station, passing by the pneumatic doors leading to the outside. As Teri passed by the doors, she realized that the sun had risen high and bright despite what had happened to her the night before. People went on with their lives as evidenced by the cars lining the parking area about 50 feet away. As her eyes took in the scene in a passing glance, something flashed briefly in her consciousness setting off alarms deep inside her traumatized brain. However, her brain had dealt with too many alarms in the last few hours and therefore, numbed itself to the sound.

Teri wondered briefly what her mind was trying to tell her, but then went back to focusing on getting through the next few hours. As the door closed behind the solemn group entering the nurse's lounge on a beautiful Richmond morning in August, the sun glinted off the windshield of the copier company van. The same company that had serviced Teri's place of business for the last three years.

Chapter 6

Sitting around the table usually reserved for hurried meals and the reading of orientation manuals, sat a group of people with different agendas. Teri, still somewhat shell-shocked, took in her surroundings and dissected them. Anything not to think about what she was about to undertake until absolutely necessary. She read the names on each nurse's locker and studied the photographs, quotes, and occasional celebrities that adorned most. She wondered about those lockers that had nothing but a name. Were they a new employee, an outsider, a loner?

Sergeant Patterson studied each person at the table: Teri, the two officers responding to the scene, Kate and the detective that would be taking the statement. He knew Kate well enough to know that she would want to be leaving as soon as possible. Per protocol, she would only need to be present long enough to assure chain of evidence on the sexual assault evidence kit and Teri's statement to her regarding knowing the identity of her assailant. Kate would be dismissed from these proceedings before Teri gave her statement so that any future testimony from Kate would not be considered biased.

Kate was aware of the burnt coffee smell permeating the room. She knew the road ahead of Teri and did not envy her the journey. This morning would be just the beginning. She wanted to quickly give her statement regarding Teri's proclamation, then join her colleagues for the rest of the shift. She knew they desperately needed her in staffing and the sooner she could take on a part of the workload, the better.

With a determined look passing between Sgt. Patterson and the lead detective, the detective cleared his throat and addressed those at the table and in the room.

"Okay, I think we can go ahead and get started. Ms. Tuscadero, I know that you are anxious to get on with your day here at the hospital." He addressed this last bit to Kate standing by the door. Kate did not miss the quick, worried glance that Teri gave her.

"Well," Kate started, "following protocol, I don't want to be in the room for Teri's testimony and I explained the reasons for that earlier. So, it would make better sense for me to go first instead of trying to come back later."

"Right." said Detective Ted Corning. He set up the tape recorder, stated the time, date and those present at the taping and began. "Ms. Tuscadero, do you certify that you delivered the sexual assault evidence kit directly into the hands of a waiting officer?"

"Yes, I do. The sexual assault evidence collection kit was given to Officer Sandra Beck of the Henrico County Police Department," stated Kate, who had been through this part of the proceedings too many times to count.

"Officer Beck," Detective Corning said turning slightly to face the female officer, "do you attest that the same sexual assault evidence kit passed from your hands into the hands of a certified crime scene unit officer?"

"Yes," stated Officer Beck, "I personally handed the sealed sexual assault evidence kit directly to CSU officer Brent Taylor. The evidence kit never left my hands or sight and was not tampered with in any way before reaching CSU Officer Taylor." This was not Officer Beck's first time at this particular rodeo either. Detective Corning smiled at Officer Beck before turning back to Kate.

"Ms. Tuscadero, please state your involvement in these proceedings."

"I am a sexual assault nurse examiner. I examined Ms. Teri Sanderson in accordance with the procedure regarding the collection of a sexual assault evidence kit with Ms. Sanderson's permission," Kate explained.

"And did Ms. Sanderson make a declaration to you regarding the identity of the person who she claims assaulted her?" guided Detective Corning.

"Yes, she did," Kate answered, "she said, 'I know who did this to me. I saw his face and I know who did this'."

"Ms. Sanderson, please state your full name," Detective Corning addressed Teri.

"Teresa Sanderson and that's what I said. I told her I knew who it was because I saw his face, and I recognized him. I also said that I had scratched him and probably had his skin under the nails of this hand," added Teri.

Detective Corning had at first winced as Teri rambled on after her name, but seemed satisfied with her statement. He asked Kate, "Did you take samples from under the nails of the left hand that Ms. Sanderson is now indicating?"

"I did...immediately, after her statement. Then, I proceeded with the collection of other items indicated by the sexual assault evidence collection kit."

"Thank you, Ms. Tuscadero. Is there anything else you would like to add before we dismiss you?" Detective Corning paused for her response.

"No thank you, and if you have no other questions, I will be leaving the proceedings at this time," Kate said more for the tape recorder than clarification of his statement.

"Very well. Thank you, Ms. Tuscadero for your time and your input to these proceedings. You are free to go," finished Detective Corning.

Kate slipped out during Detective Corning's explanation of her leaving the room and stating once again, who remained to witness Teri's upcoming statement. She was glad to be out. She had barely cleared the nurse's station when Eileen caught up with her.

Eileen walked quickly with Kate as she swiped in on the time clock under the ER code, dismissing her SANE duties and billable time as such. Eileen could barely contain herself during the mundane act. As they headed back towards the hub of the ER, Eileen asked, "So, is it the same guy? And did she see him?"

"Eileen," Kate warned in a singsong voice, "you know I can't discuss anything about this particular patient because it could go to court and I don't want to jeopardize *anything* with this one, capisch?"

"Darn it! Okay," whined Eileen. "Well, maybe I'll just ask the copier guy."

"Do what?" Kate stopped by the white eraser board to see which patients she would be picking up.

As soon as Eileen had secured the nurse's lounge, she had known that Kate would be available within the half hour. Therefore, being the charge nurse for the shift, she had already broken down the assignments, giving Kate two existing patients and holding two open rooms for incoming patients who would then be assigned to Kate.

"Oh yeah, the copier guy was servicing the copier right by the exam room and I could tell he was stalling to find out what was going on," Eileen explained.

Kate was half-listening while she picked up the clipboards on the two patients already in exam rooms. So, her only comment to Eileen was a non-committal "uh-huh."

As Kate checked returned lab work and assessment sheets, Eileen continued, "Yeah, my fault really. I'm the one that asked him to have a look at it because it was putting this line down the left side of everything. Right down the center of where the vital signs are written in. Anyway....I kind of played a nosy Nelly when I realized he was eavesdropping and trying to figure out what was going on in there."

Kate smiled at her good friend. "Hey, don't worry about it. I'm sure he didn't get much with the door shut. He was gone before she came out, right?"

"Oh yeah, by a good five minutes or so. He never saw her," Eileen assured her, knowing they were both thinking the same thing....media.

"Well, there you go! No harm, no foul. So, you want to tell me a little bit about these two train wrecks you dumped on me or what?" Kate asked as she playfully shouldered her friend.

***

Back in the nurse's lounge, things were progressing smoothly. The officers had given their statements and had been dismissed. After a brief break while someone made fresh coffee, the tape was flipped to the other side for Teri's portion. Teri declined the coffee, but asked for some ice water instead. Her throat was still quite sore and water with crushed ice would be more soothing, she thought.

When she had the water in front of her and had assured Detective Corning that she was ready, the recorder was turned on. Once again, the date and time were given, as well as those individuals who remained in the room.

"Ms. Sanderson," Detective Corning began, "We are taking a statement from you here today to present to the district attorney's office. Should the district attorney feel that we can proceed..."

"What do you mean 'if we can proceed'? Why wouldn't we? I already told him (indicating Sgt. Patterson) who did this. Aren't they arresting him right now?" Teri's voice had risen in pitch with each question, and she turned to look at Sergeant Patterson for an explanation.

"Ms. Sanderson," Sergeant Patterson was quick to reassure her, "We will certainly be speaking with the copier company today. Together with your statement, a positive identification and what the kit will give us......Well, I would be hard pressed to see why it wouldn't proceed...."

"Sergeant," stuttered Detective Corning, "we certainly cannot give any guarantees at this point," he finished indicating the tape recorder with a nod of his head towards it.

Sergeant Patterson could see the victim coming apart at the seams while he and Detective Corning argued semantics. So, he intervened in the interest of the victim. "What Detective Corning is trying to explain is the normal protocol for all statements taken. All are presented to the district attorney. It's just how the system works. All cases presented with sufficient evidence, like positive identification and hopefully good DNA are the good ones. DAs are not likely to turn down a gift like that. Don't you worry. You do your part and we, sure as hell, will do ours." He finished with a warning glance to Detective Corning.

Teri seemed somewhat placated, but asked again, "You'll get him today, though. You'll arrest him today?"

"Ms. Sanderson, if he can be found today, he will be in an interrogation room today," stated Sergeant Patterson.

"Okay," Teri turned around to address Det. Corning. "So, what do you need me to say?"

Detective Corning using a calm tone said, "If you could start by telling us what you did today or yesterday."

"You mean....starting when?" Teri asked.

"Did you go to work?"

"Yes."

"Anything different there? Copier serviced yesterday?"

"No. It's only done about once a month; not sure which day, but not yesterday."

"Okay, fine then. Did you go anywhere after work?"

"Well, it was Thursday, so I did my grocery shopping at Food Lion."

"Do you always shop for groceries on Thursday? At the same store?" Det. Corning was also making notes, which made Teri a little nervous.

"Yeah, the store's a zoo on the weekends and I don't want to go on Friday nights. I don't get paid until Friday, so I just go on Thursdays because I know it won't show up in my account until Friday or after." Teri explained as Detective Corning scribbled away on a legal pad.

"Okay, so you get groceries. Did you go straight home?" Detective Corning continued.

"Well, yeah. I had refrigerated and frozen foods...so, yeah," Teri said.

"Notice anything strange when you got home? Anybody hanging around? Anything like that?"

"No...other than it was raining hard by the time I got home and I got soaked getting the groceries in. If he was hanging around then, I wouldn't have noticed him," Teri said as Detective Corning scribbled on his paper like an accountant on the set of Scrooge.

"What did you do after you got home?"

"You mean after putting the groceries up?"

"Did you do that right away?"

"Yeah."

"Then yes, after putting up the groceries."

On and on it went and Teri thought she would lose her mind from all the mundane facts of her boring, single life: eating a frozen dinner, eating a slice of cold pie with a glass of milk right before bed, watching the Thursday night line up by herself. She was almost embarrassed. When she mentioned that she went to bed after the 15 minute preview of the "tonight's news" like she did every weeknight except Fridays, Detective Corning scribbled on his pad again.

"What do you keep writing? I mean, isn't that why we're recording this? Doesn't this thing have a rewind button?" Teri snapped.

She was becoming agitated again. She was tired and hurt. She was scared and bruised. She wanted to go home and sit under a scalding hot shower until the water ran cold, but did not think she'd be clean even then. She wanted this part to be over so she could be alone and just, just...be alone.

"I'm just making notes to help me with my interview with this guy, hopefully, later today. See if anything matches up. It's just to help me help you," Detective Corning said softly. He was married and had two teenage daughters at home.

"Oh," Teri said seeming contrite, "I'm sorry...I...sorry," she ended quickly.

"Hey, don't worry about it. You have the right to ask me anything you want. Are you okay to continue right now or do you need a break?" Detective Corning asked.

"No, I'm okay," Teri said opening her eyes a little wider for a moment, sitting up straighter in the chair and tucking a piece of drying hair behind her right ear.

"Okay, tell me when you knew something was wrong," Detective Corning directed.

Teri took a deep breath and tried to calm her suddenly racing heart. In flashes of memory, she could see the shadow in the corner of the room confirmed as a man by the passing lights of a car. Her cries echoed in her ears and her jaw throbbed with the memory of the first blow. The sudden panic threatened to overtake her as she looked at her splayed fingers, cuticles white as she pressed hard on the table before her.

She forced herself to concentrate on her left hand. The hand her mother was always picking up and examining for the missing engagement ring that was never there. She looked at the hand that she had tried to push him away with but ended up scratching him instead. She looked at the hand that was going to nail the son of a bitch. Then the steel resolve that had peeked out earlier now came to stand in the door of her mind.

She looked up and began with determination, "I woke up because I just sensed something wasn't right. I thought I saw a shadow in the corner of the bedroom, but I wasn't sure. Then a car passed by outside and a beam of light showed me that there was a man in my room..."

She told the story of her assault with few interruptions for clarification from Detective Corning. She did so without faltering and only pausing to sip at the iced water in front of her to soothe her traumatized throat. Sergeant Patterson and Detective Corning saw in her their Golden Goose.

She had seen him and taken away a piece of him. She was determined to see him prosecuted. As she spoke, she continued to protect her left hand as if it still held the damning evidence beneath its nails. When the statement was complete and the tape recorder cut off, she turned to Sergeant Patterson with steel in her eyes and said, "Okay, I've done my part. Now you do yours. Go pick up the son of a bitch and arrest him. I want him to pay for what he did to me."

Chapter 7

Tommy was elated as he walked back to the van. The day had been smooth so far; nothing but general maintenance on all copiers and no complaints. That had to be a first! It was just after 2:00 and he was ready to turn in the van. Normally, he would just eat up the rest of the time on the clock. He had no problem cheating THE MAN; hell, once he'd even gone to a movie in the middle of the day. But today was special. He needed to go "window shopping" this evening. He laughed at his own witty use of the media moniker. He would turn in the van, claim he didn't have a chance to take a lunch today - which was a lie - and beg off early for today. He was a model employee. He never missed a day of work and never called in sick. His dweeb of a supervisor would have no reason to deny his request. Feeling superior and in command, he sniffed hard three times in succession and tossed the clipboard on the passenger seat beside him.

He would have time to jump in his own car, run home to change out of his now damp shirt and be back in time to sit in front of Allison's office complex with time to spare. If he did not spend too much time at home, he could even spring for a burger combo to enjoy while following Allie -- his chosen name for her - around for the evening. *It's a plan, then*, he thought. It was like the gods approved of his activity and could not wait for the next show. Pulling out of his last stop, he anticipated being back at the shop by 2:30. Smiling at his good fortune, he waited for the car coming down the road to pass him, then pulled out into traffic; anxious to be back at his "real work."

***

Detectives Corning and Benson stood inside the supervisor's office at Copier Services, Inc. They had arrived at the company less than 30 minutes earlier and had been able to surmise the name of the probable suspect in the Teri Sanderson case. According to company records, Thomas "Tommy" King serviced the copiers at Ms. Sanderson's office on a monthly basis and had been for over a year. He was working today and expected to report back to the office by 3:00. The detectives had decided to await his arrival. t was now 2:30. While they were waiting, Detective Benson asked the supervisor if Mr. King serviced other offices - knowing the answer would be yes. The supervisor adjusted his glasses and stated that yes Mr. King did have other accounts, but perhaps they should discuss that with him and why did they need to speak to Mr. King again?

They reassured the supervisor, Mr. Pansington, that they merely had some questions for Mr. King regarding a case they were investigating. It was nothing to get overly excited about. They had declined the coffee they could smell burning when they had entered the office. To put Mr. Pansington at ease, Detective Benson had asked what a copier that collated would cost, suggesting interest in something he knew nothing about.

In the middle of discussing the advantages of color copies, Mr. Pansington's eyes shifted to the bay area and licking his lips quickly, he said, "He's back already." The two detectives rose out of their chairs as the supervisor came around his desk, adjusting his glasses once again.

Detective Benson turned and smiled at the supervisor. "That's him in the van?"

The supervisor stopped to make sure, looked up at the slightly taller detective and stated, "Yes, that's him."

The two cops passed a look between them and Detective Benson said, "Okay, we thank you for your time. We'll just go have a chat with him. If that's all right with you, of course."

The supervisor, who seemed eager to cooperate with the police, nodded his assent. "Sure, no problem at all. I'll go ahead and clock him out then."

Detective Benson gave Pansington a quick smile. Then he and Corning headed out to the van.

Tommy was noting the time on his clipboard when the detectives joined him by the van. It was obvious that Tommy had spent the last half-hour or so in a hot van in August with no AC by the shirt somewhat plastered to his back.

"Mr. King?" Detective Corning asked.

Tommy turned with a disgruntled look that quickly turned to surprise when he faced the two men. "Yeah?"

Corning asked, "Are you Thomas King?"

"Yeah. What's this about? Who are you guys?" Tommy asked as his eyes scanned the two. He noted that one stood slightly behind the other. Cops!

"Mr. King, do you know a Teresa Sanderson?" Detective Corning asked.

"Who?" Tommy asked, feigning confusion.

"Teresa or Teri Sanderson?" repeated Corning.

Although Tommy's heart had doubled its rate, an accomplished liar, he appeared baffled but calm on the outside. "I'm not.....sounds kind of familiar. Can you help me out a little and tell me where I might know her from?" he said smiling at the last question.

"You service the copier at her place of business," Detective Benson said, pretending to consult some notes, "a place called Co-Op Electrical."

"Oh, okay. I know who you're talking about. I really don't know her, per se. I know who she is, but we're not...you know...I mean, it's like 'hello, how are you?', 'good and yourself'...you know, that type of thing." Tommy played it up well.

"I see," said Corning with downcast eyes. He looked up to make eye contact with Tommy for his next question. "So, you would have no reason to be at her townhouse last night. No reason at all."

"What?! No!" Tommy denied vehemently. Then he asked, "So what's this about anyway? Something happen to her?"

"Now, why would you ask that, Tommy? What makes you think some harm came to her? Would you have any knowledge of something like that?" Corning said, a barb in his tone.

"What? Come on, guys. I told you I didn't know her that well. I just assumed something happened to her for you to ask...for you to be here. I mean, Christ!" Tommy feigned bewilderment as he reached his right arm back to slip his hand down the back of his slowly drying shirt and pull it away from the damp skin of his back. In doing so, the collar widened just enough for the two officers to see what appeared to be an injury on his right upper chest at the collarbone.

Detective Corning's pulse quickened and Benson, sensing his partner's interest, stepped back in cover mode. Detective Corning modulated his voice to sound casual and asked, "Hey, Tommy. What happened to your chest there?"

Tommy's heart turned to ice and the humidity in the air evaporated as the sweat on his body went cold. "What? Where?"

Both Corning and Benson had caught the paling of Tommy's complexion and the sudden dilation of his pupils; sure signs of alarm and guilt.

"Right there on your chest," Detective Corning said pointing it out. "Yeah, when you reached your arm back like that, I couldn't help but notice that you have some type of injury to your chest. Pull your shirt over. You'll see it."

Tommy had no intention of letting them see the scratch marks. "Oh that," he said chuckling weakly, "that's nothing. It's all right."

"Wow, looked pretty bad to me. What happened, man?" Corning asked in a conversational tone.

"I said it was nothing. What do you guys want anyway? What's this all about?" Tommy said, bordering on belligerent.

"Mr. King," Detective Benson said switching tactics, "we need to know what you were doing last night between the hours of 11p.m. and approximately 4 a.m. this morning."

Tommy pretended to be nonplussed by the question. "Well, I was sleeping, of course. Why? What was I supposed to be doing?"

Benson knew he had something. *Man, this guy makes it too easy.* The cop realized that by taking notice of the scratch marks on Tommy's chest, they had thrown him.

"Mr. King, I haven't accused you of anything......yet. Why are you assuming guilt? Is there a reason you might feel guilty about something?" cajoled Benson.

"Well, you're asking me about..." Tommy was not thinking clearly now, and he was afraid to say anything else. "Never mind, never mind. I was sleeping."

"Mr. King, would you mind coming down to the police station and answering a few more questions?" asked Detective Benson.

"No, I can't right now. I got things I got to do. Maybe tomorrow, huh?" Tommy asked, already thinking of picking up his shopping cart and changing stores by nightfall.

"Mr. King, I'm afraid we're going to have to insist. You see, you were named as a person of interest in the rape of Theresa Sanderson and you're going to have to come with us," Detective Corning explained.

Tommy stared at both for a few seconds and then made a break for it. Benson had anticipated this all along and was able to cut him off after only a few feet. They struggled briefly until Benson could get the cuffs on him and drag him to his feet. Detective Corning read him his Miranda Rights and finished with the obligatory, "Do you understand these rights as I have read them to you?"

Tommy merely nodded his downcast head, sweat-soaked hair hanging in his eyes. "Is that a 'yes', Mr. King?" asked Detective Corning.

"Yes, I understand what you said," Tommy answered, refusing to raise his head. His shirt remained on by just a few buttons and was skewed and twisted severely to the right. Displayed red and angry on his right chest, were three parallel lines showing broken skin scabbed over in some areas.

Detective Corning couldn't help himself. "Are those scratch marks on your chest there, Tommy? Care to explain those?"

Tommy picked up his head then, eyes shining through wet strands of hair, to Detective Corning's surprise Tommy was smiling like he knew a dirty secret. Then the smile turned into a sneer and Tommy's eyes filled with hate.

"I want a lawyer," was all he said.

Chapter 8

Hospitals are like any other small community in that it does not take long for tragic or exciting news to filter up or down through the ranks. So, it was with the news of the capture of the Window Shopper. Although he had been arrested and was currently being held until a DNA match could be proven, he was already guilty in the eyes of those in the know.

There were several nurses married to or "seriously dating" many of Henrico's finest. Therefore, all it took was for one officer to tell one girlfriend and *whoosh* the news of the capture was like a California brush fire. When it was found to be the one and only copier repairman that had been servicing the copiers in the ER for the past year, two camps pitched tents. One camp was startled to learn that the good-looking, charismatic young man was capable of such heinous deeds. The other camp, of course, had always suspected "there was something not quite right about that man."

This was the atmosphere of debate that Kate walked into that September morning when she reported for the 7 a.m. shift. Kate was the charge nurse this morning and as such, met with Eileen to receive the charge nurse report. Eileen recounted the status of those patients currently in exam rooms and the triage report of those still waiting to come back. Kate mentally assigned each patient an acuity level to aid in assigning patients to the oncoming day shift nurses. Acuity levels had to do with the estimated number of nursing hours each patient would occupy, stability factor and an educated guess on which patients would be admitted and which patients would be heading home with advice and possibly, a prescription.

With the business end of things completed, Eileen was quick to change the subject, "So, I guess you heard that your Window Shopper's been caught."

Kate was aware of the current river of rumors flowing through the hospital, but as yet had managed to stay ashore. She pretended to be busy as she made notes on her assignment sheet and replied, "I did hear that they have a person of interest in connection with that case, yes."

"'Person of interest' she says," Eileen mimicked as she rolled her eyes at her friend. "Hey, we're not in the courtroom. Don't you believe it's him? Don't you hope it is?"

Yes, thought Kate, *God, yes!* Then this nightmare would be over for everyone. Well, she corrected her thoughts, everyone but those left to testify. However, to her friend she answered, "I just hope they have the right guy in jail. I don't think the Window Shopper's next victim would live through the attack."

Both nurses walked over to check the equipment together: the code cart, the locked automatic medication dispenser and the bank of monitors. Eileen talked while Kate made the necessary notations on the corresponding checklists.

"I can't believe it was the copier guy!" shared Eileen.

Well, thought Kate, *I guess I know which camp she pitched her tent in.*

"I mean, all those times…" and she visibly shuddered, "I just knew there was something about him."

I stand corrected, Kate smiled inwardly.

"Oh my God! You know what I just thought of?" Eileen emphasized the import of what she had to say by grabbing Kate's arm.

"Remember, with the last one….that morning?" she continued, searching Kate's eyes for comprehension. It was obvious by Kate's blank stare that she was trying to remember, but Eileen could not wait for her to catch up. "He was here! Remember? He was fixing that copier right beside the exam room she was in. Remember? Because I had the feeling he was eavesdropping on that situation and trying to get a look at that woman…" She stopped, her eyes going even wider. She took a sharp intake of breath. Now she had Kate's attention, because she did remember. She knew where her friend was going with this.

"He knew somehow she was here, and he was going to…what? Try to get in and finish her off? Even so, how did he…? Did he know she knew…? Do you think it was just coincidence, or…?" Eileen couldn't finish, so fast were the thoughts spinning in her head.

Kate was worried as well. How much had he heard? She was trying to recall each conversation she had at the doorway with the officers. How long had he been there? Did he realize that Teri had seen him? Was he even the right guy? Question after question, worry after worry.

"He was gone before she came out, right?" Kate asked Eileen.

They were both silent a moment, recalling that morning. Finally, Eileen visibly relaxed as she said, "Yeah, I remember. It was right after that female officer took the kit from you that I noticed he was listening. That's when I interrupted him and made him hurry up and finish. I remember he headed off towards the main hospital before you and Teri came out. I'm sure of it."

Kate sighed with relief. How screwed up that would have been if he was the guy and Teri had seen him. Some defense attorney could say that Teri's traumatized mind had zeroed in on the first strange male she had seen...yada,yada,yada. It was always a battle of wits when it came to proving or disproving rape.

It all boiled down to consensual versus non-consensual sex. "Sure we had sex, but she wanted it," the accused could say. What about the bruises and torn tissue? "She likes it rough. She begged for it," was the comeback. It was generally taking the notion of "innocent until proven guilty" and running with it.

As a SANE nurse, training cautioned on trying to prosecute a case. Better to just report on the collection of the sexual assault kit. They were not forensic scientists, nor judge and jury. They were the collectors of fluids, hairs and fibers. They could report on tissue damage and location. It was left to the forensic scientist to testify on DNA matches and other forensic evidence. However, SANE nursing was new to the East Coast and many of her well-educated colleagues had been tripped up by a savvy defense attorney while trying to play prosecutor.

Kate made assignments and went about her shift in the busy ER. For a Tuesday, it was steady but not overwhelming. Eileen had stayed over for an in-service on a new IV pump the hospital would be integrating over time. Slowly, the clock moved forward from 7 a.m. to 10a.m. Kate had all but forgotten the animated conversation of earlier.

She saw Eileen exiting the conference room and gave her a silent, "still here?" with raised eyebrows. Eileen, handbag slung over her shoulder, came to say a final good-bye.

"Are you back tonight?" asked Kate.

"Nah. I'm off tonight. Plus Jimmy's got football practice later this morning, so..." Eileen left unfinished the working mom's lament.

Kate was giving her friend a supportive smile, when she saw the process server enter the ER. She had seen enough of them now to recognize one when she saw them. Somehow, she knew he was looking for her. Her suspicions were confirmed when she noticed the desk monitor catch her eye and nod her head in Kate's direction.

Shit! thought Kate, *here we go.*

Both she and Eileen watched the man approach them and ask, "Ms. Kaitlin Tuscadero?"

Kate responded, "Right here."

"This is for you," the gentleman stated as he handed over the official envelope. "Have a good day!"

As he turned to leave, Eileen commented, "Cops and servers. 'Here's your ticket or subpoena....have a good fricking day!' What's with that?"

Kate quickly glanced over the subpoena. Well, the DNA must have come back a match because they were going ahead with the arrest of one Thomas King. Her presence was requested at the Criminal Courts building of Henrico County at 9:00 a.m. on September 24th.

"It's him, isn't it?" Eileen asked.

"Well, they seem to think so," answered Kate.

"They called you to testify on the kit, right?" prompted Eileen.

"Yep. Happy birthday to me," sighed Kate as she folded up the official document.

"Oh, man! You have to testify on your birthday?" Eileen looked to her friend and received a sad nod. "Hey, well look at the bright side." Eileen smiled in a wicked way.

"Huh? What?" said Kate, already thinking ahead to what would be required of her.

"You always try to take your birthday off. Now, you won't have to. Mr. Process Server Man just handed you your excused absence!" laughed Eileen.

"Har-de-har-har," was Kate's only response.

Chapter 9

Tommy sat across from his public defender, feeling he was being misrepresented, and they were only ten minutes into their second meeting. He had spent a harrowing first few nights in county lockup. But if his cellmates were to be believed, he had to do whatever it took to stay out of "the pen" where he would be considered a bride on the auction block. Evidently, rapists were not well thought of in prison populations.

"Mr. King, at this point it is not a question of whether you had sex with Ms. Sanderson, but rather was that sexual encounter of a consensual nature. DNA proves you had sexual relations with her. Another wrinkle is the injuries she sustained during your sexual encounter of which there is ample photographic evidence," said the exhausted and frustrated Public Defender, Sandra Derringer.

"Well, I can tell you she wanted it, and she liked it rough. She begged me to slap her around. That's how she got off, she said," explained the well-rehearsed Tommy. One of his cell mates had admired the fact that he was sitting next to the infamous Window Shopper. Being a lower grade rapist himself and beating the rap twice, he had spent the previous night educating Tommy on the finer points regarding the charge of rape.

"See, they got these rape kits now where they collect all the evidence they are going to need," schooled the professor of crime. "They got your jizz -- you use a condom? Oh, that's good....good man! Like your pubes get all mixed in with hers, body hairs and shit. All that's DNA, man! DNA will screw your ass! They know it's you then -- ain't no denying it. Naw, you're only defense is to admit to being with them and make it look like they wanted it."

Tommy must have looked worried because the professor asked, "You play a little slap and tickle with her?" At Tommy's raised dead stare, the professor continued, "Course you did. Sometimes you gotta smack them around a little to get them to realize you ain't playin'. Well, then *your honor*, she likes it rough, what can I say?"

However, the way the public defender was looking at him, Tommy did not think that strategy was going to work. "And the ligature marks around her neck?" asked PD Derringer. "Her testimony is that you strangled her to the point of unconsciousness several times. Now, she can't prove unconsciousness, but the marks show strangulation."

"Yeah, I thought that was a little out there! She called it, um...auto...auto..."

"Autoerotic asphyxiation," supplied the deadpan PD.

"Yeah, yeah, something like that," said Tommy.

"Autoerotic asphyxiation is performed on oneself, but I understand your meaning. So, you're saying she was into that and you complied. You strangled her during the act of *consensual sex* per her request?"

"Request? Shit! She damn near demanded it. Said it was the only way she could get off," crowed Tommy, rolling with the lie.

"Uh-huh. And how many times do you think you strangled her?"

"How many times?"

"Yes. How many? There was more than one ligature mark suggesting more than one attempt at asphyxiation."

"Oh, uh...shit. I don't know. Till she came, alright?!"

"Okay, okay. I'm just asking some of the same questions the DA is going to throw at you. You need to be prepared for those types of questions. Now, during these repeated asphyxiations, did she at any time lose consciousness?"

"Well, yeah."

"Are you sure?"

"I'm pretty sure I know when the lady beneath me has stopped moving, yeah."

"You like to do this asphyxiation ritual a lot? You do this with all your sexual encounters?"

Tommy, sensing a trap, answered, "Hell, no! That ain't my thing. I'm what the ladies call a 'sensitive lover'. That was her deal, not mine. I was just making sure the lady was satisfied." He finished with a grin and rocked back in his chair. His smile and bravado faltered when he saw the response of the PD.

"Mr. King," said the PD as she closed her eyes briefly and breathed deeply, "if I am to defend you, you have **GOT** to be honest with me. I don't care if you're guilty or innocent of the crime of which you've been accused. No, no...That's not quite right. I care to the extent of knowing the truth. Because, guilty or innocent, the truth will help me to prepare a viable defense for you. We...**YOU**...cannot afford to be tripped up on the stand by being caught in a lie."

"But I am telling you the truth," Tommy sputtered as his chair legs slapped down hard upon the tile floor.

"Oh? Is that so?" baited the PD.

"Yeah! That's so!" mimicked Tommy.

"Well, then tell me, Mr. King. If erotic asphyxiation is not 'your thing', and it was specifically for the 'lady's benefit', as you infer; if this was your initiation into this type of thing? Tell me, Mr. King. How is it that you could strangle Ms. Sanderson into unconsciousness and not kill her? Or were you trying to kill her and just couldn't go through with it three times? Conversely, was it an accident the first time and just play time the other two? Explain that to me, Mr. King"

"Dumb luck?" Tommy tried his "aw gosh, baby, you got me" look that defused most women.

"Dum-?" started the PD, but then began to pack up her legal pad, pens, and other paraphernalia.

"Hey," asked a startled Tommy, "where the hell are you going?"

"Mr. King, I do not have time for bullshitters or frat boy antics. When you decide to be straight with me and be serious about your own defense, call me." Turning to the locked door, she yelled, "Guard!"

"Hey, fuck you, bitch!" yelled Tommy.

As the guard opened the door for the frustrated PD, she looked back at Tommy's red, sweating face and got a glimpse of the monster. Within the safety of the well-built guard and an open door to freedom she retorted, "Dream on, Mr. King. I'm out of your league."

Chapter 10

Kate sat outside of the courtroom awaiting her turn to testify in the case of the Commonwealth of Virginia versus the defendant charged with rape in the first degree. The media sat in the courtroom as well; anxious to keep the public informed of the progress of the case against the alleged Window Shopper. The case was in full swing now and three other women had come forward willing to testify against Tommy with the aid of sexual assault kits collected via their claims of rape. Those cases would later be tried separately.

Kate looked over her notes written during the collection of the sexual assault kit of Teresa Sanderson. She wanted to make sure that she remained objective on the stand and reported on the collection of the kit only. She had not slept well the night before. Although this was not her first time on the stand in a rape case, it was the first time that she would be testifying in such a high profile case. Vinnie had tried to ease her worries by taking care of Izzy after dinner with a messy bubble bath and an acted out bedtime story. She and Vinnie had made love long after Izzy was asleep and Kate had pretended to fall into a contented sleep. However, once Vinnie's snores became rhythmic, she had slid from beneath the body-heated sheets to look over her notes "one more time."

She knew she was a small piece in a very big puzzle and the case did not rest solely on her testimony. However, she also knew that rape was a difficult crime to prove and defense attorneys took advantage of any omission or mistake made by anyone for the sake of his or her client. One of the tenets of sexual assault nurse examiners was to report only on the collection itself and not imply guilt or innocence. The words were, "Semen was found in the vaginal vault." The words were not, "The defendant obviously raped the complainant because we found his semen inside her."

Kate was jerked from her reverie by the bailiff stepping into the hall and calling her name. She followed him to the front of the courtroom, trying not to look at the media or over at the defendant's table. She stood in front of the judge's bench and placed her left hand on the Holy Bible.

"Do you swear to tell the whole truth and nothing but the truth, so help you God."

"I do."

"Please watch your step and take a seat in the witness box."

Kate tried to relax as the prosecuting attorney approached the witness stand. She answered all the introductory questions about who she was and her expertise in this case as it pertained to the collection of the sexual assault kit. She recounted her training, her years of experience and the documented number of sexual assault cases she had collected during her tenure as a sexual assault nurse examiner. She allowed herself to be led through the testimony by the prosecuting attorney, staying clear of accusatory words or phrases. She kept her eyes on the prosecuting attorney and tried not to look at either Tommy or Teri.

Tommy listened to Kate's voice and found it pleasing to the ear. It was soft and low with a hint of an accent not of Richmond. It suggested she was not "Old Richmond." But her voice did hold a mild Southern influence. She had use of a large vocabulary, but tempered it to fit the audience to whom she was speaking. She was a nurse, which could lend itself to so many fantasies. He looked forward to exploring those fantasies in more detail later tonight alone in his cell.

Kate took a deep breath and let it out slowly as the defense attorney approached; trying to do so without making it obvious. The defense attorney opened with, "Sexual assault nurse examiners are a relatively new branch of nursing, are they not, Ms. Tuscadero?"

Kate wondered how much longer this would be the opening question of all defense attorneys. The supposition proposed that a new area would be fraught with problems leaving too much room for errors; too much room for some innocent defendant to fall through the cracks. It was a question Kate heard in and out of the courtroom and one she was prepared for.

"Although new in Virginia, it has been in practice in other states for a number of years. Each sexual assault nurse examiner must complete extensive training under a certified sexual assault nurse as well as hours with other services such as the police department. Only certified nurse examiners are allowed to take any collections for a sexual assault kit," she testified.

"Thank you for the history lesson, Ms. Tuscadero. A simple 'yes' or 'no' would have been sufficient," stated the attorney.

Kate wanted to retort *it was your question,* but was sure she could be construed as a hostile witness, so remained silent. She tried to appear calm and superior, but felt the butterflies taking flight in her stomach awaiting the next question from the defense attorney.

Tommy was impressed with the way the nurse handled herself. She appeared calm and self-assured on the stand. Only a true hunter like himself was aware of the quick, flickering pulse showing itself at the base of her throat. Also, the fact that she kept her hands safely trapped in her lap to keep their trembling hidden was a dead giveaway. He had spent much time purposely bringing women face to face with fear and therefore, could notice the fine nuances of it.

"Ms. Tuscadero, did the complainant tell you that she had been raped? Did she actually use the word rape?" the defense attorney continued.

"No, she did not use *that* word," answered Kate.

The defense attorney did not bite. Instead, she continued, "Did the complainant, at any time, name my client as her attacker?"

"She did not tell me his name, although..."

"Thank you, Ms. Tuscadero," interrupted the attorney.

And so it continued throughout Kate's time on the stand. The defense attorney did her best to lead Kate down the road of rough sex versus non-consensual sex. However, Kate had testified enough times and been taught well during her training. She let the kit do the talking for her. She stayed out of the deep, dark woods full of trees named "consensual", "guilty", "force" and "intention". To every question aimed at causing her to pass judgment, she would only respond, "I can only testify to the actual collection of the sexual assault kit items, to do otherwise would be acting outside of my scope of practice."

On a few occasions, she requested permission to consult her notes and notwithstanding a few objections from the prosecuting attorney, believed she had provided a thorough testimony based on the collection of evidence for the kit.

Tommy had stopped doodling and had started to pay close attention to this portion of her testimony. What was this about a rape kit and what exactly was she saying? She spoke of the ligature marks and bruises he had left all over Teri's body. *Oh, how he wished he could have seen that!* He was glad he was seated behind the table to hide the raging hard on he obtained from the image.

As she continued, he lost his hard on as it was replaced by a cold sweat. The worry he felt was compounded by the furious writing done by the aides of his attorney seated at the table. With every word out of her mouth, even an idiot could read through the lines! She was making him out to be a monster. With DNA, there was no doubt he had engaged in sex with Teresa – he had admitted that some weeks ago. However, there was still the option of Teresa going along with and even requesting rough sex. The stupid bitch on the stand was ruining that. Why didn't his retard of an attorney shut her up?!? Christ! Obviously, all women were dumb bitches that needed a man to tell them what to do.

The prosecutor had just a question or two on cross for clarification, but Kate was able to step down after about 30 minutes of testimony. She tried to keep her eyes straight-forward and not look at either Teresa Sanderson or Thomas King, but she could feel his eyes upon her. She turned her head to the right as she pushed through the polished wooden gate. Her steps faltered for a millisecond when she met the eyes of the accused.

Thomas King was impeccably dressed in a tailored suit, with a fresh new haircut. Together with wire-rimmed glasses, he appeared to be part of the legal team and not the accused. When he looked Kate in the eyes, the façade was broken. The predatory look in his empty eyes had Kate feeling as if she had been marked and tagged for a later hunt. His look said, "You'll be sorry."

The trial was far from over, but in Kate's mind Tommy's look removed all doubt. Kate had no problem believing that the man sitting at the defense table was capable of torturing and raping women and if the other cases came to trial, she would have to face him again.

Tommy caught Kate's eye and took a psychic photograph of her face. He had better beat this rap, or he was going to hold her partially to blame. He knew he had made a connection with her when he saw her falter as she passed through the gate and her face drain of color. But, as she passed, he caught the eyes of Teresa, and slowly he felt his testicles try to crawl their way into his lower belly. There was no fear on her face. With dawning dread, he saw instead a look of triumph.

Chapter 11

Tommy sat in the holding cell awaiting transport to the state penitentiary. His mind raced with dead end options in a frantic need to redirect it from dealing with the reality of his situation. His trial for the rape of Teresa Sanderson had lasted a little over a month. Before it was over, charges had been brought against him on three of the other four women he had sexually assaulted. His lawyer kept trying to get him to plea out on those cases, but he had wanted to see how he made out in the first trial.

Public Defender Derringer explained that with the culmination of a collected sexual assault kit, damaging testimony from Teresa, the graphic photos of Teresa's injuries taken by that interfering bitch of a nurse and the testimony from his "instructor" from county lockup, he was going to jail. Only his length of stay was open for discussion. He was better off to plead guilty to lesser charges on the other cases before the verdict came through on the first case.

"As long as doubt is still swinging in the breeze, you maintain the option of pleading to a lesser charge," explained PD Derringer. "But if you continue to wait on this and the verdict of guilty is handed down - which I really don't see how it's going to come out any other way, Tommy - that option is going to disappear for you. Those other women are going to want to press charges to the fullest extent of the law. They will smell blood - your blood - with a guilty verdict and be unwilling to plea down. You do what you want. I will do the best I can based on any decision you make.

However, as your lawyer, I have to tell you that your option of seeing the outside of a jail before you are 50 is dwindling fast."

"But I didn't rape anybody!" Tommy swore petulantly.

Sandra Derringer leaned back in the plastic chair provided for counsel in the cinderblock room. She stared at Tommy with resigned frustration. She kept one arm on the table; pen in hand poised over her legal pad. She wiggled the brass pen quickly between two fingers over the pad as she thought of how to crack this nut.

"Oh, Tommy," she sighed. "If only you had kept up that claim while sitting in your jail cell instead of feeling the idiotic need to brag to your cellmate. Then he wouldn't have testified against you, further impeding our snowball chances in hell of getting you declared innocent of forcible rape."

"I told you! He was lying! He was only trying to save his own skin!" Tommy sputtered.

"Oh, I agree with you about him trying to save his own skin. And you handed him the perfect opportunity. A jail cell confession. For crying out loud! He knew details never shared with the press. Details only she, you and the police would know," she chastised.

"He only did it to save himself," Tommy all but muttered, refusing to look her in the eye anymore.

"Redundant," she said. Now, she sat forward with both hands on the table and took on the pose of supplication, trying to get Tommy's attention. "Hey," she called to him.

He looked up wary, but upon seeing her apparent earnest plea for his attention, raised his head and opened his ears.

"I'm giving it to you straight, Tommy. This case is all but sealed up. I believe with all my heart that the jury is going to return a verdict of guilty. You need to let me keep these other cases from going to court and plea out for you. Let's plead you guilty on lesser charges. Sure, you're going to do jail time. We can't help that. However, we can keep your jail time down to a point where you will be out somewhere down the line. Out of jail in time to live your life a little. I'm trying to help you out, Tommy. You have to let me."

"How much time are we talking?" asked Tommy.

"Hard to say..." she hedged.

"Take an educated guess," Tommy said a bit too sarcastically for her liking.

"It really depends on this court case sentencing for Rape I, but with the others...you're probably looking at serving 15-20 years," she concluded.

"15-20 years! You have got to be shitting me!" Tommy exploded.

Before he could backtrack completely, she quickly interjected in the midst of his tirade.

"Listen to me! That's based largely on the guilty plea in this case. Rape I carries a five to life term. That range allows for, 'oops, I'm sorry, was that your daughter?' to acts of savagery. Your act tends toward the savage end."

Upon his attempt to take umbrage at the last statement, she held up her hand for silence and continued, "Now, the judge will hand down sentencing, and you are required, by law, to serve 86% of that time....period. That's going to be the bulk of your time. We, or you, plead out the other three on lesser charges, which carry smaller sentences, and we can greatly cut down on your time."

Tommy's mouth filled with air again and his lips formed the shape for the word "but", then died in a puff of air as she continued on.

"But..." she held up a warning finger. "But, if you decide not to plea out and the other three go to trial, AND you lose, you're looking at three other sentencing trials for Rape I. That could be up to 20 years apiece. Even at 86%...well, you do the math."

With that final statement, she pointedly smacked her pen down upon her pad of paper, crossed her arms and leaned back in her seat. Tommy's eyes frantically searched the cement walls for arguments. She could see him multiplying and trying to figure it out. She gave it time to sink in. She had given it her best shot. She had explained it to the best of her ability. She believed he was guilty of the savage rape of all the women, but she was his lawyer.

It was her duty to look out for his best interests. She could rest easy tonight knowing she had done just that.

Even so, secretly, she hoped he would maintain the jackass mentality that he had been showcasing since the trial began. She really, *really* hoped he would pass on this and take his chances. Because if he did that, no one would have to worry about Thomas King, aka "The Window Shopper, again for a very long time.

Tommy's head hung now remembering the instant he had realized he was not walking away from this one. The trial had ended and he had received 15 years. He had taken the deal suggested by his lawyer and pleaded out on two cases before the verdict had been handed down on the first case. The third bitch had been decent enough to commit suicide before his decision had been broadcast, thank God. As promised, the sentencing was better, but with good behavior and time served, he was looking at approximately 17 years.

Seventeen years for doing nothing that those bitches hadn't asked for! The rage surrounding him was suffocating. He was blinded by it. The woman who insisted on calling herself his mother had been there for the verdict and the sentencing. She had sat in the back row, trying not to be recognized and he had not acknowledged her. While waiting to head back to county lockup after sentencing, she had been given permission to approach him. She had been crying and clutched a tissue in her left hand, her arm crooked to hold her old lady purse. In 24 years, he had never seen her cry on his behalf and he doubted the tears were real now. Nevertheless, she was his mother and he yearned for some contact from someone who knew him.

The sheriff's deputies looked upon her with pity as she approached her wayward son. They put her age at about 75 or better and figured Tommy as a "late surprise". Hard living had taken a toll on the 49 year old woman approaching them and she played it up to get closer to her son. When she reached him, she straightened her stooped posture and raised her haughty, pointed chin. Without warning, she spit in his face and then used her tissue to wipe her mouth.

As the deputies hurried him away from her and toward the loading dock of the courthouse, she yelled after him, "You ain't nothing but trash, you hear me! I should have let them vacuum you out of me when I had the chance. I will always hate myself for not doing that. You hear me, you piece of shit? YOU ARE NO LONGER MY SON!"

Tommy rode in the back of the van with his mother's spit drying on his face. The deputy riding with him never even offered a handkerchief, tissue or even a damn paper towel to wipe it off with. Tommy hated his mother! He always had. He hated them all.

As he waited to be picked up and driven into the pits of hell, he started to plan how they would all die - every worthless woman ever thrown into the way of his greatness. That would be his salve to pack his wounds over the next few years. That would be his master plan. He had plenty of time to work on it. He had the next 17 years.

Chapter 12

Kate heard about Tommy's conviction and sentencing for each case as they happened from Bill. He would drop by the ER for the weekly roster of Henrico PD officers covering the ER during the 11-7 shift. He always had time for a cup of coffee and the sharing of his take on current events. Whether it was local or national politics or who was going to the Super Bowl this year, Bill had an opinion.

When it came to The Window Shopper getting "what he damn well deserved" he was an expert on the subject. Being "on the inside" of this particular case and "knowing all the players", it was his favorite subject of late. Not one instance went by on one of his visits that the subject did not find a way into their weekly conversations. Kate figured that Bill not only considered himself the liaison between the police department and the hospital staff, but the big, bad world in general.

During the day and early evening, there was security staff that manned the hospital. As the last administrator left the building, the security staff was backed up and eventually replaced by a Henrico County Police officer as evening became night. They generally stayed in the ER, but could be called wherever they were needed throughout the hospital. Kate had a reason to be thankful for their presence on more than one occasion. Bill Patterson carried the responsibility for staffing the hospital, and he took the position seriously.

Kate was finishing up a 12 hour shift and looking forward to getting home in time to bathe Isabella and read her a bedtime story before tucking her in. She loved the smell of her daughter's freshly washed skin and hair and craved the cuddling of story time. On the days that she worked, Vinnie picked Izzy up from his mother's on his way home from work and fed her dinner. But Kate insisted that bath time and story time were hers. The only time she missed it was when she was called in for SANE duties, but that was a rare occurrence. She was tying up her loose ends and finishing her charting when Bill came through the pneumatic doors.

He picked up the previous week's log sheets and dropped off the roster for the following week. This act would normally only take a few seconds out of his daily routine. He took the chance to grab an always-fresh cup of coffee - heavy on the cream and sugar - and visit with some of the nurses. He validated this as keeping up good public relations. However, everyone knew it was because he was somewhat lonely after the death of his wife of 26 years to cancer. They all indulged him on every visit and Kate was no exception.

"Bill!" she exclaimed, "come and talk to me a minute."

He finished stirring the sweet mud he called coffee and sidled over to the counter where she sat charting. "You about ready to go home aren't you?" he said.

"I'm giving it my best shot. How are things with you?" Kate stopped writing to smile up at him.

"Well, I can't complain...much" he said with a smirk as he sipped at his coffee and Kate chuckled appreciatively.

"Anything new? Having a good week?" she asked.

"Same old thing. Holidays are over, so it ought to be quiet till spring fever hits the highschoolers."

Kate nodded at his statement. The feast or famine roller coaster of the ER ran somewhat in sync with the police department. When people became crazy, someone usually ended up hurt.

"So, I guess you heard old Tommy's off to the big house now. Yeah, he's probably playing house with some big sum bitch right now," he said and chuckled into his cup as he took another sip.

Kate shuddered, in spite of herself. She would never forget the look he had given her as she left the stand that day. The oldest genes coursing through her recognized the predator in Tommy and had sent out a warning along all the nerve endings in her body. She had told no one, but had struggled with nightmares for a few weeks after that day. The anger and hate that shone from those eyes bore into her subconscious mind and flashed horrific scenes across the stage of her dreams almost nightly.

To Bill, she feigned mild interest and said, "Well, I hope we've seen the last of him. I find it hard to believe that he didn't get life for all of those rapes."

"Oh, don't you worry. If he makes it out of prison alive, which statistics say is slim to none, he'll be a broken man. He'll probably do at least 20 years or so. He'll be jumping at his own shadow or drinking or drugging himself into oblivion," he assured her. "I've seen it a hundred times, Katie. These sexual perverts are nothing but bullies that prey on the weak. When they spend enough time being the victim, they're broken. Maybe we'll get lucky and he'll figure out a way to kill himself," he finished as he took in the last of his coffee.

"Well, I had better be getting these logs back to the clerk before I clock out for today. You take care now," he said with a wink before turning to walk out, waving to his many female fans along the way.

Kate stared at the chart before her, not reading it but hearing the last words spoken by Bill. *"These sexual perverts are nothing but bullies that prey on the weak."* The word "bully" caused an almost physical reaction from Kate. She was a champion for the weak. Nothing would enrage her more rapidly than witnessing someone stronger taking advantage of or harassing someone weaker. Some of the only reprimands she had received on the job were due to her "unprofessional" behavior in situations such as those.

She had a difficult time controlling her temper and subsequent actions whenever bullying was present. Whether it was a husband suspected of causing the broken arm of his wife or a child cowering whenever a parent walked into a room, Kate saw red. She suspected that Vinnie had convinced his mom to watch Izzy on the days Kate worked in order to keep her out of jail. It was an unspoken understanding that Kate would probably kill someone suspected of harming Izzy. Because of what Kate did for a living, she knew that monsters were real, and she would be unable to expose her little girl to that. It was a personality trait *(flaw)* that Kate recognized in herself and dealt with as best she could. She was willing to stand up to any bully, no matter what. She had always been that way. *Well...not always*, a shameful voice spoke up from the back of her mind. And once again her mind brought out Emily as exhibit A.

When Kate was six years old, her family relocated to Richmond, Virginia from Chicago. That summer, all of the children in her neighborhood had a good laugh at her expense because of her weird pronunciation of certain words. Being painfully shy anyway and thin-skinned, she had been hurt and withdrew further into herself. She was miserable about the prospect of going to school with those same children and stayed on the merry-go-round when the bell rang that first day.

She was not missed at first, and she was trying to figure out a way to get out of school and not get into trouble with her parents. Then she saw a girl about her age quickly walking up the sidewalk, clutching her Bobby Sherman lunchbox in front of her like a shield. She was sniffling and walking with her head down. Kate felt drawn to her and quickly moved to intercept her.

"Hi, what's your name?" Kate asked, falling into step beside her.

The girl glanced at Kate quickly and looked back down at the sidewalk. "Emily."

"My name's Kate and I'm scared too. We can be scared together if you want," Kate said, desperate for a friend.

The little girl named Emily stopped and stared at Kate for awhile. Then she smiled and said, "Okay."

The angels favored them that day and placed the new friends in the same class. From that first day, Katie and Emily became inseparable. Emily spent many nights over Katie's house, but Katie was never allowed to spend the night over Emily's house. Emily's mother had left the family when Emily was four. Emily explained that it was too hard on her father to watch "two girls." Katie's mother seemed to agree and understand.

Both girls survived elementary school and entered middle school with all the squealing anticipation of a "tween" girl. Under Emily's friendship, Kate felt accepted and blossomed into a fairly confident girl - at least, around Emily. Both girls were avid tomboys as they approached their teens, with Emily being the most stubborn in refusing to wear make-up, dress provocatively or act "all girly girl".

They were in their first year of middle school, when Emily started to miss a great deal of time due to sickness. She would miss several days after starting her period and suffered from one stomach malady after another. Soon, she developed bags under her eyes and many of the teachers thought she was using drugs. When Emily was feeling better, she was exuberant and bordering on wild. When she was ill, she pulled away from everyone including Kate.

As spring began to chase away winter one Friday afternoon, Kate walked to Emily's house to drop off make-up work. She had tried to call Emily, but had not gotten an answer. She hoped to catch her awake and maybe visit for awhile. She went without her parents' permission, because they would have never allowed her to enter "a sick house."

When Kate arrived at Emily's house, her disappointment was evident by the slowing of her steps and the drooping of her shoulders. Emily's father was home. His truck's tailgate was sticking out from behind the house. She knocked on the front door, but no one answered. She decided to walk around to the back of the house. Maybe Emily's dad was working out in the backyard.

Kate found no one in the backyard, but saw the backdoor open through the screened-in porch. She entered the porched-in area and tried to see into the kitchen. She meekly called out, "Hello?"

Not getting a response, Kate looked at the books and papers in her arms. *I'll just put these on the dinette table in there and leave a quick note,* she thought, *no harm in that.* She entered the house and listened for any signs of life. She thought briefly about going up to Emily's room and peeking in on her, but was afraid she would be caught by Emily's dad who obviously had a quick and irritable temper. She knew his room was off the kitchen, but the door was closed. Was he in there? Was he sleeping? Could he be sick too?

Kate was rethinking her decision to come into the house uninvited when she heard Emily's dad say from the other side of the door, "Just stay right there, baby. I'm going to get a glass of water, and then I'm going to show you some things. I think you're ready," and laughed in a way that made Kate's skin crawl.

Oh my God! He has a woman in there, and they're probably doing it! She was frozen! She jumped and gave a little cry of surprise, clutching the books and papers to her as the door opened. Emily's dad stood before her shirtless and barefoot. He had obviously donned a pair of jeans to come into the kitchen, but had not bothered to zip them all the way or buckle his belt.

"What the f...?" he started to say.

Kate was stammering over a response when the door swung back open to show a startled and flushed Emily sitting up, clutching a wrinkled sheet to her seemingly naked body.

Kate looked from Emily to Emily's dad as a sick realization dawned upon her. Her arms became weak and the books and papers she had been holding fell to the floor. She turned to bolt, but Emily's father yelled, "Hey!" and caught her by the arm. She fought him briefly, but then he smacked the back of her head and yelled "HEY!" again.

She stopped her struggling and looked past him to Emily. Emily begged Kate with her eyes and shook her head slowly.

"Hey, girl, look at me!" Emily's dad said, digging his fingers into the soft flesh of her upper arm.

Kate's heart got stuck in her throat, and she tore her eyes away from her friend to look into the eyes probing hers.

"You're going to keep your mouth shut about this, missy. You hear me? Or so help me God, I will hunt you down and beat the living shit out of you! This is something between me and Em. She don't mind it. Do you, pumpkin?" he called out to Emily, although his eyes never left Kate.

"No, Daddy, I don't mind. Don't hurt her. She won't tell anyone. Will you, Katie?" Emily begged.

Kate looked to Emily. Emily's eyes shone with tears, and she mouthed the word "please" to Kate. Kate looked back to Emily's dad, but could not keep eye contact, so great was her fear and confusion. "No, sir. I won't say a word. I promise."

"You believe her, Emily?" Emily's dad called out again without taking his eyes or his hand off Kate.

"Yes, Daddy. She won't tell anyone. She promised. Just let her go, please, Daddy. I'll do whatever you want from now on. Just, please, please, let her go," Emily begged and began to cry.

"Now, now, sugar. You don't need to cry. I'm not going to hurt your friend here. I just want to make sure she understands. You understand, don't you, girl?" he asked Kate.

"Y-yes, sir," Kate managed.

"Alright then. You go on," he said and looked back to smile at Emily. Emily turned her back to them and her shoulders shook with silent sobs. Turning back to Kate, he leaned in close. He smelled of stale cigarettes and sweat. He dug his fingers deeper into the soft flesh of Kate's arm, causing her to wince. "You tell anybody and I'll kill the little slut."

Kate's eyes flew up to meet his and any doubt was removed. Her bowels turned to water, and she could only nod.

He let go of her arm and said, "Now, pick up those books and put them on the table over there."

Kate did as she was told as she listened to the tortured sobs of her friend. Emily's father poured himself a glass of water and watched her closely. As she turned to walk out, she looked once again into the room towards Emily.

"Go on, now. Unless you want to join us this afternoon" he said with a smirk.

Kate rushed out of the house and ran most of the way home. She kept her word and never told her parents. She refused to take Emily's call that afternoon or for the next two days. Her mother wondered if the girls had quarreled, but figured they were teenagers and best friends and would eventually work it out.

Emily was not in school Monday or Tuesday morning. Somewhere around 1:00 o'clock, Kate's mother showed up at her biology class with Assistant Principal Morley. Emily had slit her wrists and bled out in a bathtub the night before. Kate's scream was drowned out by the bell to change classes. She sank into her mother's arms as curious students filed past.

She could not speak up in the days leading to the funeral or those first few days back to school. She was too ashamed of her silence; convinced Emily had killed herself because of it. Kate could have saved her but was too afraid to speak up. Emily's dad just skipped out on the rent one summer night and that was the end of that town story. Kate had never told anyone, not even Vinnie. After that day, she never backed down again. She supposed it was why she pursued SANE nursing - so she could speak up for the victims of bullies and monsters.

Kate blinked away the moisture from her eyes and forced herself mentally to change tracks. That was a long time ago. She believed that she had dealt with those demons over time. *No need to dwell on it*, she reminded herself. Her job was done. The Window Shopper was behind bars and good riddance! She would move on and in another year or so it would be just another chapter of her life seldom remembered. With that comforting thought in her head, she finished her last chart and prepared to give report to the oncoming shift.

Chapter 13

Time flies. Anyone who has lived past the age of eight knows this basic fact. Whether times are good or bad, time moves on. Sometimes that's a good thing as in "time heals all wounds." And sometimes, it's not as in "Six months?! That's not enough time! I still have so much I want to do with my life!" Time, i.e. life waits for no one and nothing. In essence, time flies whether you're having fun or not. The next 15 years passed more rapidly for some than others, although the days still contained 24 hours and the weeks, seven days.

On the first night Tommy spent in jail, he was greeted by a welcoming committee of four inmates who took turns beating and raping him. Tommy was enough of a celebrity, it seemed, that he was well known to the prison population before he arrived. Unfortunately for Tommy, one member of that population was the cousin of the woman who had committed suicide rather than testify. The prisoner had never been close to his younger female cousin, but he was very close to his mother. When his mother cried during her visit and said her heart was broken by this tragedy that had befallen her sister, Emilio regretted every tear. She went on to say how much she wished that Emilio had not been in prison because he could have taken care of things for the family; been a man. He consoled her by telling her not to worry, that "the worm" would pay. So, while his gang worked over Tommy that first night, he watched with satisfaction. He had made a promise to his mother and by Dios, this worm before him would pay for his sin against Emilio's family. Then, when Emilio was ready to leave this place, the worm would die.

Two weeks after Tommy received his initiation to prison life, Kate Tuscadero and Sandra Derringer literally ran into each other at one of the Ukrop's grocery stores. They disentangled their shopping carts and apologized to each other. They were about to go their awkward, separate ways, when Kate complimented Sandra's purse. True, she was looking for something to say in leaving, but she was a connoisseur of handbags. She didn't spend money on clothes or shoes, but she could validate a big expenditure on a well-made purse. Therefore, her appreciation of the black, soft leather Coach bag slung over Sandra's shoulder was genuine. Sandra began to validate the money she had just spent on it and Kate asked where Sandra had found such a bargain. Before they knew it, they were talking over coffee in Ukrop's cafe. It was the beginning of a new friendship for both women.

Two years after the case was finished, Bill Patterson was sitting at a stoplight at Broad Street and Parham when his right arm began to tingle and a pressure developed in his chest. He removed his arm from the steering wheel and flexed his fingers, trying to stop the numbness creeping into his arm. Slowly, he became aware that he was perspiring profusely and becoming short of breath. When the car behind his cruiser tentatively gave a short tap on their car horn to alert him the light had turned green, Bill knew he was having a heart attack. He was within a three minute ride of the hospital, so he drove himself to the emergency department. After stabilizing him, he was sure every nurse on duty that evening came by to chastise him for driving himself to the hospital during a cardiac arrest. A few tests and a cardiac catherization later, it was determined he had indeed suffered a myocardial infarction and would need cardiac bypass surgery. All the years of rich foods, smoking and caffeine had caught up with him. He retired from active duty shortly after the surgery was done.

Four years after spitting in her son's face, Tommy's mother returned to her condo to find her latest boyfriend tearing the bedroom apart obviously looking for something. They argued and she refused to admit to taking the large amount of money she had found earlier in the week. She vehemently denied spending that money as she thought of putting down a deposit on a new Benz and spending the rest on liquor. They were so busy yelling at each other that neither saw the dealer's representative until the gun was pointing in their direction. Without being able to come up with the cash or the whereabouts of the cash in the time allotted by the representative, they were both disposed of per the dealer's instructions.

When Tommy heard about his mother's demise in prison, he muttered an uninterested "thanks" to the chaplain whom had come to tell him, then "your deal" to the men waiting to see if he was still going to play. The chaplain shook his head and said a prayer for the "poor woman, this poor child of God." Finally, the woman who had claimed all those years to be "a champion of God" on Sunday, but headed the political campaign of the devil during the week, finally got to meet God face to face, and He was NOT pleased.

Seven years later, Teri Sanderson finally had a chance at happiness. She had worked through the pain of being a victim and had been determined to be known as a survivor. She was made of tough stuff. She went back to school and obtained a degree in communications. She was working in radio and was a nighttime diva giving out sage advice to the lonely and the hopeful. She met a good man, and they made plans to marry. They were going to hold off on announcing their engagement until they had a chance to tell her parents during Christmas.

She was returning from a successful dinner meeting where her program had been picked up for syndication. She dialed her love on her new cell phone and drove a little too fast in her excitement. As she drove down the straight lane of Ridgefield Parkway, she shared the good news with her future husband. By the time she saw the small white dog, she only had seconds to react. She dropped the phone and swerved to miss the small dog. Her car jumped the median and sped into the oncoming lane.

In her panic, she stomped on her cell phone, which had landed to lean against the brake. Her well-heeled foot slipped and hit the gas. She continued across the lane toward a residential street that opened onto the main road. Parked on the side of the street, in preparation of repairing the road the following day, was a bulldozer. Teri's car hit it traveling approximately 40mph, crushing the front of the car. For awhile, the frightened and unharmed pup stood watching the car in shock. When the car caught fire and the woman began to scream, he ran in the direction of home. By the time the fire truck arrived, Teri Sanderson had been dead five minutes. The radio world mourned her passing.

Eight years after sentencing in The Window Shopper case, Kate found out the reason she was always tired and feeling nauseous every now and again. It wasn't a vitamin deficiency or the flu. She was pregnant. She and Vinnie had been trying to have a baby since Isabella was three, but it seemed it was not to be. After three miscarriages, they had decided to stop trying. Neither was interested in trying fertility drugs. If it was not meant to be, they figured, it was not meant to be. They had Izzy and she was quite a handful. For a few years following that decision, they took careful precautions and just enjoyed their spirited little girl.

However, when Isabella turned 11 earlier this year, Kate felt comfortable enough to leave her with her parents for a week while she and Vinnie spent some alone time together. They had taken a trip to Emerald Isle. They rented a beach cottage somewhat secluded from everyone. They spent the week being just a couple again, flirting and chasing each other in the surf. After a very romantic dinner, a few too many Coronas and the recognition of a breathtaking sunset, they had walked down to the beach together. As they stared out at dolphins making the lazy trek home, they recognized the gift of each other. What started as a simple, loving kiss became the dance of lovemaking in the sand. Man and woman coming together surrounded by nature's glory. What could be more natural than this?

Well, obviously, procreation, damn it!!, thought Kate. Part of her was thrilled, but part of her worried about both Vinnie and Princess Izzy's reaction. She decided to tell them both after dinner. Whether it was nerves or hormones, her stomach would not let her enjoy the special meal she had fixed for her family. She had worried all day how to break the news and had come up empty. Finally, when it looked like everyone was about to go about their evening and leave her to stare at an empty table, she spoke up.

"Wow, Emerald Isle was really great, wasn't it, honey?" she stammered.

Vinnie's eyebrows knitted in confusion, but he answered, "Sure was, babe. Seems like a while ago now, doesn't it? But next time, we'll all go. Right, Izzy?"

Isabella was picking up her plate and glass, preparing to put them on the kitchen counter like every other night. "But you guys said it was isolated out there. I'd rather go somewhere fun."

Vinnie was about to comment, but Kate interrupted him, "Well, it seems we brought back another souvenir." Kate groaned inwardly thinking, that's so corny!

Isabella's eyes lit up and she put the plate and glass back on the table. For some reason, her mom and dad had saved a gift for her until now. She did not know why, but that didn't matter! What could be so special to wait until now? She was giddy with anticipation.

Vinnie gave her a look that said *what in the hell are you talking about?* He was waiting for some clue from her.

Kate took a deep breath and said, "I'm pregnant. I'm about 13 weeks along, according to the doctor and well, I'm due in March."

Both Vinnie and Isabella's mouths dropped open in the exact same way. *They really do favor each other*, thought Kate.

Isabella began to jump up and down and squeal with excitement. She clapped her hands together in joy. "A baby! A baby!" she exclaimed.

Vinnie's reaction was a bit more reserved. They had not told Isabella of the miscarriages because she had been too young to understand. He was worried about his wife and her emotional health should she have to deal with another. But she glowed. She actually glowed and he could guess when this child was conceived. It had been a beautiful moment; an act of pure love. He knew in his heart it would be okay. His eyes misted up with joy, and he moved to take his pregnant wife into his arms.

Nestled against him, Kate pondered whether she should tell him it was a boy. In the end, she decided not to but was content to bask in the moment. Held in her husband's loving arms and hearing the excited giggles of the impending big sister, she was quite content.

Eleven years passed and Kate became the head of the SANE program at the hospital. Her nursing duties changed to education and administrative ones, which suited her life better now. Robbie was a very rambunctious three year old and Isabella was every bit the hormonal teenager. Kate's duties included training future SANE nurses, doing workshops to educate police officers, EMTs and ER staff. Her predecessor had retired earlier that year and had named Kate as the new head. They were big shoes to fill, but Kate was dedicated to not only keep the program alive, but expand it as well.

She celebrated with a dinner with her family at the decadent Cheesecake Factory. After having Robbie, it was a little harder to keep weight off, but she allowed herself a slice of cheesecake nonetheless. While Isabella pouted about not being able to have a cell phone of her own, Robbie could not decide which area of the restaurant was the most interesting. Kate sipped at her coffee and closed her eyes while tasting the rich mixture of creams.

Later in the week, she and Sandra met for drinks at their favorite watering hole. They had become good friends over the years and made a point to get together whenever they could. They spoke of Kate's family and Sandra's career. They made plans to get together again soon and walked to their respective automobiles: Sandra's Jaguar and Kate's minivan.

Fifteen years later, someone added something wrong, and it slipped through all the checks and balances afforded to the underpaid. Release papers came up and were signed by all the appropriate people for Thomas King. When the word came down to Tommy, he quickly covered his surprise. He was afraid to believe his good luck and would not breathe easy until he was standing on the other side of the razor wire fence. On April 15th, he got that chance.

Tommy King was a free man, and he was ready to execute the plan that had been brewing for 15 years. First he needed some wheels, and he needed to get laid. Then, and only then, when he could think straight, was he going to set his plan in motion. He sniffed hard and quick three times, an old habit that refused to die. Then he lit a cigarette, inhaled deep and blew it out slow. Smoking was a new habit he had picked up in the shit house, and he was hooked.

The day had finally come for his revenge. The bitch was going to die, and she was going to die slow. Teri Sanderson was going to regret the day she opened her mouth. Tommy was going to make sure of that.

Chapter 14

On the day Tommy was released, Kate was on her way to Robbie's school and was driving a bit erratically. She was running late to sit down with Robbie's teacher to discuss some concerns she and Vinnie had. After a brief and heated discussion with Vinnie, it was decided that he could clear his schedule after all and attend this meeting. Kate was trying her best to keep an open mind and not let her normally analytical mind present too many scenarios.

Robbie was now seven years old and in elementary school. He had a relatively severe speech impediment and was difficult to understand. Even as parents, Kate and Vinnie would sometimes need Robbie to repeat a phrase several times before translation kicked in. His speech had been delayed and when it finally began to present itself, there was obviously something wrong. The normal cute mispronunciations were exaggerated, leading Kate and Vinnie to seek professional guidance. After several referrals to, yet another, specialist, it was determined that Robbie's palate had formed too high in his mouth for correct speech patterns.

The explanation given to them by a speech therapist was that while learning a language, the brain took signals from the forming of certain sounds to make words. For example, to form "L" the tongue curls toward the top of the mouth, connecting with the hard palate slightly behind the front teeth. With repetition, the developing speech center of the brain recognizes that, in simple terms, "when I want the 'L' sound, this is where I place my tongue" and stores that information in muscle memory. Eventually, one no longer needs to think about it, the tongue just "knows" what it is supposed to do.

However, in Robbie's case, his palate formed extremely high in his mouth. When learning language and trying to form sounds to create words, his tongue rarely hit the same spot twice in a row. Therefore, his brain did not get the opportunity to create a muscle memory for language. The news had at first, been devastating. With speech therapy, progress could be made, but Robbie's speech would never be "normal." Alternative ways - such as spelling simple words, hand motions, substituting words, and so forth - were being taught to help Robbie make himself understood.

Therefore, last night when Kate ran a tub of water for Robbie to take a bath and returned later to peek in on him, she was shocked to see a dark, angry bruise on his left arm. Since Robbie was old enough to bathe and dress himself without difficulty, Kate did not necessarily see Robbie's body undressed. Shocked at the dark color and size of the bruise, Kate asked, "Robbie! Where did you get that bruise, honey?"

Robbie continued to play, but asked, "Wah booz?"

"The bruise on your arm, sweetheart," Kate answered, pointing to his small upper arm.

"Oh, dat. Shool," he answered.

Kate knew that "shool" was Robbie's word for school. She found that odd. The school sent home little notes about any little mishap common to children that age. When Robbie jumped from the merry-go-round and skinned both knees, Kate received a short note explaining what had happened and the clinic treatment that had been given. When Robbie ran into an opening door because he was not looking where he was going, a note accompanied him home that day to explain his little busted lip. So, Kate was surprised that something could have occurred at school to leave a bruise of that size and yet, no note explaining it.

"At school, Robbie?" she clarified.

Robbie smiled. "Yeah, shool."

Kate squatted by the tub and took up the washcloth to wash Robbie's small back. Trying to sound like it was no big deal, she asked, "That's a pretty big bruise, buddy. What happened?"

Robbie continued to scoop bubbles into his lap, but answered, "Tika heh me."

"What, honey?" Kate asked.

Robbie looked up at her then, unconsciously knowing that when misunderstood the first time, he needed to look at the person listening and try to speak more clearly. He repeated, "Tika heh ME."

"Tika heh you?" Kate was trying to decipher what a "tika heh" was. "Mama doesn't understand. Can you tell me a different way or show me?"

Robbie said it again, "Tika HEH ME" and took his fist and brought it down into the water with a great deal of force, causing water to splash them both. This caused him to break into gales of laughter.

But as the water dripped off Kate's face, she understood what her son was saying and did not find it funny in the least. "Tika hit you?"

"Uh-huh. Momma, you all weh," he said and he laughed again.

"Robbie, honey, look at Momma for a minute," Kate said as she quickly wiped her face. "Who is Tika, honey?"

"Tika meeeeen," Robbie said as he made a monster grimace.

"Is Tika someone in your class?"

"Uh-huh. See seh by me. See heh me ah da time. See mean."

Kate sat back on her heels hard. How could this be going on and the teachers not be aware of it? She had emailed Robbie's teacher last night and informed her that she and Vinnie would be coming by at school's end today to speak with her about something of great import. At first, Vinnie had complained that he had to meet some investors in Charlottesville today and why couldn't Kate handle this on her own?

After some discussion reminding Vinnie that he was one of the parents of one Roberto Tuscadero and the life partner of Kaitlin Tuscadero, Vinnie decided his client meeting could be moved around. Kate had left work early for a "family emergency" and was now heading to Robbie's school. Kate realized that now was not the most opportune time to be taking off work early, for she was in line to be named head of the SANE program for hospital corporate. But, she was a mother first and anyone who knew her was aware of that.

She arrived at the school and, not seeing Vinnie's truck, debated waiting for him. A quick glance at her watch showed her she was just a few minutes early. By the time she looked up, she could see him pulling into the next available parking space. The bell had not rung yet to dismiss school, so the parking lot was relatively empty of people. Vinnie greeted her with his customary, "Hey, babe" and gave her a quick kiss.

They walked into the office and after a short wait and the ringing of the final bell, they were told they could wait in a conference room off to the right. Soon after, Robbie's teacher and classroom aide came in and pleasantries were exchanged. Kate could barely control her impatience through the banalities. When all were seated, Robbie's teacher, Ms. Kutchins asked, "I received your cryptic email this morning. What concerns do you and Mr. Tuscadero have?"

Kate bristled at the word "cryptic", but answered calmly, "Well, I guess my first question is who Robbie would be referring to when he says 'Tika'?"

Ms. Kutchins and Amy, her classroom aide, exchanged knowing glances. At that exchange, Kate's maternal hackles rose. Ms. Kutchins replied, "That would probably be Patinka, one of our other students."

"Oh, okay," said Kate. "Then my second question would be: How long have you been aware that she is hitting Robbie?"

Again with the team glances, then Ms. Kutchins spoke, "Well now, Ms. Tuscadero, I'm not sure what Robbie has said, but I can assure you that it isn't quite like that..."

"Quite like what?" Kate demanded. "Is she hitting Robbie? Were you aware of it?"

"Well," hedged Ms. Kutchins, "Patinka is one of our ESL students placed in the class. She speaks little to no English. She sits next to Robbie in class, and we feel due to frustration on her part, she sometimes lashes out...nudging Robbie in the arm."

Kate could feel Vinnie's hand lay softly on her leg under the table. Kate was not going to take the signal to calm down, "Nudging him? I'm sure you are both aware of what I do for a living. Rarely have I seen 'nudging' leave a big, dark bruise on someone. Yet, this is what I found on Robbie's arm last night while he was taking a bath!"

Now it was Amy's turn to speak. "Well, Ms. Tuscadero, at first it was just kind of a poke. I think because Robbie was right there, not because of Robbie. We would try to redirect her, and if she did it again, she was put in time out in the corner of the room. She has been more aggressive in the last week or so. But, every time she does it, she is reprimanded."

Now, Vinnie's hand began lightly to pat Kate's leg under the table. "Every time? You mean to tell me this has been a regular occurrence? Why the heck didn't you just separate them?" Kate could feel her blood pressure going up at the thought of Robbie being punched on a regular basis, and she, being completely unaware of it. Did they not move him or send one of their short little notes home because they realized the ludicrous nature of it and knew Robbie would not speak of it?

"We really don't think there's any malice in it. She doesn't understand the language, which is why we put her in time out. We don't want to move her because it might confuse her, or she may misunderstand the reason behind it," explained Ms. Kutchins

Kate barely heard Vinnie's "Oh, Lord" as she pushed back her chair and stood up. Even as the right side of Kate's face began to tingle with probable explosively high blood pressure, she addressed the startled pair before her, "I don't pretend to be an educator with years of university knowledge behind me. Nevertheless, just a few years of parenting – no, even babysitting for God's sake - taught me that disorderly children need to be handled. Disorderly children that hurt others need to be stopped. It appalls me that someone with your background would allow something like this to go on in your classroom. It confuses me that I get little colorful pieces of hand-written paper to explain every little 'mishap' that has occurred since Robbie began school. However, he becomes a punching bag for some little psychopathic BRAT, and I have to discover it on my own?!"

"Now, really Ms. Tuscadero..." began Ms. Kutchins.

"Shut. Up," Kate warned. "This is what's going to happen. I'm going to go home to my son and tell him that the next time that

'Tika' looks like she's revving up to sock him one, he's to give her the international symbol for 'back the hell off'." Kate demonstrated this by raising a fist to the side of her face. She left it in the air as she continued, "Then if she hits him again, I'm going to tell him to haul off and hit her back with everything he's got. Hit her in the same place with everything he's got, you hear me? I figure he's got the right at this point. And don't you **dare** punish him in any way. I don't want to get a phone call from you, a warning letter from the school or any repercussion for that action. If you cannot protect my son, then by God, you will allow him to protect himself. Do I make myself perfectly clear?"

Neither woman facing Kate spoke. They both appeared to have had day-old corn cobs shoved up their backsides. Kate dropped her fist, placed both hands on the table and leaned forward. "Do I?" she repeated.

Both women bobbed their heads in unison, but continued to say nothing.

"Good," Kate snapped. She bent down to retrieve her purse and opened the door of the conference room to leave. She looked back at Vinnie, who smiled up at her in his lazy, laid back way. Vinnie turned to the stunned educators in front of him and said simply, "Ladies" then he too, rose from his seat to leave.

At the door, he turned and said, "Oh, and regarding what she said," he nodded to the retreating figure of his spitfire of a wife, "she isn't kidding and I'm behind her 100 percent on this one. You may want to do something about this before it gets really hairy, huh?"

The next day when Robbie came rushing into Kate's arms from his Nana's backyard, he was all excited to tell his mom about his big day at school that day. It seemed that 'Tika was moved to the other side of the classroom and that he, Robbie, was the line leader for the "hole of nesh week!" Kate oohed and ahhed at the appropriate times during Robbie's rushed announcement. She gave him a big hug and watched as he skipped-ran to her new Jeep Cherokee sitting in the driveway. Her children were her life and nothing caused Kate to lose her cool more than the thought of someone intentionally harming them. Vinnie often teased her, saying she was like a mother bear with cubs. Maybe so, thought Kate as she thought of her behavior the previous day.

She had met with corporate administrators earlier today and had discussed the possibility of taking over the leadership of the SANE program. This position would be for all five hospitals in the Richmond area under the corporate umbrella of PHCH, Professional Healthcare Community Hospitals. She was asked if she believed that being a working mother would affect her ability to carry out the duties necessary for that position.

Kate very much wanted the position and had spent the last few years preparing for it. However, she wanted no misunderstandings in the future. Therefore, her answer had been, "I see no problem whatsoever. I am a mother first. It is my most important job because I am raising future adults with the ability to survive and contribute to this society. Being the best mother I can will always take priority over everything else. However, I have trained and spent a great deal of time preparing for this position. I believe because I refuse to adjust my priorities shows how dedicated I can be to something I believe in, and I believe in the growth of this program within Community Hospitals here in Richmond." She figured that this answer may have cost her the position, but didn't really care when she saw Robbie's face beaming at her from the other side of the passenger back window.

Chapter 15

While Kate was verbally spanking Robbie's teachers, Tommy was looking through a *Trading Post* to secure a vehicle cheap while drinking a rancid cup of old coffee at a fast food joint in Richmond. He had gotten a bus ride back into Richmond via Greyhound. He had walked to the nearest 7-11 and purchased a *Trading Post* with the limited cash the jail had given to him. Although he wanted to eat, he bought only coffee.

He knew he needed to secure a job, but he figured he would need wheels first to take him back and forth. He had been gone for a long time and automobiles cost a hell of a lot more now than they did 15 years ago. Tommy found a Toyota Truck about 10 years old that fell into his price range. He had a few dollars to his name thanks to his long dead mother.

It seemed his mother had taken out a life insurance policy on both of them years ago. Probably, because she was hoping something would happen to Tommy once he landed in prison. However, fate had smacked her in the face and Tommy could now reap the benefits of her greed. The money had been held for him until his release, without interest, of course. Therefore, in addition to the $200 the prison had given him, he had over $50,000 now sitting in a savings account at one of the major financial branches in Richmond. He also had a halfway house to stay in until he could secure a job and living quarters of his own.

The house was located in The Fan area of Richmond and was nothing more than a small apartment with a kitchenette, small bedroom and adjoining living space. There was one bathroom on each floor to be shared by six "residents." There were three floors and Tommy's unit was 4M, which he assumed was on the third floor. He had not been there yet, but had heard from a bus mate what he could expect. He still had plenty of daylight left, and he had to check in by 6:00 p.m. This gave him enough time to play at being a good contributing citizen and use the time to find a paying job. He was to check in with his parole officer by 9:00 a.m. the following morning at the Henrico County Courts Building out on Parham Road. So, it was a no brainer, he needed a vehicle. He wasn't going to blow through his "inheritance" by continually paying bus fare.

Tommy was familiar enough with Richmond to realize that the Toyota seller was also located in The Fan area. How convenient, mused Tommy. He could hit the bank at the corner and get set up there. Take out the cost of the Toyota plus a little title and tag money. Check in with the halfway house and get settled there and be standing in line at DMV before closing time.

Tommy did not care what kind of shape the Toyota was in as long as it ran. He did not care what kind of job he got, as long as it had flexible hours and gave him an alibi. He didn't mind sharing a bathroom with a bunch of guys or living in a small space for awhile. Hell, he'd been doing that now for the last 15 years, he thought to himself. Tommy knew it was all temporary. He didn't plan on sticking around. He was going to find Teri Sanderson, kill Teri Sanderson and get the hell out of Dodge. If he could find her quick enough, he may not even need the job. He didn't know where he was going after he finished Teri off. Maybe Mexico first, then...well, he didn't think any further than that.

With the sigh of a satisfied man, Tommy slurped down the sugary concoction now cold in his Styrofoam cup, then crumpled it his hand. It felt good to crush things with his bare hands. He could not wait to feel again what warm flesh felt like crushed between his strong fingers. He sniffed hard and quick three times as he stood up from the table. Tossing the crumpled cup into the waste receptacle with "THANK YOU" stenciled upon it, Tommy pushed open the glass doors and walked out into a sunny day. Looking up the street, he slapped the folded *Trading Post* against his hard thigh.

He had stayed in shape during his prison years. He had, in fact, become leaner and definitely meaner. Becoming a wiry, lean mass of muscle in prison had allowed him to escape the grasp of those who would do him harm repeatedly. One greaser from down Me-hi-co way had been related to one of the chicks he had toyed with. It turned out she was the one who had offed herself rather than face him at trial. The greaser was the same one who had greeted him that first night in prison. After taking years of both physical and sexual abuse from or because of this one guy, Tommy had risen to a position to prepare food. After getting the idea from some prison show, Tommy had continually fed the grinning greaser ground glass until he finally coughed up rivers of blood and died on the dirty cafeteria floor. His "boys" knew who was responsible, but Tommy just smiled and waved his serving spoon at them. No one bothered him after that. Oh, the occasional bleeding heart faggot that wanted to give him one for womankind would give it a shot. Sometimes they got him, but more often than not they got beat back. He was a survivor and he had proven it in that hellhole.

As Tommy walked to the bank a few blocks down the street, he planned his evening. He was going to get his financial affairs straight and check in at the house. He would find and hopefully purchase the Toyota truck in the paper. He'd drive it over to the DMV and take care of that business and be back at the halfway house to be safely tucked inside by 6:00.

Then once he figured out a way to do it, he was going to sneak out and hit up one of the strip clubs close by. He needed to get laid, and he needed to kill. He wanted to take his time with Teri and plan it out well. He had 15 years of pent up rage screaming to be let out. He needed to let off some steam on some waste of a human life before going after Teri. Yes sir, beamed Tommy, it was shaping up to be a bee-oo-tiful day!

Chapter 16

Kate could hardly contain her excitement as she walked out of the boardroom of the administrative offices. She walked calmly through the halls on the way to her office. Smiling, she greeted people she knew with a quick, "Hey, how's your day going?" or "Hey, working hard?" Kate worked in a relatively small hospital by today's standards, and therefore, it was easier to know just about everyone who worked there. By the time she had made it back to her office off the hallway next to the nursing staffing office, she had greeted about 15 people and stopped to briefly chat with three more. Even as she made quick chatter about someone's new grandchild or another's recent promotion, she could not wait to get to her office and on the phone.

The position was hers! Although the official announcement would not be made until later that week, she had been offered the position she had been grooming herself and her department for. She was now the Director of the Sexual Assault Nurse Examiners of Professional Health Care Corporate Division, Richmond, Virginia. She would head up the SANE program for all five PHC hospitals in Richmond ensuring adequate staffing and consistency; two areas lacking in the current program in Kate's opinion. This would be her goal as director. Well, her first goal, at least.

Finally, she could reach her desk and call Vinnie first. She called his cell phone, glancing at the clock to check the time. It was almost 3:00, so she should be able to catch him. After a few rings, he picked up.

"'Lo, babe. How's your day going?" he opened with his usual salutation.

"Vinnie! I was offered the position of director!" Kate blurted out, unable to contain the urge to share.

"Whoa! Congratulations, baby! Did you accept?" he said, and she could hear the smile in his voice.

"No, I told them it was just an honor to be nominated. Yes! I accepted!" she laughed.

"I'm proud of you, Katie. I know this is what you've been hoping for. You're the woman for the job. How could they not offer it to you? So, how do you want to celebrate?" he asked.

Kate leaned back in her chair soaking up the moment. "Hmmmmmm," she mused. "A weekend at the beach house, before it gets too cold. We'll go down Friday night and come back Sunday evening. What do you think?"

"Whatever the lady desires, the lady gets" answered her knight. "This weekend?"

"Possibly, I'll have to see what the kids' schedules entail. Check with Izzy, that kind of thing. I want the whole family to go. Izzy's so caught up in her first year at VCU, I'm not sure if she'll be willing to come along," Kate said.

"Oh, I'm sure she will when she knows the reason. I'll call her and see what she says," said Vinnie. Kate knew that father and daughter still had a special relationship she could not touch. She supposed when Isabella became a married woman or a mother, she would get her back. But for now, she remained her daddy's girl. Kate also knew that if Vinnie asked, Isabella was more likely to come.

"Okay, that would be great. Whatever weekend works for her then," Kate said, adding, "Well, I'll see you at home tonight. Love you."

"Love you too, babe, and I'm proud of you," Vinnie said softly. "And if you're lucky, I might just show you how proud after Robbie's gone to bed."

"Ooooh, stop teasing," said Kate laughing. "Fingers crossed."

She hung up with her husband and immediately tried to see if she could get Sandra on the phone. Sandra had been pulling for Kate to get the position and Kate wanted her to be included in the first few people to know. Unfortunately, she received Sandra's voice mail and left a quick message to call her back. She did not want to leave the news on voice mail.

She looked around her office and began to mentally pack and rearrange her office items in a more organized way. She knew generally where her new office was going to be located but not the precise location. The previous director had operated out of another hospital. Kate, when asked, had elected to stay here. The person taking her place would also be occupying her office. Therefore, it would be necessary for her to move.

She had over an hour left in her day, but was too excited to do much work. She wouldn't be moving for at least a week so there was no point of packing now. Kate decided the occasion called for a Snickers bar and grabbed her wallet out of her purse to make a quick run to the vending machines closest to her office.

As she made her way down the hall toward the ER, she said hello to a few people here and there. She stopped in the hall to speak with one of the radiology department heads coming out the imaging room. TJ smiled when he saw her coming down the hall and waited for her to come up beside him.

"Rumor has it that they offered you the new director's job," TJ said out of the side of his mouth as they walked along. He could have been a mole in some forties spy movie.

"TJ!" Kate said with a laugh. "Is there anything that goes on in this place that you aren't aware of?" She was constantly amazed at TJ's ability to know it all before the rest of the hospital. For possibly the one hundredth time, she wondered just who he was sleeping with or how many pots he had his spoons in.

"Not much," he said. "Why? You heard something?"

Kate laughed and playfully nudged his shoulder with hers as they walked. Ever since she was a new nurse starting out at this particular hospital and TJ had stepped in when an irate physician was chewing her out, she and TJ had a very comfortable and special relationship.

Kate laughed and said, "Never before you, TJ, never before you."

"Where you headed?" TJ asked.

"Going to get a Snickers bar. Want one?" Kate said.

"A Snickers bar? What? No champagne? Baby, now I know Vinnie's going to do better than a Snickers bar. Am I right?" TJ's eyes twinkled atop his slow, easy smile.

"But of course," Kate shot back.

"I knew it! You did get it." TJ smiled, as Kate realized the trap she had stepped willingly into.

"Yes, shush. Look, it's not official yet, so don't say anything, TJ. Seriously. You know admin likes to do the big notices and everything," Kate pleaded as they stopped in front of the vending machines in the ER waiting lounge.

"My lips are sealed until you tell me to open them," TJ said as he pretended to lock his lips with an imaginary key and throw it away.

"Thanks. You sure I can't buy you a treat for being such a good boy, then?" Kate asked. It was her turn to put a twinkle in her eye.

"Allow me. It's your big day. I should be treating you." TJ quickly dug in the back pocket of his scrub pants to pull out his wallet. "One Snickers bar. I tell you what. It being such a big day and all, hell, you can have a drink too," he joked.

"A drink too? Be still my heart! Coke Zero, please," Kate said.

"Coke Zero? With a Snickers bar? Seriously?" TJ smirked, but hit the correct button anyway.

He handed over both as though handing over the queen's jewels, with a courtly bow. "Madam, your treats."

Kate laughed and willingly accepted both prizes. Over TJ's bent back, she saw Eileen standing by the ER main desk. Her friend had become the Director of Nursing in Emergency Services within a year of Kate becoming head of the SANE department. Their working relationship remained a close one due to SANE operating out of the ER. She wanted to include Eileen in the small group of people who would hear the news before the rest of the hospital.

TJ finished his bow and gave a warm smile as he said, "Congratulations, Kate. Really. You deserve it."

Kate mocked a bow to acknowledge the compliment and said, "Thanks for my celebratory goodies as well."

"Hey, can't anyone say I don't know how to treat a woman to the finer things in life. Caffeine and chocolate on me, baby!" TJ winked, saluted her with the films he held in his hand and turned toward the physicians' desks in the ER.

"Eileen!" Kate called to her friend.

Eileen looked up from making some notations in the staffing book at the nurse's station and smiled. Closing the book and handing it back to the desk monitor; she slipped her pen in her white lab coat pocket and joined Kate at the vending machines.

"What's up? You slumming?" Eileen joked with a wink.

"Just collecting the finer things in life," Kate answered back showing Eileen the candy bar and soda.

Eileen smiled. "Oooh, what's the occasion for you to both eat junk food AND at such a late hour? Aren't you afraid you'll ruin your appetite for dinner, little girl?"

"Well, that is true," Kate said as she bit off her first bite of her candy bar. She pretended to give this point a great deal of consideration. "I mean, Vinnie is probably going to be taking me out for a celebratory dinner tonight. I really should be saving some room..."

Eileen looked a bit confused at first. Then her eyes widened and she clutched Kate's arm. "You got it, didn't you?!"

Kate smiled and nodded her head. Quietly, she and Eileen did a subdued happy dance on the carpeted area in front of the vending machines.

"Well, not to be undone," Eileen started. "I think you and I should have a celebratory lunch after the big announcement and the dust has settled a bit. What do you think?"

"Oh, absolutely!" Kate smiled. "Well, I've stalled as much as I can. I need to get a few more things done before I can get out of here today. I guess I better be making the trek back to my office."

"Yeah, walk off that candy bar, girl," Eileen called out as they turned to go to their respective offices.

"You're just jealous," Kate teased as she took a big bite of her candy bar seemingly out of spite.

Eileen laughed, kissed two fingers and patted her butt as she turned away. Kate laughed and walked back to her office. By the time she made it back, the candy bar was gone and Kate was washing it down with the diet soda, wishing it was the real deal.

Her voice mail light was on and Kate heard Sandra's voice teasing her about leaving messages and then disappearing. She quickly called her back and shared the good news with her. After promising, yet another, celebratory meal to Sandra ("with alcohol, sugar, and lots of it") she rang off. She hung up the phone thinking that by the time she finished all these celebratory meals, she might not be able to fit into her new office. She looked at the clock and saw that it was close enough to call it quitting time, and she locked up to go pick up Robbie.

As she walked to her car, she felt light and almost giddy as she realized that all the hard work was paying off. Of course, her new position would carry with it a great deal more responsibility and be more time-consuming, especially at first. She had big ideas for the program and was anxious to initiate them.

She climbed into her car and searched for the appropriate CD to take her to Vinnie's parents. She pulled out of the parking lot singing to one of her favorite songs and loving life. *Sometimes,* Kate thought, *life just rocks!*

Chapter 17

When Sandra heard about the early release of Thomas King, it was by accident. She was checking in with the office receptionist after a morning court session when she heard two coworkers discussing Mr. King.

"Turns out he was released too early because of some paperwork," one said.

"Damn! I wonder whose head will end up rolling for that one?" the other worker asked.

"The lowest guy on the totem pole, I guess. But, it's technically legal now, so..."

"Wow. Talk about a lucky son of a bitch. What was he in for anyway?"

"He was that rapist here in Richmond. What did they call him? The Window Dresser? No...that doesn't sound right..."

Sandra's auditory filter, which had been trained to catch words and phrases important to her and her career gave a sharp, internal BLEEP. She looked up sharply and asked, "The Window Shopper? Thomas King?"

"Yeah! That's him! Know him?"

"Yeah, I know him," Sandra said as she grabbed her laptop bag by her feet. She hurried to her office and made a few quick phone calls to verify the information and find out what the hell had happened.

After she finished with her last fact finding phone call, she sat back in her chair and blew out the air in front of her. *Son of a bitch!* she thought, *how in the hell does something like this happen?* She had been around in the legal field long enough to know that crap like that happened all the time, but normally not in such a well known case. As she continued to think it through, she had to admit that it was a well known case *15 years ago.* Further, it was a well known case locally only. Sandra doubted that it had made it beyond the surrounding counties in the news at that time. Still, it tweaked her sense of justice to know that it had happened nonetheless.

Her coworkers were correct. It was a stupid error. A person could make it his or her mission to see it reversed. However, the error merely caused the sentence to be shortened by a couple of years. She could rightfully fight to have him returned to prison to serve out the minimum sentence. However, even if she won that argument, by the time the case made it to trial, defense could easily argue "time served" and it would all be a waste of the taxpayers' money. At least that's what the DA's office would say and her office would not touch it.

She was in a private law firm now and doing quite well. She had recently made partner and this would not be her Mount Everest. Through her phone calls, she found out that Teri Sanderson had died from a tragic car accident some years ago. There would be no need for an anonymous phone call to her. The only person who needed to know TODAY was Kate.

Sandra leaned forward in her seat and quickly dialed Kate's office number. After a few rings, she received Kate's voice mail. She did not want to leave a message of this import on her voice mail. She decided to leave the message, "Hey, it's Sandra. Look, I need to talk to you as soon as you get this message. I've got some really big news to tell you, so call me as soon as possible, okay? If I'm not in, call me on my cell. It's that important! Okay, talk to you soon."

She knew Kate never had her cell phone on at work. She used a hospital pager there. It was one of the things about Kate that drove Sandra insane! She knew she could have Kate paged at the hospital, but thought better of it. Kate was normally paged for emergencies only, and she did not want to frighten her. Was this an emergency? Well, yes and no. She did not think Kate was in any real danger, but she thought she should be made aware it anyway. Sandra decided it could wait until Kate called her back.

In the meantime, she decided to place a "safety call" to Bill Patterson. Bill had been long since retired from the police force, but had started a private detective service. He was a damn good detective and Sandra had used his services many times. They remained friendly in a sometimes unfriendly business. What Bill would call a "heads up" call, she called a "safety call" because in her line of work in criminal justice, it always paid to be safe rather than sorry.

Bill picked up on the second ring. "Patterson Security Services."

"Things that slow that you're answering your own phone?" Sandra joked.

"Hey! Nah, Cindy's at lunch and I forgot to roll the number over to the answering service. Good thing, though, huh? How're you doing?" Bill said.

"Well, I received some interesting news just a few minutes ago," Sandra started. "Seems Thomas King was inadvertently released early. Got out yesterday. God knows where he is."

The other end of the line was silent. Sandra began to wonder if Bill had put her on hold without her knowing. Then Bill spoke quietly, "How in the hell did that happen?"

"Seems some paperwork had a wrong date on it, not caught by anyone in time. Anyway, he's out and there's not a lot anyone can do about it now."

"Not a thing anyone *wants* to do about it, you mean."

"Yes, well...anyway, I made a few phone calls and that's the deal. He's out."

Again, it was silent on the other end of the line for a moment and then Bill asked, "Kate know yet?"

Sandra could tell, by the way Bill asked, that he had not forgotten. No one associated with the case would forget Tommy King. Thomas King was a true psychopath and readily displayed all the personality traits of a psychopath. Psychopaths did not heal; they did not see the error of their ways. Psychopaths did not stop hurting people, they just changed hunting grounds.

Soon after Tommy arrived in jail and began attending the mandatory counseling sessions required by the state, he was a very wordy individual. He was full of rage and fantasies of revenge. He continued to insist that he had only been giving each of the women whom he had traumatized what they were looking for in the first place. He was convinced that having a woman lawyer had screwed his chances of a fair trial. He preached that if a male doctor had examined Teri Sanderson that night in the ER, then he would have determined that Tommy had only been fulfilling Teri's desire to be handled roughly by a strong, virile man. Tommy had stated that he would see "all of them pay for caging [him] up like some damn animal." He had named Teri, Sandra and Kate, as well as a few others.

All of those years ago, Bill had contacted Sandra out of his worry for Kate. They had discussed things like parole hearings and testifying at such events. Now, that opportunity had been taken from them, and they were stung by it. It had been a very long time since either had revisited the subject of Thomas King, but neither had forgotten.

So, to Bill's question of whether she had been able to reach Kate yet, Sandra answered, "No, I got her voice mail. I left her a message to call me. I didn't say what it was, but I let her know it was important. I'm sure I'll hear from her today."

"Well, he had to check in with a parole officer," Bill thought out loud. "I'll make a few phone calls and find out where he's at and get back to you. Want me to try Kate?"

"No, no. I don't want to upset her. I'm sure I'll talk to her today. Just let me know what you find out, okay?"

"Yeah, you bet. We'll all do lunch," Bill deadpanned, then, "Listen, let me know if you can't reach Kate. She probably ought to hear it from one of us. It's going to shake her up. She had a hard time with that one."

"I know. You're right and I will. Thanks, Bill," Sandra said in a way of good-bye,

"Yeah, anytime," and he was gone.

Sandra tried to concentrate on the computer screen in front her after her phone call with Bill. She had a few ongoing cases and needed to spend time on each one. She found herself staring at her phone and willing it to ring. It remained silent, taunting her with every passing minute.

***

Kate gathered up her leftover PowerPoint handouts and prepared to head back to her office. She had just completed her last training session on consensual versus non-consensual sexual encounters as the Director of the SANE program for the hospital. She was sure she would be involved in more training in her new position, in fact, insisted on it, but it would be on a bigger scale.

One of the training session participants approached her as everyone filed out of the classroom. It was obvious he wanted to ask a question, but politely waited for an invitation to do so from Kate.

"Did you have a question, officer?" Kate asked as she continued to put away her laptop and accompanying cords.

"Yeah, I was wondering..." the officer began, "were you the SANE nurse that helped nail The Window Shopper?"

At the mention of the name, Kate dropped the coil of extension cord she had been holding. The name brought back to her mind the look he had given her as she left the witness stand that last day. Many times, she had received threatening looks from defendants and had been able to shake it off. However, the look that Tommy had turned upon her...

Although Kate was not a devout anything, she did believe in God and by direct correlation, Satan. She was an active participant in life around her and had therefore, been able to witness, firsthand, good and evil. She had no doubt these or the entities that championed them were real. Therefore, when Tommy had locked eyes with her, she had found herself looking into the eyes of evil. It was Emily's father all over again. She felt she was looking into the eyes of a demon residing in the body of what may have once been a human being. In her lifetime, she had withstood the stare of a demon on three occasions and the memory of all three still caused her to shudder. Thomas "Tommy, the King Snake" King, a.k.a. The Window Shopper, was one of those.

With the officer watching her now, she mumbled "oops" and stooped to pick up the cord. She composed herself before standing and glancing at his name tag: HOWARD W. RATHER. Wrapping the cord once again, she answered him, "Well, as SANE nurses, we do not decide guilt or innocence. Our focus is on the gathering of and the presentation of the contents of a sexual assault kit. But, yes, I was the testifying SANE nurse on that case."

She studied the officer in front of her. "How old were you when all that happened?" she continued by asking. "You couldn't have been any older than, what? Elementary school?"

"Yeah, probably in the third grade or so," answered the young man.

Wow, I'm getting old, Kate chuckled to herself. Out loud she said, "Well, why the interest? Or should I say, do you have a question about what we covered today as it pertained to that case?"

"Oh...well, when I found out you were teaching the class, someone told me that you were partly responsible for sending The Window Shopper to jail. I looked up the case and realized how big it was at the time. I just wanted to meet and congratulate you, I guess," the officer said with a smile.

"I see," said Kate. "Well, I appreciate you taking the time to say something, but I really can't take credit for that. The last victim is really the hero in this case. Because of her courage - that's why he's behind bars today. Who knows what would have happened if she had chosen to remain silent?"

"Huh," pondered the officer. "Well, I hope she had a happy ending then. Let me guess. She went on to marry and have 2.5 kids."

Kate smiled sadly as she remembered the day Bill gave her the news of Teri's death. "No. She ran her car off the road, hitting some type of construction equipment, I think. Anyway, she was killed instantly. It was a few years after the trial, as I recall. Teri Sanderson was the real hero. And of course," Kate added with a grin, "all the fine police officers who made it their mission to keep a clean chain of evidence and play it by the book. SANE nurses are a piece of the bigger puzzle. Sometimes even a corner piece. But a piece of the puzzle just the same."

"You're too modest, Ms. Tuscadero," the officer said and added, "Well, it was nice to meet you all the same. Great PowerPoint by the way."

"Thank you. It was great having you in class and meeting you as well." Kate smiled and watched him leave.

In short fashion, she gathered up the rest of her belongings and headed back to her office. She needed to check in with her voice mail, since she had been gone most of the day, and then head home. Once she arrived at her office, she dumped her laptop shoulder bag into a visitor's chair and placed the white binder of PowerPoint notes on the bookshelf. She had two quotes framed in her office. She had placed them so that she would have to see both every time she came in.

The first was about principles and was one of her favorite quotes by Thomas Jefferson. It read:

"In matters of style, flow with the current...in matters of principle, stand like a rock."

This was placed on the opposite wall from the door, and she saw it every time she walked in. It had been given to her by the previous director before vacating the position. It would follow her to her new office.

The second spoke to integrity, and it was on the wall opposite her desk, so that she saw it before she even sat down. It read:

"Integrity is one of several paths. It distinguishes itself from others because it's the right path and the only one upon which you will never get lost." M.H. McKee.

Kate had found the sign in one of those anything shops down in Carytown while shopping with Isabella. She was going to give it to Isabella for her dorm room; kind of like a maternal "hint, hint." Isabella had glanced at it, wrinkled her nose and said, "Too wordy" and had gone back to try to find an outlet to plug in a used Panini grill. Kate just could not seem to put it down all the way to the register. At Isabella's questioning glance she had responded, "It's for me. I like it."

She checked in with her voice mail and heard Sandra's cryptic message. *She's already made partner*, she thought, *does she own the law firm now?* Kate loved her friend, but she was too career-oriented. Sandra had dated throughout the years, but never anyone more than twice. She politely, but firmly, refused all attempts by Kate and Vinnie throughout the last few years to introduce her to their known single male friends.

At one time Kate had wondered if Sandra was gay and had finally felt comfortable enough in their long-standing relationship to ask her outright. Sandra had almost expelled Scotch and water through her nose. At first, Kate thought that Sandra was furious for asking, but then saw her laughing.

"You think I'm gay?" Sandra asked. "Let me guess. This comes from me choosing not to marry and have the offspring required to carry on some man's name?"

"Well," began Kate, "it's not that you're not married...not really. It's just...you never seem to have any relationships...long term relationships with men."

Before Sandra could form an answer, Kate said, "You know what? Never mind. It's none of my business, and it was rude of me to say anything. I'm sorry. Forget I said anything."

Sandra gave Kate her courtroom stare which made Kate feel as though she were a criminal with evidence mounted against her in plain view, denying she had done the crime. Kate hated that look!

"You're right. It *is* none of your business, and it was rude. Not like you at all, actually," Sandra said in a tone Kate recognized as the beginning of a summation.

"I only asked," Kate interrupted, holding up her hand in a silent plea for leniency, "because if that's the case, Vinnie and I could stop trying to find Mr. Right for you..."

"I would almost claim homosexuality for that alone," Sandra commented.

"Okay, not Mr. Right, per se, but...I don't know...male companionship. Oh God, I wished I had never started this conversation," Kate said and took a healthy gulp of her wine.

Sandra smiled and leaned forward. "Hey, it's okay. I am every bit of a woman that loves the attention and particular attributes of a man. I just don't want a long term relationship with one and I most certainly do not want children. I love my job. I am married quite blissfully to my job."

She dipped her finger in her drink and leaned back to say, "You know, marriage isn't for everyone and no one should be forced to enter into anything that sacred, or designed to be that sacred, if their heart's not in it. Don't you agree?"

Kate admired her friend for her tenacity and her rapier wit. She admired her for her strength and her ability to freeze fire if the need arose. Once when a man commented to Sandra that she had balls of steel, Sandra had replied, "Oh honey, I don't need balls. I'm a woman. I'm made of steel."

Kate raised her glass in answer to her friend. "Here's to remaining faithful to the love you so choose: man or career."

"Hey, don't forget. I work at my relationship too," said Sandra, "many a night I've been up all night."

"Yeah," agreed Kate, "but when I'm up all night in my relationship, it's because I'm getting laid."

"Touché," laughed Sandra as they clinked glasses again.

Kate laughed at the memory as she waited on hold for the connection to Sandra to go through. Her smile died on her face at Sandra's first words. "Kate, he's out. Tommy's out."

Chapter 18

Tommy lay in his bed reliving his first 24 hours of freedom in his mind like a fantasy revisited by a horny teenager. He had accomplished quite a bit in his first 24 hours. No one could call him lazy or as his dead mother used to say "a waste of space." At the thought of his mother, his empty stomach shifted the hot acid around reminding him that he had yet to eat. He made a mental note to find his mother's grave later today and piss on it.

Yes sir, in his first 24 hours he had checked in with the halfway house and secured a room. He had checked in with his overworked parole officer whom he was meeting with later this week. He had gotten his finances straight and paid cash for a decent pickup truck which neither his parole officer nor the homo that ran the halfway house were aware of. He secured some decent threads, managed to get laid and had squeezed the life out of another whore last night. As AC/DC sang; he was Back in Black as a hunter.

When he had checked in to the halfway house, he was a bit pissed that his room was on the third floor of the rat trap the state considered habitable. The dump didn't even have an elevator. There were three flights of stairs to carry himself and anything he thought he could carry up to his room. The fag that had showed him to his room yesterday acted like Tommy should lick his mock croc boots for allowing him to stay here. Yeah, right! Even with his drug/alchie whore of a mother, he had never stayed in anything so squalid.

It was a furnished room with a kitchenette against the left wall. 'Kitchenette" being a two burner gas stovetop oven. The oven itself looked like it hadn't been touched, or cleaned for that matter, since the Nixon administration. The refrigerator/freezer had to be the same one that had been here since electricity had been added to the building. The chrome handle was rusted in spots and the ice so thick in the freezer, it was unusable.

The other "furnishings" included a beaten up old dresser and a metal-framed double bed. The dresser drawers were shit. The top two stuck and you couldn't open the bottom one too far or it would fall out completely landing on unsuspecting toes. The bed was halfway decent if you didn't remove the sheet to take a real close look at the mattress. The mattress itself sagged so much in the middle, Tommy would bet that he would spend most of the night fighting gravity to stay out of that hole. He assumed he would have to test that theory tonight, because he had not slept here last night.

He lay in that hole now as he was in no hurry to go job hunting. He smoked to override the stale, moldy smell coming off of the cheap, worn carpet lining the entire apartment. He had waited his turn earlier to use the full bath in the hallway. Evidentially, each floor had one bathroom shared by that floor's residents. Each floor, when filled to capacity - which was always - housed six "residents." According to the "resident manager" - some loser that had never had the balls to move on - using another floor's bathroom because yours was "occupado" was "not encouraged." Whatever. Tommy didn't plan on staying long.

When being given the grand five minute tour, Tommy noticed the one window in the apartment led to the fire escape. He also noted that the window had been nailed shut and commented on it.

"That's so you guys have to go by the front desk to check in and out," said the homo. "A lot of guys were sneaking down the fire escape and getting into all kinds of trouble."

"Isn't that breaking some kind of fire code, Einstein?" said Tommy, who stood a good six inches taller than the manager. "Why not just put bars on the windows?"

"Because," said the manager after taking a deep breath and rolling his eyes at Tommy's tall, lanky frame, "people were removing them from the outside and going about their merry way. This ensures compliance," he finished, indicating the nails. "Inspections are done once a week and we'll know if they've been removed," he added.

Tommy smirked at the brown-nosed little twit. He had known guys like him in prison; busy little rats eager to do the big cat's bidding. He despised the pathetic displays of borrowed power these mewling little twits tried to pull off. Normally, he would have bitch slapped the guy until his attitude toward him improved. But, he played nice because he knew it was not for long.

"So, what day are you going to bounce quarters off of beds there, boss?" Tommy said as he smiled a shark's grin.

"It's a random thing," shot back the manager.

"But once a week," sassed Tommy.

Missing the jibe, the manager confirmed, "Once a week."

What an idiot! thought Tommy. One of his errands had been to pick up superglue and black model paint. He had removed the nails, sawed through them and glued them back into the holes just enough to seem nailed in. Using the model paint he painted the windows around the places where marks showed his earlier removal of the nails. The window now appeared to be nailed shut, but in reality opened quite easily.

Last night, after showering and getting ready for bed, he had returned to his room and gotten decked out in a few of his new clothes. Dousing himself in his favorite cologne, he made sure his room door was locked and left via the fire escape. He walked the five blocks to where he had parked his pickup. The Fan was still very much alive at 11:00 and he doubted anyone had taken particular notice of him.

He had driven out to a well-advertised strip club and sat in the back where it was darker for those requiring a little more anonymity for their lap dances. When she walked out to perform her number, he knew she was the one. She danced to one his favorite songs, Ted Nugent's Stranglehold. He considered it his "school song" in a way.

Her name was Cashmere. She had long, thick, wavy brown hair. Its ends touched her sweet ass when she laid her head back showing her long, soft neck. Her face was nothing special - Tommy had seen better - but her body was worth every cent she had poured into it. Her breasts were too symmetrical to be real, but flawless in their fullness and beauty. Nice flat belly but not too skinny. *Nothing said "crack whore" like a skinny bitch*, thought Tommy. Nah, this girl had that little pooch right below her belly button that screamed "FEMALE" to Tommy. Nice, full ass sitting on top of average legs. But those legs were hairless and stuffed into hooker heels so how could they not look good?

She danced and gyrated her hips exhibiting all the right moves to make the monkeys sitting around the stage beg to stuff money under her thong. She played them all like fools as she danced to Ted's magnificent guitar. What stood her apart from the other dancing sluts, in Tommy's eyes, was her total disregard for the men. It was all about the song for her. Anyone could see that. She would be dancing like that to this song in her bedroom alone. It wasn't for the money; it was because the song turned her on. At that moment, Tommy had no intention of killing her; he just wanted to break her; to dominate her, to make her his own.

Tommy knew strippers. She would circulate the room after her dance, offering herself for lap dances. A few eager droolers would paid the extra money to see her up close and personal. He left before her song was over. Tommy finished his watered down drink in one swallow and left a decent, but not stand-out tip.

He sat in his pickup truck watching people come and go for over an hour before she came out. She had changed into a T-shirt and jeans ensemble, complete with cross trainers on. *How cute*, smirked Tommy, *the whore's supposed to be the girl next door*. He followed her to a West End luxury apartment complex and watched to see which apartment she entered.

Leaving the apartment complex, he drove across Broad Street to leave his pickup in one of the store parking lots there. Although a decent truck, it would stand out like a hog in a field of horses in the apartment parking lot. He returned, by foot, to the apartment complex. Being very careful, he made his way to her apartment. The apartment was dark by the time he was standing in front of the sliding patio door.

He did a quick perusal of the outside framework and looked along the inside of the sliding glass door as much as his limited view would allow. He saw no evidence of an alarm connection pad. He did see the bar across the track preventing the door from sliding. *No problem there*, he thought. He'd been popping doors off tracks since he was 13 and continually being locked out of the apartment by his drunken mother. But it could be noisy, so he decided to give it an hour.

Later, the door popped easily off the frame and he was able to catch the safety bar before it fell. Stepping inside the kitchen, he listened for any indication she had been awoken by his entrance. Other than the ticking of the electrical appliances, he heard nothing. Tommy breathed a sigh of relief that he did not hear the padding of doggie feet either. Quietly, he walked across the kitchen and entered the hall, keeping an ear to the slightest noise.

Pausing to look into her living room, he noticed the treadmill sitting in the corner facing the TV. *Into working out, huh? Thinks she's strong.* His eyes stopped on a baseball bat leaning in the corner near the front door. He had to put a hand over his mouth to stop the laughter that threatened to erupt. *She intended to hurt whoever came after her, did she? Well, well, we'll just have to see about that won't we?*

Slowly, he began to ascend the stairs, careful to stay to the outside so as not to step on any loose and worn boards. Once at the top of the stairs, he had a choice of four rooms. One was obviously a bathroom and stood directly in front of him. The other three doors were shut. *Damn it!* He should have cased it long enough to know which of the rooms she slept in. If this had been in the good old days, he would know what time she got up to pee every night. But this was a release of tension thing and Tommy had a second of doubt.

To his right, his peripheral vision caught a swift movement low to the ground and his heart lurched in his chest. Then a pair of glowing yellow eyes stared back at him from the midst of a black shadowed demon. Slowly, his rational mind recognized the shape of a startled Persian cat staring back at him. *Damn fur ball,* thought Tommy, *liked to scare the shit out of me!*

From a room to his left he heard the muffled sound of a TV. It was so low that Tommy had not heard it at first. He remembered now. Many single women fell asleep with their TVs on, he wasn't sure why. He figured it made them feel less alone and maybe gave them a false sense of security. When in reality, for hunters like him, it was like a big, neon arrow saying, "She's in here!" Tommy smiled and sniffed hard three times in succession in anticipation of the lesson to be given.

She was still sleeping, even after he opened the bedroom door. The light from the TV lit up the room in varying shades of darkness. She was sleeping on her belly, the sheets twisted around her legs. Tommy almost tripped on her cast off shoes lying forgotten on the floor. His adrenaline saturated heart skipped a few beats as the stupid cat darted by him into the room. In a fit of anger to compensate for the shame of being startled by a cat, Tommy kicked out, connecting with the ball of fur.

The kick was a solid one and propelled the cat across the room to crash against the opposite wall, which contained two windows side by side. The cat slammed into the cheap apartment blinds shouting out a frightened and angry screech of pain. This, of course, woke up Sleeping Beauty.

Before she could turn all the way over, Tommy jumped onto the bed and straddled her back, pushing her head into the pillow with enough force to cut off her air supply and get her attention. The other hand held one arm behind her back, shoving her grasping fist far up between her shoulder blades. Her screams were muffled by the pillow completely covering her face.

"Shut up!" Tommy said in a husky, angry, low voice. He said this leaning his full top weight upon her back and hissed into her ear.

She heard him and proving her intelligence, stopped struggling and listened. To reward her, he released a bit of pressure from the back of her head and she wrenched her head to the side to draw in a breath.

Quickly, leaning his body forward again, he laid his stubbly cheek against hers and said in the same menacing voice, "You scream, bitch, and I will shut you up and kill you slow. Cooperate and be a good little slut for me and I will let you live. You understand, you just nod your head."

Now the crying started and Tommy hated that. Not because it touched any part of him, but because it ruined their beauty with the reddened, puffy eyes and snot coming out of their noses. She did not scream, but neither did she do as she had been told.

Tommy grabbed a handful of that long, luxurious hair and jerked her head roughly and repeated himself, "You understand? Are you going to be a good girl?"

She nodded her head and said, "Y-y-yes, yes, I underst-st-stand."

Then it began. Tommy took his time and he practiced his long dormant art of strangling to the point of unconsciousness and using pain to bring her back around. At one point, she broke her part of the bargain and began to scream. But Tommy stifled the sound with one of the pillowcases shoved in her mouth. All the hate and anger that had built in him for the past 15 years was allowed to peek out and show itself to the once beautiful stripper.

All the beatings and repeated rapes that Tommy had suffered had taken the fledgling psychopath that had entered prison and turned him into a heartless maniac intent on inflicting pain. Even as he tortured this girl, he knew he was holding back on the full extent of his rage for his intended Teri. This girl begging him to please stop beneath him was just a human release valve to allow him to let out enough steam to be able to think and plan.

When he finally strangled her to the point of death, it was almost with a type of reverence for the service that she had provided for him. It was probably why he covered her dead, naked and bruised body up before turning to complete his mission. He found scissors in the downstairs kitchen drawer and returned upstairs to cut off a strand of that long, beautiful hair. But instead of keeping it as a treasure, he used tape found on her computer desk to tape it to the headboard.

He used the bathroom off the bedroom to brush out his hair and check himself for any marks - there were none. Smiling at his reflection, he regretted that he would not be there to watch the faces of the detectives as realization dawned upon them. This time he did not worry about leaving evidence or hiding what he had done. He wanted the word to get out. He wanted Teri to know he was back. He wanted her to know that she was a dead woman borrowing time.

He had no intention of getting caught or going back to jail. He would get away clean and live on the money he had stashed away down in Mexico somewhere or he would be killed trying to get there; but he was never going back.

Before leaving the bedroom, he looked back at the woman lying across the bed the way most people would look at a pile of discarded clothes recently worn at a gala affair. It was a much needed and anticipated event, but it was over and it was good to be rid of it. To Tommy's surprise, he saw the injured cat lying beside his mistress watching Tommy with cautious eyes. His anger spent for the time being, Tommy left the cat softly mewling next to the dead stripper.

Back in his stale state-supported apartment, Tommy extinguished the cigarette in the aluminum ashtray sitting on the nightstand. He knew he would need to leave the apartment and find another place to hide out by tomorrow afternoon. There would be no job hunt. There would be no checking in with the parole officer. Tonight, he had started the clock ticking on his mission of revenge. Within the next few days, he would find and kill Teri before they thought to put guards on her. Within a week, he would be sitting on the Gulf Coast of Mexico drinking Mexican beer. Once in Mexico, he would blend in with the other American beach bums and he would have his choice of young, unimportant senoritas to play with now and then. There were plenty of women down there; a few missing here and there would go unnoticed.

Although wired from tonight's festivities, Tommy forced himself to listen to the street noise outside and lay still in the hole of his mattress. He needed to get some sleep so he could be ready to roll tomorrow. He had places to go, people to hunt and one very special snitch to kill slowly. *Yep*, Tommy thought, *a master's work is never done.*

Chapter 19

Tommy sat in one of the many Internet cafes in the Fan District waiting his turn to hop onto a computer. He nursed his cup of high dollar coffee and looked around the college hangout. Because of its proximity to Virginia Commonwealth University, the Fan District was home to many college students. As Tommy sipped at his plain coffee, he watched through the plate glass window as the normal crowd went about their day.

Two cute little things went by chattering and laughing about inane topics, Tommy assumed. One had a book bag slung over her right shoulder. The other girl seemed to prefer using a messenger bag to organize her crap. Privileged little stuck up princesses, no doubt. Tommy had gone through his teenage years being rejected and laughed at by the beautiful girls. After awhile, he stopped trying to be nice and started to hone his skills on hunting. He practiced on all those high school cheerleaders and popular girls by following them home at discreet distances. He knew their daily routine better than their own parents. He would go so far as to stand at the foot of their bed while they slept, but no further. He reserved his rage for small animals then, but practiced the art of the hunt on the girls.

He was never missed at his house and by the age of 16 he was practically living on his own. He was determined to finish high school, but knew there was no college in his future. That did not stop him from going though, he thought as he watched a homeless man wake up to a hot day in the Fan. Right here at VCU, Tommy realized that many of the classes were so large, they were held in auditoriums. By nervous trial once, he found that he could sit in one and never be questioned. So, he did many times. He continued the hunt during those days, watching the college girls.

College girls were more reserved; at least during the day. At night, after a few beers in the local meat markets masquerading as bars, they could be a little wild. Nothing worse than a loud, obnoxious drunk co-ed; unless you needed them that way. Before graduating to the status of The Window Shopper, Tommy had taken his skill training a little further with a few drunken co-eds.

Never stooping to picking them up at the bar (*that was amateur stuff*); Tommy continued to case each co-ed. He knew if they lived alone in an apartment mommy and daddy had paid for. He knew what night the roommate had a night class. All three chosen women had been cased for about three to six months before Tommy had allowed them the privilege to be with him. There were several others that did not pan out once the research had been done. One had a boyfriend that spent the night in no particular pattern. One had a big dog sharing the apartment with her. One girl showed herself to be gay and Tommy did not want any part of a woman who wasn't into men.

He was never angry when months of work would reveal a dead end. He realized that this was what hunting was all about. Sometimes, a good hunter had to realize when he couldn't take the shot and wait for the perfect opportunity to present itself. Tommy took great pride in the care in which he selected his victims.

Finally, some artsy-fartsy woman removed her fat ass from a bench seat, vacating a computer terminal. Tommy quickly sat in the warmed seat and used the code he had paid for to log on. Tommy had become quite proficient at the computer while in prison. Inmates were allowed to visit the computer lab on certain days at certain times if that privilege was granted. Of course, there were filters on every computer. But that didn't stop the self-professed computer hackers from cracking that code. Once found out, they were banned for the remainder of their stay. Tommy played nice.

Having come from copier repair, Tommy was a machine type of guy and recognized potential when he saw it. From the first few difficult-to-read rolled up pieces of facsimile paper that Tommy spied in the computer lab, he knew. That machine, later called a fax machine and computers were going to be big. The prison was always a step behind the market as far as the newest technology was concerned, but they had it nonetheless. Tommy played around on the computer, dreaming of the day he could be free and hunt again.

Eventually, his unwaning interest brought about the attention of the prison and his counselor finally asked the question Tommy was waiting for.

"So, Tommy, I noticed that you're spending a great deal of time in the computer lab lately. Researching anything in particular or just checking it out? What's that all about?"

Tommy displayed his best honest face and answered, "Well, you know I was a copier repairman before, right?"

After a nod from the counselor, Tommy continued, "Well, that wasn't just a paycheck for me. I really enjoyed what I was doing.

Machines and how they work have always interested me. When these desktop computers started coming out, it was another machine to try to understand. I believe they are going to be big and there is going to be a job market based on it. I want to learn all I can about them, so maybe when I do get out of here, I'll have a chance to work on them."

He could see that his little speech had convinced the counselor by the way the counselor was looking at him as a parent would look at a child finally recognizing a hidden talent. The counselor smiled and doodled a little bit on the desk pad in front of him. "Well, Tommy, that's great! I think it's wonderful that you have found something constructive to do with your time here. And I agree with you. I think computers are going to be big. At least, I hope so. I bought some stock in McIntosh myself." He paused here and Tommy was convinced he was in the clear; the counselor's curiosity and warning bells had been silenced.

"You know what, Tommy? What would you say if I told you that you could spend even more time in the computer lab and concentrate on developing the skill you are already working on? Maybe take some classes, earn a degree in computer technology? Would you be interested in that?"

Tommy was taken aback. He had anticipated the question only in preparation of throwing off worries of why he was always in the lab. As someone who was not used to anyone giving him a break, much less a hand up, he was speechless for a minute.

Obviously, the counselor took this as a sign of self doubt, because he said, "Rehabilitation starts with whom?"

Tommy knew the tune of this song. "Me," he answered. The look on the counselor's face read *good dog*. Tommy had to work hard to keep his features unchanged as his rage flared at the patronization. *Be careful, doc, this dog bites!*

"That's right, Tommy. That's what we've been talking about. I am more of a guide. You have to be the trailblazer. I am very encouraged by your interest in what will probably prove to be a very lucrative business path. I'm going to recommend college courses for you aimed at computer technology. Interested?"

Tommy knew how this song ended as well. "Oh yes, sir! Thank you! I would like that a lot! You don't know how much it means to me to have someone in my corner for once!" Tommy thought that last bit may have been a little over the top. But from the self-satisfied smile on the prick's face, he could see the song had been well played.

He had graduated from the kitchen to computer lab assistant. He was given almost carte blanche for the remainder of his stay. He played very, very nice and never overstepped his boundaries. While he earned his degree in information technology, he learned what ISP stood for and banked it. He learned which search engines were most reliable, updated most often and could navigate through most with lightning speed. As strong as the desire was, he never once ventured into looking up old friends; mainly one Teresa Sanderson.

But he was out now and close to using all that knowledge to hunt down his prey. He looked upon the computer as a newly required, well-bred hunting dog and he could not wait to undo the leash. He sat in the warmed seat and logged on using the code the Internet cafe owner had given him. He had only purchased 15 minutes worth of time, but figured he would probably need half that much. The minute he entered the code, a timer displayed itself in the bottom right hand corner: 14:59..14:58..14:57.

Tommy went directly to his favorite search engine and typed in the name TERESA SANDERSON just to see what popped up. He knew it would be like searching for a penny in the ocean, but he had to satisfy the child-like impulse he had denied himself all those years in prison. No surprise, those two words returned 28,324 results. Now, he would get down to business. Shifting in his seat, he sniffed hard three times in succession so loudly that it earned him a rude stare from the uppity bitch beside him. Let her stare, he thought. He couldn't help it. He had waited years for this one moment of many and great was his excitement.

13:13..13:12. As the timer ticked away the seconds, Tommy typed in the web address for the *Richmond Times Dispatch*, the local newspaper. He figured by now Teri had gotten married and had a few brats to clean up after. He would have no idea of her married name. Nights lying awake waiting for this moment, he had formulated a plan.

12:59..12:58. Once the page had completely loaded - *outdated piece of shit!* - Tommy immediately navigated to the archives. He would be looking for notices; specifically wedding announcements. He had no way of knowing whether she had remained in Richmond. But he knew that often brides placed announcements in the paper of their hometown if the parents still resided there. Once he had her married name, it was a matter of cross-referencing the poor dupe who had married Tommy's sloppy seconds and get an address. Once he had the address, ol' Miss MapQuest would be glad to show him how to get there. Then Teri would pay for opening her slut mouth.

12:10..12:09. Once the archive page had loaded and Tommy had clicked on NOTICES, he typed in her name: TERESA SANDERSON. Once again, the rotating hour glass mocked him silently - *not yet, not yet, not yet*. He sniffed three times again, anxious to have the "where" in his hands.

11:48..11:47. Finally, it was there. The page loaded slowly, taking time to make sure all the advertisements were correctly placed. Christ!, thought Tommy, for an Internet cafe, they need to upgrade their...what the hell is this?!

11:10..11:09. He was looking at an obituary page, for Pete's sake! Now he'd have to use the back browser and...then he saw her name and his bowels started to roll as ringing started in his ears, drowning out the white noise of the cafe. He read:

SANDERSON, TERESA, 27, of Henrico, died Thursday, June 11, 1995. She is survived by her fiancé, Bruce Wilson; by her parents, Shirley and Glen Sanderson and her sister, Carol Sanderson. A memorial service will be held Saturday, June 13, 2 p.m. at St. John's Cathedral. Funeral services will follow at 4p.m. at Hollywood Cemetery. In lieu of flowers, the family asks that donations be made to Victims of Violent Crimes to which Ms. Sanderson devoted much of her time.

This couldn't be the same Teri! It couldn't be! Even Fate couldn't be that cruel! To have waited 15 years for revenge and be cheated out of it...when? Just a few years after he had gone in? All those years of not daring to type in her name to find out where she was and keep track of her to make her easier to find. All those tortured nights while his ass bled onto his mattress after another brutal rape, dreaming of making her pay for his time in jail. SHE COULD NOT BE DEAD!

9:58..9:57..9:56. Precious seconds slipped away as Tommy's eyes read the obituary over and over. Quickly, his fingers started to tap-tap-tap over the keys searching out the information he needed. Using the date of death, he used other search engines and avenues known to him to find out if this was indeed her and how she died.

Over the next few minutes, he found it all: the fatal car crash, the hints of possible suicide, the vehement denials from the family; every piece of detail surrounding the untimely death of Teresa Sanderson. The final reports stated that the reason for the crash would never be known. Tommy didn't give a rat's ass about the reason for the crash. She was dead! He was like a child coming down to an empty living room on Christmas morning...he was crushed.

4:21..4:20. He didn't know whether to scream in rage or cry in frustration. For the first time in 15 years, he had no idea what he was going to do next and he was mentally incapacitated by that thought.

He left the computer terminal without signing off, sacrificing three minutes and 23 seconds that he had paid for. He was going to consume large amounts of alcohol until he passed out. When he awoke, he would decide what to do with the rest of his pathetic life. He left without looking back, headed to the nearest store selling alcohol.

The young college student watched him leave, sliding quickly into his vacated spot. This was the only way he could spend time on the computer. He had to wait around and catch someone giving up the rest of his or her time. Normally, the people in the Internet cafe kept an eye out for his kind, but he was dating one of the girls behind the counter. She gave him a sly wink to let him know he owed her a favor and continued to wipe down the tables.

He noticed the list of plots in Hollywood Cemetery still on the screen and wondered who the famous person was with the last name beginning with "S". Many historical and famous people were interned at the beautiful cemetery on Cherry Road. He did not want to spend any of his dwindling time solving that particular mystery. He quickly typed in the Internet address for Hotmail and logged into the email account of one TNTMAN.

Chapter 20

For a few seconds after Sandra's opening sentence, Kate didn't breathe. "Kate, he's out. Tommy's out!" bounced around in her head and her mind refused to touch it, let alone grab hold of it. So long was her silence, Sandra asked, "Hello? You still there?"

"Sorry," Kate said and swallowed with an audible click. "When did he...I didn't even know he was...But then again, I guess I wouldn't necessarily...What?"

It was not that Kate didn't know immediately who Sandra was speaking of. Kate did not remember many of the individuals who she had testified against. There had been many throughout the years and Kate had not testified herself in over five years. But some cases she never forgot; not one whimper, one predatory glance, not one self-satisfied smirk. In Kate's career as a SANE nurse testifying on court cases, there had been three that haunted her still. But she refused to travel down that worn path of regret now and forced herself to participate in the conversation that Sandra had started.

"Sorry, you sucker punched me there, Sandra." Kate tried a laugh, but it came out weak and frightened; a lost kitten instead of a courageous lion.

"I'm sorry. I should have worked on my opening statement a little," Sandra said, attempting humor. She was never very good at humor in tense moments with friends.

"No, no...I just didn't realize it had been that long, I guess," Kate said. "For some reason, I thought he got more time. Frankly, I'm a little surprised at my own reaction to something like this...or for the urgent call." The last she said almost as a question as realization of the real passage of time pressed itself upon her logic.

"He got out early," Sandra started.

"How? No...let me guess...good behavior?" Kate said attempting humor herself.

"That's why I'm calling. Not as a warning or anything really." Sandra paused here as if thinking that through, "but more as...Oh, I don't know. I'm pissed is what it is."

"Well, he was bound to get out. He didn't get life or anything," Kate said relaxing. Sandra was just venting on another of her "justice didn't quite fit the crime" issues. Kate had talked Sandra down from the fictional ledge of vigilante justice many a time.

"No, that's just it. Personally, after getting to know the psychopath, I would have buried him under the jail and thrown away the key. But he got what he got. Okay, done deal, right? But, that's just it," she repeated and Kate could picture her friend leaning on her massive desk, shoulders hunched forward in emphasis of what she was about to say. "He got out too early. It was a real cluster on the paperwork side. He got out *two years* earlier than he should have!"

"What do you mean 'earlier than he should have'?" Kate's perception of justice was: although justice may be blind, the woman wasn't stupid.

165

"I mean, that even if he had been the warden's play thing, he had to serve 17 years. It's been 15! He was released on a technical error. I don't have all the particulars yet, but I'm looking into it, trust me!"

"Oh, wow! Of all people! Well, what happens now? Can you legally put him back in? How does that work?" Kate wondered aloud.

"Trust me, I'm on it. But, Katie," Sandra started, but hesitated. She knew she could be brass and somewhat of a bitch at times. She was a high powered female lawyer in a boys' club profession. But when it came to her close friends, who were her family, she could be tender as well as direct.

"Yeah?" Kate knew what Sandra was going to say, but allowed her the time she needed.

"I spent enough time with this guy to know that he is a true psychopath - the real DSM VI definition of the word. He is not going to stop. He enjoyed it too much. I know he was released back into Richmond. I'm sorry to say, it's only a matter of time before he starts back up again. If we're lucky he'll skip town and start his games somewhere else."

Kate said nothing, but silently hoped that Sandra was right. She did not want another serial rapist in Richmond and she particularly did not want one with Tommy's history. She shuddered to think of all of the pent up rage that existed within him now; 15 years later.

"If we're unlucky," Sandra continued as if reading Kate's mind, "he'll pick up where he left off. I hesitate to consider how vicious he has become in prison. Another thing, Katie. I've known a few nut jobs like this one. They tend to be the vengeful sort. He'll see whoever put him away as a fly in the ointment of his perfect world."

They were both silent for awhile as that image sifted through their collective consciousness. Kate's mind worried for Sandra because she knew Teri Sanderson was out of the picture. Sandra's mind tried to remember the woman who had seen his face - *started with a T or S?* - and for her friend that had collected his DNA to prove it.

They both started speaking at the same time, "What was the name of the wo-"; "Teri died some years ago..."

They both stopped. They were silent for a second or two and both started again, "It was Teri Sanderson...", "She's dead?" Now they both laughed at themselves and Sandra said, "You first. You're the one with all the information."

"I just heard a few years ago that Teri Sanderson died in a freak car accident. No one really knows what happened there. But she's gone. I wonder if he knows that," Kate anguished.

Sandra wondered herself and was now more concerned for both of them. She answered Kate, "Don't know. I spoke with Bill Patterson earlier and he is going to check up on Tommy's whereabouts. Hopefully, we'll hear from him soon. In the meantime, I just wanted you to know so..." She did not know how to finish that thought.

Kate could hear the worry in her friend's voice and said, "Listen, you free for lunch in the next few days? Let's catch up and dig into this a little more."

"Hmmmm...I can do an early lunch tomorrow...about 11:00?" Sandra said.

"Sounds good. Where?"

"Can you come down here?" Sandra asked meaning downtown.

Kate was going to be teaching some classes at the Red Cross building down there tomorrow anyway. It was why she had suggested it in the first place. She would be in Sandra's "neck of the woods".

"I can and I will. I'm teaching a class down there, so we need to be wrapped up by 1:00."

"Darling, the day I take more than an hour for lunch will be the day some judge decides to hold court in a restaurant. See you then. Oh, and Katie," Sandra paused for effect, "you be careful."

"You too," answered Kate and rang off with Sandra. She hoped for them both, it was an unneeded caution. Her mind was left with the placement of Tommy in her personal hall of shame. After the incident with Emily, Kate had championed the cause for those unable to speak for themselves. She knew it was one of the reasons for her becoming a SANE nurse so that she could stop the sexual abuse from happening or at the very least put the abuser under a microscope.

In Kate's career she had three cases that replayed on those lonely, sleepless nights she had every so often when other stressors were closing in on her life. The first was one of the first child cases she had worked. The kit collected on a quiet little girl pointed to evidence of repeated non consensual penetration. The terrified child would not name her abuser, but through investigation and persistence, the abuser was found out. It was the little girl's soccer coach who often gave the young girl a ride home when the parents were unable to get to a practice in time. The picture that masqueraded through Kate's mind on those sleepless nights was the horrified and guilty look that crossed over the mother's features when she found out who had been harming her child. The cry of anguish that escaped the mother's throat was raw and open in its intensity. Kate would see that face and hear that cry in her mind and remember her escaped thought at the time, "Better her than me. Please, Lord, never me."

The second case involved a woman who was being raped and beaten on a regular basis by her husband. Kate saw her when the couple sought medical attention after one "love fest" had gotten out of hand. The couple claimed that the woman had been beaten and raped by a home intruder while the husband had run up to the store for beer (on his breath) and cigarettes (in his pocket). Through interrogation and collection of the kit with a sample from the husband (to rule him out), the truth became glaringly apparent. However, the woman refused to admit that her own husband was abusing her. Kate did everything but call the woman a masochistic coward and the woman finally not only admitted to the crime, but agreed to press charges as well. Before the husband was even arraigned, the woman went home and hung herself from a rafter in their garage. A note pinned to her pajama top read, "Sorry for betraying you, my darling."

Finally, the case with Tommy had crossed her path. It was that day in court and the look he bestowed upon her. The look that made her falter in her steps to leave the courtroom; something deep inside of her, something asleep to modern woman and a push button world. It stirred in recognition of the possible approach of death. It was the same look that Emily's father had laid upon her and her soul recognized it and she was that frightened teen all over again. It was the look of pure evil. It was the look of a child watching an ant silently scream under the laser stream of sunlight through a carefully aimed magnifying lens. It was the look of the wolf who has separated the yearling from the herd and takes it's time closing in; tasting and savoring the fear wafting off of its trapped prey.

It was this thought that stayed with Kate. She would never forget that look or the promise within it. If Sandra was right and Tommy decided to seek vengeance among his accusers, she would be the yearling and she would be in grave danger. Because she had met the wolf and looked into its eyes; and he was hungry.

Chapter 21

By the time Tommy arrived at Hollywood Cemetery, he had a fairly good buzz on. He had switched from beer, after the six pack was gone, to stronger liquor. He was about halfway through his bottle of Tequila now. He had not had access to alcohol for quite some time while in prison, so his tolerance for the stuff was not what it once was, he was pleased to discover. Tommy had never been a hard drinker or even liked it very much. But when times were bad and he needed to self-anesthetize, it was his drug of choice. But even through his alcoholic haze, he knew if he wanted to get into the famous cemetery with his alcohol, he would need to play it smart.

When Tommy was a little boy, his mother would sometimes bring him out here. The old witch liked this creepy place for some reason and Tommy knew she was buried out here as well. He had a fairly good idea where, but he would look for her grave later.

From his frequent trips here as a boy and later as a torturing ground for small animals (*because who enters a locked down graveyard at night?*), he knew this graveyard like his own backyard. In reality, this was the only constant "backyard" he had growing up. Although his residences changed as often as the rent was due or until his mother's current flame tired of them both, Hollywood cemetery had always been there. *How freaking poetic is that?* thought Tommy as he took another gulp of his golden Tequila.

He knew the graveyard closed at sundown and the gates were locked until dawn. There was a fence around the perimeter and in some areas, it was quite precarious to be on either side of that fence. However, to someone who had practically grown up in the cemetery, Tommy knew all its secrets. Even 15 years ago, the neighborhood was settled all around the cemetery and there would be no more expansion of either the cemetery or the neighborhood. What perimeter was not surrounded by houses was bordered by the rapids of the James River. It was a cemetery that mixed a Civil War Monument among ornate Victorian mausoleums. Moss covered crypts stood next to freshly dug graves.

Through his quick search online, he knew the plot and location of Teri's grave and he was anxious to confirm that she was indeed gone from him forever. Part of him wanted it all to be a clever ruse to keep her from him devised by the police and her loving family. But even as drunk as he was, he knew this was a desperate thought. He waited for the last car to leave the cemetery office area for the night and made his way to one of his favorite places to enter illegally.

There was a bit of overgrowth from vines gone unattended for some time, but Tommy could see that the access had not been altered in over 20 years. It was comforting in some small way to know that some things remained faithful and constant in Tommy's world. After a little work on his part and a quick furtive glance to make sure no curious eyes watched him, Tommy entered the graveyard close to where Teri's grave would be located.

Again, enjoying the irony of his life, Tommy wondered at the fact that the two women most responsible for his FUBAR life chose to be laid to rest in the same damn graveyard. Life was a riot. Tommy chuckled again and he knew it was the alcohol that kept his rage on the jovial side of things. He wondered if the sentries that used to cruise through the graveyard at night still did. Many a time when Tommy was too small to defend himself, he would escape the wrath of his mother or the advances of some pervert she was screwing by spending the night in the graveyard. Again, who would bother him in a graveyard? Tommy had spent a few nights in the massive mausoleums with their old iron gates. The gates meant to keep curious adults out allowed little boys in need of sanctuary in. From his nights spent here, he knew that there was a night crew that made it harder for frat boys and other pranksters from vandalizing the graveyard. He also knew how to avoid them.

Darkness approached swiftly and Tommy moved quite easily toward his destination. *She would be near the dog*, thought Tommy, one of the easiest landmarks within the cemetery to find. He had entered a good little walk from her; at least by following the curving asphalt drive winding through the many sections. He could cut across several gravesites and reach her quicker, but he wouldn't. *Tommy King was many things*, he thought, but he would be damned if he would walk on a bunch of strangers. He did have some manners about him, after all.

Tommy saw the dog coming up on his right and knew that her plot would be somewhere to the left. Tommy knew all the stories surrounding most of the landmarks of Hollywood Cemetery. He had taken the tour many times, falling in with the tourists, always thought to be someone's child. One of his favorites was the story behind the cast iron dog he was quickly approaching.

There were a few different versions based on which tour book one read, but his favorite story and the one he chose to believe went something like this: The daughter of a prominent Richmond citizen died at the age of three from scarlet fever. She always admired a cast iron dog in the home; in some versions of the story treating it like a real dog, petting it and hugging it. The dog was cast to be as big as a breed of dog known as Newfoundland. When the little girl succumbed to the fever in 1862, the dog was placed at her gravesite - at least in Tommy's favorite version.

Some versions stated that the father placed the dog there long before she even died. Other versions had the dog belonging to a grandfather or even a store owner. Tommy chose to believe that it was the father and he was a sly one. "Oh, my poor, lovely daughter has left me. I'll give her the dog she so admired. Boo hoo hoo."

In reality, the Civil War was cranking up and the Confederate Army was looking for cast iron to melt down and make bullets and cannon balls. Hell, the old man probably loved that stupid iron dog more than her and just did not want it to be melted down. The man had probably paid a tidy sum for it. Tommy turned toward it now and bent drunkenly before it. " 'ello puppy. How's the corpse watching going, huh?" laughing at his own wit.

He did a lurching about face and walked over the plots directly across from the cast iron dog. He did not know exactly which grave it was, but he did know the general area. Although the cemetery was extremely large and spread out over many acres, there was a method to the madness. To those familiar with the layout, as Tommy was, it was not as confusing as it would at first seem.

After searching for only five minutes, he found it. A rectangular piece of polished gray marble set into the ground. Simple, but elegant in design, it had a carving of a lily on the left and a carving of a dove on the right. Centered was the name **TERESA SANDERSON** with an artist's rendering of a cherished photo possibly taken not too long before she died. The artist's rendering was set upon a polished piece of white marble raised in an oval shape; similar to a jewel. Under this was simply carved the birth and death dates for the girl who lived a short life.

Upon finding the grave and seeing the serene, smiling face staring up at him, Tommy fell to his knees. Partly because his drunken legs were having trouble balancing his continuously weaving body, but also because of the desolation of the confirmation that the stone imprinted upon his mind.

"No, no, no, no, no!" sobbed Tommy. To anyone looking on, he would have appeared to be a heartbroken lover. Even if caught after hours in a place he was not supposed to be, anyone would have paused graciously at his supposed grief before escorting him out of the graveyard.

But Tommy cried not in grief, but in frustration borne out of a stolen dream of revenge. Part of what kept him going all those nights lying on his prison cot were the fantasies of making Teri Sanderson pay for betraying him. A silent sob froze Tommy's mouth into a cavernous grimace as a string of saliva escaped down his chin. He stared at her smiling, serene face and rage built up within him like lava within an active volcano.

His grimace became an angry snarl and then a roar of rage as he unleashed years of pent up anger upon the cool marble. The tequila bottle shattered as Tommy brought it down with lightning force, attempting to break the smile painted on the white marble. Not even a chip appeared and this angered Tommy even more. With his hand bleeding thick red splatters upon the stone from the multiple cuts upon his hand, he beat upon the marble with very little effect.

The skies seemed to share in his anger and they opened up with increasing wind, slanted rain and sharp cracks of thunder. Tommy did not even seem to notice and if he did he would have thought it was justified. As lightning lit up the darkened graveyard around him, he looked for something to destroy that stupid, smiling face!

About 10 feet away stood a stone grave marker in the shape of a cross. Tommy stopped stomping on the marble and stumbled over to the cross. He paid no heed to the name or inscription engraved upon it, but tried to take it with him. The rebar springing from the base of the gravestone some two feet down anchored it to the spot for which it was intended.

Tommy would not be denied and with chords standing out upon his neck and sinewy arms and veins bulging in his forehead, he screamed as he pulled with all his might. Slowly, the cross headstone began to move and when it let go, it came loose easily. As the lightning flashed in the sky and the wind caused the trees to dance to the music of the thunder, Tommy walked back to Teri's grave.

Over and over, he brought the cross headstone down upon the marble, first cracking the oval rendering and shattering it into a multitude of colored mosaic pieces. But he did not stop there. With her face gone, he set to work on the name, then the lily and finally the dove. When he was done, the grave was destroyed; desecrated beyond repair.

With his rage spent, the boiling Tequila mixed with the convenience store burrito channeled its way up his esophagus and he vomited several times into the wet grass around him. He crawled over to the nearest tree and leaned against it, closing his eyes to the light show that continued around him. As the storm moved over the graveyard, Tommy's storm was over and exhaustion from his rampage and the effects of the alcohol finally caught up with him. He fell into a drunken sleep just 20 feet from what remained of his broken dreams.

Chapter 22

The day broke like most late spring days right before the humidity of summer realized it was supposed to make an appearance along the banks of the James River. The sunlight was instantly bright as it peeked over the horizon and lay like diamonds over the water and dripped through the leaves of the old trees of the graveyard. Tommy awoke to the sound of a faraway lawn mower and realized that the grounds personnel would be getting an early start on the constant upkeep of the cemetery.

His head was still fuzzy and felt like it was stuffed with wet cotton, the sludge of his pulse slapping its hands against the walls of his temples. His mouth was dry and with each exhale, Tommy tasted the regurgitated alcohol and burrito. He went to push himself up from his slouched position against the tree and his hands reminded him of the torture he had put them through. At first, Tommy held them up, squinting against the early morning sunlight; confusion apparent upon his face.

Then, he remembered and he looked over toward the carnage he had created. In the morning light, it was a harsh reminder of his loss and he moaned as he tried to raise himself off the ground. He needed to clear out before anyone saw him. He needed coffee. He needed to clean his hands and wrap them. He needed to decide what to do now.

Looking out for ground crews, Tommy made his way over to the area of the graveyard where his mother used to brag that she would be one day be buried. He finally found the area as cars began to enter the graveyard; some visiting loved ones buried there, some with tourist maps in their hands. When there was no one within watching distance, Tommy unzipped his pants and released the hot first morning urine at last. With immense satisfaction, Tommy pissed all over the name of the woman who had cursed the day he had been born and daily reminded him of that fact.

With at least one promise completed, Tommy zipped up and did a quick, mental map of where he was and where the closest exit would be. Before anyone should happen upon him, he left through another exit well-known to him since childhood. He turned in the direction of the halfway house. He had a long walk ahead of him, but that would give him the time he needed to think. Coffee first though, he thought. With at least one goal to keep his feet moving, he was on his way.

***

Kate prepared her manikins and learning materials for her 1:00 CPR/AED class. It was close to 10:00 in the morning and she would need to leave by 10:30 to make her lunch date with Sandra. Kate was never late and always allowed herself enough time to find parking in the limited space on Cary Street. During the week, Carytown traffic was not quite as bad as during the weekend, but parking spaces could still be hard to find.

They had decided on Moshi Moshi at 11:00 and Kate had purposely forgone breakfast to be able to have enough room for Moshi's phenomenal cuisine. She wanted to be sure to get there early enough to secure a table outside. The day was turning out to be the perfect weather for eating outside; sunny but cool. Soon, it was would be summer and the stickiness would drive most customers into the arms of the air-conditioned indoor dining area.

She locked up her reserved classroom and quickly descended the stairs to sign out at the lobby level. She hated to give up her parking spot at the Red Cross building, but it was too far to walk in heels. She was able to navigate her way down the myriad one way streets and find a parking space about a block from the restaurant. To her delight she was able to secure a table outside. She ordered herself an iced tea and let the sun fall across her uplifted face as she waited for Sandra to arrive.

***

Tommy washed his hands in one of the many water fountains found throughout the city. He decided his hands would be better off left open to the air, as most of the cuts were clotted off and already scabbing. He ignored the pain and thought about his two main concerns: where to get decent coffee cheap at this hour and what to do with the rest of his time. His plan had been a simple one before. Find Teri Sanderson, torture and kill Teri Sanderson and get the hell out of Dodge via Mexico to live out the rest of his life raping women and getting drunk on Tequila.

He had no intention of going back to the stuffed shirt way of life, with or without a damn degree. He had even taken Spanish lessons while in prison and had plenty of practice with some of his cellmates. He was employably fluent, but only learned the language in anticipation of luring young senoritas his way. He supposed he could go on to Mexico, but it no longer held the allure of escape it once had. Now it merely seemed like a consolation prize and part of him fought against the belief that this was it.

He decided to walk off his hangover and have a plan in mind before heading back to the rat trap otherwise known as his current living quarters. He made up his mind to take the long way around and go through Carytown and hit the McDonald's there where the coffee was guaranteed to be fresh and strong. Besides, he consoled himself, the sexy little VCU girls shopping down there may help to raise his spirits a bit. He could occupy his mind with fantasies of wrapping his hands around their self-entitled little necks. That brought a brief smile to his lips and his gait became a little jauntier.

***

Sandra arrived at the table in her normal whirlwind style. "Girl! Let me tell you about the adventure I just had in finding a parking space in this theme park!"

She flopped into the chair, dropping her briefcase on one side of her and her large black leather Coach purse on the other. This dramatic entrance drew a few glances from people passing by, but Sandra either did not notice or did not care.

"Had to circle a few times, did you?" Kate said with a smile over her iced tea.

Sandra adjusted her chair, shrugged out of her expensive black suit jacket and leaned forward, crossing one long leg over the other. She held up one lacquered nail and said, "Once. I circled once. The rest of my ride through the fun house we call downtown parking was spent waiting for some rich biddy to load her many purchases into her Bentley and vacate some prime real estate parking."

"And where is this prime real estate spot you waited a few minutes for?" Kate asked.

"It was five minutes," Sandra said splaying five well manicured fingers, "and just two blocks that way," she finished as she managed to flip her long blond hair over one padded shoulder and removed her Gucci glasses.

"Oh, I see," primped Kate, smiling. "I myself never circled and found a parking space wide open right over there."

Sandra sat abruptly back in her chair and stared at Kate for one second before saying quietly, "Bitch."

Kate laughed with abandon as Sandra pretended to ignore her and order water with lemon from the befuddled waiter. Kate wiped under her eyes with her drink napkin while Sandra pretended to study the scenery around them.

"You are such a riot!" Kate joked with her friend.

"Shut up, skank," Sandra shot back and Kate broke into laughter again. Then, Sandra leaned forward again to bite into the meat of their meeting. Kate did not know if Sandra realized it or not, but this was a big tell of Sandra's.

"Okay, listen," Sandra started as she symbolically shooed the hilarity away with her right hand. "We know that Teri is no longer with us."

The laughter died in Kate's throat, but she said nothing.

"I know," Sandra continued as if reading her mind, "I'm sorry to say it like that, but we need to move on."

Kate was speechless as her mind wrapped around the cruel irony of life. Teri had survived a violent attack, only to be taken out by an auto accident. Nothing was funny anymore.

"Her dead and him alive doesn't seem right. I know," Sandra said and Kate began to wonder a little at Sandra's ability to read her. But then again, that's what made her a killer prosecutor; that ability to read people and see lies unspoken.

"Do we know if Tommy knows she's gone or if he's even interested?" Kate asked.

"According to Bill this morning, Tommy spent a lot of time on computers in prison. Even got a damn degree, courtesy of the state. And the prison monitored what he accessed via the Internet and he never hit anywhere near her name. They, the prisoners, were allowed to access certain news media for world events, but were prohibited to look up anything happening in their hometown. Per Bill, this is more because of gang related issues..." Sandra left it and sat back in her chair as her drink arrived. They both ordered their usual lunch orders and waited for the server to leave before continuing.

"Anyway, Teri Sanderson is no longer with us and Tommy may or may not be aware of that fact," Sandra continued. "In a way, she's probably better off."

"Sandra!" Kate admonished.

"Well," Sandra said looking only slightly offended, "think about it. Tommy has a vendetta and she has a family." She paused here, plucking at her napkin. She began to speak as the server returned with their lunch orders, but stopped. They went through the ritual of "Need anything else" and "No, I think we're good" and the server went back indoors; probably to smoke another cigarette by the wafting odor clinging to him, thought Sandra.

"Do you really think...?" Kate started as she stirred her soup, creating intoxicating aromas to tease her nose and palate.

"I know it was fifteen years ago, okay? But I'm telling you, Katie. I remember that guy. Do you know I never showered more in one day than when I had to deal with that piece of trash? Evil, I'm telling you, pure evil, that's what that man was. Pass the pepper, please. You understand what I'm saying or no?"

As close as they were, Kate would not admit to her childlike fears when it came to Tommy King. Instead, she just nodded her head and passed the pepper.

"Anyway, that's all I meant by that remark about being better off. Hell, I was his lawyer for Christ's sake! At least it's just me and no little rug rats at daycare to worry ab--, oh shit! I'm sorry!"

Kate must have paled quite considerably as the thought of Tommy turning those wolf eyes on Robbie or Izzy played across the theater of her imagination. She tried to smile and wave off Sandra's horror at what she had said, but the smile was tremulous at best and her hand suddenly felt heavy.

"Okay, here's what I think will really happen, okay?" Sandra spoke quickly and firmly as if she were telling Kate that the puppy dropped at the vet's office would live, damn it! Would live! "Best case scenario, he'll have had the evil beat out of him in prison and will be all meek and mild by now."

At Kate's dubious look, Sandra continued, "Or...he'll take a few days following up on Teri, find out she's no longer here to take his revenge out on and just skip town. Seriously, that's what I think will happen. He'll have a little temper tantrum, screw something and then jump parole. Bye Bye, Mr. Hyde."

"But what if he..." Kate was finally able to breathe again, but could not stop the sense of foreboding left with her at the thought of being on Tommy's list of "People Most Likely to Want to Look Up."

"Okay, stop! You are going to be the last person he would think of. You made a brief appearance on his stage of destruction and, sorry darling, but you just weren't that important."

"Gee, thanks," Kate said, trying to follow suit on lightening up the mood.

"Now me," Sandra pretended to plump her hair, "I, as always, was the star attraction."

"Supporting actress is more like it," barbed Kate.

"Damn, you really are a bitch!" bit back Sandra and they both laughed in earnest again.

"Hey, you know what...screw this water with lime crap. Hey, hey...yeah, darling, could you bring me a very cold martini, extra olives. Thanks, darling."

"My, my...you have court this afternoon?" Kate asked.

"Shut up, mother. Besides, if I'm going to go play with the big boys, I need a big boy's drink!" This time Sandra allowed herself to join in the laughter with Kate.

***

Tommy walked with his large, strong coffee (four sugars, two creams) and strolled down Cary Street toward the cross street that would take him to his new neighborhood. The day was unbelievable in its glory and it, together with the coffee, was clearing the dreary cobwebs from his head. Somewhere around first block or two down Cary and about halfway through his coffee, he had formalized the sketch of a plausible plan.

He would check in with his parole officer, pack up his shit and catch a bus out of town. Once he made it to Tennessee or so, he would catch a plane to Mexico. He had enough money to get a decent place and get started down there. He was sure with his handle on the Spanish language and computer skills; he should be able to secure a job somewhere. His computer skills would also allow him to become whoever he wanted to be. He would take a little time in the Nashville airport changing who Thomas King was.

With a plan made, he began to enjoy his walk through colorful Carytown on this beautiful day and took in the sights and sounds around him. Many of the vendors had some of their wares outside of the shops on the sidewalk and Tommy browsed here and there. He came upon a vertical rack of sunglasses and hats and thought *now, these would come in handy down in ol' Me-hee-co*. He circled the rack, trying on different pairs of sunglasses and hats, admiring his good looks in the plate glass window. He saw a knockout blond throw the hair over her shoulder in the reflection in the glass and his blood went cold.

Without turning around, he removed the sunglasses slowly and stared at the two women sitting at the table. *It couldn't be! No fucking way! Those bitches!* He recognized them both within seconds of each other. The blond was his lawyer -- *his fucking lawyer!* -- and the other woman was that nurse lady that testified against him and talked Teri into opening her slutty mouth.

He turned around now, keeping the brim of the cowboy hat he wore down as he made his way back to the rack. He pretended to continue to look as he watched them across the street at the outdoor cafe. They were obviously friends by the way they laughed with each other and joked. Only close friends were that comfortable with each other. He continued to watch as the conversation became quiet and the blond leaned forward, at one time touching her friend's arm.

At that touch, Tommy almost slammed his fist into the hat rack. All along they had been in it together. Teri, the lawyer, the nurse...they had all conspired to trap him and put him in the dungeon. They were probably all lovers or some shit! What a fool he had been! He had probably been set up! Yeah! Teri had offered herself as some sacrifice so that these two could get to him and unjustly set him up to fall. Son of a bitch!

Well, they would pay! He was not going anywhere until he made sure both of them paid for what they had done. The old hatred seeped back into his bones and he calmly paid the merchant warily watching him now for a hat and pair of glasses. He ducked inside the diner across the street and bought a Coke. He sat at the window seat and watched the two conniving women cackle through their lunch. When it was over, he was disappointed to see they went in two different directions.

First the cunt lawyer, he thought and he followed her to her black Jaguar, jotting down the license number on his Styrofoam cup. Tommy dumped the rest of the soda out and tore out the part of the cup with the number on it. He set off for the nearest Internet cafe. He had a new plan now and he was anxious to get started.

Chapter 23

Even though it was late spring, Sandra was never one to tolerate even the slightest hint of humidity. Now that the sun was high in the sky and her black Beemer had been sitting in it for over an hour, she habitually cranked up the air conditioner soon after starting the car. She checked in with her administrative assistant via cell phone while her car smoothly idled and slowly cooled. Finding no new news, she did a quick check of mirrors and pulled out into Cary Street traffic.

As the performance engine cried at the inability to show its capabilities, Sandra turned her CD player back on to practice her fledgling Spanish. During the drive in and around town to different appointments, Sandra liked to listen to instructional tapes or books on tape to keep her mind occupied, yet fresh. She learned long ago, that silence often led to contemplation and contemplation often led to frustration, or worse, remorse. As an added benefit, learning a new language or negotiation strategy kept her mind sharp - but the key word was occupied.

Sandra had been a defense attorney starting out in the district attorney's office and had graduated to being a well-known prosecutor in an established law firm just five years out of law school. Even while being given the tour of the firm, her objective was clear: which of the partner's offices would be hers within 10 years. She had beaten her own goal by three years and was well satisfied with her large office. She knew what it took to secure a partner position within a law firm and retain that position and she played the deck skillfully.

Her position afforded her the life she promised herself growing up all those years ago. She had come from a comfortable middle class family, but being one of four children, she had not been able to have some of the things many of her friends took for granted. Her family had moved into a neighborhood slightly above their income level, which meant that she attended school with children that got whatever they wanted. Her friends drove brand new sport cars for their sixteenth birthday. She shared the family's paid off station wagon with her older sister. Her friends wore all the new designer styles and conversations between her female counterparts revolved around which store carried the best brands in the most variety of colors. She had one pair of designer jeans which she begged for and faithfully threw into any available laundry load so that she could wear them repeatedly throughout the week.

As soon as she was able to work, she put in as many hours as legally possible for a minor and spent her money buying just enough of the "got to haves" to pass as privileged. She attended all the "right" parties and no others. She joined the "right" clubs, but only the top three. Luckily, studying was not as necessary for her to hold her honors position as it was for some of her siblings. She paid for her undergraduate tuition with the help of her parents and some out of her own pocket by working full-time while attending school. But she also looked into and applied for every scholarship, grant or tuition assistance program she could find.

She graduated with honors and had no problem transferring or finding funding for law school. She applied for and secured a low-level job in a law firm to gain experience. This would be a second job in addition to her full-time student status. They were hard years that left no time for social activities except those mandated by office functions or client relations. But, in Sandra's mind, it was all worth it. She had everything she had ever wanted and the means to obtain anything that had, up till now, escaped her radar. Throughout high school, undergraduate school and while working as a "go fer" in that first law firm; Sandra learned that money may not BE everything, but it sure BOUGHT it.

Her Spanish language tapes were not keeping their part of the bargain by occupying her mind as they should. She listened to the struggling male student on the tape totally botch what the instructor had just taught him.

"Quiero ir.....ire?...quiero ire, pero no puedo por-kay....por-ka..."

Sandra had very little patience for ignorance or time consuming people. "Quiero ira pero no puedo porque tu es un pendejo...you idiot!" And with that she tapped the knob to switch over to FM radio.

Disappointed, she did not find music, but instead heard the news. "In local news, this hour, a woman was found strangled in her town home today. Our sources here at the complex state that a friend of the slain woman, being concerned after the victim did not show for a child's birthday party, found the woman dead in the bedroom. The friend declined to be interviewed by the media. In other news, some leads on the 7-11 robberies this afternoon....."

Sandra clicked off the radio and continued to navigate through downtown traffic. Unbidden, a shiver traveled from her scalp down her spine, creating a sense of hyper alertness within her. The car was now a bit too chilly and Sandra turned off the air condition. One did not have to be too savvy to realize the mind had automatically made the connection between Tommy's release and this unfortunate strangle victim. She was quite sure one had nothing to do with the other. Even someone with Tommy's overwhelming desire to torture would not be that stupid. One thing she had learned while working as a defense attorney: psychopaths tended to be methodical, smart individuals.

She berated herself for allowing her mind to wander. Since she could spell the word, Sandra lived a disciplined existence. Everything she did had a purpose. She had a routine that allowed her to maintain what she had and a routine that would help her to achieve her next goal. She pushed the button on the console again to bring up the CD where she had so rudely left off. In the seconds it took for the CD to commence, she apologized to it as if it were a true entity.

"Lo siento para mi maleducado antes de. Por favor, seque."

Obviously, she was forgiven because the stupid male student did not seem bothered by her earlier insult at all as he continued to struggle with the sentence the instructor had asked him to say in Spanish. With years of practiced discipline, Sandra concentrated on the lesson on the CD for perhaps the fifth time. She did not often get to use Spanish among her clientele, but it did come in handy with some witnesses. She listened to the last three CDs of the eight CD set about every six weeks to keep the language fresh in her mind. She also attended a Spanish meet-up group about once a month in various eateries throughout Richmond. The group met more often, but Sandra allowed herself one gathering a month and never missed it. Discipline and routine; it was her mantra for life. Perhaps she should have known better than anyone: psychopaths thrive on routine.

***

Across town, Bill Patterson had spent the morning doing surveillance for a client. It was one of the many cases Bill was working on at the time. He did not particularly like confirming cheating spouses, but it did pay well. Had he known how well private detective work paid for someone with his skills and background, he may have retired a bit earlier. But the hours were longer and more irregular than being a cop ever was. With his two assistants out in the field, Bill had committed the afternoon to paperwork. He had hated paperwork as a cop and he hated it now, but it was a necessity of any business owner. Of course, now there was a computer program to handle any aspect of his business, but the monotony was still the same.

The office phone rang and glad for the interruption, Bill answered, "Patterson Security Services."

"Hey, Lt. Patterson! Officer Rather," was the excited voice on the other end.

Bill smiled at the unchanging enthusiasm of Officer Rather. He commented, once again, on the officer's use of his previous title,

"Rath, son, you don't have to call me lieutenant anymore. I retired, remember? Opened a little detective and security agency? Ringing any bells?"

There was a good-natured chuckle on the other end before Officer Rather replied, "I know, I know. It's just a habit I can't seem to break. I guess you'll always be a lieutenant to me."

"Damn! The least you could do is promote me per protocol and in honor of my exemplary service."

That got a real laugh from the other end and Bill could just picture the all-American kid turned man putting his hand to his belly while he laughed. It was something the young officer did all the time when his laughter was sincere. When he was trying to pretend he got the joke, but found no humor in it, his hand never moved from its original position.

For instance, when a classmate asked him what the "W" stood for in Howard W. Rath. And just say, young Howard were to answer "William." Perhaps said classmate, named Satterwhite, would now jerk that line to set that hook and say something like, "Oh, I thought maybe it was "would"...like in, Howard Would Rather suck dick!" Imagine if everyone in the class thought that was funny, yes, funny indeed. Everyone except Howard, that is. Well, that hand would just stay put. Oh, Howard would laugh to show what a good sport he was about it, but that hand would never move. His nickname became "Wood" in the academy and he continued to take it all in jest, but that hand never came near his stomach.

Bill had seen potential in Howard and frailty. He had taken the young rookie under his wing and soon Howard's fellow officers saw the same potential. Particularly when Howard was able to display those abilities in besting his previous tormentors. Without breaking any rules or going against any protocols, Howard was able to set up the rookie responsible for his unfortunate nickname. When Satterwhite went after the bait, Howard tugged hard. Howard might have taken the bait and gotten hooked; but Satterwhite was gutted, stuffed and mounted. After that, Howard's nickname was changed to "Rath" as in "beware the wrath of Howard." Bill could not remember what became of Satterwhite.

Howard "Rath" Rather went on to become one of Henrico's finest and most decorated officers early in his career. One of his gifts was the ability to smell a rat and the reputation for having a pretty accurate gut. After Bill had retired, he had continued to keep in touch with Officer Rather and be a sounding board now and then. Bill knew that Howard was up for his detective shield and he wanted to see him achieve it. He assumed that was the reason for the call.

"What's up? Ready to quit the force and come work for me?" Bill teased.

"I'm keeping that in the options file, lieutenant. No, the reason I called...well, you got a minute? You're not with a client or anything, right?"

Bill had to laugh silently. Many people thought private detectives still operated like the old Sam Spade movies. Truth of the matter was that very little correspondence took place in Bill's office. He was either meeting clients in neutral venues or corresponding by email. But he answered politely, "No, I'm free at the moment. What have you got?"

"Remember that Tommy King case from years ago?"

Bill was stumped. He was sure that Rath was going to ask him for his opinion or draw upon his years of experience. He was not prepared for hearing Tommy's name again in such a short time frame.

"Yeah, I remember a little bit about it. Why?"

"Well, we got this call the other day - over at those townhouses out by Ridgefield - you know the ones?"

"Yeah, I know them."

"It was a woman. She had been raped and strangled in her apartment. Found by a concerned friend the next morning. ME's still working on the exact time of death."

Bill knew where this was going, but he did not lead Rath on. "Yeah?"

"Okay, so I was at the scene, working it with homicide and it's got all the marks of that Tommy King character. She was strangled multiple times by the ligature marks on her neck. I mean, this poor girl was tortured for what the ME thinks were hours. It wasn't kinky sex gone wrong, either. That room showed all the marks of a violent crime."

"Huh," Bill grunted, trying to force the acid from his quick and cheap meatball sub at lunch from making it past his throat.

"Okay, so our guy Tommy's in prison, right? And this is just some copycat. Wrong! Turns out Tommy's been let out due to some legal screw up and guess where the prison bus dropped him off?"

"Ridgefield?" Bill cracked weakly.

"Nah, we're not that lucky. But last known is in Richmond. Here's the clincher, though. You ready?"

Bill said nothing.

"Remember when we talked about chain of evidence and his name came up regarding tokens? He had stashed his in some speaker box and in particular, a lock of the last victim's hair? Well, guess what was stuck to the headboard with some tape?" asked Rath.

Bill was silent, his mind spinning.

"A lock of the girl's hair! Taped there like he didn't give a rat's ass if we figured it out or not. Scissors, he probably used, lying right there on the night table. Fingerprints all over the damn bedroom and a jimmied glass door downstairs! What the hell do you think that means?"

Before Bill could answer, Rath continued, "I think it means that he doesn't care if we know. Because he's on a final spree after being bottled up all those years and he doesn't have any intention of getting caught...or doesn't care. I checked with his parole officer and nothing. Checked in once and he hasn't heard from him since. Never showed for two job interviews and hasn't been back to his apartment. We've got a warrant on him, but he's nowhere to be found. So, what do you think? Think he's going to hang around or do one and split?"

Bill's mind was already three steps ahead. As Rath had gone through checking with Tommy's parole officer and Tommy's living quarters, Bill had been checking them off on his own mental list. He knew from looking into it, that Teri Sanderson had died in a car accident several years back. She'd been buried here in Richmond...where was it?

Before he could mentally go any further, Rath persisted, "So, what do you think? You knew him. I know it's been a long time, but what do you think?"

Bill asked, "When was this girl attacked and how long after his release did it happen?"

He could hear taps on a keyboard on the other end. Rath answered, "She was a stripper. We think that's how she was noticed...ah, here it is. He was released on Monday and she was attacked Tuesday night, early Wednesday morning. He probably hadn't been out a full 24 before she hit his radar. Shit!"

Bill's mouth answered while his mind raced, "Let's see, this is Friday...I think he's long gone, possibly right after doing her. Could be the reason for the gift he left us. That's what I'm hoping anyway."

"You think if he stays, he's just going to pick up where he left off?" Rath asked with hard held excitement.

"I think if he stays it's because he has a reason to stay and that reason would either be one last rampage before going out in a blaze of glory, so to speak or be because he's after vengeance for those who put him away," Bill answered.

"Which one do you think it is, lieutenant?"

"What's your gut saying, Rath? You've been at the crime scene. You've looked at his priors, checked his prison sheet, talked to the parole officer. Right now, what is your gut telling you?"

"My gut says he's staying and he's just starting, one way or the other. And if its vengeance, then God help them."

Bill closed his eyes and saw Katie's face. "God help us all, Rath."

Chapter 24

Sandra's day had been a busy one. She had spent the morning in court on three cases for three different reasons. One was a request for a continuance....DENIED. One was a request for time served and the defendant to be released to his family while awaiting trial.....DENIED. The last was a waste of her time as the defendant had decided to change her plea to guilty to the obvious surprise and displeasure of her defense attorney. It was what Sandra would call a "backhanded win" - a score for justice but not very lucrative for her or her firm. But all in all, three up to bat, three homeruns for her team. Not a bad score in the game of justice.

Lunch with Kate had been informative, as well as fun. Snatches of their conversation and of much earlier conversations with Tommy kept invading her mind during her afternoon courtroom case. Several times, she had to resort to scribbling everything the defense attorney was saying, as well as each witness, in order to force herself to pay attention. It was something she had not done since her beginning Public Defender days. Back in those days, fresh out of law school and still wet behind the ears, she had frantically written down as much as she could verbatim of everything said. She was so afraid that she would miss something important, vital to her case; something obvious to someone with more experience. However, what she found was that she was so busy writing, that she missed multiple opportunities to object as well as the time to hear what was being said.

This afternoon's case was a slam dunk - off the record - and she felt she was merely going through the motions to satisfy due process. And although she knew that it was just that kind of slam dunk case that could sneak past a lawyer to sit with a smirk on the "insufficient evidence" shelf, she knew this case was sewn up before the lights were turned on in the courtroom this morning. Therefore, her mind, always anxious to be solving the next "big dilemma", chewed at the bit of boredom.

She remembered Tommy's face and how it reminded her of a sky; open with the "aw shucks, ma'am" innocence of a young cowhand one minute and thunderous with barely concealed rage the next. From the moment she sat across from him those many years ago, she was aware of the bullshit being slung her way. But she had to admire his ability to cover and recover quickly. She wondered how much more adept he had become, how much harder, how much rage boiled within him over these last 15 years.

She had ridden in silence, allowing her mind the freedom to flow uninhibited at last. Her brows knit together as she passed through the columns announcing a neighborhood of the "better than average". Most of the large, brick homes had lights strategically placed throughout their landscaping as if to say, "'Oh we know we're untouchable and we're really not afraid of anyone invading our space. It's just its pretty, right? And it gets so very, very dark at the top." Her house was easy to spot among the rest, because although she had the strategically placed lights (they came with the house when she purchased it), she did not have them on a timer.

Sandra was warned by her colleagues, both in her earlier days as a defense attorney working for the public defender's office and now as a prosecuting partner, that sometimes bad people did very bad things to good people. Her job could create enemies; justified or not. Security measures were a favorite topic of conversation among her peers during the mandatory holiday meet and greets. Gated community or not? Which security company did one use and what was the response time? You haven't tested it? Well, you must, you really must because otherwise, how do you know you're getting your money's worth? Safe room or no? Motion sensitive lights or timer lights or both? On and on it would go.

Sandra was seen as lax or downright stupid because she never invested in the security measures someone of her status and profession could and should employ. In Sandra's mind, as long as she was doing the right thing, she had nothing to worry about. Oh, she knew there were demented people out there that were convinced that everyone else owed them a life. But to pay a monthly fee to a security company, build a safe room, light up her outside property like some prison yard during the great escape? Well, to her, it screamed guilty conscience. Or worse reeked of weakness and fear. She was neither of these things and she would not portray herself as otherwise. So, she decided to forego the usual security measures adorning those of her status.

She turned into the driveway of her darkened house and hit the remote on her visor for the garage door. Some would see it as a security measure; as that once the car door closed on the garage, the side door opened into a privacy fence enclosed backyard. And she did prefer the detached garage to the attached variety for security reasons, but for her it was all about convenience and creature comforts. She liked not having to get out to open the door, that's all.

She picked up her briefcase and coat out of the passenger seat. Locking up the garage, she was already thinking of the unopened bottle of Sangria waiting for her and what she was going to create to eat tonight. She walked through the darkened backyard and up onto the deck. She unlocked the door and let herself into the black and shadowy silence of her den.

There was no waiting lover or spouse to inquire about her day. No homework to check or drawings to attach to the refrigerator. No cat or dog welcomed her home. Sandra's hours were too long for any pets, although a **BEWARE OF DOG** sign graced the gate of her fenced in yard. The sign was given to her by her mother as a plea to "at least give the burglars and rapists pause before they just come on in." Sandra walked into a quiet, empty house and the tension of the day melted off of her like a layer of ice under the sun's rays.

She laid her briefcase and coat on the couch to be carried upstairs later and slipped out of her heels into a pair of well-worn moccasins sitting by the door. She spent a few minutes choosing a few choice CDs and placed them carefully into the CD changer of the state-of-the-art sound system. Soon, Stevie Ray Vaughan wooed her with bluesy melodies of longing. Sandra smiled and went to the front of the house turning on lights as she went. Flipping on the portico lights, she did a quick peep before opening the door to retrieve the mail in the box attached to the brick effacement.

Shutting the door securely behind her and locking it as an afterthought, she briefly scanned through her mail while singing along with Stevie and sashaying her way to the kitchen. She laid the mail on her cafe table in the kitchen and went about the business of pouring herself a glass of Sangria. Sipping it while trying to put on an apron, Sandra continued to sing and dance around in her kitchen. She pulled out the ingredients necessary for an easy to make pasta dish, swinging her hips and dancing with the spoon. She laughed at herself as the music and Sangria helped to warm her stiff neck muscles. She looked a bit self-consciously at the bay window across from her but was secure in the fact that she cavorted for an audience of none.

She was wrong.

Sitting in the shadows by the back fence was Tommy, smiling at her wanton display of sensuality just for him. He had seen the sign about the dog earlier in the day when he had found the address provided by DMV from her license plate. *God, he loved the Internet!* At first, he had been a bit put off by the prospect of having to figure out how to get around a big dog. But persistence had paid off as it always did.

Wearing a non-descript navy jacket and a navy blue cloth baseball cap, he had put some junk mail on a clipboard and driven right up to her front curb during the day. He had rung the doorbell and knocked on the door and received no answering bark from inside. He had pretended to listen at the front door as if hearing someone

inside and said, "What? Oh, come around back? Okay, ma'am."
In case any privileged and bored rich housewife was peeking
through the neighboring curtains at him. He wanted a plausible
reason to go around back. Pretending to study his clipboard, he had
walked around the side of the house to the privacy fence gate. He
had rattled the gate door and knocked on it. No sound of running,
padded feet approached the gate. No barking or even curious
doggy panting did he hear. He tried a few more times with the
same result.

Normally, he would have stored the information from this
reconnaissance mission and come to play another day. But he
knew his time was short. He had heard the police had found his
stripper earlier today. He needed to move on this one faster than he
had in the past. He needed to find a way in and figure out if she
had a routine that he could use.

He had found his way to the back of the house through an easement
and had jumped to look over the fence into the backyard. He found
a few things missing from the backyard in addition to the big dog.
There were no doggy toys, no doggy house or evidence of a
bedding down spot. There were no food dishes or water supply for
an outside pet. Tommy figured it was a safe bet that there was no
dog. Maybe there had been, but he doubted it. It would be just like
the lying bitch to pretend she had something that she loved and that
loved her back.

As she continued to make herself something to eat, Tommy
made mental notes. He had researched her on the Internet and
found that she was neither married nor had any children. She was a

partner in her law firm of "Snag 'Em, Cheat 'Em and Ruin 'Em." She rarely lost a case and she seemed comfortable in front of a camera. Soon after railroading him, Tommy was not surprised to see that she had given up the pretense of defense attorney and had followed her true calling of nailing the innocent. From his casing of her house and her routine today, he saw that she was not as security conscious as her neighbors. It would be an easy break in.

He also noticed that encased behind the glass and brick of the house, her singing and dancing was like watching a movie with no sound. Normally, one might have found it comical and some less intelligent yokel may have decided to record it and put it on YouTube. But Tommy smiled with dirty delight as he realized that as much as he could not hear the music; neither would any of the neighbors hear the screams. At the thought, Tommy sniffed hard and fast three times in anticipation of the kill.

Chapter 25

There were several clues that Isabella was home for the weekend. One was the two navy duffels peeled down like skinned sausages, spilling their multicolored assortment of wrinkled clothes onto the utility room floor. Another was the strategic attempts of reclaiming ownership throughout areas of the house: a used glass and plate by the sofa in the great room, a lonely pair of ear buds clinging to a discarded iPod on the dining room table and a hoodie slung over the stair banister. But perhaps the most obvious, or at least the loudest, was the sound of angry tones being traded in the kitchen. Yes, Isabella was home for a visit. Let the debates begin!

Kate remembered when Isabella, Little Izzy, was all smiles and curls; bouncing into a room to show Kate her newest drawing or to give her thighs a "gwate big hug!" Isabella and she used to be so close, doing "girly" things and enjoying "pampering parties" on Kate's days off and on rainy Saturdays. Isabella was so animated and full of life, she was addictive. Kate loved the time she spent with her beautiful daughter - up until about the age of puberty. The hormones circulating throughout Isabella's body reacted like a kind of poison, turning her into a moody and surly young woman.

At first, it was just the deep sighs and "I just need to be alone for awhile, Mom." Kate could name the *day* Isabella quit using "Momma" and started using "Mom"; the week before sixth grade ended. Isabella was looking back after being dropped off at school. Her little friends' eyes lit up as they saw Isabella getting out of the car. Without saying a word to Kate, Isabella waved at her friends and started to shut the car door. Kate said, "Have a great day, honey!"

Isabella turned to look back at her, somewhat distracted and said, "Okay, Mom, bye" and she was gone. The last vestiges of Kate and Vinnie's little girl fell away as she swung her long curls over her left shoulder and greeted her ladies in waiting. Kate knew it was a rite of passage, but it stung nonetheless.

But in those days, when Isabella's body was awkwardly trying to adjust itself to womanhood, Isabella still relied on her mother to walk her through the dark valley of comeuppance. They spent a few nights eating chocolate chip cookies and discussing boys and make-up and the perils of peer pressure. Kate sat at the very same table that graced the dining room now and assured a tearful, heartbroken Isabella that there were not only other fish in the sea, but she would most likely throw a few back before she caught the right one. But the first love lost always hurt the most and Kate validated that and promised Isabella the pain would fade in time. For a very short, sweet spot of time, Isabella was less of a daddy's girl and sought out Kate's advice and guidance. Kate drunk it in like the fine champagne it was because she knew this particular bottle would soon be empty.

Not only did the bottle become empty, but it fell to the ground and shattered as Isabella entered high school and damn near demanded her independence. If Kate said up, Isabella went down. If Kate suggested left, Isabella just knew that right was the only way to go. Kate was not sure who said, "Raising teenagers is like nailing Jell-

O to a tree" but whoever did was a genius and a parent. Once Isabella started to drive, Kate said good-bye to long nails. Kate and Vinnie came to the conclusion that curfews were invented by parents who valued sleep. Because neither could do so until they heard Isabella's Volkswagen Rabbit pull into the driveway and her key turn in the lock of the side door.

Isabella decided to attend Virginia Commonwealth University after graduating from high school and pursue a degree in psychology. There was a bit of a debate on whether she would continue to live at home or in a dorm. Of course, Kate and Vinnie could not see the logic of Isabella living in a dormitory or an apartment when the University was just 20-30 minutes away from the house. Isabella, on the other hand, could not understand how they could *not* understand why she *had* to live away from home. Enter compromise 116 (or thereabouts): Kate and Vinnie would pay tuition, books and the apartment rent and Isabella would pick up car insurance and all utilities for the apartment. Sign here.

Therefore, Isabella lived in the Fan area of Richmond, close enough to the University to ride a bike to her classes. She shared the third floor apartment with three other college students who split all utilities and rent with her. All in all, it was not a bad deal, because Isabella was out of the house (a win for Isabella), but close to home (a win for Kate). The night Kate and Vinnie lay down to sleep after moving Isabella into her third floor apartment without an elevator, they lay resting their old and tired bones. As sleep began to creep over them, Vinnie said, "Well, at least with her out of the house we won't be lying awake at night waiting for that door to open to tell us she's back in and safe." Kate stayed awake for at least another hour envious of Vinnie's snores after that statement. She realized that now she would not know when and if Isabella was safe in her bed night after night and that scared the hell out of her.

And even though the apartment house Isabella lived in with about 40 other college students had a laundry room and the Fan area sported several relatively clean Laundromats, Isabella still brought her color-sorted mountains of clothes home to wash about every other weekend. So, she could "visit" she said. She lied. She washed a few loads and spent the rest of her time out of the house or on her cell phone making plans to get out of the house. Every time she visited, Kate tried to be on her best behavior and not nit-pick too much. However, Isabella was a wild and sometimes impetuous child. Kate was not yet ready to let go. The mother in her still felt she had to step in between her careening daughter and life's brick walls. She was content to let out quite a bit of slack in those proverbial apron strings, but she was damned if she was going to cut yet.

So, there they stood; the mother and her grown daughter, about the same height but unable to see eye to eye. Isabella was no longer the chubby little cherub with the bright eyes and bouncing curls. She was long and lean with the awkwardness of puberty over with the curves landing in the right places. Her naturally auburn curly hair was worn loose and long, cascading down her back to just below her shoulder blades. It was her crown of glory and she knew it. Dark lashes framed her father's chocolate brown eyes. The nose and smile were her mother's; her skin had just a touch of the olive to complement her features. She was striking in the promise she held in her youth. But what Kate saw in moments like this was the same stubborn little spitfire Isabella had been since she had heard the word "no."

"You can be the most stubborn individual and that is NOT a compliment. Individuality and spitefulness are two different things, Isabella. Why are you fighting me on this?"

"Mom, why are you fighting *me*? Whose life is this anyway? I want to live the life I want, not the life you want for me. When are you going to get that?"

"Isabella, stop being so overly dramatic. I am not asking you to live a life contrary to who you are or - whatever you're making it out to be. This is a perfect opportunity for you to build a resume, get some experience and maybe learn a little something in the process. How could you not even consider it?" Kate tried to keep an even tone in spite of her growing exasperation.

"Because, Mom, it's all summer in the middle of nowhere dealing with a bunch of angry delinquents. Not how I planned on spending my freshman....freshman, hello?...year!" Isabella answered as if talking to a slow child. "That's something I would maybe do in my junior summer. Not now. Not when I have the opportunity of a freaking lifetime!"

"Isabella, travelling to Europe is a fantastic opportunity, I grant you that. I think everyone should do it once if given the chance. But, this opportunity at the Counseling center is a limited time offer. I pulled some strings because I thought it would be something you would jump at the chance to do. Europe can wait, this won't."

"Oh my God..." Isabella was beginning to crank up a real freak out, when Robbie came busting through the front door. He had been out around the neighborhood riding bikes when he had seen Isabella's car in the driveway.

He ran into the house calling, "Izzie, Izzie.....Izzie!"

Isabella's face took on an amazing transformation as she heard her little brother calling for her. "Robbie, in here, dude!"

Robbie adored his college-aged sister and the feeling was mutual. Kate's heart softened and her blood pressure returned to normal as she watched the two interact.

Robbie rounded the corner and began to run to Isabella, but hesitated slightly. He was eight going on nine, after all, and perhaps effusive shows of emotion were no longer appropriate. But Isabella was having none of it.

"Come here you," she said as she grabbed him to her and hugged him closely, lavishing slobbery kisses all over him complete with wet, smacking sounds, "Mmmmwah, mmmwah..."

Robbie pretended to be appropriately disgusted, but laughed and squirmed only so much. Trying to sound serious, he said, "Izzie, stop. Stop, Izzie."

Per tradition, Isabella sealed each kiss with a tickle before letting go of her brother. "What's up, coolness?"

"Did mom ter you dat I got a 'kateboard?" asked Robbie.

"Dude! That's awesome!"

"Yeah, 'n I can wide it. I can, Izzie," Robbie bragged.

"Wow, you are just too cool! You have got to show me later, okay? Promise?"

Robbie was beside himself with joy. "Yeah! I can show you 'ow if you wan me thoo"

"Well, I'm kinda talking to Mom right now about something important. How about you hang out with your friends for a little while longer and here," Isabella said reaching into her back pocket, "when Mom and I are done, I'll call you."

Robbie looked at the cell phone he had just received as if it were Excalibur itself. With the utmost sincerity, he said, "I woan bwake it, I sweah, Izzie."

"Hey, I know that. That's why I trust you with it. Call you in a few, dude."

" 'k, Izzie. I'm coo, huh?"

"You are the coolest dude I know, by far," Isabella responded to that question as she usually did.

With this installment of affirmation secure, Robbie raced back out of the house yelling, "Hey guys! Hey guys, lookit dis!" no doubt showing off the cell phone. Isabella watched him and smiled when she heard him bragging.

"Well, I'm sure you made his day by giving him that cell phone, but you realize he could break it out there riding his bike or that skateboard," warned Kate.

Isabella rolled her eyes and turned to address her mother. "See? That's what I'm talking about, Mom. I knew it would rock his world to give it to him and that's why I did it. If it gets broken, well hell...that's what I pay the insurance on it for. It's just for an hour or so and it made him unbelievably happy for a minute. Sometimes, you just got to do what makes you happy and live in the moment. It's what makes life worth living."

Now it was Kate's turn to roll her eyes, thinking *Spoken like a true college student with little to no worries and no rush to take on the real world*. That's what she thought. What she said was, "Isabella, I do understand, honey. You want to go to Europe with your friends for a month during the summer break. But Isabella, what I'm trying to explain to you is that Europe will still be there next year and the year after that. This opening in Jarrett is this summer only and you are only allowed an interview as an undergrad because I spoke so highly of you."

"But did you ask me if I wanted to do something like that this summer? Did I ask you to find me a job? No, on both counts, Mom. That's the thing. You assumed I would just fall at your feet for getting me this great opportunity. I'm sorry you went through the trouble, but that's on you. You didn't ask me before you did it and I'm not going to do it just because you set it up." With that, she walked out of the kitchen to check on her last load.

"Hey!" Kate said, going after her, "I thought you might appreciate the opportunity to work with teens with psychological difficulties so that you could get a feel of that world. You are the psych major who wants to work with adolescents. Why wouldn't I think that you would want to immerse yourself in that environment where only upper grads normally get to tread and get paid for it? What was I thinking?"

Isabella, who had been tossing clothes from the washer into the dryer, paused to answer, "You were thinking of what you would like to do. Of how you would have spent the summer. Of what an opportunity this would have been for you if you had been the psych major wanting to work with adolescents. I, on the other hand, want to spend the last few years of my dwindling student life.....playing, alright? I want to be able to be sitting in some office later not regretting a damn thing. That's who I am, Mom."

With those dark eyes pleading for understanding, Kate saw her little Izzie again and it was hard not to cave in entirely. "I don't know, Izz...Isabella. I may have jumped the gun on this one, but I still believe it is an opportunity you shouldn't pass up. Besides, who is going to fund this European vacation?"

The pleading was replaced by frustrated anger in Isabella's eyes, but before she could speak, Vinnie announced his arrival with his usual, "Yo!" at the front door. Both women sat in frustrated silence as Vinnie made his way to the utility room after Kate's "in here" gave away their location.

Vinnie took one look at both of the women he loved and pretended to machete his way into the room. Neither woman asked about his antics. They knew this old joke about having to cut the tension between them. The joke had been a common one since Isabella's high school days.

He hugged and kissed both. Then he asked the loaded question, "So, what's the problem?"

Isabella mumbled, "Nothing" as she continued to stuff the dryer with angry jabs.

Kate's smile did not reach her eyes as she said. "We're fine."

"Okay then," Vinnie said as he backed out of the room. "Play nice, ladies."

They could hear him joking around with an excited Robbie and they both silently agreed on a truce.

"What are your plans for tonight then?" Kate asked.

"This is my last load. I'm going back to the apartment. I've got some studying to do and I'm working on a paper for Lit," Isabella said speaking in clipped tones.

"Well, can you stay for dinner? We're having Seafood Yum Yum Salad," Kate said. She knew it was one of her daughter's favorites and she didn't want Isabella to leave while they were both still somewhat angry at each other.

Isabella stopped to inquire, cocking one eyebrow at her mother, "With or without a side of lecture?"

Kate had to smile in spite of herself, "Your choice."

Isabella pretended to give it some thought. "Hmmmm, without, I think. I'm trying to cut back," she said as she patted a flat belly.

Isabella turned the knob on the dryer and gave her mother a brief smile before passing her in the doorway. "Yo, Robbie!" she called, "ready to show me that skateboard, dude?"

Soon they were outside after Isabella dutifully let him return to his friends without her so she could call him on the cell phone. Robbie must have been putting on quite a show from all the applause and cheering he was receiving from Isabella.

Vinnie joined Kate in the kitchen, coming up behind her at the counter while she chopped an onion. He nosed aside her curls to nuzzle the nape of her neck and drop butterfly kisses upon it.

"I have a knife," Kate playfully warned.

"I know and it's making me hot," Vinnie continued to play.

Kate laughed, put down the knife and turned to receive his full attention. After a restoring hug, he asked, "So, the offered summer position didn't go over too well, I take it?"

"No, you were right. She hated the idea. Maybe if you had come up with it, we could have sold it." She pretended to pout.

"It was a good idea, baby, just a bit industrious for our Izzie."

"No, she's talking about some trip to Europe this summer. I really think she would have gone for the Jarrett thing if not for that." Kate explained.

"Oh, okay, sure," said Vinnie smiling in that sexy way of his. "And who's funding this little excursion she has planned?"

"That's when you walked in. *You* can ask her. I swear, it's an exercise in frustration sometimes just to have a logical conversation with that girl. She can be so hard-headed."

"Mmmmm, sounds like her mother," joked Vinnie.

Kate cocked an eyebrow at him and smirked. "Vinnie, the knife is still within reach."

"Mmmmm, I know. It's being this close to danger that makes me so horny!" he said, settling his lips on her throat.

Ah, hell, thought Kate as she let herself enjoy his advances, *sometimes one did have to just live in the moment.*

Chapter 26

Officer Rather had been very busy in the last few days. Because he had been one of the first responding officers to the stripper killing, he was part of the investigation. Although he had other duties, he was allowed to spend time off of the clock investigating all possible leads...unofficially. At least in Rath's mind. There were policies and procedures to be followed, but Rath had a good gut; everyone knew it. He was working toward his detective shield and when it came right down to it, as long as the case was solved by the police department, everything else was semantics. Rath would make sure every "T" was crossed and every "I" dotted. But for now, Rath's gut was telling him that not only was Thomas King responsible for the stripper's death, but there was more to the story.

The questions posed to his mentor Bill Patterson refused to go away in his mind until answered. Why so blatant? The perpetrator - Tommy in Rath's mind - leaving prints, fluids, fibers and the hair taped to the headboard showed no attempt to cover his tracks. One theory would be that he just cracked. Tommy was a monster honed into a sadistic killer by "the system". He was going to go on some kind of killing spree until he was taken out in every escaped con's wet dream -- a shootout.

But Tommy wasn't an escaped con. He was let out free and clear. Tommy was a justified and certified psychopath and they typically had IQs off the chart. The most natural and true course of action for a psychopath who has not lost the taste for blood was to lay low for awhile and cover all tracks of any killings. Rath had studied the type. His long range plans included becoming a profiler and he had spent many nights gleaning what he could from professional online journals and criminal record sites regarding sociopaths and psychopaths.

With 15 years of planning, Tommy would have come up with one hell of a plan. But what was it and how did the stripper fit in? Rath had gotten identification on the woman and checked out her place of employment. Her stage name was Cashmere and she worked at one of the mid class "gentlemen's clubs" on the Southside of Richmond. Her real name per her driver's license and rental agreement for her luxury apartment in the West End was Elizabeth Justice; Beth to her family.

She had lived two distinct and separate lives. She was 25 years old and was using the money made from her weekends stripping to pay her tuition at MCV, Richmond's teaching and trauma hospital. She was in her third year of medical school and had been in the top five of her class. Her fellow "exotic dancers" knew of her journey to become a doctor, but Rath doubted that her colleagues in the hospital knew from where her tuition money came.

Rath had sat down to speak with many of her "friends" at the gentlemen's club after paying a ridiculous amount for a plain Coke on ice. One of those "friends" had been an obvious advertisement for breast augmentation named Cherry.

"I appreciate you taking a minute to talk to me, Sherry," Rath said trying to keep his eyes above the buxom stripper's neckline.

"It's Cherry. Yeah, no problem. I really liked Cashmere. She was really cool and very, very smart. But not like stuck up smart, just that quiet kind of smart, you know?" she asked sincerely.

"Yeah. Were you working the night she was here last?"

"Yeah, I go on right after her which kind of sucks....or did...because she did this one number to Ted Nugent's Stranglehold. That was a real hard act to follow. Anyway, that's the number she did that night for her final stage show and then I went up," Cherry explained while adjusting her too small, sequined top.

"Did she hang around? Talk to anybody?" Rath asked while he pretended to take notes.

"No, she never hung around after. It used to piss Roger off to no end. But she said, 'You hired me to dance and serve a few drinks between numbers. I'm fulfilling my part of the contract. Once I'm done dancing, I'm done. Don't like it, I'll go dance somewhere else'. She was a trip! She knew Roger would never fire her. She was one of his 'elite' girls." Cherry talked fast, looking around the bar for an eavesdropping Roger.

"What do you mean by 'elite girls'? Was there a little something going on between her and Roger?" Rath forgot about the lack of clothes on his interview subject for a minute. This could be another lead.

Cherry laughed and asked, "Have you met Roger? He's slime! Oh God, don't tell him I said that alright?"

At Rath's wave of understanding, she continued, "No, an 'elite girl' just means a girl that brings in a lot of clientele or repeat clientele. Those girls who hold a reputation for being quite the entertainer. Cashmere had two numbers she did and both were....well, I don't bat for the same team or nothing like that....but they were hot, okay?"

Rath suddenly wished he had been able to catch one or both of those numbers. But instead of commenting on her last statement, he continued his questioning. "Did you happen to see anyone in particular take a special or particular interest in her that evening?"

"No, not really. Hell, I've known guys to pause a freaking lap dance to watch her do her thing, okay? Having somebody watch her every hip pop would not be new, believe me," Cherry said with just a hint of envy.

"Okay. Did you happen to notice anyone leaving the same time or right after she did?"

"Nah. I had to go on right after her, like I said, so I wouldn't have noticed anything like that."

"Okay. Listen, if you don't mind me asking...about how much does one make, on the average, for a night's work here?"

"Well, I'm sure you're asking about Cashmere, so I'll tell you. I only heard her mention it once when she was relatively new - before she realized that it's not polite to brag. In one night, that bitch pulled in $3,500."

"Damn!" Rath said before he could catch himself.

"I know, right? I've never pulled that out of here, but it can be done if you're good at it and you make them believe it's for real. Did they steal it?"

"What? Who?" Rath was thrown for a minute.

"Whoever killed her? She would have had her money on her from the night's take. She would have had some hiding place at her house, but it would have been there until she could hide it legally."

"I don't really know. I'll have to look into it." He was silent for a minute and thought, *Hey, can't hurt.*

"Listen, one more thing," he said as he pulled out the release photo from prison for Tommy. "You see him in here that night?"

"Yeah, I saw him," Cherry said nonchalantly.

Rath almost dropped the photo. "You sure? That particular night?"

Cherry caught on and her eyes widened. "Yeah! See, I'd never seen him before and thought maybe I could get a lap dance or two out of him, because he looked hungry, you know? Then Cashmere comes on and he was hypnotized like all the rest. But he didn't lick his lips or rub himself or any of the other stuff I normally see. He also didn't spend one single dollar on her and that, my friend, is highly unusual for Cashmere! He just watched her."

"Did he leave when she left?" Rath asked.

"No! That's just it. The first time I ever saw it. He left before she finished! That's really why he stuck out in my mind. No one has ever walked out on Cashmere to my knowledge."

"How long before she finished did he leave?"

"Well, I don't know if you've ever heard the song, but it's a longass song! God, it goes on for like…10 minutes or something. So, he leaves like….ummm...that part where Ted Nugent starts singing again. I don't know, like near the end. So, if you take her finishing up, changing and then leaving...he was probably gone a good ten minutes before her," Cherry finished.

To sit and wait for her to leave, no doubt, thought Rath. He thanked the fine Cherry and gave her a twenty dollar bill for her time.

Sitting in his car, he called a fellow investigator and asked him to check on the robbery angle by seeing if any cash was recovered at the scene. After securing a venti mocha latte at Starbucks, he heard back from the investigator that a large roll of money was recovered from the night stand, totaling $2,850. No robbery.

He figured that Elizabeth had been a convenient kill, something to let off the steam. Someone like Tommy might have figured that she would not be missed for awhile or it wouldn't warrant much investigation, in Tommy's mind. But wouldn't it have been more prudent to dispose of the body and give himself a little more time? And why not abduct her from the gentlemen's club? Why make the kill zone her apartment? None of that made sense if this was to be the first of many.

And that's when Rath started to try to think like Tommy. That was what good profilers did. They studied their subject enough to be able to try to put themselves inside of the perpetrator's mind. Rath had read and re-read Tommy's file and had gotten a good idea of Tommy's life up until he was put away for the rapes. Tommy was an excellent exhibit for the nature versus nurture debate. Some psychopaths were created and Tommy could very well be one of those.

So, Rath had retraced Tommy's supposed steps. He checked out the halfway house to which Tommy had never returned. He found the closet and dilapidated dresser empty of any belongings. Obviously, Tommy had moved on. No one seemed to know when he had left, because he had sequestered himself in his room one afternoon and had supposedly never left. At least that was the adamant statement of the manager of the halfway house.

The effeminate man had been self righteous in his indignation that he had somehow fallen short of his responsibility as manager. He showed Rath the log that each resident had to sign in and out of whenever they left or returned; "no exceptions". On the top of the page, two days ago at approximately 1:10 p.m., Tommy had signed back in. With an increasingly reddened face, the manager could not find where Tommy had signed out earlier that day or the day before. The last entry for Tommy showed him returning to the apartment house. Oops!

The manager was then very accommodating about letting Rath check out Tommy's room. Rath gave the room a thorough look as the manager prattled on.

"Perhaps Mr. King did manage to leave earlier that morning without signing out. I will definitely have to speak with David about that and I will, believe you me. I can assure you, officer, that all of us take our responsibility very seriously here and such oversights are dealt with immediately and measures are employed to..."

"What about this?" Rath had been looking out of the only window to a fire escape. "Couldn't he just come and go this way?"

The manager swallowed a few times, sensing a trap and trying to decide how best to shine the light on this mess, "Well, you see...we will hopefully be getting bars for each window...very soon, actually. But in the meantime, we have had to take rather crude measures to ensure that...for a very short time, of course. Anyway, the windows are nailed shut and in case of a fire, of course, one could break out the window or...anyway, that is currently not a viable exit...for now..for..." he did not finish. His jaw dropped suddenly.

Throughout the manager's stumbling explanation, Rath had seen the nailed shut window and at first been a bit angry at the crudity of security measures and the evidence of a blocked fire exit. He had merely meant to test the strength of the nails by giving the window a hard push up. He was just as surprised as the manager at the ease in which the window gave way. Upon close inspection and with the manager breathing heavily over his shoulder, Rath discovered the clever ruse. *One for Tommy*, he thought.

Leaving the manager explaining, again, how "this matter would be dealt with immediately," Rath checked a few more avenues to find that Tommy had gotten hold of his mother's meager holdings. He had not opened any bank accounts or made any big purchases...on record, anyway. No weapons bought through legal measures, no transportation. He had to have transportation. A quick check showed no stolen vehicles in the approximate area in the last two weeks.

Rath sat outside of the halfway house trying to figure it out. Tommy was running, maybe already gone. But Rath's gut said *No*. The empty halfway house, not checking in with his parole officer, blowing off job interviews and the attainment of cash with no known purchases like a car or other anchoring items screamed "Runner". But Rath's gut said *No*. Killing Elizabeth, aka Cashmere, in her apartment with no regard for evidence and leaving a cold, signature calling card said, "One for the road, suckers!" But Rath's gut said, *No*.

Rath did not understand it yet, but there was something going on. He still felt from all he knew about Tommy that he would be the vengeful sort. What would he do when he found out that Teri was long gone, out of reach? How would he settle for that? Rath thought Tommy would be enraged and feel cheated, but then what? How would that manifest itself? Rath's gut remained silent; it did not know. It did not have all the answers, but it did whisper this: *It's not over*. And that was what kept Rath going.

Chapter 27

Location, location, location. According to a well-known real estate motto: location is everything. Deciding to take a shortcut home that ends in an accident where a newly paid-off car is totaled: location. Passing three convenience stores to choose a neighborhood store and walk in on a robbery in progress: location. Claiming "shotgun" in the car about to be T-boned on the passenger side by an 18 wheeler: location. Trying to be in two places at one time and unavoidably making the wrong choice: location. In life, sometimes it's all about location.

Take Rath and his developing detective gut. He was right when he assumed that Tommy was still in town and would remain to take care of unfinished business. He was right when he figured that said unfinished business would revolve around his being caught, arrested and thrown into jail for 15 years. He could easily receive a gold star for thinking it would be Sandra Derringer or Kaitlin Tuscadero.

He had checked on the other victims of The Window Shopper and found that out of the five only two remained. Teri had died in an auto accident. One of the other victims had committed suicide before the trial had started. In fact, she had a male relative in the prison that Tommy had been incarcerated in. Rath wondered if they had ever crossed paths. One of the other victims became involved in drugs and died of an accidental heroin overdose.

Of the two that remained, one had moved to Florida with her parents shortly after the trial ended and had married there. The only other known victim had married a Navy man and lived on base in Norfolk, Virginia. Therefore, Tommy remaining in Richmond -or so Rath was convinced - meant that his unfinished business was there as well. Rath discounted the police officers that had arrested Tommy, because Tommy liked the ladies. Like all bullies of women, Tommy felt insecure and unworthy around other men.

When choosing between Sandra and Kaitlin, Rath had used simple logic. Sandra was Tommy's defending attorney. Yes, they had lost the case. But in Tommy's eyes, she would have been on his side; not against him. Therefore, Rath logically assumed that when Tommy made his move, it would be against Kate. That was why Rath was parked a few houses down from Kate's house in an unmarked car doing surveillance on his own time. He drank chai tea from a thermos and ate a sandwich that he now wished he had put a little more thought into when making.

He had followed Kate home from the hospital and remained to watch the house. He had his police band radio in the car turned down low to listen for any other activity of interest. Should he hear something that required his attention in a professional capacity, he would give up his post at Kate's house. But for now, he had no intention of leaving. He knew in his gut that Tommy was coming for Kate. It was just a question of when. The only time she was not protected was when she was home alone - before her husband arrived home. Rath took it upon himself to be the barrier between Kate and Tommy.

Vinnie was obviously running late tonight, because he had not yet made it home. Therefore, Rath sat eating a very dry turkey and cheese on wheat sandwich and sipping lukewarm tea. He waited and thought, *would tonight be the night?* A couple of times he had heard dogs barking at other houses and heard what sounded like a big dog barking behind Kate's house. Good for them. Good to have a big dog. They were the cheapest and most reliable alarm system one could have. However, nothing came of those warning barks from Kate's dog or the others. Most likely the dogs were answering other barks in other neighborhoods unheard through Rath's cracked car window.

Rath was a patient man. Tommy would show. He was sure of it. He was willing to bet that Tommy would only show when Vinnie wasn't around. He was sure of that, as well. Tommy would come and Rath would be his welcoming committee.

But sometimes, it all comes down to location. Rath's gut was right - Tommy was still in town and bent on revenge. But he was not anywhere near Kate's house. He was sitting outside Sandra's house awaiting her arrival home so he could kill her.

***

Sandra returned home a bit later than usual. Her whole day had been pushed back by one meeting running a little later than normal. The partners were celebrating a big win and she had joined in the celebration with a couple of Scotch and waters. By the time she had been able to pull herself away from the group, the other office staff had gone home for the evening.

She quickly took the elevator down to the building garage. She was trying to think of her closing argument for the next morning. She had a long night ahead of her to write a convincing rebuttal. Adjusting the strap for her laptop more comfortably on her shoulder, she hit the lock release button on her key. Her car winked back a hello to her.

As she drove home, she realized she would need some coffee for the long night ahead. The defense had put on a dazzling show and she knew the jury was most likely divided down the middle. The defense had successfully portrayed the accused as someone to be pitied and possibly excused for his actions. *Over my dead body!* thought Sandra.

Once she arrived home, she pulled into her garage with the first couple of paragraphs already written in her head. She wanted to hurry into the house and get those onto the laptop before she lost the words. She hated to admit that her mind was a bit more fuddled from the few Scotches than she had at first thought. *That coffee will need to be strong*, thought Sandra as she tried to fit her key in the lock while her laptop strap continued to slide down her right arm.

She was concentrating so hard on getting the big key into the tiny slot; she did not hear the soft thump some yards behind her in the grass. Nor did she hear the quick approach of booted feet closing the distance as the door lock finally relented. She had time to mutter, "Finally" before she was hit from behind, the force propelling her and her attacker through the back door.

Suddenly, all senses were on high alert. She heard the door being kicked shut behind her. She smelled the body odor of the man who held her arms pinned down by her sides. She could taste the Scotch-flavored bile shoot into her mouth from the force of her abdomen hitting the back of the couch. She could feel the wet warmth of his harsh breaths exploding from him, parting her hair on the back of her head. The problem was she could not see who was doing this. Once the door was kicked shut and she had swallowed the regurgitated Scotch, the mystery was solved when she heard, "Welcome home, bitch!"

With the knowledge that it was Tommy, came dread and extreme fear. At the very core of her, she knew it was going to be a fight to the death. Several conflicting bits of advice flashed in rapid succession like some bizarre slide show through her brain regarding how to respond to an attacker. Become dead weight versus stand your ground and fight. Scream "Fire! Fire!" versus ask him what he wants and give yourself time to plan an escape. Do what he says, throw up on him, tell him you have AIDS, cry, kick him in the balls, pluck out his eyes with your thumbshithiminthesolarplexusthroatnose......the thoughts began to talk over each other in her head. But one main theme screamed above the others:

GET AWAY NOW!! RUN!!

But she could not. He had her arms pinned to her side and her body bent over the couch. Her feet were no longer on the ground and her hair lay like a frenzied curtain over her face. She became still feigning submission, waiting for him to relax enough to give her a chance of escape. She could make it to the front door, get outside and scream her fool head off. It was not the best of plans, but until something better presented itself, she was sticking with it.

But after his first phrase spit out beside her ear, he had not spoken again. Somehow that was more frightening than spitting obscenities at her. Neither did he move except to assert his hold on her at the slightest movement. What was he doing? What was he planning? What the hell was he thinking? She heard him sniffing continuously like he had a bad cold. Even in her moment of panic, she remembered the strange tic he had when nervous, excited or angry. He had not changed and Sandra tried not to think of what that meant for her.

Quickly, Tommy moved one hand to grasp both of hers behind her back. He pushed up causing her shoulders to scream in protest. With the other he grabbed a handful of her hair and jerked her head back.

"I'm sitting here wondering if I want to waste my cum on you, you know that? You're such a cold bitch; you probably got ice for snatch. But then again, maybe you need a man to teach you some respect. Is that it?" Tommy spoke with quiet rage.

Then he used the fist that held her hair to nod her head. "Oh! You want me to slam you hard, dontcha? You little two timing slut!"

The hand holding her hair released it and started to reach under her designer skirt. She began to struggle then, ignoring the fire that ignited in both shoulders when she did so. Fear turned to anger, "Still can't get it up unless you're raping someone, Tommy?"

She was released for just a second so Tommy could turn her to face him. She barely registered the change 15 years had made on his appearance before he punched her in the mouth. Her legs buckled from the pain and impact.

Tommy grabbed her by the throat with one hand and brought her up to face him. Through tearing eyes, she watched Tommy as he grinned at her.

"Oh, I'm going to enjoy this shit," he said accompanied by a hard punch to her stomach.

Before her body had completely recoiled from the punch, Tommy pushed her face into his quickly rising knee. Sandra felt and heard her nose fracture.

"Learned that little move from my mom's Southside boyfriend number three," Tommy crowed as Sandra slid down the couch's back, blood pouring from her broken nose and busted lips.

Tommy grabbed her by the hair and pulled her around to the front of the couch towards her CD player. "I know how much you like musical accompaniment, so I brought along something I think suits this moment between us well. It's 'Crawl' by Kings of Leon. Fitting, dontcha think?"

With no answer from Sandra, he shrugged his shoulders. "Ah, that's alright. I like it and it's my party, isn't it?"

As he looked for the right buttons, he spoke in a conversational tone to her. "Yeah, my mom, she dated a lot of assholes through the years. Every single one of them liked to smack her around a little bit. When she wasn't there, then little Tommy did just fine as a fill in. Learned quite a bit watching her get her ass kicked or being the pinch punching bag. Now, I'm going to share those lessons with you."

Sandra wanted to cry, but even broken and bleeding she would not give him the satisfaction. She remained silent, refusing to look at him. Till she could no longer try, she would fight him. She promised herself that.

"See, you worked me over pretty good. Pretending to work for me, fighting for my rights, working to keep me out of jail. BULLSHIT!" Tommy screamed in her face now, pulling her head back to look at him. "The whole fucking time, you and that holier than thou nurse were plotting to put me away. You never intended to help me out. You and that bitch framed me!"

Sandra laughed then, spitting blood onto his face, just inches from hers. "You are such a fucking idiot. You can't be framed for a crime you actually committed, dumb ass!"

Tommy backhanded her then and blood sprayed onto her beautiful, expensive cream carpet. *That's going to be a bitch to get out*, she thought. She prayed for escape and in lieu of that, unconsciousness.

"Just for that, I'm going to take my time with you. You hear me?" Tommy said, close enough to feel his angry spit on her cheek.

He stood up then and for a moment, Sandra hoped for a chance to pull what strength she had left to escape. If he would leave the room for just a minute to go get a knife or something, for Christ's sake! Then she could make it to the front door just twenty feet away. If he would just leave for a minute, she could do that. She would use everything she had in her to do that.

But he did not leave. He punched the power button on the CD player and turned up the volume. A song Sandra had never heard of began to play. But she heard the words and she knew she was going to pay for whatever sins Tommy felt she had committed.

Tommy kept his promise and took his time. Sandra did not lose consciousness for some time. When he finally left, Sandra was barely alive. She knew she needed help immediately if she wanted to live, but she was nearly blind from two swollen eyes. She could not rise, but only flail her battered arms around. She reached around the floor beside her, sticky with her own blood. Her hands ran across her suit jacket and she felt the lump of her cell phone inside a pocket. She promised herself she would stay conscious long enough to call 911 using her broken fingers no matter how painful. That was a promise she kept.

***

Rath heard the call about the time his thermos was giving up the last of his chai tea. He recognized the address and swearing, turned the key in the ignition. He raced down the darkened road, hitting his palm against the steering wheel. "Son of a bitch! Son of a BITCH!"

He had bet the wrong horse. He had been watching the wrong house. His gut had failed him and he had been at the wrong location. And whether dealing in real estate, fate or police work, sometimes location *was* everything.

Chapter 28

Kate was cleaning up from dinner when she thought she heard a car start up abruptly outside and race down the street. She walked to the front of the house and looked outside at the darkened and empty road. She hated that some of her neighbors took no heed of the residential area and its corresponding speed limit. With Robbie being the typical mile-a-minute boy, she was hyperaware of cars going way too fast to stop in time for a child in the street.

Robbie was at Kate's sister's house tonight. There was no school tomorrow because of a teacher's work day, so Kate had allowed him to spend the night at his cousin's house. Her sister was taking the day off and had agreed to have Robbie overnight. Robbie and his cousin Allie were inseparable. A regular fric and frac, they were.

So, Kate's dinner had been a romantic one planned for just Vinnie and her in the absence of Robbie and their college daughter. But Vinnie had either forgotten or something had happened, because he had not shown. Kate had tried his cell phone twice and was put directly to voice mail. She was a little worried because Vinnie was not the inconsiderate type; quite the opposite. On the other hand, where was he? And why was he not answering his cell phone?

Kate walked around the house, straightening this and that, trying not to worry. She tried to ignore the feeling of doom that pervaded her mind. She tried to watch a rerun of *Seinfeld*, but could not keep her eyes off of the clock hanging on the wall directly above the

TV. She tried Vinnie's cell phone again and was put directly through to voice mail. Either his cell phone was off (rare for Vinnie Tuscadero) or dead. This just added to Kate's file of evidence for a conviction of worry.

After watching 45 minutes of two episodes of *Seinfeld* and not being able to give a synopsis of either, she turned the TV off. She decided to listen to some music to help ease her mind. She chose a collection of Stevie Ray Vaughan's slower blues. The first song to play was "True Love is Gone." Kate walked over to skip to the next thinking, *not the best song right now*. The phone rang and Kate jumped, startled by the intrusion. She turned off the CD changer and ran to answer the phone in the kitchen.

Please be Vinnie, she prayed, *please be Vinnie and be alright*. She glanced at the caller ID display and her breath caught in her throat. It was the hospital calling! She was no longer one of the SANE nurses on call. The only reason the hospital would be calling her was...

"Hello?" she managed to get out.

"Kate. It's Eileen. Honey, I'm afraid I have some bad news for you"

Kate's eyes closed and her heart began to pound in her chest and ears. She could not speak.

"Kate?" Eileen repeated.

"I'm here. Go on," Kate steeled herself.

"Kate, it's Sandra. She's been viciously assaulted. She's here and she's asking for you."

Kate's eyes flew open. "What?!"

"Sandra was just brought in. She was attacked at her house and she's...Kate, she's in bad shape. She's asking for you, honey."

Kate was already reaching for a notepad and scribbling a short message. "Okay, I'll be there as soon as I can."

"Okay, just look for me when you get here... and Kate?"

"Yeah?"

"Sweetie, you need to hurry."

Kate swallowed a sob and managed, "I'm coming."

She grabbed her purse and keys and ran out of the house. Backing erratically out of the driveway, she became one of those people she hated as she raced up the street towards the hospital.

Sitting on the kitchen cafe table was a hastily scribbled note to the missing Vinnie. It read, "HOSPITAL. KIDS OKAY. SANDRA"

***

Vinnie was just about finished glad handling one of his clients when that client mentioned that the late meeting had saved him from his wife's meatloaf. Vinnie was giving the obligatory chuckle when he remembered. *Oh shit!* he thought, *Kate's waiting a "special" dinner on me!* He checked his front pocket and found no cell phone. Saying a quick good-bye, he hurried over to his truck. There sat his cell phone in the passenger seat. He picked it up and found that the battery had died.

He had pulled up to the meeting place, planning on charging his waning battery on the cell phone, but had never plugged it in. Starting up the truck and plugging in the phone, he saw three missed calls from Kate. *Crapola, I am a dead man!* thought Vinnie.

Kate had called him earlier in the day to let him know that Robbie would be spending the night at her sister's house. Therefore, she would be fixing a "dinner extraordinaire" and hoped he would be able to make it home at the usual time. Translation: Child is away, want to play?

He had, of course, promised that he would be home right after work and teased her about what they might find to do with all that alone time. He listened to her only voice mail:

"Vinnie, hey. Just wondering what happened to you. I thought you were coming home right after work and your dinner's getting cold, bud. Can you just call me and let me know you're all right? Okay...bye."

Yep, he thought, *dead and buried*. He and Kate had been married long enough that he could translate any message based on content and tone. The message he had just heard would translate in the language of marriage as:

"Hey, Vinnie, third time I'm calling you. Guessing something must have happened to you for you to be a no-show on a romantic dinner. Your dinner's getting cold and so are your chances for dessert. You better call me and have a good excuse ready. Consider yourself warned. No love, just bye until I hear what you have to say for yourself"

And the truth shall set you free, he thought. He would just admit to being a total idiot and forgetting about the special dinner. His last client of the day had walked in and threatened to pull his business over an imagined faux pas. Vinnie had spent the better part of an hour smoothing his feathers and another half hour just "being friendly" and shooting the breeze. *No other excuse babe, just plain forgot. I am sorry, but I plan to do whatever you want to make it up to you.* Kiss, kiss, hug, hug.

Kate was not one to hold grudges or demand groveling for the slightest wrong. She would just want to know why and probably ask for the details of the meeting. In the end, she would take his side on the business end, tease him by telling him he owed her a back rub "free of charge" (with that eyebrow of hers raised) and she would reheat the dinner. But Vinnie still felt like a shit. Especially when she did not answer the house phone.

Knowing Kate, she had climbed into a hot, sudsy tub to ease her tension. She would not jump out of the tub to answer the phone when years of experience had taught her to keep her cell phone close to her at all times. Vinnie tried that now and waited through her voicemail greeting. Not answering the cell either? *Something's up*, thought Vinnie as he headed towards home.

***

Kate arrived at the hospital within minutes of receiving Eileen's call. She jumped out of the car, dropping her cell phone out of her jacket pocket on the way. It fell into her seat unnoticed, as she quickly shut the car door behind her. She ran to the emergency room entrance, surprised to see both Bill and that prodigy of his....what was his name?

"Ms. Tuscadero..." started Rath.

"Kate..." said Bill at the same time.

Kate did not stop, but rushed past them, leaving them no alternative but to follow her. She was recognized immediately by the nurse at the front desk and buzzed through to the ER. Rath and Bill followed closely behind calling, "Kate, wait just a second..."

Kate saw Eileen and ran to her. "Where is she?"

Eileen touched Kate's arm to get her to look at her. "Kate, you have to calm down first, before you go in there." Kate shook off Eileen's arm.

"Kate," Eileen repeated without raising her voice, but just looking steadily at her.

Kate knew what Eileen was saying. She had uttered the same words to frantic mothers, angry fathers and other friends and family members of sexually assaulted victims throughout the years. The victim was still in a state of shock right after an attack and very sensitive to any energy brought into a room. Calmness needed to be preserved. Kate knew this as a professional but was having a hard time practicing it as a friend.

"Quickly, before you go in, I'm going to let you know what you're going to see. She's asking for you, but..." Eileen stopped Kate from rushing blindly forward, "you know you need to go in there prepared and in control of yourself. For her sake, Kate."

Kate took a shuddering, deep breath and said, "I know, I know. Okay, what happened?"

Eileen looked to Rath and Bill standing quietly by. Rath spoke up as the officer responding to the scene, "Ms. Derringer appears to have been attacked in her home soon after arriving. She was beaten severely and managed to call for help. She's saying it was Tommy...Thomas King, who did this."

Kate's shock was evident in her wide eyes and audible, quick inhale. "Tommy? Tommy attacked her?"

"That's what she's claiming. She states she got a good look at him before..." Bill faltered, "before he...before she was unable to see clearly..."

"Oh my God!" Kate said on an exhale.

Eileen spoke now, "Kate, I'm going to give this to you dry, okay?"

Kate nodded her head realizing that it was the quickest and easiest way to hear it.

"X-rays show fractured facial bones including nose, cheekbones and jaw. Her right hand has multiple fractures consistent with a crush type injury. She is suspected of having some internal injuries and her abdominal tap showed immediate blood. She has some broken ribs resulting in a flail chest. She is being prepped for surgery, so that's where we're going. We don't have much time, but she insists on seeing you first."

Kate took in the information and a part of her died with each recited injury. She imagined what her beautiful friend would look like now and held a hand to her mouth to stifle the sobs.

"You ready, honey?" Eileen wrapped an arm around Kate's shoulder.

Kate nodded her head.

"We'll be right here when you get back," called Bill.

Kate was led to the holding area for surgery and put on a hat and gown quickly to be able to enter into the room where Sandra lay. Kate stood in the doorway, looking at the battered and bruised body that lay on the stretcher before her. Most of Sandra was covered with a sheet, but her face was grotesquely bruised and swollen, with caked blood everywhere. Kate pulled upon the steel in her resolve and went quickly to Sandra's side. Tenderly, she laid her palm on Sandra's forehead thinking her unconscious.

"Kayyy," Sandra mumbled.

"Shhhh, sweetie. Don't try to talk. I'm right here. They are going to take you into surgery and you'll be okay."

"Stah lyin'. It uhs hin. It uhs Tonny. I saw hin, Kay," Sandra said, trying to talk around her broken mouth.

"I know, sweetie, I know and we're going to make sure he pays for this. Bill and Rath are here and we're going to get him for this. I promise you that."

"Kay. He dint ape me. I dint let hin. I dint let hin ape me, da son o' a ditch!"

Kate was openly crying now and said fiercely, "Good for you, Sandra. Now, you rest and ..."

"Kay"

"What, sweetie?" Kate gave a silent "wait" signal to the nurse trying to take Sandra to surgery.

"Your nex. He's conin for you, Kay. Kill hin...kill hin!"

Then they could not wait for her anymore and Sandra disappeared beyond the double doors leading into the operating suite. That was the last time Kate saw Sandra.

Chapter 29

Vinnie returned home to an empty house and Kate's car missing from the driveway. *This isn't good*, he thought. He went into the kitchen and saw her hastily scribbled note. He kept trying her cell phone, but it would ring for a few seconds and go straight to voice mail. The only number he had for the hospital was her office number and he knew it would be useless to call.

As he headed for the door to drive to the hospital, he wondered what had happened to Sandra. Car accident? The woman drove that expensive car of hers like it had wings. Kate's writing had a hurried, bitten off quality to it. If it had been a car accident, a minor fender bender, Kate would have called to leave another message for him. Or at least, she would have written a more descriptive note.

No, from the look of the note, it was bad and Vinnie knew that some car accidents could be very bad. He shuddered to think that one of the many social rejects that Sandra had put away had come for their own brand of justice. Somehow, he believed it was something along these lines. He tried not to think of someone hurting his wife's sassy friend as he hastily climbed into his truck.

Because to think about something like that happening made it way too easy to think of someone coming after his own wife and that was a nightmare that Vinnie did not want to visit. Kate was the hothead in their relationship and he tended to be the salve and voice of reason. But Vinnie would kill anyone who came near his wife with intent to do harm and he would not even change his rate of breathing.

***

Kate waited a little over an hour before one of the surgeons she had known personally for many years came through the operating suite doors, head hung low. He did not need to speak. It was written in the slump of his shoulders, the deepening lines on his forehead and the lines forming parentheses around his mouth.

Kate confirmed softly, "She's gone?"

"I'm sorry, Kate. I know she was your friend. But there was just too much damage in too many places. She had sustained a massive amount of trauma to the head as well. There was just not much we could do. I'm sorry," the surgeon said quietly.

Kate nodded her head and tried to keep herself together. "Thank you for trying, Dr. Rowland."

They both moved in separate directions; Dr. Rowland to the surgeon's lounge for some much needed coffee and Kate back toward the ER. She had dropped her purse and jacket at the front nurse's station when looking for Eileen. Her keys were in her jacket along with her cell phone. She needed to call Vinnie, she needed to see...she needed to...she needed....Oh God! Her knees buckled slightly and she leaned against the closest wall in an empty hallway. She wanted to lie down and sob, but she could not. It was all so surreal; like some nightmare that she could not awake from.

As she rounded the corner, Eileen was speaking to someone on the phone and said, "Here she is, thanks."

"Kate, I am so sorry. Why don't you come into the nurse's lounge for a minute? Honey, you look like you need to sit down. I'll get us some coffee..." Eileen started.

"No, I have to get home," Kate answered as if unsure if that was what she needed to do or not.

Rath and Bill had been alerted to her arrival back in the ER. Kate was surprised to see them and did not remember them being there before. She turned to Rath over Eileen's protests about going home. Kate saw only Rath and Eileen was just background noise.

"She said that Tommy King did this. She said she saw him and she named him. Why are you still here? Why are you here and not locking his ass up? Is he already in custody? Are you here to tell me that? Because if you sit there and tell me that my friend was beaten to death by that bastard and you don't have him. I am going to lose...my....SHIT!" Kate felt herself becoming unglued.

Eileen was at her side so quickly, Kate jumped when Eileen touched her. "Kate, honey..."

Kate whirled on Eileen, shaking off the hand on her arm. "Shut up, Eileen, and stop calling me honey like some child that has lost her damn balloon! Did you see her face? Her beautiful face? Did you see what that...I have to go home." Kate spun around and headed for the nurse's station to grab her jacket and purse. Eileen, Rath and Bill followed right behind her.

"Kate, whoa...Kate, I don't think you should drive home right now. Maybe Bill can give you a ride home," Eileen said as Kate hurriedly put on her jacket, first inside out, then right side in.

"Kate, I can even follow behind you. I don't think you should be alone..." Bill started.

"I'm next. That's what she said. I'm next. That's what you're thinking too, isn't it? Well, you know what. Let him come. I dare him to..." Kate could feel angry tears starting and she knew that once she started crying, she would not be able to stop. She stopped talking abruptly and started slapping at her pockets. She found her keys, but could not locate her cell phone.

She flung her purse on top of the counter and busied herself with looking for her cell phone through the deep recesses of it. "I can never find this damn thing when I put it in my purse. That's why I never put it in there. It's black and it just gets lost when I put it in there. Sandra says that if I would stop buying suitcases for purses then I could...."

Kate sat down hard in a rolling chair with her purse in her lap. She hugged it to her as she wondered aloud, "Why would he kill her? She was his lawyer and defended him. Why would he do that? The rage that he inflicted on her fa... Why would he do that?" She said this last quietly, all out of steam, defeated. She posed the question to Bill, her old friend.

Rath spoke up. "Well, I've actually been giving that a great deal of thought lately and..." He faltered from a pointed look from Bill and continued, "but perhaps now is not the time, sorry."

Kate looked from Rath to Bill then back to Rath. "No. Now is the perfect time, Officer Rather. I need some answers. If you've figured this all out, then I need to know."

Rath received a slow, warning shake from Bill standing behind Kate. He paused to figure out how best to proceed. "I haven't got it all figured out yet, Ms. Tuscadero..."

"Kate," Kate interjected.

"Kate," Rath continued, "but I do agree with what your friend, Ms. Derringer, told you. I do believe that if his intent is revenge, then you are probably included in that plan and therefore need police protection."

"I'm sorry, what?" Kate was taken aback. Things were moving too fast for her. She looked to Bill for guidance.

"Kate, Officer Rather is right. I think it's best if you let us put a protective detail on your house for awhile until we can locate Mr. King. It won't be for long and it would make me feel a whole lot better knowing we had you covered," Bill reasoned with her.

"Okay, whatever you think." Kate was not going to play the femme fatale and trusted Bill's opinion when it came to police matters.

"Could I give you a ride home, Ms. Tuscadero...or maybe Lieu...Mr. Patterson?" Rath suggested.

"No, no. I'm fine to drive and I don't want to have to worry about my car tomorrow," Kate said, forgetting about her missing cell phone.

"Well, then. You won't mind if I follow you home then?" Rath asked.

"Sure," Kate said and turned to her friend. "Eileen, I'm so sorry. I didn't mean to..."

"Shut up. Now we're even. Don't worry about it. You go home and take care of you. Is Vinnie there?" Eileen said as she hugged Kate.

Kate had forgotten all about Vinnie and his unexplained absence. Had he ever made it home? Did he get her message?

Kate rushed to her car and saw her cell phone sitting and waiting for her. She was relieved to see a message from Vinnie. While Rath waited patiently for her, she listened to her voice mail:

"Hey babe, it's me. Don't hang up. [slow laugh] I got caught up in a client and lost track of time. I expect full repercussions when I get home and I know that I will spend about the first hour making it up to you. 'Course that's really not punishing me...okay, on my way now and I'm really sorry, babe."

Then:

"Kate, I'm home and see your note. Why aren't you picking up? Okay, talk to you soon. Call me when you get this message."

There were no more messages waiting for her. She assumed he was at home waiting for her to bring news of what had happened to Sandra. She did not know if she was ready to speak yet of what she had seen and heard. She did not know how she was going to tell him about the way Sandra had died or about the police protection. She did know that she needed to get home. She needed his strength.

She pulled out of the parking lot with Rath following a discreet distance away. As she pulled out into traffic, Vinnie's truck entered the parking lot from the other direction. They did not see each other. Vinnie parked the truck and headed into the ER. Kate headed home to an empty house.

***

Tommy was sitting in the woods across from Kate's front door. In the darkness, he was indistinguishable among the dark shadows from trees and undergrowth. He had left his truck four houses down. As he sat and watched the house, he wondered if he should move the truck to another street. He had seen who he assumed was Kate's husband come home and leave shortly after. *Wonder what that was about?* thought Tommy, *and where the hell was Ms. Kate?*

He was seriously considering stretching his legs and moving his truck when a car slowly approached Kate's house and turned into the driveway. *Ah, has the queen bee returned to the hive?* Tommy watched as she got out of her car, and then turned to look at the car arriving close behind her.

Hmmmm, not hubby. Who might this be? thought Tommy.

From his position in the woods and the quiet of the night, he could just make out their conversation.

"Did you want to come in? Have some coffee? Have you had dinner, Officer Rather?" Kate asked.

"No, ma'am. I'm fine, Ms. Tuscadero. But thank you," answered the average built younger man.

"Kate, please. Everyone calls me Kate."

"Okay, Kate. Then you can call me Officer," shot back the smooth talking cop.

She smiled at that. Then Rath said, "I'm just kidding. Everyone calls me Rath."

"Wrath?" she asked.

"Yes, Rath. R-A-T-H, from Rather. Long story. Anyway, I'm just going to follow you inside and make sure everything's okay. And I guess introduce myself to your husband..."

"Oh, yeah. His truck's not here. I guess I can call him and find out where he is. But come on in," she said and started for the house. She added, "You sure you don't want some coffee or something?"

Their voices faded as they walked toward the front door, but Tommy was no longer interested in their inane chit chat. Police protection? How in the hell did they know about Sandra so fast? No way that bitch had lived! She was not dead when he left her, but damn near it. Truth of the matter was, he did not get much enjoyment out of kicking a dead horse, so to speak. Once she became a sack of broken bones, his rage was spent. Besides, he figured she'd be dead by morning; long before anyone thought to come and look for her.

Before he had time to explore this mystery, her husband returned. His truck came barreling down the road and he practically jumped the curb before cutting off the ignition. Kate and Rath came to the door as Vinnie came running across the lawn. He grabbed onto Kate and kept saying, "Oh baby, I'm so sorry. I'm here now. Are you okay? I'm so sorry, baby."

"Mr. Tuscadero, I'm Officer Rather..." Rath began.

"I know who you are and why you're here. Bill Patterson told me everything. I just missed ya'll at the hospital and he told me about Sandra." He was speaking to Rath, but at the mention of Sandra's name, he looked back to his wife. "Baby, I'm so, so sorry".

"Okay, well. I'll be here for the next hour or two..." Rath started, but Vinnie was walking his wife back into the house.

Rath walked back to his car and radioed in his position. He looked to the house and thought about the fishbowl effect that lit up rooms inside of a house on a dark night created. He could see Vinnie and Kate in their living room.

Tommy could as well and he thought that Mr. Tuscadero might be a problem. He was a tall drink of water as his dead, musty mother used to say. Big old husband, real dog in the backyard and a cop in the front. Could be a problem getting to Ms. "Kate" as everyone called her.

Suddenly, another car, a little red VW Rabbit, came pulling up to the house. *Why it's a party!* snickered Tommy. The laugh died in his throat as he saw the vision that exited the car. Running up to the house, was a flirty young thing with long, tanned legs and curls in her hair just like Kate. She was wearing a hooded sweatshirt open and flying behind her. On her little peach bottom she wore running shorts. *Mmmmmm, mm, just look at little sister as Stevie Ray Vaughan used to sing.*

At the arrival of the car, Kate had peeked out again and Tommy heard the fine piece of meat say, "Mom!"

Well, well, well. Looks like Kate's got herself a little girl. Tommy sniffed hard and fast three times as a new plan began to present itself.

Chapter 30

Isabella was on her way to Jarrett, Virginia. The radio was off and she was lost in her thoughts; only interrupted by the occasional "remain on the current road" from her GPS system that her father had gotten for her last Christmas. Since the drive was mainly down I-95 South for many miles until an exit dumped her into a relatively rural area, all was quiet inside the little Rabbit.

Isabella was worried about her mother. She had been almost inconsolable after her friend Sandra's death. Her father was trying to hold her mother, who kept walking away from him talking about some guy named Tommy. How Sandra had defended him and he had done "that" to her. Isabella was not sure what "that" was, but she knew that Sandra had been assaulted and had died as a result of the assault.

She had called her father earlier to see if he could float her a loan for a concert she wanted to attend at a venue downtown and he had been on his way to the hospital. All he knew at the time was that something had happened to Sandra and it was probably pretty bad because her mother had rushed to the hospital. Her father assumed it was probably a bad car accident and was going there to be there for her mother. Isabella had been minutes behind both, because Sandra had become kind of like a reckless and defiant big sister to her. Many times when Isabella felt her mother was being too unbending on something, Sandra would give her a quick shake of her head and then a conspiratorial wink. Usually, within days, her mother would give in or at least offer a compromise.

Sandra once told her, "You and I are a lot alike, kiddo. We're both free spirits that know what we want in life. Don't let anyone tell you that you can't do something. Don't let someone else's fears and doubts instill a lack of confidence in you. Fulfill your dreams. To do otherwise is to cheat yourself and destiny."

Isabella's vision blurred as her eyes filled with tears over her surrogate big sister that was now gone forever. The two days that had passed since that terrible night seemed to blend in a blur when the ripple effect of Sandra's death hit them all. Isabella had been just minutes behind her father leaving the hospital. Eileen had seen her come in and at first, was confused.

"What are you - ? How did you know - ? Izzie, they have all gone home. Your dad just left," Eileen said.

"What happened? Where's Sandra? What happened to her?" Isabella looked around the ER as if Sandra's manicured hand would wave to her from one of the curtained rooms and she would say, "Over here, kiddo!"

Eileen looked worried. "Isabella, how did you know to come here?"

"I called my dad about something else and he told me that Sandra had been brought to the hospital and was really messed up. Mom was supposed to be here." She stopped to look around, forgetting Eileen's previous statement. "But, he was coming here to be with Mom and....where's Sandra?"

Eileen was silent for a minute, trying to figure out if and how she was going to tell Isabella about her mother's friend. Isabella felt the unease crawl up her spine and settle like a spider on her crown. Her eyes teared up in anticipation of horrible news. Looking just like her mother, she laid a hand on her chest as if to still a frantic heartbeat and asked, "'Leen, where's Sandra?"

Eileen's heart broke a little when Isabella used the nickname she had called Eileen as a small little girl visiting her mother at work. She did not want to be the one, but she knew how much Sandra had meant to the family. She placed a hand in the small of Isabella's back and guided her to the nurses' lounge a few feet away. As soon as Eileen's hand touched Isabella's back, it was if she had touched a release valve for tears, for they flowed quite easily.

Once away from prying eyes and ears, Eileen broke the news to Isabella. "Honey, Sandra is dead. She was viciously assaulted by someone and her injuries were just too extensive. They took her to surgery, but she did not survive. I'm so sorry, honey."

Isabella cried freely for a few minutes. Then with reddened eyes, she asked, "Where is everyone?"

"Well, your mom went home after she found out. We asked her to stay, but she insisted on going home. One of the officers here followed her home, though. Your dad..."

"Why did an officer follow Mom home? Are they worried about her?!" Isabella's reddened eyes widened.

"No, no, just because she was upset, honey. Nothing more than that," Eileen lied. She was not going to be the one to explore that can of worms with Isabella. She would find out soon enough.

"Oh...Dad?" Isabella asked.

"Well, your dad got here just after, I mean within two minutes, of your mom leaving. He only stayed long enough to find out that Sandra had...had passed and then he too took off out of the door for home. You probably missed him by about a minute. I'm sure they are all at home. Are you okay to drive?" Eileen asked.

"Yeah, yeah. I'm fine, thanks." And she had left.

She had arrived home to find her mother ranting about this guy Tommy and her father trying to control his anger and, yes, fear. Seeing her father afraid made her afraid. No one would tell her what had happened. Her mother kept pacing and ranting and then crying and then ranting. Isabella had never seen her so out of control. She had looked to her father for direction. He had walked over to the sound system and started playing this slow Stevie Ray Vaughan blues type of song. Isabella had questioned her father's motives with a look that said, "Are you out of your mind? Music? Now?"

But it worked. He had walked over to her mother and stopped her from pacing. She had tried to get around him for a minute, then out of his arms saying, "Vinnie, let go of me! Vinnie, stop it! Let go!" But her father had held on in his calm way, pulling her gently ever so closer; shushing her and saying lowly, "It's okay, baby. It's alright. Come 'ere."

Her mother had slowly melted into him, drinking in his strength. She held onto him fiercely and began to cry hard. At first her father just swayed back and forth, letting her shatter while he caught all the pieces. Then the swaying became a slow dance of comfort and after awhile her mother quieted, but did not let go. During that time, Isabella could hardly breathe. For the first time, she saw her parents as a couple, united against whatever came and she was humbled by the strength in that.

She had gone outside to sit on the front porch. Suddenly, a voice came from her right.

"Don't be afraid," it said.

Isabella had let out a little yelp and had turned to see a good-looking man emerge from the shadows.

"I'm Officer Rather. I followed your mom home. I didn't mean to scare you," he said as he continued to come closer.

"It's okay. I just wasn't expecting anyone to be out here," Isabella excused him, and then said, "Why are you still here? Is there something wrong? Is my mom in some kind of danger?"

"How is everything in there?" Officer Rather said looking into the house at her parents' slow dance.

"Hey, don't do that!" Isabella snapped.

He looked surprised and guilty at the same time. "Do what?"

"Completely ignore my question, for one. As for another, spying on my parents in a very private moment!" Isabella needed to vent on someone and conveniently, there stood some young rookie.

"I apologize for not answering your question, Ms. Tuscadero. There is a small chance that the man that attacked your mom's friend may be planning something for your mother. I'm here mainly as a deterrent and to just check out a few things. And I was not spying on your parents; I was merely concerned for your mother," he explained.

"Well...is she in danger? I mean, are you guys going to provide police protection for her?" Isabella insisted.

"Yes, ma'am. We intend to watch your house when your mom is home until we can locate Thomas King. Do you live here as well?" Rath asked as he could not help but notice Isabella's natural beauty and therefore her attraction for Tommy.

"No, I'm going to VCU and live in an apartment down there with some roommates."

Rath did not comment, but merely waited her out, waiting for her next question. But Isabella was out of steam at the presence of calm manners and lack of anger in the tall, slim officer. "So, why aren't you in uniform? You are a police officer, right?"

He had a slow, sexy kind of smile. "Yes, ma'am. But I'm actually off duty tonight. I just happened to be in the area when...well, at the hospital. So, I volunteered to follow your mom home. I've seen her speak. I really admire her."

Isabella started to study him a bit more. He did not present himself in a cocky way but was obviously sure of who he was and what he wanted out of life. He carried himself that way and it was evident in the way he spoke, never breaking eye contact. Isabella found herself drawn to him.

Thinking back to the talk on the porch, Isabella wondered if it was merely "damsel in distress" syndrome for both of them. He was the protector that night and she was part of those affected by tragedy. He had explained who Tommy was and the part he played in both Sandra and her mother's past. He did not stay long after that. He said he was going to run the plates of all the cars on the block - why, she had no idea - and was going to do "a little digging". He did give her his card and took time to write his cell number on the back. Isabella was fairly sure that he was being a bit more than professional.

Now, as she turned off of the highway onto her intended exit as prompted by her GPS, her thoughts returned to her destination today. She was headed for the interview her mother had begged her to take. Part of the reason she was going ahead with the interview was her mother. She wanted to do something to please her right now; she could not deny that.

But the other reason she was headed to the home for troubled girls stuck way out in the country was because of Sandra. As she mourned Sandra in her own way in her tiny room in her shared apartment, her roommates and a few 20 friends partied away right outside her bedroom door. Amidst the loud music and raucous laughter, Isabella hugged her pillow and stared at the poster Sandra had given her on her graduation night. The poster that stayed plastered to her door so that it was the first thing she saw every morning.

Isabella loved the beach. If it paid well, Sandra would kid Isabella sometimes, Isabella would be a professional beach bum. Her mother was the same way and Isabella was sure that genetics had something to do with that. But ever since Isabella could say "beach house" she insisted that one day she would have one. Isabella was ecstatic when she once saw a picture of beach huts placed out over the water in some luxury vacation spot. She used to expound Sandra about how she was going to "live in one of those and you can come visit whenever you want."

Sandra had smiled at Isabella in that way she had which made you feel like she was about to tell you a particularly juicy secret and said, "I just bet you will, kiddo. But don't expect me to come stay at one of those unless it includes catering, salon services and a place to store my many bottles of wine."

So, for graduation, Sandra had found one of those inspirational posters that read "DESTINY" and in smaller print below, it read,

"Destiny is not a matter chance; it is a matter of choice." W.J. Bryan

Those inspiring words lay beneath a picture of one of those beach huts of Isabella's dreams situated at the end of a long wooden pier over crystal light blue waters. It may have been meant to be a gag type of gift, because Sandra had also given her a silver charm bracelet that had a #1 dangling from it. She had explained, "You've accomplished the first step in your destiny by graduating high school. Now, fill this bracelet with the rest."

These memories and more flowed through Isabella's mind as she mourned her mentor and big sister figure. But the word "destiny" stuck out in her head and she thought about it long and hard. Her end goal, her destiny, she believed was to become a child psychologist who would change the way the justice system and society viewed child abuse.

She wanted more than anything to go with her friends to Europe this summer and was not sure that opportunity would present itself again. However, this summer position in Jarrett was another step toward her destiny. She had seen the notice and had mentioned something to her mother about it, but had disregarded it because they were looking for someone with a degree in psychology.

Her mother had made some phone calls or something and suddenly, she had the opportunity to interview. Part of Isabella's refusal to do interview was she wanted to go to Europe, true. But the real reason she had argued with her mother was that she was afraid to fail. If they wanted someone with a degree would they not also expect some kind of knowledge that she did not possess?

She stared at her poster and she could imagine what Sandra would say: "Is Europe part of your destiny? Is going to Europe a step toward achieving your destiny? No. Is this position in Jarrett a potential step toward your destiny? Uh, yeah. Smarten up, kiddo. Obtain your goal, your destiny, and *then* reward yourself with Europe. And if you never get there, does it matter? Does it really matter in who you want to be? Who you want to become? Does it?"

Isabella spoke out loud, "No, Europe is not part of my plan, my destiny." So, she made her mind up then and in the late hour, wrote a request to a professor for a letter of recommendation for the position in Jarrett. The professor of psychology was one that Isabella admired and who had shared with her his belief that she would make a fine psychiatrist one day.

So, here she was waiting to hear the next spoken directions from her GPS to take her to the next step in her destiny. She was a little put off on how out in the middle of nowhere this place obviously was. *Well, no partying at the local clubs for me this summer,* she thought. Well, no matter. She was sure she would have a few days off here and there.

Listen to me! Acting like I already have the position, she laughed at herself. She would have to wait to see if she was offered the job, then she would share the good news with her mom and silently with Sandra. How surprised her mother would be that she, Isabella, had actually changed her mind and gone with her mother's suggestion.

In spite of the emptiness of the area, Isabella's spirits began to lift a little in anticipation of the adventure. She still had Officer Rather's card in her purse as well; Howard Rather, read the card. She wondered what he went by: Howard? Please, God, not Howie. She'd find out when she brazenly called him later tonight and asked him out. She did not know whether he was part of her destiny or not, but he would make an interesting sidebar, nonetheless.

Per her GPS system, she was less than a mile away from her destination, another step toward her destiny. The knowledge gave her a little thrill. She would give it her best shot and the rest was up to those listening. Like the poster said, she had been given the chance, she had made the choice to go for it and destiny would decide.

But destiny does not belong to any one person. Isabella was still too young to grasp that concept. By contrast, destiny is a complex woven fabric that includes many people and many events. One individual is but merely a thread in the great tapestry of life and sometimes, destiny and one's place among it is not what one imagined at all. In words Isabella would easily grasp and Sandra may have muttered, sometimes destiny could be a bitch.

Chapter 31

The two men who were going to play significant roles in the tapestry of Isabella's life had spent the last two days with two entirely different agendas, but still linked. The good and the bad. The white knight and the dark shadow. Both had been very busy and both were working out their own personal dilemmas.

Rath had run every plate on every car sitting on Kate's block the night of Sandra's death and had won the lottery. Most of the cars belonged to residents of the street on which they were parked. A few had turned out to be friends visiting or others having business on that street; three as it turned out. It was interesting to Rath to discover on a license plate sweep of a particular street how few people visited each other as opposed to meeting somewhere else outside of the home. One car ended up being abandoned there. In fact, neighbors reported seeing it there for over a month, but because no one knew his or her neighbors anymore, no one had thought anything about it. Each assumed that it was a long term guest of the other.

But one car, or truck rather, had turned out to be a twisting road of deceit. But the end of that road had been paved with pay dirt. The license plate on the truck belonged to a Ford Explorer with two flats down in The Fan area of Richmond, not far from Tommy's supposed new residence. Checking for stolen vehicles matching or coming close to the truck's description had yielded nothing.

But remembering Tommy's mother's meager legacy to her son, Rath played a hunch. He checked back through the *Trading Post* and other well-known and easily accessible trader venues and looked for someone selling a truck matching the make, color and approximate year of the truck in question. He was able to narrow his search down to two vehicles. One vehicle had been sold to a man and his son and upon further investigation checked out.

However, the other belonged to a man who claimed he had sold it, for cash, to someone fitting Tommy's description but going by the name of Jude Silver. Rath caught the irony, but he downtrodden man did not. He had turned over the title and a handwritten receipt for the cash and had asked very few questions. He was not a fount of information regarding Tommy either. The gentleman claimed the buyer was nice enough about it and did not waggle too much about the price. "He didn't even seem to mind the cab being a little dirty either because he knew the true value of a big truck like that" exclaimed the man."

The seller had fulfilled his part of the bargain by turning in his old plates and notifying DMV of the transfer of title. But Tommy, or someone fitting Tommy's description, had never purchased new license plates or registered the truck through DMV. Rath was 99% sure it was Tommy driving that truck. Which meant that he was 99% sure that Tommy had been in that neighborhood that night; the night Sandra had died. He was 100% sure he knew why. Based on what he had learned about Tommy and psychopaths in general, he knew that this twisted perp had come to gloat and drink in the misery he had caused.

Of course, the truck was gone now, but Rath did not doubt that Tommy's next plan of assault would be on Kate. He was so sure of this fact that he had taken vacation time for the next week to work on this particular case. It was not his case but belonged to a detective friend of his, Andrew Grisham. With Andy's permission, Rath was allowed to help in a non-professional and definitely unpaid capacity. Rath would take the opportunity both because he believed it would be good experience and because he believed in his gut that Tommy was creeping up to the door. Rath wanted to be there to answer it.

Kate had gone right back to work and while she was safely ensconced within the hospital walls surrounded by witnesses, he did his footwork. But at 4:00 p.m. he was waiting in the parking lot for her to walk to her car sometime after 5:00. To his knowledge, he was the only one following Kate home the last two days, but he could be wrong. Tommy could park his truck on another street and walk in. Rath would be waiting for him.

Currently, he was parked across the street from Kate's house watching every vehicle that came down the road. He had been wrong the last time and had sat outside of the wrong house while Sandra had been beaten practically to death. He would not be wrong again. When Tommy came calling this time, he would be waiting for him.

***

Tommy had been a busy little bee himself in the last two days. With his first glance at beautiful Isabella in those running shorts, he knew she would be his next victim and he began preparation for the hunt. It started with noting the VCU sticker on her back windshield. Not taking anything for granted, he made a note to check VCU's computer files and see if one....hell, what was her name? He was sure it was still Tuscadero, but what was her first name? He decided to hang around even after the lovesick rookie left.

It was obvious from their body language that Kate's daughter and the young cop had taken an interest in each other. Well, sometimes tragedy brings people together, thought Tommy. Too bad the stupid cop would never get to taste that little treat. Tommy was intent on making Kate suffer. If losing some lying lawyer friend caused this kind of drama, imagine what snuffing out the life of her little girl would do. *Hot Damn! That was going to be suh-weet!* thought Tommy.

The cop and the girl never spoke loud enough for Tommy to hear her name from his position in the woods across the street, even in the stillness of the night. However, he was relieved when the cop left first and the daughter went back into the house to visit for awhile. She did not stay long and her father walked her to her car. *Aw, such a protective father*, thought Tommy.

They hugged. *Hugged for Christ's sake! What child over 12 still hugs their parents?!* As she started to pull out of the driveway, her father called, "Izzie! Izzie! Isabella!"

She stopped, rolled down the window and said, "Yeah, Dad?"

Her father seemed to have changed his mind and said, "Just be careful. I don't want you alone, okay? Keep yourself around other people."

Tommy could not see her face, but she was silent for a few seconds. Then she said, "Okay, Dad. I will." Then she drove off into the night – all alone.

Isabella. Isabella Tuscadero. Good name. Almost had a movie star quality to it. She had that girl next door look to her as well - if the girl next door happened to be a knockout! Pity to snuff out the life of such a fine piece of ass, but c'est la vive!

He had run to his car and managed to catch up with Isabella's car via an adjoining road. He followed her to her "home" down in the Fan area of Richmond. It was more of a very lively and noisy apartment building acting as a dormitory. After watching the house for a few hours, Tommy realized that he would be unable to get to Isabella here without plenty of witnesses or worse, intervention. No, it had to be quiet and she had to be alone.

So, he had left that night and later gained access to a computer once again and hacked into the University computers to pull up her academic record. He looked over her schedule to see if she had any night courses and was surprised to see that she was a psychology major. *Well don't that beat all!* thought Tommy, *a damn head shrinker!*

He began to check her grades and projects. He read a few of her online papers and checked her email. That is when he hit the jackpot! There, just a few days ago, was a letter written to some professor she was probably banging asking for a recommendation for some job in Jarrett, Virginia. Tommy had never heard of the place. He did a little Google satellite on the address of the girls' home she spoke about in her email and found that it was situated in a very rural area of the state - as these facilities often are.

That's it! he thought. That was how he was going to get her alone. He needed to know the time of the appointment. He secured the number of the girls' home and called the day before the appointment and spoke to an office assistant.

"Yes, hello," he spoke in a businesslike manner. "I am the assistant for Professor Reed here at Virginia Commonwealth University School of Psychiatry. He wrote a recommendation for a student of his coming to see you tomorrow, a Ms...Tuscadero?"

"Uh, yes. We are expecting an Isabella Tuscadero tomorrow afternoon at 4 p.m. for an interview," said the helpful office assistant.

"Right, right. Well, could I have your fax number? I want to make sure you have a copy of this letter of recommendation from Dr. Reed, in case she does not have it with her."

"Uh, sir. You or, I guess, the professor already faxed a copy of that letter this morning with the understanding that Ms. Tuscadero would be bringing the hard copy with her tomorrow," replied the assistant.

"Oh. Well, what does he need me for?" Tommy said and managed a self-deprecating laugh. "I guess my work is done, huh?"

The assistant laughed along with him and said, "Looks like it. But you're welcome to fax another if you like," and she laughed at her own humor.

Smart ass bitch, thought Tommy, but instead said, "No, no. Wouldn't want to work too hard. Heh, heh, heh. Alright then, bye now."

An appointment at 4 p.m. would put her travelling alone back down those country roads to the Interstate in the near dark. Perfect. He had left early this afternoon and had, in fact, been sitting in this exact spot when Isabella's red VW Rabbit went by on her way to the appointment. At that time it was 3:30. She was a punctual little thing; he would have to give her that. He had settled in to wait her return down this lonely stretch of road.

It was now 5:15 p.m. and he had to pee something fierce. But he was afraid to step out of the truck and take a piss. She could be coming down the road at any minute. He wanted to make sure he was in the right place at the right time. At least one of the two men in the tapestry of Isabella's life had it right that night.

Chapter 32

Rath sat in his car listening to the neighborhood sounds around him waiting for Vinnie to arrive home and thinking how he would go about attacking Kate if he were Tommy. They believed that Tommy had studied Sandra's routine and had surprised her as she entered the back door of her house. Her keys were still in the door and her coat and briefcase had fallen just inside the doorway, probably from the impact of being hit from behind or forced through the door. This meant that Tommy had been watching from the backyard hidden in the shadows of the trees or sitting in the tree branches above the privacy fence enclosing the backyard.

He did not think Tommy would enter Kate's house from the backyard. She, too, had a privacy fence surrounding it. However, inside was a very large dog. Rath had met the dog during a walkthrough of Kate and Vinnie's house to inspect for security worries. The dog's name was Bear and it fit him well. He was a long-haired black German shepherd that looked more like a pony, but had thick black hair like a black bear. Kate laughed at Rath's obvious discomfort and explained that he had been named Bear as a puppy because he resembled a black bear cub. "The name still fits though because he's just a big ol' teddy bear, aren't you?" Kate nuzzled Bear's neck and ruffled his fur. She did not have to bend far to do it either, Rath noticed. Bear obviously adored and belonged to Kate and although he readily accepted the attention lavished upon him by his mistress, he kept a steady eye on Rath.

Yeah, just a big ol' teddy bear, thought Rath, *a teddy bear with big shiny teeth*!

No, Tommy would not be entering through the backyard and making it to the house in one piece. Rath sat and looked at the front of the house through the eyes of a predator. The living room window afforded a good look into the house. As evening started to fall and Kate turned on lights in the house, Rath was able to track her movement. He would need to speak to her about that, he thought. He also wondered if at this moment, he was the only one watching.

***

Tommy sat and tried not to think of his expanding bladder or the need to empty it. He wished the little bitch would come on already. Knowing his luck, she was probably taking a tour of the place or worse yet had packed a frigging sleeping bag to "try it out". Son of a bitch! He could not wait any longer. Hopping out of the truck parked on the wayside of the rural road, Tommy walked to the other side of it and unzipped his jeans. Ah, sweet relief! Giving it a final shake, he hurried and climbed back into the cab.

What was taking her so long! It was going on 5:30, for Christ's sake! Even though he was about to take her life, he could not believe that she was willing to throw it away on something like psychiatry. What a waste of her time and her parents' money! Tommy had his share of counselors and psychologists and he had a very low opinion of them.

Oh sure, the first time someone had intervened on his behalf as a child and called Child Protective Services, he had believed in hope and salvation. He had sat with the counselor and told her everything; about the beatings, the days with nothing to eat, the alcohol and constant drug use by his mother, the hiding from perverted "uncles"....everything. She had looked at him with such supposed compassion and understanding, nodding her head and saying, "I can imagine, I can imagine." Bullshit! Because if she would have had any idea, she would have locked his mom up and thrown away the key. But no, his mother had cried and spoke of *her* horrible upbringing and *her* pain and suffering and how sorry she was blah, blah, blah…and had sent him back home! Sent him back home to a very angry and vindictive witch. He never opened his mouth again. Months later, he had found out where the stupid bitch that sent him back lived and had hung her gutted cat from a planter hook on her front porch.

Then when he had to attend anger management courses and talk about how he felt about life and all that shit, some curly haired shit-for-brains had sat there in his wire-framed glasses saying, "We must learn to control our baser instincts and therefore our anger. We must remember that we are a civilized race now and rejoice in the evolvement. Because that's what separates us from the animals." He never listened to Tommy. He just likes to listen to himself talk for 50 minutes of each 60 minute session. The first 10 minutes were filled with the same thing, "How are we feeling today, Tommy? What issues are we dealing with that have caused us anger in the last week, Tommy? What could we have done differently, Tommy?" And what was with that "we" shit? That used to just twist his nut every time it came out of that wimp's mouth. And every 50 minute lecture would end with "you see Tommy, that's what separates us from the animals." Once Tommy's court appointed time was up, he watched as some paid lowlifes showed the waste of space what animals were capable of. Worth every penny, in his book!

Then there was the....headlights! Headlights coming down the road belonging to what looked like a compact little car. Could this be his future headshrinker? Yes, Tommy believed it just might be. Tommy started the truck, but left the headlights off for now. The sky was just beginning to give up its light and headlights were for the safety conscious. But soon...soon.

***

Isabella was both thrilled and a little anxious on her ride back to Richmond. She had felt good about the interview from about ten minutes into it. The Director had spoken of what she believed the center for girls should be about and her views on the girls who were sent there and what they needed. Isabella was relieved to hear that the center's mission statement went along with her own moral code and beliefs when it came to abused, neglected children.

The Director and she had just swapped opinions, ideas and dreams for the future of troubled youth for the first 30 minutes. Then, with some surprise registering on her face, the Director had stated, "Well, I guess I should get to conducting an official interview, shouldn't I?"

The interview had gone on another 45 minutes and Isabella was invited to tour the facility. She was very impressed with what she saw and took note of how the residents treated the Director; with respect. All the residents were polite, although a little leery of Isabella. Before the tour was over, Isabella silently prayed that she would be offered the position.

She hated to admit it, but her mother had been right. This was the opportunity she had been looking for and a summer there would teach her more than a semester's worth of psychology courses. Isabella was quietly ecstatic when offered the position. The Director had said, "I know your mother well. However, I was reluctant to grant even her daughter an interview because I was really looking for someone with the credentials to take this position. My plan was to offer the position on a trial basis for both of us through the summer and then hopefully be able to offer that person a permanent position. Your mother spoke so genuinely about your drive and enthusiasm for this type of work, well, I just had to meet you and find out for myself. I must say, you have impressed me so far, Ms. Tuscadero. I believe that you are exactly what these girls need right now. I know you were considering Europe for the summer, but I do hope you will give this position some consideration as well. We would be very lucky to have you, I think."

Isabella responded after a millisecond of consideration, "I don't have to take time to think about it. If you are willing to give me the opportunity to prove that this is what I was meant to do, then I will most certainly take you up on it. When can I start?"

Now, with a feeling of euphoria, she could not wait to get back home and tell her mother, and yes, maybe even thank her. She thought about calling her, but wanted to see her face. She wondered how she was going to sit on her excitement all the way back to Richmond. She was so excited; she paid no attention to the blue pickup truck idling by the side of the road as she flew by it.

***

Rath was relieved to see Vinnie's truck cruising down the street as dusk fell over the neighborhood. Rath wondered if Vinnie's slow approach was his norm. With his limited interaction with Vinnie, Rath supposed that Vinnie's slow driving was an extension of his laid back personality. As Vinnie pulled into the driveway, Rath stepped from his vehicle to meet him.

Rath could see Kate looking out of the window and once again reminded himself to speak to Kate and Vinnie about the visibility they were affording everyone, but possibly and most notably Tommy. Tommy was a predator and predators stalked their victims. No need to advertise. With all the house lights on, if Tommy was watching, he had a clear view of his next victim.

***

It did not take Tommy long to catch up with Isabella's speeding Rabbit and he now had a clear view of her mass of curls from the rear view window in the fading light. He rode without headlights, slowly creeping closer to her car. The element of surprise was his specialty and he wanted to toy with her a little first. Sure, he would snuff the light right out of her scientific head, but first he was going to have a little fun.

Isabella was thinking about her earlier promise to herself and was trying to keep her eyes on the twisting road in front of her, but locate her cell phone and Rath's business card at the same time. Her plan was to call him under the guise of looking for someone to celebrate with and invite him to take her to dinner. She was fairly sure the attraction was mutual and he would cave in after a few rounds of word play. Then she would stop by her parents' house, tell them the good news, swing by her place to freshen up and knock the socks off one Howard Rather.

There! She had located her cell phone and found his card in her wallet. There printed in his block lettering was his cell phone number. She checked the road ahead of her to find a relatively straight portion, but it looked as if she would need to....what the hell?

***

In one quick moment, Tommy turned his headlights on to bright within two car lengths of Isabella's car. With a chuckle, he noted the slight swerve showing he had caught her off guard. He almost pitied her ignorance as a hand came out to wave him around. He crept even closer...

***

Damn local yokel! Where the hell did he come from? She must have been in la-la land not to notice anyone behind her. She could barely see with those damn bright beams right in her back window.

She would never be able to see her turnoff with that going on. Isabella stuck her hand out of the car window to wave him around and it looked as if he had gotten the message because he pulled closer...

***

....until he was able to give her back bumper a little tap and he could imagine her frightened yelp. As suspected, she hit the gas and tried to get as far away from him as....

***

....she could. Her heart was racing and her mind flew to all the documentaries and horror movies she had watched revolving around lonely women on long stretches of deserted roads playing cat and mouse with some in-bred psychopath. Her mouth went dry and she kept flicking her eyes to her rear view mirror. To her horror he was gaining on her and it looked as if he was going to...

***

....he slammed into her again. This time her car swerved wider showing her panic and Tommy sniffed hard three times in succession to celebrate his triumph. The chase was on. He had to see her face. He fed off of the fear. He backed off enough to give himself some room to swing around her. He could see her frantic movements inside the car and wondered what she was up to.

***

Police! Rath! Call Rath! shouted Isabella's panicked mind. She grabbed for her cell phone and flipped it open. She did not think to dial 911, but tried to steer through the curves at a high speed and dial Rath's number at the same time. 3-3-5...5....Curve! Her tires bumped roughly over the soft shoulder of the road as she swung too wide through the turn. She was afraid to slow down, yet she continued to dial. With relief, she heard it ringing and looked up to the rear view mirror. He was coming around! Maybe it was over...maybe he was done playing...maybe...

***

Rath's phone vibrated in his pocket and he pulled it out to look at the caller ID as Vinnie continued to expound the finer points of GPS systems. He did not recognize the caller, but his gut said *ANSWER IT*, so he did.

"Officer Rather"

"RATHHHH!" a woman screamed. "Oh my God! Please help me!" The woman on the other end was hysterical and crying. His skin crawled with apprehension and he started to say something, but the woman continued, "Rath! He's going to push me off the road! He's trying to knock me off the road, Rath!"

"Isabella! Where are you?!" He tried to remain calm, but his heart pounded and his breath began to come quicker. Vinnie was looking at him with alarm and looked like he wanted to grab the phone. Rath was already moving toward his unmarked cruiser, Vinnie close behind him. Kate came to the door of the house and said, "Vinnie?" But no one answered her.

"Rath! I don't know. I don't know where I am.....aaaiiiiyyy! I'm going too fast, but I can't slow down. He's trying to run me off the road! *What do you want? What the hell do you want, asshole!* (this screamed to someone else). Rath! He's riding right next to me. He's looking at me and laughing! Rath!" She was screaming and crying, breathing hard, panicking.

Rath was in the car and unsure of where to go. "Isabella! Isabella! Tell me where you are! Tell me where you are and I'll come to you. Where are you?" Vinnie had climbed into the seat next to him and could hear his daughter screaming on the cell phone. Rath knew he needed to get Vinnie out of the car, but he also knew that there was no army that could do so now. Following instinct, he handed the phone to Vinnie, "Get her to tell you where she is!"

"Isabella! It's Daddy. Where are you, sweetheart?" he said surprisingly soothingly, but his face and waving hand said, "go, go!" They took off toward the main road with Kate looking after them with confusion.

"Dad? Dad! I went on that job interview at Second Chances in Jarrett and I was coming back and this guy is...Daddy!" Then nothing but screaming...

***

Tommy saw the cell phone in her hand and was instantly enraged! Who the hell was she talking to? The police? Damn her conniving ass! He slammed the truck against her little Rabbit and she did not have a chance. The car slid over to the side of the road and up a steep embankment. But the incline was too steep and the car too light. With the amount of speed she had accumulated, Isabella's car was airborne for a few seconds.

It was a beautiful sight, thought Tommy. Then with a sickening crunch, the car came down at an angle on its nose and toppled a few times before heading over the embankment down into the trees below. *Hot damn, that was something*! Tommy thought. He pulled over to run back to where her car had left the road. He could see the trail the car had left as it fell even in the dark. About 20 yards away, he could see the blinking turn signal on one side of the upside down vehicle.

Wonder if she survived that or if she's even in the car? Tommy thought he better be sure. *Can't leave a job half done, now can I*? He was thinking of how to best navigate his way down the steep embankment in the dark when his peripheral vision caught something. He looked to his right and could see two sets of lights coming from the direction they had just traveled. Son of a bitch! he thought as he looked at his parked and running truck just 20 feet away. Son of a BITCH! He would just have to go. The bitch was probably dead anyway or would be shortly. He doubted anyone would see the turn signal light of Isabella's car that far off the road.

He ran back to his truck and fled the scene before the approaching vehicle could spot him. He ran with lights off and no brake lights until he had gone around another curve. Once out of range, he hit the lights and accelerated. He wanted to pick a good spot outside of Kate's house to watch the upcoming drama unfold.

***

"Isabella! Isabellaaaa!" Vinnie's calm veneer evaporated as he screamed into the phone. "Oh my God, dear God, please God, not my baby girl. Please God, plea..."

"Vinnie, what happened? Vinnie!" Rath drove with practiced speed to the closest Interstate interchange.

"I think someone just forced her off the road! I heard her screaming and now there's nothing! Just silence! Oh my God! Oh my God!" The reality of "what if" was settling on Vinnie and he was crumbling under the weight of it.

"Vinnie, did she say where she was?" Rath tried to stay in control.

"What? Uh yeah, yeah. Something about a job interview in Jarrett. It was something Kate set up for her, but we didn't think she was going. Some home for girls or something,"

Rath ran through his knowledge of juvenile facilities..."Second Chances?"

"Yeah! That was it! Do you know where that is?" Vinnie grasped at the smallest offering of hope.

"Yeah, buckle up and hold on," Rath said.

***

The man and his son in the truck traveled back from the baseball practice thinking about dinner. The boy watched the darkness fly by his side window, lost in the missed catch of an earlier game. He saw the flashing yellow light down in the woods and called his father's attention to it. Luckily, the man was the type of father that listened to his son.

Some minutes later, they used the son's cell phone to call in a car accident out on Route 119 just past Route 621 travelling toward Eagle's Nest high school. When the 911 operator asked, "Are there any injuries?"

The man looked at his son and said, "Well, ma'am, it's a young woman and I think she might be dead."

Chapter 33

Kate looked after the speeding car with Vinnie inside of it and her stomach fell. She ran back into the house and called Vinnie's cell. It went directly to voice mail. Damn it! Trying again, she ran out of the house and checked the drink holder inside of his Explorer and there sat his cell phone, lighting up and showing her face on its display screen. Damn him!

Hanging up, she punched in another set of numbers dialing Isabella's cell phone. Same thing; directly to voice mail. Like father, like daughter. She tried to think if Isabella had any night classes this semester. She normally did not keep up with her daughter's schedule, but she usually knew about the night courses because they were the ones that would coincide with family events. She did not think Isabella had a night course this semester, but in her growing panic, she could not remember. She hung up again and dialed Isabella's apartment, praying someone was in and could remember how to answer a land line.

Finally, Isabella's roommate, Marie answered. Kate thanked God silently that it was Marie that answered the phone. Isabella and Marie were friends as well as roommates and therefore, Marie may know where Isabella was.

"Hey Marie. It's Isabella's mom. Is she there by any chance?" she asked trying to sound unworried.

"Oh hey, Ms. Tuscadero. No, she had some interview out at a girls' home or something. Oh shit! Oops, sorry. But I wasn't supposed to tell you that," Marie said.

Kate was confused. "What? Why not?"

"Because she didn't want you to know she was trying for it in case she didn't get it I guess. Don't tell her I told you, okay?" Marie begged.

"Scout's honor. Do you know what time that was?" Kate said hoping it was later this afternoon and Isabella was safely out of town and harm's way.

"Ummmm...I think around 4:00? But I could be wrong. Said she'd be back in time for dinner maybe. Why? Something wrong?" Marie asked.

"Oh no. Just trying to see if she was home. I was going to ask her something, but I'll try her later, " Kate lied and made some pleasant small talk with Marie before hanging up.

She felt better knowing Isabella was not sitting in her apartment or worse walking around downtown with Tommy on the loose. Robbie was safe in his room upstairs. But she could not figure out what would make Vinnie jump into Rath's car without a word to her....unless it was his baby girl? *Oh Vinnie!* she thought, *where are you and what the hell is going on?*

***

Vinnie sat staring straight ahead trying to keep the nightmare images crowding his mind at bay. He prayed to God and begged Him to please, please, let his baby girl be alright. Rath did some phone calls back and forth and finally he was patched through to the local police in Jarrett. Rath had put on lights and sirens and they were barreling down Interstate 95 towards the Jarrett exit. Vinnie could only hear Rath's part of the conversation, but it did not sound good. He tried to keep his heart quiet enough to hear what was being said.

"We have reason to believe that a motor vehicle accident may have occurred involving a red Volkswagen Rabbit and a young woman by the name of... When?... Where exactly is that? And that was how long ago? No, I'll find it, thanks. I'll call you back if I need to." Rath hung up the phone and would not look at Vinnie, although his knuckles were white as he gripped the steering wheel.

"Tell me," Vinnie said.

"I think we just need to get there and..." Rath started.

"Just tell me," Vinnie repeated.

Rath stole a quick glance at Vinnie and tried to decide what to tell the father sitting next to him. He was having a difficult time dealing with the information himself. He could not fathom how Isabella's father was going to take what he had just heard.

"It's not good, Mr. Tuscadero," Rath warned.

Vinnie closed his eyes as his bowels became water sending cramps through his belly. With a mouth that suddenly had no moisture left, he said, "Okay. What did they say?"

Rath took the exit and knew he had about five minutes before they arrived at the approximate location the dispatcher had relayed to him. "They have an accident involving a red Volkswagen Rabbit and a young woman. There is no other vehicle at the scene that was involved in the accident." Rath gave it to Vinnie dry, trying to keep his own emotions out of his voice.

"Is Isabella...the young woman...is there any word...do they know," and Vinnie could not hold it together any longer. His voice cracked and he stopped, knowing the flood of his fear would come out in wracking sobs if he continued with that line of thought.

Rath had been told that initial reports from a civilian reporting the accident stated that the woman was possibly dead at the scene, but ambulance crews had not radioed their assessment. Rath did not want or feel the need to give a "possible" so he told the truth he thought he should, "Ambulance had just arrived and there was no word yet. We should be coming up on it pretty soon. Do you need me to pull over?"

Vinnie just looked at him and Rath drove on. They saw the sky lit up with flashing lights before they came around a curve and confronted the scene of the accident itself. Vinnie was searching for her car, but could not see it amidst all the many different emergency vehicles on scene. Rath navigated his way through using his lights and stopping just once to flash ID.

They could see firemen and ambulance personnel standing on the side of the road and looking down an embankment. Rath spoke before Vinnie could react. "You are here because everyone assumes you are an officer. Do NOT get out of the vehicle. Let me find out what's going on and I'll come back to you. You can't do that and I will keep on driving. Clear?"

Vinnie looked over at Rath and seemed to size him up and gave a curt nod. Rath had no intention of driving on, but he could not let Vinnie know that. He found an area to park on the opposite side of the road past the other vehicles and walked back. He followed everyone else's line of sight and could make out an upside down license plate. It was Isabella's car. His knees went weak for a second, but he recovered. He walked up to one of the firemen and asked, "What have we got?" in his most official tone, flashing his ID.

The fireman barely gave him and his ID a glance. "Looks like this car took the curve too fast back there," he looked to where Rath had just come from, "rode the embankment, probably went airborne and then ended up down there after a few rolls. Had to have been going at a pretty good clip to do it, too. No telling what happened: alcohol, fell asleep with her foot on the gas...who knows."

Rath delivered the question he was dreading, "Is she alive?"

"Ambulance guys say yes, but it's bad. They're bringing in MedFlight for her. Trying to get her on the body board now and bring her up out of there to make the flight."

Rath double timed it back to the cruiser and an anxious Vinnie. He opened the door and said, "It's her! She's alive! They are medivacing her to MCV most likely. It's the closest trauma hospital. Call Kate and have her meet us there."

"I need to see her," Vinnie said as he unbuckled his seat belt.

"You won't be able to. They are still trying to get her up the hill. The medivac will be here any minute and if we don't get started now, they will beat us by a very large amount of time to the hospital. If we start now, we might make it there about the same time...depends on traffic." Rath had already buckled in and was starting the car.

"I just need to see her and tell her I'm here. She needs to know that I'm here," Vinnie said and started to open the door.

Rath grabbed his arm. "Vinnie...she won't hear you. She's barely alive. Don't slow them down, man. We need to go."

Vinnie paled at Rath's statement, but buckled back in and looked straight ahead.

"Call Kate. Tell her to meet us there," Rath repeated.

Vinnie checked his shirt pocket then his jeans. Without asking, Rath tossed him his cell phone and turning the car around, started for the exit back to Interstate 95.

***

It had been almost an hour since Vinnie and Rath had left and Kate was no closer to solving the mystery than the minute they had disappeared. She tried Isabella's house again about 20 minutes ago, but received no answer the second time. Isabella's cell phone continued to go directly to voice mail. By the time Kate thought to call Second Chances, the office was long closed and she was unable to get an idea of when Isabella had left. Her unease grew and when her cell phone rang, she jumped.

"Hello?" she asked.

"Kate," said Vinnie.

"Vinnie, where in the hell are y-?" Kate started.

"Kate" Vinnie interrupted her and something in the stillness of his voice frightened her very much. She remained silent.

"Baby, you need to put Robbie in the car and go to MCV. Rath and I will meet you in Emergency..." Vinnie was almost robotic, like he was reading a prepared statement.

"MCV? Vinnie, what's happened? Who's hurt? Vinnie?" Kate was asking, but already going up the stairs to Robbie's room.

"Kate....baby, it's Isabella. She's been in a car accident out in Jarrett. They are taking her by helicopter to MCV. Kate?"

Kate had gotten to Robbie's room, but had dropped the phone when she heard the word "helicopter" because she knew what that meant. They only sent helicopters when it was life threatening.

Robbie picked up her cell phone and gave it to her with a, "Here you go, Mom."

Kate managed a smile for Robbie and asked, "How bad is it, Vinnie?"

"I don't know all the details yet. Rath and I are headed to the hospital now. You'll probably get there before we do so..." he started to sound like himself again.

"Wait - Is that why you guys -- How did you know --" Kate was trying to understand the sequence of events while helping a confused Robbie into his jacket.

"I'll tell you all that later." Vinnie sounded tired.

"What? I don't understand..." Kate was still trying to figure it out as she and Robbie went down the stairs. She grabbed her keys and purse, trying to listen to what Vinnie was saying.

"Kate, she called Rath when it was happening --" Vinnie was saying.

"Wait...when what was happening?" Kate asked.

"When that maniac was trying to run her off of the road," said Vinnie as his voice cracked.

Kate did not need to ask. Her hands started to tremble with both fear and rage. She said quickly, "I'll see you there" and hung up. She hurried a scared Robbie to the car.

"Wha's wong, Mom?" Robbie said.

"Shhhhh, Robbie. Buckle up, buddy. Mommy's going to be driving real fast, okay? No more questions right now, okay? Mommy needs to think," Kate said as she tried not to scream out loud in frustrated rage.

Robbie knew by the look on his mother's face that he needed to be quiet and do as he was told. He knew something was very wrong, but trusted his mother to take care of it. She always took care of everything and did what she promised. When she was upset like this, she only saw what she needed to do and nothing else. Like now....she was driving really, really fast. So fast, she almost hit that blue pickup truck turning onto their street.

Chapter 34

Kate sat at Isabella's bedside and watched for any movement from her battered and bruised daughter. Last night had been one of the worst nights of Kate's life. Isabella had arrived at the hospital via helicopter and had been rushed into surgery shortly after her arrival. The Emergency Room physician had rattled off Isabella's long list of injuries and they had signed a generic consent for surgery. The consent had been for exploratory surgery because internal injuries were confirmed, but the extent of the damage would not be known until they opened her up. Kate remembered Vinnie's impatience with the nurse trying to obtain the signatures.

"Does Isabella have any allergies to any medications or foods?" the nurse asked.

"No, I don't think so...no" Vinnie answered after looking to Kate for confirmation.

"If Isabella should need blood or blood products...and I'm fairly sure she will...do we have your permission to administer them and do you know what her blood type is?" the nurse continued, checking boxes on the pre-printed form.

Kate answered, "O positive. She's O positive. She's a blood donor."

At the same time, Vinnie grew impatient and blurted out, "Let me bottom line it for you. Whatever you have to do to save her life, do it! It doesn't matter to me what that is, just do it. Okay? Stop stalling by asking all of these questions and just take care of her, okay?" On this last sentence, his voice cracked and he looked away from her down the hall to where Isabella had just disappeared.

Kate started to apologize to the nurse doing her duty in getting the consent, but the young lady just gave her a reassuring shake of her head and spoke to Vinnie's back, "Mr. Tuscadero, Isabella is already in the holding area of the OR and being prepped for surgery as we speak. This is just the paperwork and will not delay her treatment in any way."

Vinnie's shoulders dropped a bit and he turned to give her an apologetic smile. "I'm sorry. I don't mean to snap at you, darlin'..."

"It's quite alright. If one of you could just sign here..."

Kate signed and the long wait began. She and Vinnie had waited five long hours for the surgeon's return. Even after five hours of waiting, when Kate saw the surgeon pass through the door to the waiting room, her heart dropped into her belly and she thought, *too soon! He's back too soon!*

She and Vinnie stood when he entered the room and he invited them to sit. His news was cautiously good. Isabella had survived the surgery, but her injuries were many and severe. She would be transferred to the ICU after stabilizing in the PACU. His prognosis for a recovery was guarded.

"The next 48 hours are crucial. There is a lot of swelling on the brain and along the spinal cord. If she wakes up in the next 48 hours, we will be able to better predict the rest of her recovery. However, if she does not...well, we'll cross that bridge when we get to it. Let's hope for the best right now."

Now, as Kate sat at Isabella's bedside in the ICU holding her cold, dry hand, she willed her daughter to open her eyes. The ventilator rhythmically cycled 12 breaths a minute and her beautiful daughter lay motionless against the crisp, white sheets. Her misshapen face was bruised and swollen; one eye would probably not open even if she awoke in the next hour. Isabella's bottom lip was savagely split and the swelling there caused her to look as though she was perpetually pouting.

Vinnie had taken Robbie home after seeing Isabella in the ICU. Bill Patterson had come in during the night some time and had asked if Kate needed anything. He stayed for about an hour, not saying anything unless Kate asked him something. Just sitting and waiting with her. He promised her he would look into what had happened and get her answers. She could only nod her head and look at her broken daughter. Vinnie had called earlier to ask when she was coming home. He suggested that she come home, clean up, get some sleep and return later in the day. He would sit by the bed with Isabella until she returned. Kate refused to leave Isabella's side. Vinnie could come and sit with her, but she was not leaving. Vinnie did not argue with her and asked if she wanted him to bring anything when he came.

Kate sat now and watched the ventilator blow another lungful of air into Isabella. Her eyes teared up as she thought of how scared Isabella must have been on that dark stretch of country road with a monster behind her. Vinnie had relayed the conversation or exchange of information from Isabella. Kate had no doubt that he had censored what he could, but one thing stood out: Isabella did not know the identity or describe the individual responsible for her terror. But she did not fall asleep at the wheel or lose control of a speeding car because of an inexperienced lead foot. She had been run off of the road intentionally and methodically by a man who laughed at her terror.

Tommy....

But there was no proof of that. Without a description of the man or vehicle responsible for running her off of the road, no one could say who it was. But Kate knew it was Tommy and she tried not to think of what that meant for her or her family. Kate had faced her share of monsters and to her growing shame, she was beginning to see the coward she had always been in the face of them.

As she leaned her hot forehead against the cool skin of her daughter's hand, she remembered another broken girl long ago. She thought of Emily and her call to Kate the night following Kate's discovery of Emily's family secret. Kate had refused the call, not sure of what to say to her friend and still shaking from the warning from Emily's father. When she had looked into the monster's eyes that afternoon, she believed every bit of the threat that poured from the monster's poisoned lips. She needed time to think of a plan, she had thought back then and had believed she would have it. But Emily had taken her own life; dying alone and afraid because Kate would not stand up to the monster.

She was not Sandra. Oh God, Sandra! Sandra who did not take anything from anyone - not the "rude dude" behind her in line at the local Wal-Mart or the accused killer staring at her across the courtroom. No, Sandra had a steel pair! She had even special ordered steel four millimeter ball earrings for that very reason. Reportedly, she had offered them to a milquetoast judge in chambers once and had almost been disbarred.

When Sandra had heard of Tommy's release, she had been hopping mad. She wanted to go after the system for releasing him early and had tried to convince Kate to speak as an expert witness regarding his crimes. Kate had argued that by the time the case saw the inside of a courtroom and justice had a chance to be carried out, two years could have come and gone. And would that not just be time served? And, she did not voice this, but would that not just draw unwanted attention to both of them from the monster that Tommy most likely still was? Sandra had taken another sip of her Scotch and water and said, "Yeah, you're probably right. But it just twists my panties in a knot to know he beat the system by two years!"

Kate had backed down at the prospect of facing the wrath of the monster. Maybe because of that, Sandra had been beaten practically to death by that same monster. She had suffered alone and then died in a cold sterile operating room. The pain that accompanied the loss of her friend was still fresh enough to bring new tears.

Now, her beautiful daughter! Isabella would not have even been on that long stretch of secondary road if not for Kate. *I pushed her into that interview,* thought Kate. Isabella had wanted to go to Europe for the summer like any college aged young woman. But Kate had pulled some strings and had secured Isabella an interview with someone she did not even want to meet. She had put Isabella on that deserted road to face the monster all by herself. The burden of that guilt was almost too much to bear.

She sensed someone behind her and her back stiffened. The only noise was the rhythmic cycling of the ventilator, but Kate knew someone was there.

"I don't mean to disturb you, Ms. Tuscadero," came a familiar voice.

Kate's shoulders relaxed and she quickly wiped the tears under her eyes before turning to face Officer Rather.

"No, no, it's okay. What is it, Officer Rather? Something new about Isabella's case? And please, after last night, feel free to call me Kate," she said with a weak smile.

"Well then, please feel free to call me Rath, Ms...Kate. I'm sorry it's taken me so long to get back to you..." Rath began.

Kate started to object to the lateness he referred to but was surprised to see that it was indeed late afternoon. Almost 24 hours had passed since that horrible phone call Isabella had placed to Rath's cell phone.

"After some investigation into last night's events, I did find out a few things," Rath began.

Kate stood and they walked to the corner of the room. Her legs protested the change in position, but her back thanked her. Rath continued, "I spoke with the man that found...that called in Isabella's accident. He and his son were returning from baseball practice at the school down the road. They didn't see any vehicles leaving the scene of the accident. However, they did notice a blue truck parked on a wayside a few hours before that on the way to the ball field."

Kate just stared at Rath. He gauged how he would impart everything he had found out in the course of the day and wondered how Kate would accept what he had to say.

"Well, Kate, the description of the blue truck matches what we believe Tommy is or was driving. We know he purchased a vehicle very similar to it just after being released from prison."

Kate's hand went to her mouth and she tried to maintain a calm exterior so that Rath would continue. However, rage caused her to press her forefinger a little too hard into her top lip.

"We also have a woman returning from a Wal-Mart around the time that Isabella was finishing up her interview down the same road. She, too, spotted the same truck sitting on the wayside. However, she mentions that this particular truck and driver stood out in her mind because the man was urinating beside the vehicle. The man she describes sounds like Tommy and she did say that the picture I have 'could have been' him, but once she realized what he was doing, she 'was disgusted' and turned away."

Kate's previous fear and guilt was quickly overcome with mounting rage. *How dare he!* her mind screamed. *Come after me, terrorize me, but how dare he go after my child!* She could not answer or respond to Rath at first. Her mind would not let go of the confirmation that it was Tommy.

Rath continued, "We're going to find him, Kate. We're going to put police protection on Isabella. I would suggest that Vinnie, you and Robbie find a safe place to go until we have him in custody, although I know that you would not leave Isabella."

Kate answered by glancing at him and shaking her head. She looked back at her daughter and returned her gaze to Rath. "I need to be here," she said.

"Of course. What do the doctors say?" asked Rath.

"No change. The swelling on her brain has decreased a bit and she's not any worse, but...well, we're still inside that 48 hour window. She's strong though. She'll wake up. She will," Kate answered, then, "Vinnie? Robbie? Do they know?"

"I've already spoken to Vinnie. Robbie's fine. We have police on the house as well. We're watching and waiting, Kate. We're going to get Tommy. He's on a short leash, believe me."

Kate gave Rath a brief smile that said, "I know you think so" then returned to Isabella's side.

"Can I get you anything? Would you like me to sit with her awhile? Need a break?" Rath asked, feeling Kate's waning faith in the system.

"No, thank you," Kate answered without taking her eyes off of her daughter.

"Okay. Well, you have my number if you need me and I'll keep in touch," Rath said as he started out of the room.

Kate did not respond, but continued her vigil monitoring her daughter's tenuous hold on the here and now. Rath slipped out quietly. Kate was not even aware that he left. She was thinking of Sandra's last words to her and she was formulating a plan. The monster had gone after her child and in doing so he had given Kate the conviction she needed to stand up to him. As Kate listened to the ventilator cycle, she came to her own conclusion: it was time to slay the dragon.

Chapter 35

Tommy had seen Kate fly by him as he entered her neighborhood and his heart stopped at the prospect that she may have recognized him. But she had never looked in his direction. *Now, where was she going in such a hurry*, he giggled to himself. At first he had thought she had just received word her little girl was dead on the side of the road. He wanted to turn around and follow her car so he could revel in the pain he had caused her, but there would be plenty of time for that. He instead continued down the road to fulfill his plan of beginning to case her house.

Tommy had a husband and a brat of a kid to deal with now after eliminating the flirty co-ed. He needed to get the lay of the land in order to plan on how to best trap his quarry. It was dark now in the neighborhood and most of the neighbors were sitting like zombies in front of their HD enabled televisions. This was the perfect time to execute a flawless illegal entry.

He parked around the corner and down another side street. The street was a cul-de-sac with a long neck. It was neither an entry nor major exit point for the neighborhood. No one on Tommy's worry list should be travelling down this road thereby spotting his vehicle. Tommy was nothing if not a meticulous planner. He doubled back to Kate's house with a dog leash purchased at a thrift store earlier in the week. Tommy had found that people rarely questioned a distressed fellow just looking for his runaway dog. Sure, he was a stranger in this neighborhood. But golly, who wouldn't search the surrounding area for their beloved Champ?

He did not see anyone on his way back to Kate's house. The spring had brought sunshine and warmer temperatures during the day. However, the nights still carried the memory of winter on its soft breezes and kept the well-heeled inside. Soon he was standing across from Kate's house. The living room light was still on, but the rest of the house remained dark. He needed to check out the back of the house.

He walked down the street a few yards pretending to look into the woods for his lost pooch, slapping his thigh and calling quietly. He completed the charade for any spying eyes by standing up and looking all around. His look said, *Now, where could that rascal have gone to?* He saw no cars, no one outside and no one looking out of any of the windows of neighboring houses. He made a break for it and ran across the street and down Kate's driveway to the fenced in backyard.

There he came face to face with yet another bogus "Beware of Dog" sign hanging on the locked gate. Seemed the bitches belonged to the same pack. Tommy chuckled at his own joke. Attorney Derringer had been lying about having a dog and he just bet this one was as well. Here he was, standing at the gate, and nothing - no sniffing, chuffing or barking from the other side.

Tommy saw the woods in the back of the house, with trees both behind and *higher* than the fence. When people bought houses surrounded by trees and then built privacy fences and left the trees standing - they called it ambience. People in Tommy's line of work called it easy access. He decided to get a look at the back yard, just to be on the safe side before jumping the fence.

He backtracked down a few houses until he was able to cut between two yards to walk the easement back to Kate's house. Most of the trees closer to the fence line were little more than saplings. But there was one that showed some promise. With expert skill, Tommy climbed the tree to be able to peer in to the backyard. Kate's outside light was not on, but her neighbor's light was. With that floodlight, he could see most of Kate's backyard and saw no dog. Just a modest deck with plants, a jungle gym of wood (for the brat probably) and a picnic table.

What he did not see was any evidence of a dog: no dog house, no toys, not even a water dish. *All women are liars*, thought Tommy with disgust. He jumped from the tree limb into the yard, landing on his sneakered feet. He looked around at how the light fell over the backyard. Was the floodlight situated by the backdoor not working or just never turned on? Was it off because of the disruption to everyone's life, i.e. not on a timer? Tommy stood and pondered the thought. Best to watch for a couple of nights and learn the habits, he decided.

He started across the yard toward the door that led into the house from the deck deep in thought about what to do with that big husband of hers and the little dude. Take out the hus...

What was *that?!* All the fine, tiny hairs placed at the nape of his neck and along his arms stood straight up and seemed to scream. Tommy could have sworn he heard a noise under the deck and a...growl? Tommy was frozen in fright. Soon, two unmistakable glowing orbs appeared in the darkness beneath the deck; the low growl now completely audible.

"Son of a bitch!" Tommy spit out. He turned and ran for the back fence. Of course, anyone who knows anything about dogs would warn that you don't turn your back on a dog and run. The minute you do, you become prey. But Tommy had never been a dog lover and the feeling was mutual.

The worn out traction of his sneakers did not bode well in the dew covered grass of the early evening. They slipped from beneath him and Tommy was clawing his way back into a running position when Bear sunk his teeth into Tommy's calf. Tommy's mouth pulled back in a grimace and he screamed in pain.

"Aarrrgh! Son of a BITCH!" he yelled and swung his fist around, hitting Bear several times in the head before Bear let go briefly. Tommy jumped up and kicked at the charging Bear, catching him in the muzzle. Bear yelped and Tommy fled.

The adrenaline screaming through Tommy's veins helped mask the pain from the mauling of his leg. He heard Bear's large paws slapping the ground behind him and getting closer all the time. With agility not usually found in the human male, Tommy practically walked up the fence to grab a tree branch hanging over it. *Please God, let this hold me,* he prayed.

Although the branch dipped from his weight, Tommy held on and swung his good leg over the branch. He could hear Bear's huffing bark as the large dog propelled itself after Tommy. Tommy was able to stand and take the two steps back to the trunk of the tree. Bear's body writhed in mid air as he tried to follow Tommy's journey along the branch.

"Sweet Jesus! Sweet Je-sus!" Tommy breathed out in a high-pitched whine. That was the biggest dog he had ever seen. From the safety of the tree, he called down to the barking, frothing dog.

"You're a dead dog, you hear me! You stupid son of a bitch! You are fucking dead!"

Bear continued to bark viciously, no doubt hoping Tommy would come close enough to grab. Sooner or later, some neighbor was going to see what that racket was about. It was time to go. Tommy jumped from the tree, crying out when his left leg screamed from the impact. He could feel the sticky wetness of his jeans leg and knew he was bleeding badly. He jogged as quickly as he could down the easement and back to his car. He saw no one.

A dog! A freakin' dog, man! This was going to screw things up royally. This bitch was proving to be more trouble than she was worth. He was going to have to think up something spectacular for her ass! He'd figure out a way to make her pay for what her damn dog had just done! He would kill the dog, of course - probably poison it - but she would still pay for this injury. The injury which now screamed in agony. Shit, shit, shit! She was going to pay!

Much later when Vinnie arrived home, he made sure to take care of Bear. He placed fresh water in his dish in the utility room and measured out three scoops of food. He opened the back door and called for him. Bear came running from the back of the yard, down by the fence. *That's weird, he usually hangs out under the deck,* thought Vinnie briefly.

Once Bear was in, he drank noisily from his bowl. Water splashed onto the surrounding tiles. Vinnie was alarmed to see what looked like blood. He stopped the big dog, grabbing his muzzle to have a look. Blood-streaked water smeared his hands.

"Hey, buddy. Hold still a minute. You hurt yourself there? Get into something you weren't supposed to? That why you were hiding down there by the fence? Hold still, Bear!" Vinnie said soothingly as he examined the dog's jowls and gums. He could find no injury. He was puzzled at first, but then remembered.

"Did you go and catch yourself another squirrel or some other four legged intruder? I interrupt your carnal dining, buddy? You know how your mommy feels about you killing the little innocents of the neighborhood; especially when you eat them." Vinnie had to laugh at the dog's complete ignoring of his lecture.

"Alright, let's get you cleaned up. Don't want Mommy seeing you like this. It's the last thing she needs tonight." He wiped Bear's muzzle clean, glad to have something mundane and normal to do.

"There. Good as new. Now eat some dinner - if you're still hungry that is. I'd go out and look for it, but you either finished it off by the amount of blood there or you've hidden it. Just take it easy on the little guys, Bear. Remember, you're much bigger than they are." With that, Vinnie gave the giant dog another ruffle between his ears and went about getting the house closed up for night. He was a little surprised later that Bear had cleaned out his bowl after what he had found earlier. But then again, Bear was a big dog with a big appetite. One little squirrel was not going to fill him up.

Vinnie almost felt sorry for the little forest creatures. They did not stand a chance when Bear was in the yard.

As he prepared to sleep in his marriage bed alone, he comforted himself with one fact. At least they had a dog like Bear. With what had happened tonight and the conversation he and Rath had later...having a dog like Bear around was a very good thing. As if he felt his master's longing for him, Bear came panting up the stairs and into the bedroom. He looked to his doggie bed to the bathroom to Vinnie.

"She's not here, Bear. Just us guys tonight."

Bear took a final sniff as if to confirm his mistress's absence and went to check on the boy. Vinnie found him there later, lying outside of Robbie's door. Try as he might, he could not get Bear to come back into the bedroom. Vinnie was too tired and had too much on his mind to argue with the 130 pound dog. He let him lay. He did think it a little strange though. Vinnie returned to bed and was asleep within minutes. Bear kept vigil outside of Robbie's room, merely dosing, listening for the slightest sound that would indicate the return of the human that meant harm to his pack.

Chapter 36

A week went by and all the players were busy in their own way. Isabella beat her deadline by 48 minutes. Kate had been staying at Isabella's bedside almost 24/7. She had left only briefly for quick showers in the physician's locker room (a courtesy for one of the hospital's own) and hot coffees. Gone were her Tarrazu blends. Any caffeine laden brew would do. She had been washing off Isabella's face and telling her how beautiful she was when Isabella's eyes had opened and she had tried to speak. Kate was shocked, but immediately rang for the nurse. Within the hour, Isabella was weaned off of the ventilator and was trying to speak again. Kate was crying with relief, kissing Isabella's cheek and asking, "What is it, sweetheart?" Everyone in the room quieted down to hear Isabella's say in a husky whisper, "Mom..."

"Yes, sweetheart. I'm right here."

"You need..." Isabella struggled to speak louder.

Kate moved closer. Everyone in the room paused to hear what Isabella might say.

"You need...a breath mint" Isabella managed.

There was absolute silence for a few seconds. Then everyone laughed. Everyone, that is, except Isabella who had been completely serious and could not understand why everyone was laughing.

"And she's back," Kate said laughing through her tears. Letting the physician and nurses examine her newly revived daughter, she left to call Vinnie and Rath.

During the next few days, Isabella started to make a concerted effort at a full recovery and she was moved out of the ICU. Her injuries required that she spend at least a week in the rehabilitation department of the hospital, so Kate felt more comfortable going home in the evenings.

There was no news on Tommy. It seemed he had disappeared from the face of the earth. However, Rath and a few others were sure he was still around. Therefore, security remained with Isabella at the hospital and on Kate's house. Kate and Vinnie were taking turns spending time with Isabella in the hospital and with Robbie at home. Sometimes, in the evenings, Robbie would accompany Vinnie or Kate to the hospital to see Isabella. But Robbie was eight and full of questions, so his visits were limited to a few nights a week and about an hour each visit.

On one of the nights when Robbie and Vinnie were gone, Kate went home and sat on the back steps looking into the backyard and burying her hand in Bear's fur. Bear sat by his mistress's side, happy to have her back in the pack again and picking up Isabella's scent on her, along with a strange, unpleasant smell of sickness and death.

His mistress had not carried that smell on her for quite some time, but Bear was content in the limited knowledge that the smell did not belong to her, but merely permeated the clothing she wore. Bear stared off into the trees where the man he had bitten sat the last few nights. There was no sign of him tonight, but Bear kept watch.

Kate was lost in her thoughts; torn about the decision she had made in the hospital when it was unknown if Isabella would awaken. Suddenly, a squirrel obviously new to the neighborhood made the grave error of entering the yard scrounging for food. Bear was on the case. He dashed from Kate's side, trying to catch the quick-footed squirrel.

"Bear! Stop! Bear! No!" Kate yelled, knowing she was wasting her breath. The squirrel was able to use Robbie's jungle gym to gain access to the top of the shed and therefore, the fence. From the fence, it wound its way up one of the bigger trees to stop just above one of the branches that hung over the yard. Its furry little tail flicked with anxiety as Bear whined and barked at it from the ground.

Kate caught up to Bear and chided him, "You silly old Bear. He's escaped now. Come on back with me. Come on." Kate tried to pull the big dog away from the fence by his collar.

Bear dug his front paws into the dirt, not ready to give up the chase quite yet. As his massive head bowed down, he caught another strange smell down in the grass. He investigated in spite of Kate's insistent tugs.

"Now what?" Kate said, fearing it was the remains of the last foolish squirrel. She was usually the one to find Bear's intruders, although she would beg Vinnie to get rid of the evidence. She pulled at Bear's collar and pushed his head out of the way to see what he was sniffing. She gave a sharp intake of breath.

There on the ground, were cigarette butts recently smoked. There were only three, but they were in her yard and it was disturbing. Neither she nor Vinnie smoked. Kate did not even consider Robbie, but how in the he--

Kate looked up to the big tree where the squirrel had disappeared to and looked back to the house. She had an unobstructed view of the back of the house with its big bay window in the kitchen and six foot panel windows showcasing the family room. Her skin crawled and she looked to her furry guardian, busy once again trying to catch sight or scent of the elusive squirrel.

Vaguely, she remembered Vinnie trying to engage her in conversation one of those evenings while she sat like a zombie waiting for some sign that Isabella was waking up. He had said something about Bear killing something in the backyard...what was it he had said? Kate searched her memory.

"I think your dog made another kill last night some time," he had said.

Kate had not responded, but Vinnie had continued, "Yeah, he had some blood on his muzzle when I got home last night. Found it, really, when he was drinking his water. I looked in the backyard and under the deck, but I didn't see any 'leftovers' so to speak."

Kate did not remember if she looked at him or not, but Vinnie had ended with, "So, if you run across something, I *did* look."

Kate looked at Bear sitting on his haunches and waiting patiently with his ears straight up and his eyes focused on the tree.

"Did you take a bite out of crime, you big old Bear?" Kate said as she ruffled his fur and buried her face into the scruff of his neck. Bear took the attention, but refused to give up his spot. Kate followed his gaze up into the tree. So, Tommy had already been here. Maybe tried to get into the house? Bear got a good bite in, but Tommy had managed to escape. But he'd been back, because the cigarette butts were recent, with plain markings and still stiff on the ends.

So, the hunt was on and the hunter was not finished with Kate or her family. This knowledge helped to make up Kate's mind. She had much preparation to do. So, Tommy wanted to watch? Well, let's give him a show!

***

Tommy had spent the first part of the week trying to keep out of sight and nursing the many lacerations and puncture wounds left by Kate's stupid mutt. He could not wait to kill that son of a bitch. The first three days were hell as Tommy treated his wounds twice a day with hydrogen peroxide, bacitracin and clean bandages. If living with an abusive mother and her many boyfriends had taught him anything, it was how to care for, possibly hide and dress your own wounds.

By the third day, he could lower his right leg without the unbearable throbbing and by the third evening he could walk on it without wincing or breaking a sweat. The first thing he did was buy some ant poison as a little thank you gift for Kate's black horse. He would season some meat with it and give it to her stupid dog with glee next time he saw it.

Tommy had spent the last few nights watching the house, but that brute husband of hers was always outside with the stupid mutt. He would work on something outside letting the dog keep him company. Then he would take the Lassie mutant inside the house with him. Who lets a filthy dog in the house to live with them? These people were nuts!

Some nights, Kate was home, but she was always just coming in to take care of the dog, eat a quick sandwich or something in the kitchen. Then she would go upstairs to bed. When the little brat came home, she was taking care of him like some 'Leave it to Beaver' episode and still, the dog was always in the damn house. Tommy would sit in the tree after they had settled for the evening, trying to see a way to accomplish what he wanted.

He needed Kate alone; or at least without her husband there or the stupid guard dog. The cops out front were no worry. He avoided them every time he made his way to the tree in the backyard from the easement entrance some houses down. He could enter through the back. The deck door would be the easiest to break into. But he was not stupid enough to believe that he could take out the family dog, the protective husband, a screaming brat all in complete silence without alerting Kate or the police parked out front. Damn!

Tommy could be patient when a kill was the prize; so he watched and he waited. It was not long before he was rewarded and rewarded well.

***

Rath had spent the first few days after Isabella wound up in the ICU berating himself for a second miss so close behind the first. Why had he not even considered Kate's family? Particularly, someone young and beautiful like Isabella; who fit the profile of Tommy's other victims. Rath's infamous (but failing) gut rolled whenever he thought of Isabella suffering the fate of Tommy's other victims. He could take some comfort in knowing Isabella had been spared that kind of suffering at the hands of a maniac.

Rath did not know if Tommy merely meant to force her off the road to accost her or worse, kidnap her and take her elsewhere to violate at his leisure. Or if he had intended to force her off the road to a fiery death. Rath sincerely hoped that he had the chance to ask Tommy that question. He hoped it with all his heart. As he visited Kate that day to report the findings of the accident and looked upon Isabella, broken and pale in the hospital bed; he hoped he got the chance to ask those questions in a dark alley some night with no witnesses.

He licked his wounds over missing Isabella as a target for 24 hours. Then he and Bill Patterson sat down to brainstorm a few problem areas:

1. Where was Tommy and what would be his next move?

2. How did he know that Isabella would be on that road, that day?

3. If Kate or her family was Tommy's next target, was Isabella the warning or would he go after everyone else before Kate?

4. Was Tommy watching the house and if so, how?

None of Bill's old CI's knew anything from the street, so Tommy was not getting any help there. Richmond was a big city when you considered its many outlying areas. There was the city itself which was divided into its own special categories of The FAN, VCU district, Carytown and Churchill to name a few. Then there was the West End and East End of Richmond, the Northside and Southside and the Far West End/Short Pump area. Add in close by Mechanicsville, Ashland and Louisa and one had plenty of places to hide and not be found.

They did not think Tommy would be stupid enough to take his truck in for repairs after his bump and grind with Isabella's car, but they checked all the repair shops in Richmond anyway and the one garage near Jarrett. No one fitting Tommy's description had checked into the one hotel in Jarrett, nor any of the exit hotels along the way back to Richmond. So where was he? They did not have a clue.

On to point two in the lineup of unanswered questions. After interviewing the director that Isabella had met with and her office assistant, it was discovered that someone claiming to be one of Isabella's instructor's assistants at VCU had made a call searching for the time of Isabella's appointment. They ruled out the instructor himself by finding out that good professor was giving a lecture in front of 150 students at the time of the call and currently had no assistant.

But how did Tommy know the instructor's name and about the appointment in the first place? The office assistant stated that the caller was inquiring about a recommendation letter arriving in time for the interview. With a little more legwork, a few phone calls to the computer lab at the police station and one to the penitentiary where Tommy had done his time, a light bulb finally went off in Rath's head. They made the computer connection and began to circulate around areas of Richmond that offered WIFI services and Internet connection. They finally got lucky in two areas and placed private investigator wannabes from Patterson Investigations at both spots.

As for point three, between Bill and Rath, they covered the bases. Isabella had security at the rehab unit of the hospital; Robbie was either at school (which had been notified) or with one of his parents. The house still had police parked out front, but authorization for a parked vehicle was dwindling. It had been a week and Tommy was a no show. The department was about to change the status to low risk and have a cruiser roll by "every once in awhile". *Would Tommy know that?* wondered Rath.

Although Vinnie continued to work at his job, Kate had taken a leave of absence for the next two weeks until Isabella was home and doing well. So, in Rath's opinion, they had two weeks to find Tommy and put him away. Now, on to point four. Rath decided to check in with Kate and called her at the house. She picked up on the third ring.

"Hello?" She sounded out of breath.

"Hey, Kate, it's Rath. You okay?"

"Yeah, just trying to convince a very big dog to come inside with me when there are still squirrels in the tree," she said and laughed.

"Everything okay there? Anything out of the ordinary? Bear acting strange or barking more than usual?" Rath asked trying to sound nonchalant.

Kate thought about the bloody muzzle and the cigarettes by the back fence. "No, everything's pretty quiet here. Just trying to get back to normal and juggle getting back and forth to the hospital to see Isabella and still keep house, you know."

"How's she doing? Making progress?" Rath asked.

"She's doing great. Thanks for asking. You know, she mentioned that you came by the other day. She really enjoyed your visit. You should stop by again." Kate inwardly groaned at how awkward and meddling that sounded.

Rath smiled on the other end as he thought *Approved by Mom*. "I'll do that. So, really nothing that you can think of that's just a little off, things out of place or missing?"

A bloody muzzle and someone watching the house long enough to smoke at least three cigarettes, thought Kate. "No, nothing. You know...I was going to say. I feel bad for that police officer that has to sit outside the house. I really don't think that's necessary. It's

322

been over a week and there's been no sign or word or...anything. Besides, I have Bear here. He's certainly not going to let anyone in the house. Do you really think it's necessary to have police on the house? I mean, with Isabella while she's in the hospital and vulnerable...yes. But I really don't think we need it here, do you?"

"Well, to tell you the truth, Kate. That's going to be out of our hands here shortly, maybe even within the next couple of days. I heard this morning that they may change the police watch on your house to drive bys every few hours."

"And you know what, Rath? I'm fine with that. Vinnie and I both are. We're fine here. We have Bear, a security system complete with loud, annoying alarms...we're set. Really."

"Well, I do feel better that you're okay with it. But listen - if you suspect anything, anything at all, do not hesitate to let me know and we can bump it back to priority status, okay?"

"Okay, I appreciate that, Rath. I really do. Thanks for calling now," and the conversation was over.

For just a second, Rath's gut hinted that something was just not right about that conversation. That Kate was a little too accepting in tone and pitch of voice about pulling the police watch on her house. But he no longer trusted his gut and went with the facts instead. Tommy had gone after Isabella, probably hoping to kill her. With very little effort, he would know or already knew that Isabella was still alive. Rath's place was with Isabella and he was going to spend whatever time he could there. His gut whined that he should not entirely discount the risk to Kate, but he mentally told his gut to just shut the hell up for once.

Chapter 37

Kate sat in Isabella's room waiting for Isabella to complete her rehabilitation session for today. She flipped through a magazine without seeing the pictures. She was somewhat caught by surprise when Rath walked in.

"Oh, hello Kate. Where's Isabella?" he asked from the doorway.

Kate smiled. "She's finishing her rehab on the stairs down the hall. She should be done in about five minutes or so. Your timing is good."

Rath blushed only slightly and said, "So, how are you? Everything okay at home?"

Kate looked down for just a second and closed her magazine. When she looked back up, she was composed. "Yes, everything's good. I took a leave of absence until Isabella is out of the hospital. My predecessor is wrapping things up anyway, so I have a couple of weeks to spare. We're planning on getting away for a week after Isabella gets out, so..."

"Oh, that's right. I heard that you had gotten that big promotion. It's good of them to wait for you...or er...I mean, give you the time you need," Rath said.

"Yes, it is," Kate answered, eager for Isabella's return.

Rath was still standing in the doorway and looking down the hallway, obviously anxious for Isabella's return as well. Both were quiet for a moment. "That's a big dog you have," blurted Rath looking to fill the empty air.

"Excuse me?" said Kate.

Rath crossed his arms, looked at his shoes and started over. "Bear. He's a big dog. I went over there the other day to check out...to look for...to see the layout of your yard, you know...”

Kate nodded and Rath continued, "Anyway, I didn't even realize Bear was outside. I had been at the gate and fence for awhile, testing the handle, trying to peek over the fence, that kind of thing. Bear never made his presence known. But once I popped the latch, he came flying from under the deck all teeth and deep growling. I practically wet myself!"

Kate laughed. "That is Bear's modus operandi. He's been hunting squirrels so long in that backyard, he's learned to lie in wait under that deck and then attack when the time is right. Element of surprise and all of that, I guess."

Rath smiled and raised his eyebrows. "Well, he sure surprised the hell out of me! He is huge. I'm guessing shepherd's mixed in there somewhere, but what else?"

Kate smiled at the often asked question. "Just long-haired German shepherd. He was supposed to be Isabella's dog about four years ago. She begged and begged her dad for one and he finally took her out to some place in the country to pick one out. We had a look at the parents and the father was a horse! But, of course, the puppies were just little bundles of black fur and just as cute as they could be. Isabella picked out Bear and we brought him home," Kate continued, "The whole time she and Vinnie are 'oohing' and 'ahhing' about how Bear looks like a little black bear cub and 'isn't he so cuuuute', I'm looking at his paws thinking 'Oh dear Lord'. Turns out I was right. The vet said possibly 110-115 pounds full grown. He's right at 130."

Rath quietly whistled. "Like I said, big dog. I guess too big for Isabella to have in her apartment, huh?"

Kate smiled and said, "Rath, you obviously don't have kids. Kids don't get pets they will take care of. Kids convince their parents to get pets to take care of. Once Isabella started dating in high school and Bear required daily walks and exercise parks...he became my dog. You know, it's funny. At the vet, they still have Bear listed as belonging to Isabella, but she has never paid one vet bill. But that's parenthood. Beware!"

Kate looked up to see that Rath had probably not caught the last few sentences. His eyes were trained on who could only be Isabella. His face lit up, transforming it into that of a man invested in the well-being and happiness of the woman in his company. Kate smiled inwardly, *not bad, Isabella, not bad at all.*

Isabella was slightly breathless as she came limping into the room, followed closely by a physical therapist. Snug around her waist was the neon green gait belt held loosely by the therapist and which Kate knew her daughter could not stand. As if reading her mind, Isabella said, "I just wish you'd get one of these things in Gucci or Juicy Couture. 'Course then it might clash with the fashion absent warm-up pants my mom brought me to wear. Oh hi, Mom."

Kate gave her smart-mouthed daughter a scrunched up smirk and stuck out her tongue. It felt good to banter with Isabella again. So good, it made Kate's heart ache to think of what might have been.

"Hey Rath!" Isabella said, turning her attention to Rath. She said it in such a way that Kate knew Isabella returned Rath's feelings with interest. Isabella's bruises were taking on the green-yellow of age and much of the swelling had gone down. The lacerations and scratches were not the angry red of before, but still visible. But none of these things took away from the glow Isabella had as she looked at Rath.

"Looking good there, good-looking," Rath said, then quickly shot a wary glance at Kate. Kate smiled and started to gather up her purse and jacket.

"Mom? Where are you going?" Isabella said half-heartedly.

"You know me," joked Kate. "I just have to see you and know you are okay before I can get on with my day."

Kate waited until Isabella was seated and then gave her a quick hug and smooch on her least affected cheek. "No, really, honey. I planned on visiting with you for a few minutes, but just realized I need to take care of one thing for tonight. And since Rath's here, well...you don't mind if I go ahead and just take care of that do you?"

Isabella looked only slightly disappointed, but smiled and said, "No, I'm good. The doctor said I might get to go home by Monday, maybe even Sunday!"

Kate's heart jumped and her mind fiercely whispered *that's less than a week! You need to get busy. You have to go...now!* But she smiled and said, "Honey, that's wonderful! Your father and Robbie will be so excited. Well, let me go and get things ready for your big return."

She turned to leave as Isabella warned, "Okay, Mom, but you know that I'm not staying long with you and Dad, right? I mean, as long as it takes to get back on my feet, but I'm not moving back in."

Ah, it was good to know that the accident had not damaged her daughter's stubborn streak at all, thought Kate. "I know, honey. It's temporary. God bless us all," she said as she rolled her eyes on the last statement.

Rath laughed amidst Isabella's "Mom!"

With that, Kate gave a final wave and left hearing Isabella ask Rath, "So what did you and my mother talk about?"

"Your dog," Rath answered

"My dog?" Isabella questioned.

Kate smiled to herself as she put on her jacket while walking toward the elevator, *the state rests, Your Honor.*

Back in Isabella's room, Rath was smiling himself at Isabella's puzzled look and the irony it presented after his conversation with Kate. However, part of his mind was stuck on a puzzle of its own. He caught the fact that Kate seemed less than thrilled at Isabella's announcement that she may be able to leave as early as this weekend. He wondered what would keep Kate from being overjoyed at such news. But Isabella received his full attention when she said, "So, are you ever going to kiss me or what?" After that statement, his mind had trouble focusing on anything else.

Kate was back in her car, sitting in the hospital parking lot. She dialed Vinnie's cell phone and waited for him to answer.

"Hey, hot stuff," was Vinnie's customary answer for her call.

"Hey back at ya. How's your day going?" Kate asked.

"Pretty good. How about yours? How's our little girl?"

"Well, that's why I called. I'm about to make your day. Isabella said that the doctors told her that she might get to go home at the end of the week, first of next week. Maybe even by Sunday. I spoke to her nurse and it's confirmed. She just has to negotiate the steps...up and down...and walk one full lap around the unit and she's out."

"Wow! That's great! Knowing our Izzie, she'll take care of that before lunch tomorrow. And you're right, that did make my day, baby."

Kate tried to sound casual, "Listen, I was thinking. Instead of spending the week at home when she gets out...how about we spend her first week out at the beach house?"

"It's a good idea, it's just....with work....I'm not sure..." Vinnie hedged.

"That's just it, Vinnie. We all just drop everything and spend the week together away from all of this. Let her recuperate in peace with her family around her. Couldn't we all try to make this happen for her?"

Kate had played her final card and waited. She could hear people talking in the background and knew that Vinnie was trying to figure a way to do it. She gave him the time he needed.

"Hell, we'll work it out. Hell, yes! Let's do it. What about Robbie and school, though?" Vinnie asked.

Kate had anticipated the question. "Well, spring break starts the middle of next week anyway. We just write a note to the school explaining that Robbie will need the first few days of the week off as well. Everyone does it every once in awhile. We may not be going to Disneyland or anything, but we need the week. I don't see where it would be a problem."

Vinnie agreed and Kate wished him a good day. She started the car and left the radio off as she drove home. She had a great deal of planning to do and she did not need the distraction.

***

Tommy bought himself a pound of ground beef on sale and laced it with the ant poison. He wrapped it up in newspaper and tossed it in the seat of the Jeep Cherokee he had acquired, albeit illegally. He had noted the Jeep Cherokee sitting in the corner of a Wal-Mart parking lot for sale for the past week. He knew he needed to dump the truck. Last night, he had waited until just after 2:00 a.m., switched plates on the vehicles and had driven off the lot with the Jeep.

It was not a bad rig, despite the busted out back passenger window; now remedied with plastic and duct tape. The wires hanging down from the dash might be considered an eyesore, but otherwise the SUV was clean of all debris; one of the advantages of stealing a car for sale. The smell of the ground beef reminded him of how hungry he was and he stopped in at a drive-thru for a burger. He parked in another busy mall parking lot and took his time eating his fast food dinner.

He figured he had about two days before the Jeep was reported stolen, give or take twelve hours. Then he figured the amount of time before all the players realized it was **he** who stole the Jeep. He hoped to accomplish what he needed to before that time, but he had a few obstacles in his way. He turned these over in his head as he mechanically chewed on his burger and fries.

Kate might as well be in a castle surrounded by a moat for all the protection she had around her: a cop sitting out front, a husband and kid in the house and that damn dog. He figured the mutt was not trained to use a toilet and had to be let out to shit sometime. He wanted to present the dog with his special gift; maybe tonight. That would take care of the dog.

Tommy's eyes squinted in thought. What to do about hubby? The kid was no big deal. Tommy had gotten a few good looks at him from his earlier expeditions. He was just a little guy. Tommy could snap his neck like a twig, no worries there. But the husband? That was a horse of different color now wasn't it? He'd have to give that some more thought. As for the police officer parked out front, Tommy was unconcerned. The overpaid bodyguard had not noticed him before and Tommy doubted he ever would. Since he entered the easement at the end of the block, he was never seen near Kate's house.

Tommy's straw gave the unmistakable sound of "no soda left" and Tommy threw it out of the window, along with the other trash left over from his hurried meal. It would be dark soon and he had plans this evening. He patted the lump of poisoned meat beside him and started the Jeep. He knew it was a lot to ask, but he hoped he would be able to see the poison take effect. To see the monster that had attacked him foam at the mouth while in the midst of death throes? Man! That would just rock!

Chapter 38

By the time Kate picked up Robbie and made it home, it was almost 4:30 in the afternoon. She sent Robbie up to his room to work on his computer lesson on multiplication. She found Bear outside digging in the backyard by the fence. He was digging where she had spotted the cigarettes the first time.

"Bear, what are you doing? Stop it," she said as she pulled him away from the area. The freshly pawed up ground showed rich, black dirt; but no cigarette butts. Well that was a good thing. Maybe Tommy had not been around of late. Kate had been keeping Bear inside during the evening hours with the family because she wanted Tommy to feel free to come around. Either he had not been there the last few nights, had given up smoking or...

"Bear, you aren't eating these cigarettes, are you?" Kate worried. As a puppy, Bear was notorious for eating any and everything. Many of the early visits to the vet had been to make sure that whatever Bear had ingested would either not kill him or would eventually "pass through". The vet had explained that some of that was just being a puppy. But some of it was because Bear was frustrated or lonely and he was being destructive as a means of acting out. But would he actually eat cigarette butts?

Kate led Bear towards the house. "Come on you. Until this thing is over, you can do your business in the front yard and stay in the house with us."

At the recognizable word of "house", Bear followed his mistress willingly, licking the tobacco from his teeth and swallowing it. He had been taking the droppings from the man and devouring them for three days now. The man was never there, but he always left his droppings. Now there were none. The man who would do harm's scent markers were erased.

Kate let Bear find Robbie as she set the stage for the night. The kitchen was one of her favorite rooms in the house. It and the bathroom were the only rooms in the house that guaranteed solitude when she occupied them. Sometimes, Isabella would come into the kitchen to debate a rule or to negotiate when she had lived at home. But Kate discovered long ago that the simple phrase, "Look, as long as you're standing there, why don't you help me out?" was akin to "Abracadabra! Now you see her, now you don't".

The kitchen was perfected throughout the years of their occupancy and was set up for the chef that Kate aspired to be. A huge four paneled window across the room from the oven let in plenty of natural light in the morning and throughout the day. Kate had taken advantage of that and lined the sills and available floor space with pots filled with kitchen herbs and other indoor plants. The window looked out into the backyard and when sitting at the cafe table in front of it, one could see the backyard in its entirety. The reverse was also true. When in the backyard, one had a unobstructed view of what was going on in the kitchen; particularly at night when the lights were on. Kate was sure the view from the tree directly across from the window some fifteen yards away was spectacular at night.

Kate began to move the plants out from in front of the window onto the ledge surrounding the deck. She moved the silk flower arrangement normally gracing the cafe table and sat it atop the microwave. It didn't really fit there, but it was only temporary. The cafe table now looked bare, so she moved a butter dish and salt and pepper shakers onto it. Those were the only changes she made to that area. She didn't want to make it too obvious.

Next, she set about moving things around on the chef's block in front of the stove. She did not want anything to obstruct the view of her. She stole a glance outside to see that the sun was starting to dip behind the tree line. She turned on the kitchen lights and stepped outside to shake out the tablecloth. As she shook, she looked at the stage she had created and was satisfied. Feeling just a little nervous with her back to the trees, she quickly headed back into the house.

She checked in with Robbie and found him watching a Disney Channel movie and was assured that he was occupied for the next hour or so. One final preparation: Kate placed a call.

"Hey, hot stuff," Vinnie answered.

"Hey back at ya. Have you left work yet?" Kate asked, pulling out her iPod and searching for the ear buds.

"Nope. Probably leaving in a half hour, hour at the most. Why? Miss me?" Vinnie joked.

"Always," Kate smiled in spite of her preoccupation of searching. "I was wondering if you could stop by the store on your way home."

"Uh, sure. What am I getting? Wait...do I need to write this down?"

"No. Uh...we're out of milk," Kate said quickly grabbing the milk container from the fridge and dumping out what was left.

"Oh, okay. No problem, Mamacita. I'll call you before I leave here."

"No. I mean, you don't have to do that. I don't need it for tonight's dinner. I just want to have it tomorrow for Robbie's cereal. I'll see you when you get home," Kate said, looking out of the window into the blackness beyond.

"Okay, babe. See you soon," Vinnie said as he rung off.

Kate pulled out the ingredients she would need for dinner. As she did this she searched for the song she wanted. Quickly her right thumb pressed the forward button again and again. She normally listened to music when she cooked and had quite an eclectic taste. With over 200 songs on the iPod on a "Now we're cooking" playlist, the styles ranged from Michael Buble to Slipknot. If it was an emotional ballad, a hard driven metal song with poetic lyrics or the unmistakable talent of Jimi Hendrix; Kate loved the variety and often kept her iPod on shuffle to chase away any semblance of monotony. However, tonight, that very trait was making it extremely difficult to find the song she wanted. Finally, she ran across it and pressed pause.

She walked over to the cafe table and grabbed the butter dish, checking the level of darkness outside. It was full night now and Kate had no way of knowing whether Tommy was out there or not. She took her place in front of the stove, with her back to the window. It was time to begin.

Kate placed a skillet on the oven and tried to pretend like this was any other night and she was just dancing around making the evening meal. But as Korn's "Hold On" began to play, Kate moved stiffly at first thinking of whom she was dancing for. As the song played on and the lyrics began to melt into her mind, she began to think of Emily, Sandra and Isabella. She thought about the monsters she had faced in her lifetime and ready she was to do battle. As she let the music feed the resolve within her and leak out through her movements, she hoped that Tommy was watching. She hoped he was getting her message loud and clear: "Here I am. Come and get me."

***

Tommy made his way to the tree but stood behind the fence for a minute, listening for the sounds of the monster on the other side. He heard nothing, so he unwrapped the hamburger and held it close to the fence. No padded footsteps approached the fence investigating the intoxicating smell of raw meat. No frantic, hungry sniffing came from the other side. Damn! They had the dog inside again tonight. Who in their right mind kept any animal, but especially a dog that size, in the house? And they called old Tommy boy psychotic; go figure.

Tommy wrapped the meat up and stuffed it inside his shirt to free up his hands for the climb up the tree. He was surprised to see his target already at the stove and there was something different about the kitchen. *Why was she just standing there?* She had her back to him and she was just...*wait! What was she doing? Dancing?* She swayed back and forth; head forward, as if in a trance. *What the hell?*

Tommy had lit a cigarette in anticipation of a boring stakeout, gleaning a way in, a window of opportunity, a tell of habits. He was shocked to see the show unfolding before him. Tommy did not know what song she was listening to or what chord it was striking in her, but he wanted that song. Now, she bounced her shoulders to the left, throwing those long curls to the side as she looked over her right shoulder with attitude. *Oh yeah...talk to me sweetheart.*

Dinner preparations seen laid out on the chef's block before seemed forgotten as she put on a show just for him - and any other neighbors who happened to be looking in her direction. Suddenly, the music seemed to sweep her away as she popped her hips and swung that mane of curls back and forth, like a woman in the throes of passion (or struggling against a chord around her neck). For the first time in a couple of weeks, Tommy got a chub on.

Too soon the song was obviously over, because she yanked the ear buds out of her ears and stood breathing hard, arms straight, and hands planted on the stove in front of her. In the same stance as when she had begun. If she had been on stage, Tommy may have applauded; or at least thrown her a couple of ones to stuff down her G-string. *Damn! That was fine*, thought Tommy as he leaned back to finish the cigarette that had just about burned down on its own; forgotten.

He was sitting there when hubby walked in carrying a gallon of milk. He just about gagged when they smooched and the kid came into the kitchen, running into Daddy's arms. *Just like freaking' Ozzie and Harriet*, he thought. *Give me a damn break!* Sure enough, the mutant of Lassie showed up and they were all one big happy family.

He left about an hour later, not having any more answers than before. The damn mutt still lived, safe and sound indoors with the Cleaver family. He still had no idea how he was going to deal with the husband. But the trip had been worthwhile for the show alone.

And he did learn one thing new, after all. Old Kate had some whore in her yet and he was going to insist that she show him a little of that again before he killed her. Maybe he'd use the kid to convince her to cooperate. As Tommy walked back to where he had left the Jeep, his mind chewed on the dilemma of completing his mission, like a dog with a bone.

Whatever he did, he would have to do it soon. Tommy knew that his time was running out. He was wearing his welcome thin in his hometown of Richmond. He had left his calling card at the stripper's - probably not the smartest move. He had beaten the shit out of that lying lawyer and left her for dead - which had been the highlight of his getting out so far and who he now knew she had died later in the hospital...boo hoo. And he had not been able to kill Kate's daughter - BIG disappointment there - but the gimp was still in rehab, so maybe permanently damaged; fingers crossed. He was on his second vehicle and stolen at that. Yeah, tick tock, baby, tick tock. He needed a plan and he needed it quick.

**

Kate lay listening to Vinnie's snores and thinking about finalizing her plan tomorrow. She had to lay it out just right. She had spent the last few days trying to decide how to control the exact night of Tommy's attack. She went over the plan again and again, looking for any loopholes and what ifs. Her mind finally succumbed to the rhythmic pattern of Vinnie's breathing and the ticking of the alarm clock across the room.

In Robbie's room, Bear burped up a bit of nicotine laced tobacco. He licked his massive chops and laid his muzzle back upon his big paws content in the doggie knowledge that he had effectively removed all scent markers of the one who would do harm. And tomorrow, if there were more markers there, he would eat them again. Within minutes, the gentle giant was asleep as well. All was quiet in the Tuscadero house. Like the lull before the storm.

Chapter 39

The weekend was coming and everyone was busy making preparations. Robbie could hardly contain his excitement. Izzie was coming home from the hospital and she was going to be staying at his house for awhile. He had been to see Izzie twice in the hospital. Both times, she had looked like she did not feel good, but her smile for him was still Izzie's smile. He could not wait until she returned home and he could see her all the time; like it used to be before she went to college. He was going to be the very best helper and make things so good for Izzie that she would never want to leave again. Knowing that Izzie was going to be arriving that weekend, Robbie made a sweep of the house every day that week making sure that nothing would make Izzie sad or get in her way.

Thursday afternoon, he entered Tizzies' room where his big sister still sometimes stayed when spending the night over. All her favorite things were still there. Robbie had been in her room more since his big sister had vacated the house. Therefore, he just took a quick look and was about to leave when he saw Izzies' "sordity" cricket paddle with the funny-looking, purple letters on it. *Uh-oh*, thought Robbie *that will make her think of school and maybe make her want to leave.* He knew he had to hide it, but where? He did not want his mother or father finding it and returning it to Izzie's room. His mother was always cleaning his room, so that was not an option. He could hear her downstairs, but he took a chance anyway.

As quietly as he could, he snuck down the staircase and crept silently toward the seldom-used coat closet with the water heater in it under the stairs. His intention was to go deep beneath the stairs and hide the paddle there, but he could hear his mother coming. The paddle was half as long as he was and quite heavy. He hid it just inside the door and laid it against the wall. He hurriedly moved one of his mother's winter coats against the way in an attempt to cover it. He could still see the bottom of it, but he was running out of time. He was trying to shut the door when his mother rounded the corner.

"Oh! Geez, Robbie, you scared me!" said Kate with a laugh. "What are you doing?"

"Noffin," said Robbie.

Kate smiled and squinted at him. "Were you going to hide in the closet and surprise me?"

Robbie's eyebrows went up with the unexpected gift of an alibi and said, "Yeah, I was going to supize you, Mom."

"You stinka!" Kate laughed and grabbed him in a hug. Robbie took the second gift of her laughter and attention. Lately, his mother had been quiet and looked scared. It was good to see her smile again.

"Love you, Mom," Robbie said, feeling her need for the words.

"Awww, love you too, buddy," Kate said and hugged him tighter.

" 'kay," said Robbie and wiggled out of the hug. He wanted to make another sweep before dinner.

As his feet sounded on the stairs, the smile was wiped from Kate's face like words drawn in sand by high tide. It was replaced first by the worried lines that rented space on her forehead, then lines of determination. Endgame was near, she thought and it was time to tap the first domino.

***

Rath was dividing his time between visiting Isabella after 4:00 p.m. when all the rehabilitation was done and doing his best to locate the whereabouts of Tommy. Rath had bet that Tommy would be switching cars or at least dumping the truck after swapping paint with Isabella's car. His daily monitoring of abandoned or stolen vehicles in the area finally paid off. A Jeep, left advertised for sale in a mall parking lot, had been reported stolen. A truck matching the one Tommy had been driving was found in the same mall parking lot, but on the other side of the mall itself. There was no doubt in Rath's mind that Tommy had taken the Jeep. He had put out an all point's bulletin on the make, model and year of the Jeep, along with a photo of Tommy. Tommy was listed as armed and dangerous and to be approached with extreme caution.

Rath figured that Tommy was living out of his car. Therefore, finding him in the city and surrounding areas of a place as big as Richmond made looking for a needle in a haystack child's play. Rath had to outsmart, outguess and place himself two steps ahead of Tommy. It pissed him off to no end that the police protection had been removed from Kate's house even after the proof surfaced

Tommy was "most likely" still in town. It was not definitive and "besides, the one supposedly needing protection doesn't want it" said his superiors.

Why would Kate turn down police protection on the house? Sure, she had that dog and a man living there. But, Tommy was a psychopath. Psychopaths did not play fair, they did not feel remorse and when it came to accomplishing what they wanted, all bets were off. If Tommy wanted to get to Kate, he would have no problem taking out Vinnie and killing Robbie in front of her. Then he could kill her at his leisure. And if he decided to bring a gun to the party, Bear would not stand a chance. Of course, it would have to be a big gun. Rath figured that Kate fell into the same trap many people did. Most people assumed that if they locked their doors at night, did not open the door for any strangers and stayed together, everything would be fine. But rules and normalcy were for those who obeyed the law; certainly not for psychopaths.

As the week dragged on, Rath continued to work with Bill Patterson in trying to find their particular needle in the haystack. So far, much of their brainstorming, although creative, had been non-productive.

"What we need to do," suggested Bill, "is to think like Tommy. They taught you that, right? You want to catch a criminal; you got to think like one. So, let's run it down. He does not have anyone he can stay with and he best not check into a hotel. He's crazy, but he ain't stupid. He knows we're looking for him. He's going to lay low. So, where's he holing up?"

"I figure he's sleeping, eating and living out of his car. He can park in any of these 24 hour parking lots and not be noticed - especially if he rotates spots," Rath answered.

"Right and if he's doing that, there's not enough people to cruise those places looking for him. There's an APB on the car, so there's that. But, Tommy's going to know that too. So, maybe he's hiding in plain sight in some neighborhood," Bill offered.

"Okay. But it's got to be like an apartment complex or somewhere people don't really pay attention to each other and where the Jeep will fit in," Rath added.

Bill snorted and said, "Well, that narrows it down. You're right based on the fact that neighborhoods are not normally patrolled regularly unless they are designated as problem areas, but that leaves a lot of neighborhoods unattended."

They were both silent a minute drinking in the overwhelming nature of what they were dealing with. They were having this brainstorming session in Bill's office. Rath picked up the Rubik's cube sitting on Bill's desk and began to play with it. He had one just like it when he was about eight years old. He used to know how to solve it, but it too many years had passed.

Bill seemed to read his mind and said, "Situations like this are like that Rubik's cube there. There's a secret to solving it, you just have to figure out what it is. Okay, he knows how to hide. Let's move on. What's he after? Why is he still here?"

"Kate," answered Rath without stopping what he was doing on the Rubik's cube.

"Right. And his M.O. is stalking or casing his targets first, right?" Bill prompted.

"That's what it was before, but the stripper kind of blows that pattern," Rath said, setting the Rubik's cube back on Bill's desk.

"I still think that was just a release valve kind of thing," said Bill. "I think he couldn't help himself. It had been too long and he just couldn't wait it out. But look at Sandra and Isabella. That took planning. He knew Sandra's routine and how to get into that house. He knew Isabella was going to that interview. His normal pattern is to study his targets and plan his attack."

"Okay...let's say he's doing that. But with Kate? We thought that and he went after Isabella. Maybe it's Vinnie or...God forbid, Robbie," Rath was letting exasperation leak into his voice.

Bill picked up the Rubik's cube and began to twist and turn it in his hands without really looking at it. "I think the opportunity with Isabella just presented itself. I think if Tommy had the time, he would love to completely destroy Kate's world before destroying her. I'm thinking like him here, understand. But, time's running out and Tommy is anything but stupid. He should be gone, but I think he wants to kill Kate and he ain't leaving 'till that's done."

Rath looked on with a sardonic grin as Bill solved the Rubik's cube and placed it carefully back on the desk and said, "The secret to

Tommy is Kate. We have to figure out how he is casing her, because I believe he's doing that right now. We have to figure out how he's planning on removing the barriers in his way and more importantly, what his timetable is. Because, buddy, he's got one. I can guaran-damn-tee you that. What we have to figure out, in time, is when he's going after Kate and be there to stop it."

Rath looked at Bill incredulously. "Are you saying, wait it out and use Kate and her family as bait?!"

"Hell, no!" Bill showed anger for the first time. "That woman's been nothing but a friend to me. I'm saying that we are coming in late to this game, Rath. It's gonna be soon. I can feel it and it's keeping me up nights."

Rath took a deep breath and blew it out loudly. He shook his head. Then he had an idea. "What if he's hiding in plain sight in her neighborhood? What if he doesn't have far to go to take a peek now and then?"

"We've already had cars cruise the neighborhood. No car fitting his description ever showed on the radar. But I could put another couple of kids on it and branch out a bit - cruise every street in that neighborhood and those neighborhoods closest to it," Bill suggested.

Rath knew Bill's "kids" were private detectives working under Bill, fresh out of school and eager for even grunt work. They both agreed that this was the best they could do. The "kids" would be given word to report any and all Jeeps fitting the description of the one stolen.

"Meanwhile," said Rath, rising to leave, "I'm going to stick close to Isabella. I'm still not completely convinced he won't try to finish what he started there."

"Well, I don't think he'll waste time or effort trying to get to her in a hospital. It's too public a venue for his taste of drawing the kill out. But, you go on and keep that pretty girl company," Bill said and winked at Rath.

Rath blushed to his chagrin, and walked out into the cool breezes of Thursday's beginning dusk. He checked his watch and quickened his step. It would take him about 20 minutes to get to the hospital from Bill's and he did not want to keep Isabella waiting.

***

Tommy spent the week watching Kate and getting her routine down. Much of her early evening varied, but the show was always there during the dinner preparation. Some were better than others, but always worth the wait. Tommy never missed the dinner preparation scene. After dinner, the woman was a creature of habit. In fact, she was a bit of a night owl.

The kid went to bed around 8:30, by the light dousing in his bedroom window. A couple of nights, the kid had used some type of moving light source, probably a flashlight, to goof off in his room until almost 9:30. But, he was probably asleep by 10:00.

Kate and Vinnie usually watched TV until about 9:30 - 10:00. Then Vinnie went upstairs to bed. Kate always did the same thing once her blue-balled husband had left. She switched seats to sit on the couch in front of the deck windows (better view?) and stayed there until 11:00 or midnight. Then, she'd get up, cut off the TV and go to bed. She never turned on the light (such a considerate bitch) and was probably asleep within minutes. Poor Vinnie. With a schedule like that, the poor bastard probably never got laid anymore. *Welcome to married life, Vinnie my man,* Tommy thought as he lit another cigarette even as the last smoldered on the ground below.

The dog never got let out in the backyard anymore and Tommy had stopped bringing the poisoned meat. Maybe he was out only during the day when everybody was at work, but Tommy would be damned if he was coming back out here in broad daylight now. *Tick tock,* he thought, *tick fricking tock.*

Tommy was beginning to wonder if he should just break down and get a gun. He did not believe in them because guns ended things a little too quickly for Tommy's liking. But he was beginning to think that he was just going to have to resign himself to just taking out the Tuscadero clan in one quick swoop. He hated to deny himself the pleasure of watching Kate beg for her life, but perhaps it could not be helped. He'd mull it over one more night, for the sake of the hunt, he decided. However, if nothing changed by the weekend, his choice would be made for him.

Tommy continued to watch until Kate finished watching her TV programs for the night and went upstairs with that stupid mutt right at her heels. He took a final drag off of his last cigarette of the night and let it drop. Sleep tight, bitch, I'm not the only one running short of time.

Chapter 40

Kate was packing Vinnie's suitcase for him while he questioned the rationale of going ahead to the beach house without her. It was Friday and the late afternoon sunlight spilled in through the bedroom window picking up the burnished copper strands in Kate's hair as she neatly placed tee-shirts, underwear and socks in Vinnie's bag.

"What's a couple of days, babe? You trying to get rid of me or something?" Vinnie joked.

Kate looked up sharply and said, "What? No!" Then her shoulders relaxed and she smiled stiffly. "Of course not, silly. It's just there is no guarantee that Isabella is going to be released on Sunday. I mean, I know how these things work. It's a weekend. The rounding doctor will be an on call physician. He or she may not feel comfortable discharging her and will most likely bounce it back to her regular doctor for Monday. I don't think we all need to wait for her to be discharged. You go on to the beach with Robbie. Izzie and I will join you Sunday evening or Monday afternoon. I'm thinking more about Robbie, really."

"Is that right?" Vinnie squinted at her. His wife had been wound a little too tight lately. He knew it was a lot on her with Izzie being in the hospital, worrying about her new position at work and dealing with Robbie's rambunctiousness. But she was in battle mode. Vinnie had been married long enough to Kate to recognize the symptoms. What he could not figure out was where the battle was. She continued to insist that everything was "fine" whenever he asked and bristled with any probing. He had also been married long enough to know when to push and when to just lay back and monitor the situation.

"Katie, stop for a minute," Vinnie said and added, "Baby, please. Just for a minute."

Kate breathed out a frustrated sigh, but stopped what she was doing and looked at Vinnie.

"Come here," Vinnie said.

Kate walked over to where he was sitting and stood in front of him. Vinnie slowly ran his rough hand down her exposed arm and said, "What's wrong, Katie? What are you not telling me? Let me help, babe."

Kate gave an exasperated moan and went to turn away, but Vinnie caught her by her wrist and said, "Stop, Katie. Talk to me a minute. Stop shutting me out."

Instead of looking at him, Kate pulled Vinnie's head to her chest and invited him in for a hug. She ran her fingers through his hair and kissed the top of his head. Without releasing him, she said, "I've just got a lot on my plate right now, honey. It's nothing big, just me dealing with it all. I need these couple of days to myself. I know that sounds selfish, but there it is. I need just a couple of days to do nothing but sleep in, clean a little, visit Izzie and eat a peanut butter and jelly sandwich when I get hungry. That probably sounds mean, but that's it."

Vinnie hugged her tighter for a few seconds, then released her. "That doesn't sound mean, babe. I understand. It's been a rough couple of weeks."

He stood up and caressed the side of her face, brushing back those soft waves to slip his hand behind her neck. He pulled her forward and tried to kiss away the frown lines there on her forehead. Then, he lightly brushed the lips that had just lied to him.

"Okay, you got yourself a deal. I'll take the Robster and we'll head to the beach tomorrow morning. You and Izzie join us as soon as you can. Then we can all be together and start putting this behind us," he finished and gave her another kiss to seal the deal.

As he walked away, she began to finish packing the suitcase left unattended on the bed. He watched the stiffness return to her shoulders and the slightest jabbing motion as she placed each piece. She was angry, but at what or whom? Once he got her on the beach, they would talk. Out on the beach, sitting by the fire pit, he would get the truth from her.

Maybe it was that she would never see justice done regarding Tommy King. When she mentioned that the police protection was no longer necessary because everyone thought Tommy had moved on, he was relieved. But she had lost a good friend to that son of a bitch and had almost lost her daughter. He knew his wife; she was probably pissed at not being able to spit in the bastard's face. As for himself, he was glad that Tommy had moved on. If not, he would have been the one going to jail for killing the little shit for daring to harm a hair on his daughter's head.

As he headed down the stairs to pick up Robbie from Little League practice, he consoled himself with visions of stability returned. Once they all got to the beach, he thought, they could get busy with the process of healing as a family. As he drove down the road, he realized something else that was bothering him.

When Sandra had died, he had held Kate while she sobbed out her broken heart. They had stood in the living room, pretending to dance while he held her to him trying to soak up some of the pain for her. However, while Isabella lay clinging tenuously to life in the ICU, Kate had not shed a tear. At first, she had appeared shell shocked. Then she was enraged once they all realized what had happened. But so far, in the weeks that followed, she had not shed one tear. His wife was one tough cookie, but when the dust settled after any traumatic event, she crumbled...every time. This thought tickled his mind until he saw the sign for the Little League field and Robbie scuffling in the dirt with another boy just to the right of that sign. Then the bothersome thought about Kate was gone. Just like that.

He threw his truck into park and hurried over to the scuffling boys about the same time the coach figured out what the crowd gathering around the ball field sign was all about. They reached the two boys at the same time; Vinnie pulling Robbie away, leaving the coach to handle the other boy. Robbie seemed shocked to see his father there and slightly chagrined at being caught. But he was still angry and shooting darts at the other boy.

Vinnie was surprised to see Robbie fighting at all, but especially with Edward. Edward lived diagonally behind them across the easement and Robbie and he played together often. They were not the best of friends, but friends of convenience. They were both the same age and lived so close to one another. There was a bit of animosity there because Edward refused to acknowledge Robbie in school, but they were usually friendly enough in the neighborhood.

In Little League, where team camaraderie and sportsmanship was encouraged, there was usually little room for altercations. Both Vinnie and the coach were shocked by the outburst.

"What is going on here, boys?" asked the coach.

"He hit me!" spurted Edward, sporting a bloody nose for proof.

"Robbie! Did you hit Edward?" Vinnie asked Robbie gruffly.

"Yeah, but...he say sumpin bad 'bout mom!" Robbie looked accusingly at Edward.

"Did not!" yelled Edward.

"Uh huh!" yelled back Robbie.

"I'm going to ask you one time to tell me what you said about Robbie's mom and then I'm going to ask those who witnessed it. I hope you have enough sense to tell me the truth, son," said Coach Waterson.

"All I said was..." Edward hesitated, no doubt trying to think of the best way to say what had started this. "What I said was I saw

Robbie's mom dancing like a stripper the other night. 'Cuz she was!"

Coach Waterson looked to Vinnie's shocked expression and back to Edward. "Why in the world would you say such a thing? What in the world are you talking about?"

Robbie looked to his father to see if he was just as outraged as himself and waited for Edward to repeat exactly what he had said. What Edward had actually said was that Robbie's mom had been "dancing around like a slut."

"Because," started Edward, "the other night I was taking out the trash at my house and I saw Robbie's mom dancing around in her kitchen. We can see into Robbie's kitchen window from my backyard. Not real good, but good enough to see that she was dancing around like... those strippers on TV"

Robbie started to go after him again, but Vinnie's strong hands held him in check.

"Edward, that is NOT a very nice thing to say about anyone, but particularly someone else's mother. Now, I think you owe Robbie an apology for saying something like that," Coach Waterson suggested.

"But, I'm not the only one that thinks so..." Edward started, thinking of the man sitting in a tree that night watching Robbie's mother. Edward had not realized he was there until he smelled cigarette smoke and realized there was someone sitting in the tree watching Mrs. Tuscadero. It had creeped him out a little bit and he had quietly crept back inside. He had been about to tell Robbie about the creepy man when Robbie had sucker-punched him. But once again, he was not allowed to finish his sentence.

"Edward! That's enough of that! You need to apologize to Robbie right now," Coach Waterson said again.

"Sorry," Edward said, holding a handkerchief to his nose supplied by Robbie's father.

"Robbie, there is nothing gained by violence, son. You need to apologize to Edward for hitting him," Vinnie prompted Robbie.

"Dad..." Robbie started, but stopped when he saw his father's look. Turning to Edward, who was never going to be his friend again, he said, "Sowwy."

"Okay, I think both of you boys need to go on home and come back next week with a brand new attitude," Coach Waterson said.

Vinnie reminded Coach Waterson that his family would be at the beach the following week as the boys continued to glare at each other. Vinnie guided Robbie to the truck, secretly pleased that Robbie had stood up for his mother. Vinnie knew that Kate sometimes danced around the kitchen when she was making dinner. Perhaps he should let her know to take it down a notch. He stifled a chuckle at the thought of Kate's expression when she heard about this chain of events.

Edward waited for his mother to show up, holding the handkerchief against his nose, although the bleeding had all but stopped. *Stupid*

Robbie, he thought, *I hate his retarded guts, sucker-punching me like that in front of everybody. I saw what I saw. I was going to tell somebody about the creepy guy but not now. I hope Robbie sees the creepy guy sitting in that tree one night and pisses himself.* That thought made Edward feel a little better - not much, but a little.

Chapter 41

Kate was standing in the exam room of vet Doc Tyler with a panting Bear. She had brought Bear in on a ruse and she was having trouble dealing with the guilt. She could not bring herself to look into Bear's big, brown eyes because she knew he was wondering why she was punishing him.

She had brought Bear in without an appointment, which was never a problem with Doc Tyler. Normally, Bear only saw the vet about twice a year for annual vaccinations and other incidentals. Since Bear had outgrown his puppy antics, he had settled into one big teddy bear that rarely got into trouble or danger.

However, this morning, Kate had lied and stated that Bear had been vomiting and having diarrhea for the past few days. As she had told the vet technician who had checked them in and performed all the preliminary work, she did not know what could have possibly caused the problem. She had portrayed the necessary worry and loving concern for the technician and now waited for Doc Tyler to come in.

Bear whined and nuzzled her hand. Without looking at him, she absently stroked his massive, furry head. In an effort not to look into Bear's anxious face, she had been looking around the room taking in every nuance of it. In doing so, her eyes had fallen on what could have been a beacon in a hopeless situation. Now, she was trying to work up the courage to go through with the opportunity that had just presented itself. Every ethical fiber of her being was screaming as she considered doing the unthinkable. Sitting on the counter, possibly forgotten, was the answer to a problem she had been losing sleep on for days. It was not the reason she had come here -- *hell no! This option would have never entered her mind without some type of hint like this* -- but it was right there. Who would know?

Before her conscience could talk her out of it, she grabbed the opportunity and shoved it in her jacket pocket. Quickly and mechanically, she searched the drawers for the other half of the solution. Finding what she needed, she shoved it beside the first and tried to calm her breathing and in concert, her racing heart. When Doc Tyler came into the room, she was still flushed and trembling slightly.

"Hello Bear!" Doc Tyler said, greeting his patient first, which was his custom. "What have you gotten into that has caused that stomach of yours to get so upset, hmmm?"

Bear's tail wagged so fiercely, his butt was wagged by consequence. Bear loved Doc Tyler and became a playful puppy in the doctor's strong, caring hands. Doc Tyler continued to ruffle Bear's fur and give him reassuring pats while addressing Kate, "Well, he sure looks happy enough. Do you know how often and how much has he been vomiting and/or having diarrhea?"

Kate answered carefully, "Well, it's hard to say, really, because he does spend some time outside...but, at least once a day... that I've seen anyway."

Doc Tyler sat down on the floor with Bear, which delighted the big dog. Bear was way too big to place on the cold metal table, so it was necessary for the doctor to sit down on the floor and handle the dog. But, he was in no danger with the gentle giant. Bear knew the routine and sat back on his haunches to be examined.

"Good boy!" praised Doc Tyler, "let me have a look at those big teeth of yours." He examined Bear's teeth, gums and pink, moist tongue. Next he raised each of Bear's eyelids and did a quick check of each eye.

"He doesn't appear to be dehydrated...yet, anyway," he reported to Kate, then continued his examination. He urged Bear to stand and ran his hands through Bear's thick, black fur, pausing to palpate the dog's belly.

"Doesn't seem to have any discomfort or abnormal findings in his abdomen and his fur is supple and intact," he continued to report.

Standing, he reached into his pocket and took out a handful of liver treats, then looked to Kate. She nodded and he gave them to Bear. "Good boy, Bear. You were the perfect patient during all that poking and prodding."

Bear took the liver treats and continued to bestow kisses upon the doctor's hands. Doc Tyler gave the big dog a bit more attention. Then he moved to the sink to wash his hands.

"He looks good, Kate," he said as he dried his hands. "Let me make some notes while I ask you a few questions. How long has this been going on?"

"Um....a few days...maybe three?"

"Okay, and have you seen the diarrhea or vomit?" he continued while writing.

"Well, not really, I mean...I didn't really examine it or anything. All I can tell you is that it looked like poop...the diarrhea, that is. And the vomit was just...well, dog yak," Kate said, scrunching up her nose.

"Dog yak. I like that. Is that a medical term, nurse?" Doc Tyler teased.

"Hey! I love Bear, but I'm a people nurse. I'm not entirely sure what's normal for dogs," Kate joked, then continued. "At first, I just thought something didn't agree with him and it would pass."

Doc Tyler nodded, encouraging her to continue and she did. "But it has been a few days and I'm supposed to go to the beach tomorrow or Monday. We always take Bear with us. But if something is going on, I'd rather know now and fix it. Have **you** fix it, that is. I don't mind leaving him here and picking him up tomorrow or Monday."

"Well, I don't think you necessarily need to leave him here..." Doc Tyler began, placing his pen back in his pocket.

"No, no. We've had a rough couple of days, Doc. We've had a close family friend die. Isabella was in that horrible car accident and...well, it's just been one thing after another. I don't want to take everyone to the beach and then Bear take a turn for the worse. That would be too much for Robbie and Isabella...especially, Isabella. Bear is still her dog, you know. I would feel better if Bear was checked out thoroughly and given a clean bill of health before we take that trip. And the only person I trust to do that is you."

Doc Tyler had watched Kate closely during her impassioned speech and did feel some sympathy for her. She had been flushed and trembling, probably because of all the added stress, when he had come in. She could most likely use a day or two without one more thing to worry about. He could easily get the things he needed on an outpatient basis, but he could monitor Bear here overnight and run tests in the morning.

"Okay, no problem. Why don't you leave this big lug with me and I'll give you a call to update you tonight or tomorrow morning," Doc Tyler said.

"That would be such a load off my mind, Doc. Thank you," said a smiling Kate as she breathed out a sigh of relief.

Bear watched with confusion as his mistress left but was pacified by more liver treats from Doc Tyler and happily followed the good doctor into the kennel area.

Kate walked briskly to her car. She sat trying to forgive herself for what she had done and what she was about to do. It was no use. She would be dealing with this for quite some time, she was sure. Instead, she strengthened her resolve by mentally checking off her to do list: Vinnie and Robbie off to the beach this morning, check; Bear at the vet, check. One more thing to do and everything would be set into motion. The thought scared her, but the alternative

scared her more. With renewed determination, she started the
engine and drove toward home.

Chapter 42

Isabella sat waiting for Rath. She had finished her rehab a few hours ago. Normally, he was here waiting for her, so she was a little put out that he had not arrived yet. She had good news for him and she was not known for her patience. The doctor rounding this morning had stated that she would most likely be able to go home in the morning. She had tried to call her mother and let her know, but kept getting voice mail both at the home number and the cell. It was so frustrating. Her mother was notorious for letting her battery run dead on her cell phone and not notice. She rarely used her cell phone and sometimes Isabella wondered why her mother ever got one.

Suddenly, Isabella's cell phone began to play distantly. Rath had just returned it to her yesterday. It had been found among her effects in the car. It was undamaged and Isabella would probably never be able to look at it again without remembering that horrible night. She had hidden it away in her bedside table, but had evidently not turned it off. She reached to see if Rath was calling her; instead, it was an unknown number. Isabella's curiosity won over her trepidation as she answered the phone hoping it was Rath calling from an unknown line.

"Hello?"

"Yes, is this Isabella Tuscadero?" said a warm, male voice.

"Well, it depends on who is calling," came Isabella's sardonic reply.

There was a chuckle on the other end and Isabella was about to slap her phone shut when she heard, "Well, that's understandable. This is Doctor Tyler. I'm the family veterinarian..."

"Oh! Doc Tyler...Hi! Yeah, this is Isabella. I'm sorry. It's just it was an unknown number and I wasn't sure if...doesn't matter. Sorry."

"That's okay, don't worry about it. I heard you had a pretty bad car accident. You doing okay?" Doc Tyler asked.

"Oh, yes. I'm fine, actually. I'm supposed to be going home tomorrow." Isabella was happy she was able to share the news with somebody.

"Well, that's great. And normally, I wouldn't have dreamed of bothering you in the hospital. But I can't seem to reach your mom and you are still listed as co-owner of Bear, so..."

Isabella's eyes widened. "What's wrong with Bear?"

"Nothing major, trust me. Your mom brought him in this morning because he had an upset stomach. She left him here just to get a snout to tail work up because of your family's trip to the beach. He's just fine. No worse for the wear," Doc Tyler tried to assure her.

"Okay. Good. So, he's been sick? He's really not my dog anymore and lives at home with Mom and Dad. I'm in college now and living in an apartment, so...," Isabella tried to explain.

"Well, I just wanted to find out something from somebody if I could," Doc Tyler continued.

"I'll answer any questions I can," said Isabella, happy to have something to do to pass the time until Rath showed.

"Your mom reported that Bear was vomiting and having diarrhea. So, we ran some tests and I think we may have discovered the problem. Seems Bear has gotten hold of some nicotine," reported the doctor.

"Nicotine? As in cigarettes?" Isabella asked.

"Actually, that's the most likely source. Sometimes dogs will get into a pack of cigarettes and chew them up. I know Bear used to be quite the destructive little cuss when he was a puppy. Anybody in your mom's house smoke? Your dad, maybe?" Doc Tyler asked.

"No! Never!" Isabella said over her shock. "Mom would never have allowed it. No one's ever smoked at our house."

"Hmmm. Any friends of the family smoke and have to be banished outside to do so?" asked the doctor.

"Not that I'm aware of. I wonder..." started Isabella, but stopped.

"Yes?" prompted Doc Tyler.

"Well, without going into a lot of detail, we had police protection for awhile. Maybe one of them smoked. But they were out front and Bear..." Isabella was thinking out loud now.

"Could be something like that. Anyway, he hasn't ingested enough to get nicotine poisoning or anything. But, depending on the amount, it could have caused some stomach issues with him. We'll look at a couple of other things to cover all the bases, but I think that's what did it. Keep him away from the nicotine and he'll be fine. Can you pass that on to your mom for me?"

"Yeah, sure. Thanks," Isabella responded automatically, but her mind was busy trying to figure out how Bear would get hold of cigarettes. She was minimally aware of saying goodbye to the veterinarian.

She was still trying to figure out how Bear, who normally roamed the backyard, would get hold of cigarettes from a mystery smoking police officer stationed out front. Had her mother invited one of the officers in, then asked him to step outside to smoke? Isabella thought she would have to ask and investigate further next time she spoke to her mother.

Rath appeared in the doorway with a large bouquet of white roses and his knockout grin. "Congratulations! I heard you've been sprung!" he said.

Thoughts of nicotine-infected dogs rushed out of Isabella's mind at the sight of the roses and Rath. "How did you find that out? I was going to surprise you with the news." Isabella pretended to pout.

Rath walked over and brushed a kiss across her pouting lips, lay down his cell phone on her bedside table and looked for a place to put the roses. "I called earlier to see how you were doing..." he started.

"You called who?" Isabella asked.

"The nurses' station," answered Rath.

"You called to check up on me, huh?" Isabella teased.

"Every day," Rath said and winked at her. "Anyway, one of the nurses told me that the doctor had already been by and left discharge papers on your chart for tomorrow. So, I had to make sure I didn't arrive empty-handed. You wouldn't believe how hard it is to find white roses this time of year! Red, absolutely. Pink, you bet. Yellow, probably. But white - good luck. But white's your favorite, so I was going to find white roses if it killed me."

Isabella laughed with delight. Rath loved her laugh. Not a girl's laugh, but deep and musical at the same time. Her bruises were mere yellowed shadows on her face now and the minuscule scars would soon fade to indeterminate lines. They gave her beauty character and Rath knew he would never get tired of looking at that face.

"So, you want to just hold these until they die or is there a vase not in use somewhere around here?" Rath said, looking at the colorful garden that he had created over the past week.

"Check out at the nurses' station. They have a collection of vases out there they told me. But hurry back. I've missed you." Isabella smiled and looked at him with a promise in her eyes.

"Yes ma'am," Rath said as he smiled back and went in search of a vase.

Her phone sang out again and Isabella was delighted to see it was her father. "Dad! Guess what?"

She went on to share the good news of her discharge with him and found out that he and Robbie were already at the beach. She could not wait to go herself and wondered if Rath would be able to come. Life was starting to come back around to normal after all.

Life went on that last Saturday night. It went on for Isabella, who had visions of watching waves hit the shore with dependable regularity. For Rath, who had visions of his own that involved taking Isabella out to a romantic dinner as a nurse went to fetch a vase for the beautiful roses. It went on for Vinnie, who had visions of an intact family leaving a nightmare behind them. For poor Bear, who was wondering what he had done to spend the night in a metal cage far away from his family. For Robbie, who was still worrying about the sorority paddle and the fact that his mother might find it while packing for the beach or maybe already had. For Edward, who was wondering if the creepy guy was still out there but was afraid to look. For Tommy, who was sitting in a tree about to admit surrender when his intended prey walked out onto her deck, having a conversation with someone by cell phone. And for Kate, who was pretending to talk on a phone while wondering if the person who needed to hear the conversation was watching and listening. Yes, endgame was here and life would never be the same for any of them.

Chapter 43

Tommy had been about to leave his post among the trees when Kate had walked out onto her back deck, talking on her cell phone. Although Tommy's butt was practically numb from sitting in one spot for the past half hour, the flame of curiosity flared. Particularly, since in this quiet, upscale suburban neighborhood at 9:00 at night, he could hear every word.

"Yes, they left this morning. I told Vinnie just to take Robbie and go on to the beach and Isabella and I would join them there," Kate said, pretending to speak on her cell phone and trying hard not to look across the yard at the tree line. Every primordial nerve in the survival center of her brain sang with the knowledge of a predator close by.

Whoa! Hold up, now, thought Tommy. *Hubby and the brat are away from home at the beach? Well, well, well. Little Kate all by her lonesome? Well, ain't that just fine,* Tommy thought and smiled. He thought about jumping into the backyard from the tree now, just to see the look of fear on her face, but a smart predator knew when to pounce. Advancing on prey talking on a cell phone was not a smart move. He settled back to watch and listen.

Kate paused for what she hoped was a believable amount of time and continued, "No, no, Isabella's still in the hospital, but she should be released in the morning. So I'll pack up tonight, pick her up in the morning and head to the beach to join Vinnie and Robbie. I can't wait, truthfully." She laughed and it sounded hollow to her own ears. She hoped that it sounded real enough to her intended audience, assuming Tommy was present and listening.

It would have to be tonight, thought Tommy. Finally! But what about the damn dog? Tommy had not seen it anywhere and he had forgotten to bring anything with him. Maybe he could leave and go get something...

Kate counted to ten slowly and said, "Well, after I pick up Bear, of course. Couldn't show up at the beach without him, now could I?" She paused for a count of five and said, "Oh, I had to take him to the vet this morning." Pause for one second, then, "No, nothing serious, I hope. But they did want to keep him overnight, so I'll pick him up in the morning on my way out of town."

No dog?! Tommy could hardly believe what he was hearing. Could it be any more perfect? Sweet Jesus! His patience had paid off and he would finally be able to settle the score tonight. As soon as she got off that damn phone...

Kate was almost faint with fear at this point and counted to ten again, agonizingly slow, then said, "Well, listen, let me go. Rath, that young police officer I was telling you about...yes, him. He's due here any minute and I want to get some coffee on...you too...Thank you...okay, bye-bye." She snapped her cell phone shut and walked back into the house.

Damn it! A cop on the frickin' way! Son of a bitch! Tommy could hardly contain his rage and disappointment. He took a couple of deep breaths and closed his eyes briefly. Don't blow it now, Tommy boy. You've waited this long. A few more hours ain't gonna make a bit of difference. We'll wait for the damn cop to show and we'll wait for his ass to leave. Then, we'll kill her slow. We'll kill her real slow. That did it for Tommy. He was able to find a different position and wait it out. He had waited 15 years. What was another couple of hours?

He watched Kate through the kitchen window as she made coffee and looked at her watch a few times. He wondered if she was the type to nag. Would she read the cop the riot act for being late or was she the passive aggressive type? God, he hated those!

After awhile, Kate must have decided to watch TV while she waited. About an hour after that, it was obvious that she had been stood up. *Aw, poor little unlovable Kate*, thought Tommy. He wondered if she was having an affair with the cop she had mentioned. Wouldn't that just beat all! He would kill her and whoever she had been talking to on the phone would name the cop! Tommy had himself quite a chuckle out of that one. But he knew that by the time he was finished with Kate Tuscadero, no one would doubt that Tommy King was responsible. Not by the time he was done, no sir!

Tommy was not sure of the time, but eventually Kate tired of waiting and went through her normal routine of turning everything off and heading up the stairs. *Must be around 11:00*, thought Tommy, *just like clockwork*. Same time every night. Early to bed. But not going to rise this time.

He saw the light go on in her room. It was on for just a few minutes, then off again. Now the house was blanketed in darkness. It was everything he could do not to jump out of the tree and go racing up to kick in the deck door. *Discipline*, he thought, *discipline erases mistakes*. He would wait it out for another half hour or so. Let her get good and asleep. Then he'd go in through the deck door. The one he had watched her walk by this evening without checking the lock.

Normally, she did but not tonight. Something wiggled in his brain about that, but he stomped on it in his haste to imagine what lay ahead. She had gone back through that door into the house after her phone conversation. Had she locked the door behind her? He could not remember. Didn't matter. Locked or unlocked, he could get in.

Then he would surprise her like all the others. He would wait for her to sense something was wrong while he watched her sleep. Tommy could almost see the fear blossom on her face and he sniffed hard a few times without even realizing he was doing it. Just a little while longer, he told himself. Tommy sat back in the tree like a big jungle cat; patiently waiting for his chance to kill.

***

Visiting hours were officially over at the hospital; they ended at 9:00 and it was almost 11:00. But Rath was a police officer and anyone could see that Isabella just lit up when he was around. After all the poor girl had been through, who was going to say anything? She was in a private room, so "let it be" was the consensus of the nurses.

Somewhere around the time Kate was going to bed, Rath was trying to extract himself from Isabella. As much as he wanted to stay - and do a bit more than hold her hand - he knew she needed her rest; especially since she was to be discharged tomorrow. Isabella was trying her best to convince him to stay when a doorbell sounded.

Both Rath and Isabella stopped what they were doing; Rath with a confused look on his face and Isabella with one of surprise. She saw Rath's look and laughed. "That's my phone. It's my daily alarm...or I guess I should say nightly. I forgot to turn it off."

"You have an alarm for 11:00 at night? What for?" Rath could not help but ask.

"It's when I used to take my birth...it was to remind me to do something," Isabella said blushing, then added quickly, "Well, I won't have to worry too much about that anymore. My battery just died with the energy expended to sound that alarm. Just as well, it's been ringing off the hook tonight."

"Oh?" Rath cocked an eyebrow and Isabella laughed at his mock show of jealousy.

"No, no...Nothing like that. My dad called earlier. He and Robbie are already at the beach. I *soooo* wish I was there instead of here," she pined.

"Your dad is at the beach? Without your mom?" Rath asked.

"No, Mom's supposed to be at home, although I haven't been able to reach her. She's picking me up tomorrow and then I guess we'll head to the beach," Isabella explained.

Rath was a little alarmed, thinking of Kate at home by herself and no new information on the whereabouts of Tommy. Inside, his mind clanged NO POLICE PROTECTION? NO HUSBAND? His gut began to twist in that uncomfortable way it did when something was very wrong. But his gut had been off lately and Rath wasn't sure he could trust it. Well, at least Kate had that monster of a dog with her, he thought.

"Well, that sounds like just what the doctor ordered...a trip to the beach. How long will you be gone?" Rath asked, trying to ignore his gut.

"About a week. Maybe you can come down and visit for a couple of days," Isabella smiled coyly and Rath could not help but return her smile.

"Maybe I can. Does that big dog go with you guys to the beach?" Rath asked, wondering how protective Bear was of Isabella.

"Oh, shit! I forgot to tell Dad about Bear! Damn it! I don't know if Bear will be coming this time or what," Isabella exclaimed.

Rath's scalp began to tingle as the individual hairs began to stand straight up. Invisible fingers crawled down his spine as he asked, "What do you mean? Something wrong with Bear?"

"That was the other phone call. Bear's at the vet. They called me because technically, he's my dog, but mom actually takes care of everything..." Isabella started to explain.

"Isabella," Rath interrupted her, "why is Bear at the vet? You said he might not go to the beach, so it's not a routine checkup, I take it. He's at the vet now? What's going on with him?"

Isabella was a bit nonplussed at Rath's reaction to her sick dog, but answered anyway, "Well, that's the weird thing. Mom took him in because he was throwing up and having diarrhea and it turns out it's probably from nicotine!"

"What?" Rath asked as his face paled as the tumblers in his mind fell into place and unknowns were unlocked.

"Yeah, nicotine! The doctor seems to think Bear got into a pack of cigarettes and ate them, but nobody smokes...Hey! Where are you going?" Isabella called after him as he bolted from the room.

Rath yelled back, "Keep trying to call your mom!"

Isabella jumped from the bed and caught a glimpse of Rath turning the corner toward the elevators. His reaction shook her and she immediately returned to the room and picked up the dead cell phone. With an exasperated groan, she turned to the phone provided by the hospital at her bedside. She called home. Still, no answer. Not even the answering machine picked up. She tried her mother's cell phone next. Her call went directly to voice mail.

What in the hell is going on and why had Rath looked so scared? Not worried, but scared. Isabella did not know and that compounded her fear. She could do nothing but continue to try to reach her mother. She could not even question Rath further about what was going on. In his haste, he had left his cell phone sitting on her bedside table.

***

Tommy had waited long enough, 15 years in fact, for this very moment. The anticipation had been excruciating and now the moment was upon him; yet he hesitated. A voice, a very small voice, buried somewhere in what used to be an unscarred human being spoke up, *Maybe it's better if we just go. Leave things alone and take advantage of the freedom we have. Leave here now and never look back.* For that voice, Tommy hesitated with his hand on Kate's deck doorknob. But the monster won out with its thirst for blood, desire for revenge and the need to expend its rage; too long held in check.

Tommy quietly turned the knob and confirmed that Kate had forgotten to lock it. Well, one chick's mistake was the king snake's fortune, smiled Tommy to himself. He quietly shut the door behind him and stood still listening for any signs of movement from upstairs. He took a moment to let his eyes adjust to the almost total darkness of the room. He was standing in a great room, the kitchen to his left. The couch that he had watched Kate sit on night after night was to his right, sitting in front of the window by the door. *Not quite the perfect housekeeper when the family's away, is she?* thought Tommy as he eyed what appeared to be an afghan strewn across the seat of the couch. He turned back to listen once again and heard nothing but the ticking of the clock in the kitchen. His heart began to pick up the pace as he silently, but confidently walked toward the stairs just a few feet away.

Behind him the afghan began to shift and levitate. Had Tommy noticed, he probably would have given a little yelp of surprise. But he did not notice. Such was his concentration on climbing the stairs toward his prey. By the time he began to suspect he heard the movement of clothing behind him, there was a sharp pain in his right neck at the jugular vein. He reached up to find a small hand wrapped around (a syringe?) something, even as he felt women's breasts pressed against his back. He grabbed at the hand, pulling it away from his neck and twisting it until he heard a cry of pain.

He looked to the hand and saw an empty syringe with a short, stubby needle. He looked to see who dared put poison in his perfect body and saw Kate! *Kate?!* His mind slowly realized the trap that had been set for him as the drug took effect. He tried to lunge for her, but his feet were made of lead and he only ended up losing his balance and falling against the couch. He pulled on the afghan as if it were the rope ladder of a boat, trying to pull himself up. His vision started to blur and he was able to form the words "You bitch!" before he succumbed to the drug.

Kate stood watching the quick acting sedative take over, shaking from both fear and the rush of adrenaline as it coursed through her body. She had dropped the syringe when Tommy had tried to break her wrist. She picked it up now and looked to see if the plunger had made it to the top of the syringe. The syringe was empty, but she was unsure if the entire drug had made it into his system.

***

Rath jumped in his car and raced out of the hospital parking lot. Son of bitch! Not again! Not again! Rath knew in his heart of hearts (*screw his gut!*) that Tommy had been casing Kate's house for the last few nights; probably for as long as he had been off the radar of local police. It was how Tommy did things. Remembering the case files from 15 years ago, it had been clear that Tommy had stalked each of the women he had attacked at least a couple of weeks before each assault. He knew their routines, their work schedules, what day their trash was picked up, who visited regularly and what time they all went to bed. He knew when to attack and when he would not be interrupted in his sadistic play.

One of the pieces of evidence noted in the Sandra Derringer case was that Tommy had continued with his habit of casing his intended victims. Although he had trimmed his timeline, it was obvious he had been there for a few days. Located inside the small fenced-in backyard, directly under a well-developed tree with branches big enough to hold a man were discarded cigarette butts. The cigarette brand was KOOL and further investigation of the tree showed that Tommy had a habit of snubbing the cigarettes out in the tree, about 15mm from the filter, before casting them to the ground below. They were the same brand of cigarettes found in an overflowing ashtray in Tommy's room at the halfway house. DNA taken from the discarded cigarettes in Sandra's yard confirmed they had been smoked by Tommy.

Rath was willing to bet that Bear had found the cigarettes and ingested them which meant that Tommy had been watching Kate's house. Ingesting enough of them to cause nicotine poisoning meant that Tommy had been there for awhile. Did Tommy know that Kate was alone tonight? Did he know that Bear was spending the night at the vet?

Rath decided to take the highway, where he could push his car to 80, 85 miles per hour. Kate's house was just a mere four exits away. He should have told Isabella to call the police, not her mother. God, I'm such an idiot!, he berated himself. As he picked up speed on the highway, he patted down his pockets searching for his cell phone. He would place the call himself.

Where is my damn cell phone? he thought as he pat first one pocket then the other. It was nowhere to be found. As his car raced down the highway (three exits now), he tried to calm himself down to remember when he had last had it. He did not have time to think about it long before his car cut off on him and the power steering acted like it wanted to quit as well.

"What the f--?" Rath managed to get out as he quickly punched his hazard lights on and steered over to the side of the highway. Then he knew. The stupid car was out of gas! He had been riding on fumes on the way to the hospital, but already late, did not want to stop. He had planned on hitting the station closest to the hospital upon leaving and had passed it doing 50mph before taking the exit to the highway just a few seconds ago.

"Shit, SHIT, **SHIT!**" yelled Rath, while pounding the steering wheel. He opened the car door to get some light in the car and frantically searched for his cell phone. He had to call the police and get them to Kate's house! His cell phone was nowhere to be found and he was wasting time. He looked at his dashboard clock and noted the time: 11:28 p.m.

Chapter 44

Kate had given Tommy the normal intravenous dose of Versed calculated by a rough guess of his weight. She had injected him with 2 milligrams and that should keep him down for at least ten minutes. She had not loaded another syringe and wondered now if she should have. She slowly approached him, first kicking at a booted foot, then a jean clad thigh. She pressed hard on his shin bone with the edge of her shoe and slid it the length of his bone. No response from him, not even a grimace. He was out cold.

Kate dared now to approach him and look at his right neck. There was some redness from the injection, but no point of entry seen - thanks to the small needle. She turned his head back to the right and looked upon his sleeping face. She saw no innocence there, no peace - only the face of a psychopath that had tried to run her daughter off the road to her death. She saw the face of the man who had beaten her best friend to death and probably laughed while he did it. She saw the face that several women had not gotten the chance to see while bound, beaten and savagely raped all those years ago. She felt no pity for the man before her. Monsters had to be dealt with; that was the whole of it.

With calm resolve, she rose to continue with her plan. As Tommy lay sedated by the couch, Kate proceeded to create the signs of a struggle in her great room. She knocked over a lamp, kicked the coffee table askew and pulled one of the curtains on the back window off the rod. She pushed hard against the bookcase and the entertainment center as knickknacks rained down. Despite the noise, Tommy never stirred.

Kate went to him and grabbing him by his booted feet, dragged him to the middle of the room and closer to the front door. She looked behind her and saw that the door was about ten feet diagonally to her right - perfect. She rolled him now and checked him for any weapons. She found a pack of KOOL cigarettes, a length of corded rope and a knife. She did not stop to think of his intentions, but merely worked quickly before the Versed had a chance to wear off.

Checking her watch, she saw that three minutes had passed. Jumping up, she ran into the kitchen and grabbed some latex gloves she kept for working with raw meat. Running back into the great room, she picked up the knife after donning the gloves. Picking up a callused hand, she hesitated wondering if Tommy were left or right-handed. She did not know! Oh, shit!

She decided to bet on right, since the cigarettes were in his left back pocket and the knife and rope were found in the right. She wrapped his fingers around the knife in the correct position and carefully carried it with her to the bathroom. As she passed through the kitchen, she picked up her cell phone lying by the salt and pepper shakers on the cafe table. She needed to dispose of the syringe and time was getting away from her.

Now she wished she had drawn up a second syringe, but she had only stolen the one from the vet's office along with the vial of Versed. She could not do it now because she had disposed of the vial of Versed after drawing the first syringe. It now lay buried in a bag of garbage at the county dump. It had been a long time since she had given Versed to a patient, but she knew that repeated doses were needed to keep a patient sedated throughout a procedure.

This knowledge quickened her step and she entered the bathroom to stare at her reflection in the mirror. Kate did not recognize the woman staring back at her. The woman had haunted and fearful eyes. Her skin was pale and her hair wild and uncombed. Kate knew even as she brought the knife to her left cheek, that she would always remember the face that stared back at her now.

Without hesitation, Kate brought the sharp blade in contact with the softness of her cheek and bore down. The stinging pain was immediate, as was the blood that sprung up to kiss the knife's edge. Kate cut down and away, making sure not to cut too deep. She ran back into the kitchen, taking care to spill her blood there and not the bathroom.

She cast the knife under the rolling chef's block and stripped the gloves off her hands and placed them in the trash. Immediately, she brought her hand to her face, as if the wound had just been inflicted. With her other hand, she turned on her phone and waited the precious seconds it took to power up. *Damn! That's really bleeding!* she thought as blood seeped through her fingers of the hand pressed against the fresh cut.

Now that her phone was on, she checked the kitchen clock against her watch. It had been eight minutes since she had dosed Tommy. He would be waking up anytime now. She was sure that his rage would lend him the energy to put up a fight. Knowing the response time of the Henrico police department was about five to eight minutes, she dialed 911. She hoped with recent events, her address would flag and the response would be more immediate. In fact, she was banking on it.

"911, what is your emergency?" asked the voice on the other end.

"Help me! Help me! He's here. Tommy's here! He's going to kill me! Please..." and Kate cut herself off with a scream before dropping her phone and stomping on it. She knew the enhanced 911 would give emergency services her address and police would be arriving soon with lights and sirens. All she had to do was baby sit Tommy and make sure he was up and seemed to be fighting when they arrived.

Holding her cheek and feeling the blood become sticky even now, she circled through the dining room to go and wait by Tommy for the police. As she rounded the corner, her animal mind screamed as the breath caught in her throat. Tommy was no longer lying on the floor! He was nowhere to be seen!

***

Tommy woke up sluggish and disoriented. He was surprised to find himself on the floor in a room he did not recognize. In a mind conditioned by years of abuse, his flight or fight pathways responded quicker than most. He looked around from his vantage point on his back and saw family photos adorning the walls. *Who the hell are they?* he thought. His vision blurred briefly, then clear again. He felt nauseous and...and...drugged!

Tommy's mind then replayed the last few moments before he lost consciousness and he threw himself onto his stomach, trying to get his hands underneath himself. He listened for a moment with his eyes closed, but heard nothing. Where was she? Had she left the house and run screaming for the neighbors? Was she sitting in some rich neighbor's house wrapped in a fleece throw while they called the police? Tommy tried to get to his feet and escape, but stumbled against a wall. He was overcome with the dizziness and the nausea that accompanied it. What had the bitch given him and how long ago was that?

He looked around and saw the front door across from him, but there was no way he was taking that way out. The police were probably waiting for him now; right outside that door. His eyes frantically searched for another way out that was close by. Tommy did not think he could navigate too many corners. Then he saw another door inside the dining room. Maybe it led to a basement that had a window big enough for him to crawl out of. He could hide in the easement and make it back to his car. Did the house have a basement? Tommy couldn't remember; he couldn't think straight. At least the basement would buy him some time.

He opened the door and found it was a coat closet. Son of a bi— someone was coming! It would have to do for the moment. Tommy quickly ducked inside and pulled the door quietly behind him. He tried to burrow back into the coats and his hand brushed against something hard. He dared not try to find a light, but picked up the item and sized it up. It was some kind of flattened bat. What the hell?

Then Tommy heard her voice! She was speaking to someone and she sounded panicked, but Tommy could not decipher what she was saying. He shook his head trying to clear the last of the cobwebs away. What was she saying? But it was too late, she had stopped talking. He could hear her in the kitchen. Now the footsteps were coming this way. Tommy stopped breathing and closed his fingers around the new found weapon; ready to strike if she opened the door. But she didn't. She walked on by.

Tommy cracked the door to see it was clear. His mouth still felt like it had been stuffed with cotton and he was still a bit shaky, but his head was clearing. He saw her standing a few feet in front of him and he heard her gasp. It was a sound he fed off of and he drew air into his lungs through his nose quickly as he opened the door and raised the wooden cricket bat.

***

Rath was in his personal car and therefore, had no radio to call anyone. Slamming his car door shut, he took his rage over his own incompetence out on the hood of his car. *Stupid, stupid son of a bitch!* he thought as he slammed his fists down again and again. He stood for a second, spent, arms planted firmly on his dented hood. Think, brainiac, think!

He knew the odds of someone giving him a lift this time of night on Interstate 64 were slim to none. He remembered that his gun was in the glove compartment of his car. He never went anywhere without it. He only had one choice left and he needed to get moving.

Grabbing the gun and checking the magazine, he slammed another clip into the back pocket of his jeans. He had almost coasted to the next exit. He still had another exit to go. He broke into a controlled run. It was 11:32. Endgame was here and only Tommy and Kate remained on the field.

***

Before Kate's mind could completely grasp the gravity of Tommy's absence, she heard someone sniff behind her and instinctively ducked and darted forward. This action caused the wooden paddle swung at her head to miss it by mere inches.

"Come 'ere, you bitch! Daddy's home and he's ready to play!" Tommy yelled. His eyes still swam in his head, but they shone with malicious glee at the fear in Kate's eyes. "You think you can beat me?! You might have won 15 years ago because of your lies, but who's winning now, huh bitch? Who's winning now?"

Kate took a few surprised steps back into the now unfamiliar landscape of her trashed great room. The edge of her heel caught on the askew coffee table, throwing her off balance as Tommy advanced swinging a paddle she recognized as Isabella's. *How did he get Isabella's sorority paddle?*

She started to fall and twisted to catch herself. The paddle caught her in the right side and Kate could feel her ribs crack under the force of the blow. The air was knocked out of her as the blunt force sent her back into the coffee table.

Her back cracked against the edge of the table, even as Tommy raised the paddle again. "Coach says to swing away, baby, so I'm swinging! Ready, here it comes. Get ready to spit out some of those pearly whites! Because game's over, bitch and I win!"

Kate was trying to judge how to escape the swing, when the front door seemed to explode into the room. Tommy swung around to find a sweating and exhausted Rath pointing a gun at him and yelling breathlessly, "Police! Drop it now!"

Tommy looked at Kate, then back at Rath. Rath kept his stance as sirens began to sound down the street. "Tommy! It's over! Drop your weapon...Drop it now!" Rath repeated.

Kate was almost crying with relief, her back to Rath. She looked up at Tommy and saw that he was thinking of following the order. *No!,* thought Kate, *this was not how it was supposed to end.* Tommy would be arrested and there would be another court trial with another lawyer. He would go to jail. There was no way he would be out again...unless there was another mistake. Kate thought of Sandra beaten and trying to warn her through broken teeth. She thought of Isabella lying bruised and unconscious in a hospital bed. Kate was unable to live with the possibility of Tommy alive. As Tommy started slowly to lower the sorority paddle, he looked at her with barely controlled rage.

Kate smiled at him and began to laugh. To Rath behind her, it sounded like hysteria. To Tommy, looking into her mirthful eyes, it sounded like she was laughing at him. It was all a setup after all!

"Shut up! What the hell are you laughing about, bitch?!" Tommy yelled.

"Tommy! Look at me! Tommy…" Rath shouted, trying to force Tommy's attention away from Kate.

Tommy started to remove his eyes from her and Kate squealed with laughter, drawing his rage once again. "Shut the fuck up! What the hell do you have to laugh about?!"

Kate stopped laughing to look Tommy in the eyes. Smiling, she mouthed silently, "BECAUSE I WIN, MOTHERFUCKER."

As the blue lights played across Tommy's face, it contorted into one of monstrous rage. He screamed and raised the paddle once again. Rath fired two shots; both kill shots and Tommy dropped to his knees and fell back against the floor to lie motionless. His open eyes seemed to stare at the blue lights as they played across the ceiling. Kate started to cry with great wracking sobs, from relief and so many other reasons as well.

Epilogue

Kate sat watching Vinnie and Robbie play in the water. Isabella was still sleeping; no doubt storing up her beauty sleep for Rath's arrival later today. Kate sat on a dune, still dressed in her Capri's and flip flops. Her bright tank top camouflaged the firework display of bruises on her right side. Her ribs had been cracked, but would heal over time. It only hurt when she took deep breaths, coughed, yawned or laughed. But she did not laugh much these days.

She wore a wide-brimmed hat to help keep the sun out of her eyes, but more important to protect the skin still healing from the stitched laceration on her cheek. Stylish sunglasses completed the picture of a woman relaxing on the beach, counting her blessings as she watched her husband and child play in the surf.

Bill Patterson sat beside her and both were silent for a time, sipping their iced teas; lulled by the sound of the waves and Robbie's squeals of laughter. Kate knew why Bill was here, but did not rush him or ask any questions.

"So, do you want to know?" Bill asked. Kate merely nodded in answer, never taking her eyes off of Robbie.

"It seems that Tommy had been watching you for some time. That was confirmed by the kid that lives behind you guys...Edward? Eddie? Anyway, he saw him at least once, but was too scared to say anything. Probably figured Tommy was the boogie man come to life"

Kate remained silent, so Bill continued, "Anyway, he...Tommy that is...sat up in that tree in the easement behind your house night after night, smoking those KOOL cigarettes. That's what tipped Rath off, by the way. We knew that Tommy's brand was KOOL and he always cased his victims. 'Course you didn't know that. You took that big dog of yours in for an upset stomach. You had no way of knowing that Tommy was watching and responsible for your dog's stomach. Did you, Kate?"

Kate turned to look at Bill, her eyes hidden behind her Ray Bans. She gave a half smile and answered, "How could I? I was wrapped up with what was going on with Isabella."

"Yeah, well...Probably not the best move on your part to stop the police protection or send Vinnie to the beach without you. But you know that. I'm not going to fuss at you now. You know now, don't you, Katie?"

Kate turned back to the ocean and her answer was a bit cold. "Well, hindsight's 20/20. Isn't that what everyone says? What difference does it make now?"

"You told the officers responding that you heard a noise, came downstairs to investigate and Tommy jumped you in the kitchen. He cut you during a struggle and you somehow managed to knock the knife out of his hand. Lucky there, I'll tell you. We ended up finding it under the chef's block. Don't know if I told you that."

Kate did not answer, but continued to stare out at the ocean. Bill could see her eyes staring straight ahead, unwavering and giving away nothing from the side. He watched them carefully as he continued. "Anyway, then he gets his hands on that paddle of Isabella's and goes to work on you with that. That's where I'm confused. When and how did he get his hands on that?"

Kate's eyes looked down for just a second, then straight ahead once again. She merely shrugged her shoulders. Bill continued to watch her as he spoke. "Yeah that stumps me too. See, Robbie admitted to moving it into the closet before taking off for the beach. So, maybe Tommy's hiding in the closet, waiting for you to come on down. But why use the knife in the kitchen then?"

"What?" Kate asked and turned to face him.

"I mean, if he finds the paddle and decides to use it. Where was it while he attacked you in the kitchen? See what I'm saying? He finds the paddle and maybe thinks, 'Oh yeah, this will do just fine'. But then he jumps you in the kitchen...no paddle. I don't get that. Do you?"

Kate continued to stare at him, saying nothing. Bill began to wonder if she was going to speak when she asked, "Are you asking me to explain how a psychopath thinks? Because, I can't do that, Bill. Everything is a screwed up nightmare from the moment I heard that noise downstairs. I couldn't tell you if he was holding a knife in one hand and the paddle in the other. I just don't remember, okay?"

Bill watched Kate as she spoke and realized he loved her. Not in a romantic way, but in the way a father loves a daughter. Suddenly, it didn't matter what the truth was. Kate was safe and another psychopath had been dispatched by an officer of the law, making it a righteous kill. So, he asked instead, "Does that hurt?"

"What?" Kate seemed startled by the question.

"The stitches. Do they hurt?" Bill repeated.

Kate absently and gingerly touched the ugly laceration. She looked down and said, "Oh...No, not really. Not much anymore."

"That's going to leave quite a mark. You going to be okay with that?" Bill asked and they both knew what he was really asking.

"See my son playing in the water with his father while that big, black bear of a dog barks at the water's edge? See how even now, my beautiful daughter has decided to grace us with her presence and she's here, safe and sound? For me," she said while touching the angry laceration again, "this was worth all that. And I'll be just fine with it, don't you worry."

Bill squinted against the afternoon sun, dropped his head and nodded. Smiling, he rose from the beach chair and said, "Well, I'm going to head on back to Richmond. But you call me if you need anything, Katie, anything at all."

Kate smiled, but did not answer him as a tear slowly made it way past the wound on her face. Bill left her with her family. Vinnie and Robbie came up to her laughing as Isabella took the vacated seat left by Bill. Bear came to stand inside of their makeshift circle and shook the excess water from his coat. Amid the squeals of laughter from Robbie and the protests of Isabella, Kate closed her eyes and saw the woman in the mirror. It was worth it, she told her and the woman in the mirror turned and walked away.

ABOUT THE AUTHOR

Karen Smith Gibson lives in Richmond, VA with her husband, two sons and three dogs. She is currently working on the next SANE novel.

A Sneak Peek at Holding SANE: the next book in the SANE Series by Karen Smith Gibson...

Holding SANE

Prologue

It was now or never. Where did that stupid saying come from? Was it a movie or....? Her mind was so overloaded. It was hard to keep a train of thought long. Her usual habit of hopping on to the free thought association express was not useful to her now. She had to keep her wits about her. Her life, literally, depended on it. God! There was another one! Her hopeless situation has boiled down to one overused cliché after another.

She looked over at the sleeping woman sharing the filthy mattress with her. The woman had cried herself to sleep, much like Iris had the first week. Iris wished there was some way to take this new girl with her, but there was no time to figure out a way. The new girl, Marie, would have to stay in the dark of the cellar until she saw the light. That was how it worked. That was HIS rule and he was always right. There was no way Iris could bring Marie upstairs without setting off major warning bells. So, with a last look at Marie's sleeping form and a silent promise that she would return with help, Iris rose out of the darkness into the light of the small kitchen for what she hoped was the last time.

He was there waiting for her; sitting in his chair and sipping one of his exotic teas. He held her eyes with his own over the rim of his cup. It was as if he could read her traitorous mind. Her pulse quickened with dread. He was silent in his perusal. Abruptly, he broke eye contact with her to set his fine china cup upon the matching saucer.

"Has she finally stopped all that ridiculous wailing and carrying on?" he asked before turning his cold brown eyes upon her again.

"She's asleep now. I talked with her again, at length, about what you expect from your applicants. She'll most likely continue to need reinforcement, but I think she shows promise. I think you have chosen well this time, sir". Even as she said the words, bile rose in her throat. But she had to convince him that she was doing her best in hopes of winning back his favor. He insisted on proper speech and etiquette and, above all else, a respectful and submissive posture.

He sucked at his teeth with disdain and brought his long, cruel fingers together to form a steeple. He placed his index fingers ever so carefully against his clean-shaven chin. Iris recognized the gesture. The new girl was a puzzle to be solved...clay to be molded. She was sure his sadistic mind was now delivering creative ways to bend his new choice to his will. Yet at the same time, he was displeased that the new girl was not immediately pliant. He would perceive it as an insult to both his intellect and presumed desirability. Once again, Iris felt the pang of remorse for leaving Marie behind. Yet, this would be her only chance at escape. She had planned for this night for so long.

Her captor stared at her this time for more than just a few seconds. For the second time, Iris feared he would read her mind. Instead, he let out a heavy sigh and repeated his lecture from earlier, "I appreciate all you've done, as I said. However, my mind is made up. I'm afraid you are not the Miss Right I was looking for. I hope you were not thinking this mewling behavior of yours would earn you a place in my bed tonight".

Iris tried not to cringe or show her disgust. Instead, she dropped her eyes and tried hard to think of anything but his dry hands on her. He took her silence and downcast eyes as indicators of guilt and disappointment.

"Ah, sweet Iris. While I understand your desire, I'm afraid my mind is set in this matter. However, as promised, should you help in training this girl and bringing her up to speed in what is expected of a potential Miss Right, I will release you back into the mire from which I plucked you. No harm, no foul, as it were. Agreed?" he asked this last as he stood, signaling tonight's lesson had come to a close. He brushed imaginary lint from his creased trousers, but Iris knew he awaited and demanded a submissive response.

Iris could do no more than nod her downcast head and pray that he did not want to seal the promise with a chaste kiss to her forehead or a brotherly hug. Her churning stomach threatened to vomit her disgust and fear all over his new Ralph Lauren shirt. He seemed content with the silent acknowledgement from her.

"Well, I'm off to bed then. Make sure you clean this mess up and get yourself to bed quickly. We need to get an early start in the morning, Iris. Of course, you know the drill – break them down so we can build them up to their true potential."

Iris forced herself to look at his patronizing face with its slightly raised eyebrows and the beginnings of a smile to say politely, "Yes, sir, of course. I will clean up quickly and set up for the morning before retiring. I'll be very quiet, so as not to disturb you."

"Good girl" he smiled. He started to walk away, but then stopped and turned. He stared at her again and looked as if he were going to say something. Instead, he gave a quick smile that did not quite meet his eyes and turned away.

That had been over 30 minutes ago and Iris had not heard anything from his end of the house since then. She had cleaned up the kitchen and gone about getting things ready for morning as she had done for over the last six months. She reached inside the ceramic seashell that housed the buddy scrubber while skittishly looking over her shoulder. She removed the door key she had secured earlier in the day. She had known he would never touch or approach anything that had to do with domestic chores. She had bet her life on it.

Her heart was pounding so loudly she was afraid that it would mask any approaching footsteps. Iris quickly moved towards the utility room door. She carried the evening's trash with her, just in case. The bag of trash held in her sweating palms was if he had, indeed, read her mind and was waiting for her outside. "Oh, just taking out the trash tonight instead of tomorrow, sir" she would say. With trembling hands, she unlocked the deadbolt and passed through the door. The tremble turned into visible shaking and she missed the keyhole three times trying to lock it behind her.

She bolted for the six foot privacy fence gate. Once she opened the gate, she was brought up short by the irony of her situation. Here all along, she thought. All this time she had been about four blocks from where she worked and about three miles from home and she was overcome with wounded surprise. Deciding to take the shorter route to help, she began to run; a sobbing jog at first. But the further she retreated from the hell she had known, the faster her gait became – fueled by rage over her captivity and her lack of courage until now.

She ran for the promise of caring hands and where she knew at least one Henrico County police officer would be. She ran, leaving another victim lying in the dark. She ran knowing that without her making it to her destination, both she and the new girl, Marie, were destined to die. She ran because she could and she would keep her promise. She would lead them all back to Mimi Marie lying on a filthy mattress in a dark corner, wet tears drying on her face.

Mimi Marie…that's what the girl had called herself. "Everyone calls me Mimi Marie. It's a stupid nickname, but one that's stuck to me for a long time. Mimi Marie…" and then she had started to cry again, asking, "Why am I here? What's happening?"

So, Iris ran those four blocks chanting, "Mimi Marie and me, Mimi Marie and me, Mimi Marie and me…" as her feet slapped against the soft grass and then the pavement of a parking lot. She tried to keep her mind off of the pain shooting from her legs, so long inactive – her body sore from malnutrition and torture. She would save them both. She would lead them back to the hell hole from which she had crawled. Iris would save them both in doing so. "Mimi Marie and me....Mimi Marie and me..." she softly panted as she ran.

She could see the brightly lit entrance of the ER across the parking lot. Her chest began to feel tight, but she pressed on through the humid night. She was going to save them both. Then, suddenly, a sharp pain interrupted her joy at almost being there. It started between her shoulder blades like a knife being pushed through her chest. It moved to the center of her breastbone. Yet, still she ran, pushing through the pain. When she reached the pneumatic doors, the sensor caused the doors to open with a whoosh and everyone inside looked up.

She took two steps inside trying to spit out the words in her head so that they made sense, but could hear herself talking in disjointed sentences. The last thing she remembered before her aching chest gave way to darkness was the questioning looks of the nurses crowded around her. All of the faces had confusion drawn upon them; all of the faces but one. She clung to the hope that the one face was enough as the darkness pulled her down into an abyss of silence.

Made in the USA
Middletown, DE
13 August 2023